WITHOUT A TRACE

"I don't think you have any business going up there in the first place. If you're not scared shitless, you ought to be."

"Alan, I think *you're* the one who's afraid to go."

He almost reached for another cigarette but then stopped himself. "I will definitely plead guilty to a deep-seated disquiet about the people who rule this placid paradise. But if it'll square things with Steve, then I'll take you up to have a quick look, for my sins. But it's got to be after the weather clears."

I finally realized he was already thinking about his next loan. *Steve, beware.*

"Tomorrow then?" I wasn't going to blink, because the Peten was where Sarah ended up the first time and I was sure that's where Ramos had taken her now. Baalum.

Dupre stared at the sky a moment longer, then caved. "Maybe we can shoot for tomorrow late. *If* I can convince myself this storm has done its worst." He looked back at me. "But I gotta tell you one thing, Ms. Morgan James. We blunder in up there and end up getting ourselves 'disappeared,' we won't even get our picture in the papers. You'd better tell your immediate loved ones where you're going, and it wouldn't be the worst time in the world to think about making a will."

The way he said it, I was sure for once he meant every word.

BOOK YOUR PLACE ON OUR WEBSITE AND MAKE THE READING CONNECTION!

We've created a customized website just for our very special readers, where you can get the inside scoop on everything that's going on with Zebra, Pinnacle and Kensington books.

When you come online, you'll have the exciting opportunity to:

- View covers of upcoming books
- Read sample chapters
- Learn about our future publishing schedule (listed by publication month *and author*)
- Find out when your favorite authors will be visiting a city near you
- Search for and order backlist books from our online catalog
- Check out author bios and background information
- Send e-mail to your favorite authors
- Meet the Kensington staff online
- Join us in weekly chats with authors, readers and other guests
- Get writing guidelines
- AND MUCH MORE!

**Visit our website at
http://www.pinnaclebooks.com**

LIFE BLOOD

Thomas Hoover

PINNACLE BOOKS
Kensington Publishing Corp.
http://www.pinnaclebooks.com

For Al Zuckerman
Quite simply the finest human being I've ever met.

One

New York, New York. A blissful spring morning beckoned, cloudless and blue and pure. I was driving my high-mileage Toyota down Seventh Avenue, headed for the location shoot that was supposed to wind up principal photography for my first feature film, *Baby Love*. It was about the pain and joy of adoption. I guess directing your first feature is something like giving birth to your first child, but that gets us way, way ahead of the story.

My name, by the way, is Morgan Smyth James, after two grandmothers, and I'm thirty-eight and single and strive to be eternally optimistic. That morning, however, in spite of everything else, I was missing Steve terribly and feeling like I'd screwed up essential components of my life.

To try for some perspective, let me say I'd always planned to have a normal, loving family. Really. Find an emotionally present soulmate who cared about things I care about—okay, slim and smart and spectacular in bed wouldn't be a minus—get married on a lawn with lots of white roses some sunny June afternoon, work one or even two perfect kids into our fulfilling, giving lives. But somehow I'd managed to have none of that. I'd messed up at every turn.

In reality I had nobody to blame but myself. Eighteen years ago, just out of college, I turned down two really nice guys. My body was fertile and hormone-driven—was it ever!—but grad school loomed and my greatest fear (instead of, as now, my fondest hope) was getting "trapped" into motherhood. Also, I had the youthful delusion that life was forever.

There was, in truth, one simpatico young director I met at NYU film school whom I would have married in a minute, but after Jason won my heart he dumped me for his undergraduate sweetheart who had skillfully gotten herself knocked up during his Christmas break.

Which was when I first developed my fallback strategy for coping with bad news. After moping around in sweats for two days, cutting class and hiding in a revival house showing a Goddard retrospective, not understanding half the French and too bleary-eyed to read the subtitles, I decided to build a defense system. From that day on, I'd put all heartbreak in a special box, nail down the lid, and act as though it wasn't there. It worked then and it still works, more or less, now. People sometimes accuse me of living in selective denial (they're right), but it makes me one heck of a survivor.

And something else. I decided then and there to focus my life: I'd concentrate on learning to make movies and let the family part just play out naturally. I had the idea that whereas men's affections couldn't be controlled, a career could. Even then I realized it was only a partial truth, but I decided to go with it anyway.

Which brings us down to three years back. And a funny thing was happening. Almost without realizing it, I'd started lingering in stores to look at little pink jumpers, begun gazing into the baby carriages that suddenly seemed to be sprouting everywhere. The phrase "my baby" became the most powerful one I could imagine, made my throat swell till I'd half choke.

At which precise time, like a *deus ex machina,* enter Steve Abrams, the man who gave me hope. He came along just as I was noticing that infinite stream of wonderful guys had dwindled down to relationship dropouts, men with distant eyes and former wives in other states. We discovered each other at the reopened Oloffson Hotel in Haiti, where I was shooting a documentary about voodoo and he was photographing that country's ragged, plucky children for *National Geographic*. No ex-spouses, no need for psychic pampering. Okay, he wasn't going to win a Mr. Universe contest any time soon; he had a couple of extra pounds that, actually, I kind of liked. But he was my age, had great brown eyes, sandy hair thinning only just a bit. No Greek god but definitely a *man*. He could tune a Jeep carburetor with his eyes closed or fix a cranky hotel lock, then recite Byron (sort of) and proceed to snare the perfect Chilean red for crawfish étouffée (yes!). But I knew I loved him when I realized it was more than any of that. I felt as if I'd found the other half of myself. Just one glance across the table and we each knew what the other was thinking, feeling. We'd laugh at the same instant, then as though on cue, half cry together over the miseries of that wretched island. Sometimes it was almost eerie. And as for lovemaking, let me just say Steve didn't need a how-to manual. We were made for each other.

Maybe it's un-PC to mention it, but I also felt safe around him. And I think he felt the same. We liked that feeling. Us fending off the world.

When we got back to New York, we had to see each other every day. We still had separate apartments—thanks to the New York real-estate squeeze—but we were scouting in our spare time for an affordable loft in lower Manhattan that could accommodate Steve's darkroom, my office, and— yes—a baby. We evolved into parents-to-be, pricing baby carriages. Who could have predicted it? The joy of sharing a need. It was a total high.

Before long we decided to stop waiting for the perfect

space. We'd start on the baby anyway, our first joint project—which, we believed, would only be the first of many.

But nothing happened. Over a year and still nothing.

That was when life began to feel like a cruel bait-and-switch. When you aren't ready, you can produce a baby in a momentary absence-of-mind, whereas once you're finally an adult, accomplished, lots-to-offer woman, ready to be the mother you wish *you'd* had, your body has closed down your baby-making equipment like an unused Rust Belt factory. Fertility has calculatingly abandoned you for the Sun Belt of youth.

"Well," Dr. Hannah Klein, my long-time ob/gyn, declared, "our tests all indicate you're both fertile, so just keep trying, under optimum conditions."

Optimum conditions. There followed almost a year of "optimum conditions." Do it upside down; wait and have a cold shower while I take my temperature; no, not that way, not tonight. My mucus is thicker: Quick! Eventually we both began feeling like laboratory rats. Our once-incredible love life drifted into something only a boot-camp sergeant with Nazi leanings could be turned on by.

I think that's what finally caused Steve to go over the edge. Three months ago—a Friday morning I shall never forget—he stepped out of my shower, swathed himself in a white towel, and announced he was going to Central America to do a book. He needed time to think. The move, he explained, wasn't about us. He really wanted to spend a year down there with his Nikon, capturing the region's tentative processes of democratic transition. Besides, he was beginning to think we'd both gone a little mental about the baby.

Out came that special box of heartbreak again. I consoled myself we were just having a seventh-inning stretch, but the wisdom in that box told me I'd somehow blown it. The baby we hadn't created had become a specter hovering in the ether between us, ever a reminder of failure.

As a parting gesture, the never-say-die longshot, he left a "deposit" with Dr. Klein—for her liquid-nitrogen womb-in-waiting—enough for two final intrauterine inseminations. Later on today I was going to see her and find out if our last and final attempt had stuck. But nothing about my cycle was giving me any hope.

In the meantime, though, I had a movie to finish. We were shooting an interview at a five-story condominium building in Greenwich Village belonging to a woman named Carly Grove, who'd recently adopted. Her story was intriguing, but now—with my own hopes of ever having a baby down to two outs in the bottom of the ninth—well, now I had more than one reason for wanting to meet her. . . .

When I arrived, I lucked into a parking space right in front. Our security guy, Lou Crenshaw, was off today getting some city paperwork sorted out, but my crew was already upstairs—as director I get to arrive at a decent hour, though later on I also get to do lonely postproduction work till midnight—leaving our three vans double-parked, with a New York City Film Board permit prominently displayed inside each windshield. The building, formerly a Hertz parking garage, was near the end of Barrow Street, facing the Hudson River, and was filled with artists and entrepreneurs.

The truth was, I wanted to get the interview on film as soon as possible. I was more than a little worried Carly might decide to get cold feet and back out. She'd started to hedge when I had one last confirming chat with her last night, something about a "no-disclosure" agreement she now remembered signing. This had to be a one-take, all-or-nothing shoot.

Which was why I'd sent down the full gang this morning, not just the "key" personnel as I'd initially planned. Leading

my (motley) crew was the director of photography, first cameraman Roger Drexel, a grizzled veteran with a ponytail
who'd been with my producer, David Roth and his Applecore
Productions, from back when he did beach movies and splat-
ter films. He worked with the production manager, Erica
Cole, our lipstick lesbian, who coordinated crew schedules.
The second camera was handled by Greer Seiber, recently
of NYU film school, who was so happy to have a job, any
job, she acted as though David's previous string of low-
budget, B-flick epics were remakes of *Gone With the Wind*.

Scott Ventri, another Applecore old-timer, was key grip,
the guy who got the gear on and off the vans, set it up, and
signed off on safety regs. Today he also was responsible for
blacking out windows and setting up lights. The chief elec-
trician, gaffer, was Ralph Cafiero, who'd come down the previous day and temporarily hot-wired the circuit breaker in
the apartment to make sure there was enough amperage. He
and his lighting "crew," another bright-eyed (and cheap)
NYU grad named Paul Nulty, had arrived this morning ahead
of everybody else to prelight the "set," a northeast corner
of the apartment.

I'm always a little hyper about sound, so I'd asked Tony
Wills, who handled recording, to also come down the previous day and record the "tone" of the living room, the sound
when there is no sound, in order to have it available for editing. Today he'd run the boom mike and be assisted by
Sherry Moran, his latest girlfriend, who was mixer/recordist.
For Carly's makeup and hair, I had Arlene Morris, an old
friend from all the way back to my early days as an AD on
the soaps. . . .

I rang Carly's bell and she buzzed me right up.

She doubtless had a closet full of Donna Karan suits, but
she came to the door in prefaded jeans and a striped sweater.

A successful publicity agent, she was petite, with dark hair and eyes and an obvious don't-bug-me take on life.

"Come on in. My nanny's here to help keep Kevin out of the way." She was sounding like she'd gotten her old spunk back, or so it seemed at first. "I've completely cleared the living room."

I looked around the place, now a vision of setup pandemonium. "You're sure this is all right?"

"Well . . ." She was biting at her lip. "Maybe we ought to talk first, okay? But come on in. I'll probably do it. Maybe I just need a good reason to . . ."

As her voice trailed off, I found myself mining my brain for a sales point. Finally, out of the blue, I settled on one. "Because you're totally crazy?"

She laughed out loud. "Not a bad start. I live in total madness. It's the definition of my life."

I laughed too and looked around. No kidding. Her loft apartment was a wild mixture of stairs and galleries and levels—unconventional in every way. Also, it had a lot of in-your-face decor, outrageous posters, and African fertility masks, signs of a wonderful, irreverent personality. Then too, stuffed animals and toys were strewn all over.

"I can't really afford the rent," she declared, seeing me survey the place, "but I need the space for Kevin. I've just joined Bloomingdale's Anonymous. Twelve steps to shredding your charge plates."

Her nanny, a Jehovah's Witness from Jamaica named Marcy (who reminded me of a cuddly voodoo doll, complete with cornrows), was bringing Carly's little boy Kevin down from his bath in the upstairs bathroom.

He was definitely adopted, sandy-haired and peachy, nothing like Carly's dark, severe strands and Mediterranean skin. When Marcy put him down, he tried to walk, and I felt my envy ratchet upward a notch. He'd just started taking tentative steps, at eleven months old, and there was still a Frankenstein quality as he strode stiff-legged, arms out for balance.

I walked over, picked him up, and gave him a kiss. He looked like a Scandinavian travel poster, a cherubic vision, and I felt a great void growing where my heart had been. Then Marcy reached out and pried him from me. I hated to let him go so much I almost pulled him back.

"You're so lucky," I said to Carly, feeling a surge of yearning. "He's great."

"You know," she said, "I've been thinking about that 'no disclosure' thing Children of Light made me sign. That's their name, by the way. Like a vow of silence about them. They seemed pretty serious about it."

Dear God, I thought, don't let her chicken out. Don't, *don't*.

"So, we won't mention them. Just never use their name."

She stood a minute, mute, and then her eyes grew determined. "No, I've got a better idea. I like you. And I think more single women ought to know about adoption. So you know what? I think I'll use their name all over the damned place. I paid what they asked, and for that I ought to be able to do what I want. What are they going to do? Come and steal Kevin back?"

Then she sighed and stared at me. "Maybe, though, you could run through again how exactly we fit into this movie."

I liked to tell the story to people, just to get their reaction. There are always moments of doubt in the film-making process when you wonder if the audience for your picture is going to consist entirely of your immediate family, your backers, and your creditors.

"Well, as I tried to explain before, it's a fictional construct intended to feel like a documentary, about a career slave named Gail Crea who's based on a hundred women I know. She's got a great career, manages fund-raising for a major museum, and work is going great. But then one day she finds herself suddenly daydreaming about babies, envying mothers. She yearns for someone to take care of, has a recurrent dream she's stealing a baby out of a carriage on the street. It's demeaning."

"God," Carly said, "I know exactly what you're talking about. I've been there. Have I ever."

The truth was, I also knew it all too well. It was poignant and demeaning at the same time.

"Anyway, Gail's focused on career all through her twenties, and by her late thirties she's become a serious professional. But her personal life is still on hold. She 'meets people' at work, or some other way, and she has a couple of long-standing relationships that finally crater because the guys, make that commit-ophobes, 'need space.' Along the way, there're ghastly fix-ups and dismal dinners with what seem like a hundred thousand misfits. She becomes the Dating Queen of New York, but eventually she realizes all the men she's meeting are either assuaging their midlife crises with some pneumatic bombshell named Bambi, or they're divorced and whining and carrying a ton of emotional baggage. The fact is, she's *become* the sensible, successful professional she's been looking for all this time. This all sort of seeps in as backstory."

I perched on a stool at the breakfast bar and looked down at my jeans, and noticed that a rip was starting in the crotch. Shit, back to cottage cheese. Those horrible eight pounds I could never get rid of.

I crossed my legs. "Finally, after she gets a couple more promotions, she wakes up one morning and realizes she's never going to have a family. All the stable, rational men have disappeared. Like there's a black hole or something. Nothing's left but the walking wounded. She concludes it's actually easier to get a baby than a decent guy—which is what she starts trying to do. High concept: This picture is about how adopting a baby can enrich the life of a childless human being and, not coincidentally, bring joy to an orphaned infant."

I remembered when I'd first pitched it to David Roth of Applecore. His response had been; "Definitely art-house. Probably never get past the Angelika. A wide release is gonna be three screens where they serve iced cappuccino."

I was dead set to prove him wrong.

"So," I wound up, "I've shot the entire film, but now, thinking it over, I've decided there's one last thing I need to do. As I go through the story, at every step of the adoption process I want to cut to an interview, just talking heads, tight shot, of somebody who actually went through it. Nonfiction. The real-life happy ending. And that's where you come in."

What I wasn't telling her was, I was increasingly concerned the picture might be slightly hollow without this punch of real life.

"Well," Carly declared with a grin, *"my* ending couldn't be happier."

"Okay, want to get started?" I looked around at Arlene, makeup, who always seemed to have more on her face than in her bag. I kidded her about that a lot. But she was actually the one who had found Carly, bumping into her at a gym in the Village.

"Hey, let's go for it." Arlene grinned.

I turned back to Carly. "So how's about we prep a little while you're getting the 'natural' look?"

In the back of my mind I knew what I wanted for the interview. Something like the feeling I remembered from *The Thin Blue Line,* where people engaged in Hamlet-like monologues that told us more about them than they themselves knew, that let us really know their secrets and their fears. The interviewer was never seen or heard.

Arlene ensconced Carly at the dining room table, a weathered country French, where she'd already unfolded and plugged in a mirror with lights.

"Having Kevin has been wonderful," Carly began. "He's changed my life. Sure, being a single 'supermom' makes for a lot of bad-hair days, but no matter how much I complain, it's worth every burp."

I thought momentarily about having her hold him during the interview, but instantly decided it would be too distracting. Kevin and his wonderful eyes would commandeer the camera. A kid this cute in a scene was nothing less than grand larceny.

He came toddling in now, dragging a stuffed brown bear. Then he banged its head and tried to say its name. "Benny." His funny, awkward walk reminded me a little of Lou Crenshaw after a couple of drinks. God, he was fantastic.

"Come here, sweetie." I picked him up, inhaling his fresh baby scent, and wanted to hold him forever—while he slammed the bear against my face. This child, I thought, is too good to be true.

He was wearing a small bracelet around his left ankle, a tiny little chain, with a small silver medallion attached. It looked like the face of a cat. Funny. Carly didn't have a cat, wasn't a cat person, so why the little bracelet? And the back had a bunch of lines and dots, like a jumbled-up Morse code.

Ask her about that, I thought. But later.

Now Carly was caught up in the sound of her own voice and on a roll. While Arlene continued with the makeup, moving to her eyes, she bubbled on.

"Like I told you on the phone, I tried and tried to adopt, through a whole bunch of lawyers, but it was a nightmare. One guy even helped me put ads in newspapers all around the country, but nothing worked. I kept getting scammed by women who wanted thousands of dollars up front, then backed out at the last minute." She was getting up, looking intense. "Let me have a minute. I want to make coffee for everybody."

I followed her into the kitchen, which was the "country" type with a faux granite counter and lots of copper-bottomed pans hanging from the ceiling.

She was right about the pain of adoption, which was why her story was such a burst of sunshine. As part of the start-up research for my picture, I'd actually gone to meet an adoption attorney out in Brooklyn, a sleazy-looking guy named Frank Brasco. I'd been pretending to be a client, to find out first-hand how tough it really was. What I heard was chilling.

"I don't want to get your hopes up," he'd declared for cheery openers. "Finding a healthy, Caucasian, American baby is virtually out of the question, so naturally we focus on foreign-borns. All the same, it can take years, and there's incredible paperwork. Passports for the kid, an extended visa for you while you go there and then wait around to process everything in triplicate. Bribes, corruption, you can't imagine." He sighed and adjusted his toupee, as though the very thought made him weary. "And that's just the foreign end. Here you have the INS, the Immigration and Naturalization Service. They give bean-counting paper-pushers a bad name." He examined me closely. "Not Jewish, I take it. 'Cause if that's what you're looking for, you may have to wait for the Messiah."

Now, almost a year and a lot of experience later, I knew full well how right he was. Which was what made Carly's story so fantastic.

"So how did you manage to get Kevin? You said it only took a few months?"

"Well, to go back to the beginning, I didn't start out wanting to adopt. But when the guy I was planning to marry got cold feet—after four and a half years, the louse—and there was nobody else on the horizon, I decided to just have a baby on my own. You know, find some smart, good-looking hunk, seduce him, and get things going the old-fashioned way, or if that didn't work, then I figured I'd just go to a sperm bank. Who needs an actual man, right?"

She took out a white and green bag of coffee beans, labeled Balducci's on the side. I was still holding Kevin, who threw Benny onto the floor, then began to sniffle and point.

But Carly seemed not to notice as she shook the coffee beans into the grinder. "Well, getting a baby the fun way turned out to be moot, because it seems I have some kind of uterine condition—which meant I couldn't get pregnant, or even do an in vitro. Bottom line, if I wanted a baby, I had to adopt."

She pressed the button on the coffee grinder, sending a blast of whirring through the kitchen. In seconds it was over and she was tapping the batch into her Braun. "So that's when I started on the attorney thing, got worked over good trying to adopt as a single mom, and finally heard about Children of Light."

"The adoption organization? What do you know about them?"

"Tell you the main thing," she said, "they're the place that can make it happen." She reached over and poked Kevin's tummy. "Right, big guy?"

Sure looked that way. What a cutie.

By now the spacious living room had been turned into a mini film set, with two 35-mm Panaflex cameras set up, windows blanked out, lights and filters in place, and a video camera and monitor. Having tested the boom mike and the tape recorder, Tony and Sherry were ready.

Carly announced to everybody that coffee was available, and I handed Kevin over to Marcy. Then together we marched into the living room.

"Okay," I told her, "we're going to be filming, but ignore that fact. Just look into the back of the camera and talk to it as though it were me."

"Hey." She grinned. "You're dealing with a pro. This is my thing."

I looked around at the cameras and the grips. "Okay, guys. Roll sound." There was a retort as the clap stick used for synching whacked out the start of the shoot. "Scene one, take one, Carly Grove interview."

She proceeded to hit the ground running, recounting in great detail her story of many disappointments. She finally got to the point where she was trying to adopt the baby of a woman in a Memphis jail, and then even that fell through.

"Which was when my main lawyer, Chuck, just gave up and recommended I hock the family silver, take a Valium, and try this place called Children of Light. Where you go when all else fails. So I gave them a call."

"And what happened?" It sounded too good to be true. "Did they seem . . . in any way unusual?"

She looked at me, as though puzzled by the question. Then she shrugged it off. "Well, first they tried to get me to check into their clinic—it's this place up the Hudson—to let them see if my 'condition' could be cured somehow, using his special techniques."

"His?"

"Goddard. Dr. Alex Goddard. He's a kinda spacey guy, but he's the big-shot presiding guru there." She remembered the camera and turned back to it. "I told his staff I didn't have that kind of time, and anyway nothing could be done. They were pretty insistent, so I eventually ended up talking to the man himself. He sort of mesmerizes you, but I finally said, forget it, it's adoption or nothing. So he just sent me back to the peons. Checkbook time."

I stared at her, hungry for details, but she didn't notice, just pressed on.

"The money they wanted, I have to tell you, was staggering. Sixty thousand. And believe me, they don't give revolving credit."

I thought about the figure. It was the highest I'd heard for getting a baby, but it wasn't totally off-the-wall. Terrific babies don't drop from trees.

Carly was still going strong. "It took me almost half a year to scrounge it together. A lot of credit lines got maxed. But when I finally did plunk down the loot, sure enough, I had Kevin in less than three months. I don't even know where he came from. They took care of all that, but I do know it was probably out of the country, because of the blank INS forms I signed. But then, who cares? With a deal this good, you don't press for details, right?"

Carly Grove had a mutual love affair with the camera. The footage was going to be fabulous. The only problem was, it sounded like an "infomercial" for the adoption miracle wrought by this doctor named Goddard.

When the interview began to wind down, losing its punch, I suggested we call it a day. With the time pushing two o'clock, I wanted to get the film to the lab, get it developed, and take a look at the rushes. I also had a doctor's appointment, not to mention a meeting with David to bring him up to speed on what I was doing. But surely he was going to be pleased. The interview, with Carly's honest intensity, would give the picture spine and guts. Just as I'd hoped.

You could always tell by the reaction of the crew. Even Roger Drexel, who usually hid his thoughts somewhere in his scraggly beard, was letting his eyes sparkle behind his Panaflex. Scott was also grinning as he struck the lights and Cafiero ripped up the power lines, now taped to the floor. Everybody was in wrap mode, flushed with a great shoot.

I followed Carly into the kitchen, where Marcy was feeding Kevin some Gerber applesauce. The time had come, I thought, to spring the next big question, out of earshot of the crew.

"I hate to put you on the spot, but do you know any other women like you, single, who've adopted through Children of Light?" I decided to experiment with the truth. "God knows, depending on what happens in my own situation, I'm . . . I'm thinking I might even want to check them out for myself."

"What do you mean?" She gave me a quick, concerned look.

"Maybe I'd like to talk to them about adopting too." I realized I was babbling, my usual prelude to obsessing.

Carly's worried gaze eased up a bit, but she started twisting at her hair.

"Well, I might have another name. When my lawyer first told me about them, he gave me the name of another woman who'd adopted from them, and I talked to her a little about how they worked. She'd just gotten her baby, so I guess she was about six months ahead of me in the process. Her name was . . . I think it was Pauline or Paula or something. She's probably not the kind of person who'd take their 'no disclosure' crap all that seriously. She was adopting a girl, and she lives somewhere on the Upper West Side."

"Any idea how I could find her?"

"You know, she wrote kids' books, and I think she gave me her card. In case I ever needed somebody to do some YA copy. Let me go look in my Rolodex. I filed her card under 'Y' for Young Adult. Right. It'll just take a second."

The woman, whose name was Paula Marks, lived on West 83rd Street. The business card, a tasteful brown with a weave in the paper, described her as an author. The address included a "suite" number, which meant she worked out of her apartment.

"Mind if I take down her phone number and address? I'd really like to look her up. To see if her experience was anything remotely like yours."

Carly gazed at her fingernails a second. "Okay, but do me a favor. Don't tell her how you got her number." She bit her lip, stalling. "It's one thing for me to talk to you myself. It's something else entirely to go sticking my nose into other people's business."

"Look, I'll respect her privacy just as much as I respect yours." I paused, listening to what I'd just said. The promise sounded pretty lame. I'd just filmed her, or hadn't she noticed? "Look, let me call Paula, see if she'll agree to be interviewed on camera. I'll keep your name entirely out if it, I promise."

She reached down and plucked Kevin out of his high chair, kissed him on his applesauce-smeared cheek, then hugged him. "Sorry. Guess I'm being a little paranoid. I shouldn't invite you here, then give you a hard time about what you're going to do, or not do. I can't have it both ways."

In the ensuing tumult and confusion of the wrap, I did manage to get one more item from Carly Grove. The address and phone number of Children of Light. But I completely forgot the one thing I'd been meaning to ask about. That little amulet, with the strange cat's face and the lines and dots on the back. Why was Kevin wearing it? And by the time I got to the street, surrounded by the clamor of crew and equipment, it seemed too inconsequential to go back and bother with.

Two

Moving on, my next stress-point was to meet with my young boss, the afore-noted David Roth, who was CEO and First Operating Kvetcher of Applecore Productions, a kinda-sexy guy whose heart was deeply engaged, often unsuccessfully, with bottom lines. The issue was, I'd done today's shoot, the interview with Carly, without troubling to secure his okay. Without, in fact, telling him zip—the reason being I was afraid he wouldn't green-light the idea. Now my next move was to try to convince him what I'd just done was brilliant.

Actually I liked David a lot, and hoped the occasional tangles we'd had over the film wouldn't stand in the way of a friendship. The truth is, you don't meet that many interesting, stable men in my line of work. Our artistic goals weren't always in sync, but all the same, he'd done an enormous favor for somebody close to me and for that I'd vowed to walk through fire for him.

When I marched into his cluttered, dimly lit office, my mind still churning over Carly's strange adoption story, what I saw sent my problem-detector straight into the red. There, sitting across from him, was Nicholas Russo, a five-seven smoothie in a charcoal Brioni double-breasted, the gentleman David sometimes referred to as Nicky the Purse. Another land mine in my life. He operated off and on as Applecore's "banker" when cash flow got dicey and real banks got ner-

vous. It was an arrangement of last resort, since Nicky's loans
had to be serviced at two percent a week. Do the numbers:
He doubled his money in a year. I knew too that putting
money out to independent filmmakers was part of Nicky's
attempt at a legitimate front; the real cash went onto the
streets of Hell's Kitchen, just outside our door, where he got
five percent a week. And Nicky's overdue notices were not
sent through the mail.

He also had a piece of a video distributorship, Roma Ex-
otics, that reputedly specialized in . . . guess what. It was all
stuff I tried not to think about.

I had a strong hunch what was under discussion. The
$350,000 David had borrowed to finish my picture. We'd
gotten the loan three months ago, when cash was tight, and
we both figured we could pay it back later in the year, after
we got a backup cable deal (though I was ultimately hoping
for a theatrical distribution, my first).

Shit! What did Nicky want? Were we behind on the weekly
juice? I'd signed on with David partly to help his bottom
line. Was I instead going to cause his ruin?

At the moment he had his back to Nicky, seemed to be
meditating out the window he loved, its vista being the grimy
facades that lined the far west of Fifty-eighth Street. His
office, with its wide windows and forest of freshly misted
trees, told you he was a plant nut. Outside it was early April,
the cruelest month, but inside, with all the trees, spring was
in full cry. The place also felt like a storage room, with piles
of scripts stacked around every pot. The office normally
smelled like a greenhouse, but now the aroma was one of
high anxiety.

David revolved back and looked across the potted green-
ery, then broke into a relieved smile when he saw me. I could
tell from his faraway stare that he was teetering on the verge
of panic.

"Hey, come on in," he said. "Nicky's just put a brand-new proposition on the table."

David had a keen intelligence, causing me to sometimes wonder if he was in a line of work beneath him. (For that matter, maybe I was too.) He was dark-haired, trim, with serious gray eyes and strong cheekbones. This morning he was wearing his trademark black sweater, jeans, and white sneakers, a picture of the serious go-for-broke New York indy-prod hustler. He'd already made and lost and made several fortunes in his youthful career. My only sexual solace since Steve left was an occasional glance at his trim rear end. I also saluted his fiscal courage. His congenital shortfall, I regret to say, was in the matter of judgment. Exhibit A: Nicholas Russo's funny money.

"Nicky, you remember Morgan James, the director on this project."

"Yeah, we met. 'Bout four months back." Nicky rose and offered his manicured hand, a picture of Old World charm. His dark hair was parted down the middle and his Brioni, which probably fell off a truck somewhere in the Garment Center, had buttons on the cuffs that actually buttoned. "How ya doing?"

"Hi." I disengaged myself as quickly as possible. The slimeball.

Again, why was he here? The way I understood it, we'd signed a legitimate, ironclad note. Nicky wasn't exactly the Chase Manhattan Bank, but I assumed he was a "man of honor," would live by any deal David had with him. "Do we have some kind of problem?"

"Nah," Nicky said, "I'm thinking of it more in the way of an opportunity. Dave, here, showed me some of your picture this morning, and it ain't too bad. Got me to thinking. You're gonna need a video distributor. So maybe I could help you out."

Oh, shit and double-shit. I looked at him, realizing what he had in mind. "How's that? Applecore already has a video distributor. We use—"

"Yeah, well, like I was telling Dave, I got a nose this picture's gonna do some serious business." He tried a smile. "Whenever I see one of these indy things that don't add up for me, like this one, I always know it's a winner. What I'm telling you is, I think you got something here. He says you're figuring on a cable deal, and maybe a theatrical release, but after that you gotta worry about video. I'm just thinking a way I could pitch in."

Pitch in? The last thing I needed was some skin-flick wiseguy getting his sticky hands on my picture. Forget about it.

"Well, I don't really see how. I'm shooting this one by the book. I've got a standard Screen Actors Guild contract, and everything is strictly by the rules. If we're current on the loan, then . . ." I looked at David, who appeared to be running on empty. Maybe, I thought, I didn't understand what was at stake. What had Nicky said to him? This was a man who could make people disappear with a phone call to guys nicknamed after body parts. "Look, let me talk to David about this. I don't know what—"

"You two're just gonna 'talk' about it?" Russo's penetrating eyes dimmed. "Now that's a little disappointing, I gotta tell you, since I sent for my business manager, Eddie down there in the car, hoping we could reach a meeting of minds right here. Sign a few things. Roll that note I'm holding into a distribution deal and give everybody one less worry." He turned in his chair, boring in on me. "Like, for instance, I checked out your locations and I noticed there ain't no Teamsters nowhere. All you got's a bunch of fuckin' Mick scabs driving them vans. Now that can lead to circumstances. Inadequate safety procedures. Of course, that wouldn't have to be a concern if we was partners together. Then you'd have good security. The best."

I looked at David, who seemed on the verge of a heart attack. Why was he letting this even be discussed? Get in bed with Nicky Russo and the next thing you know he's got somebody hanging you out the window by your ankles.

Besides, ten to one the guy was bluffing, seeing if he could scare us.

I refocused. "Mr. Russo, it may ease your mind to know that our security is managed by a former agent for the FBI. He was with them here in New York till about a year ago, when he came to us full time. His name is Agent Lou Crenshaw. You're welcome to check him out. He's familiar with union issues, and he carries a .38. He also has plenty of friends down at 26 Federal Plaza. So if you have any lingering concern about our security procedures, why don't you run it by him?"

The mention of Lou seemed to brighten David's listless eyes. He leaned back in his chair and almost smiled.

He had good reason. The favor he'd done for Lou, and indirectly for me, was enough to inspire eternal loyalty. Lou would face off against half of Hell's Kitchen for David Roth.

"That ain't the point, exactly," Russo said, shifting uncomfortably. "Thing is, Roma could do good distribution for you. We work with a lot of people."

"Then why not submit a formal proposal? In writing. I'm in charge and that's how I do business. If your numbers work, then we can talk."

"Just trying to be helpful." He glared at me, then seemed to dismiss my presence. I disappeared from his radar as though lifted away by an alien spacecraft, and he turned back to David. "You know, Dave, me and you've kinda drifted apart lately. Old friends oughtn'ta do that. We ought to keep more in touch. I think we get along okay."

In other words, get this pushy broad out of my face.

"It's just business, Nicky," David said, trying to conjure an empty smile. "Business and pleasure don't always mix."

Yes! David, tell the creep to leave us alone. *Tell him.*

"Doing business with me ain't a pleasure?" Nicky Russo asked, hurt filling his voice. He'd brought out a large Havana and was rolling it in between his thumb and forefinger. "I figured we was best friends. *Paisans.*"

"We're not not friends, Nicky. We've just got different goals in life. You know how it is."

I worked my way around behind his desk and glanced out the window. The lingering day was beginning to cloud over, a perfect match for my state of mind. After this I had a late appointment with Dr. Hannah Klein. I feared she was going to end my baby hopes.

"Yeah, well," Nicky Russo said finally, rising, "I gotta be downtown in a little while, so I guess we can talk about this later."

"Okay, sure." David made a shrugging sign. Like; *Women! What can you do?* Then he got up too. "Look, Nicky, let me chew on this. Maybe I'll get back to you."

"Yeah, you think about it, all right?" He rose without a further word and worked his way out the wide double doors, stumbling through the ficus forest as he struck a match to his cigar.

"David, don't sign anything with him. *Don't.* I'll handle the Teamster stuff if it comes up. I know how to talk to them."

"Okay, okay, calm down. He was just seeing if he could push me. I know him. You called his scam with that talk about Lou. By tomorrow he'll forget about the whole thing." He looked at me, his eyes not quite yet back in focus. "Thanks. You can say things to him I'd get cement shoes for. Nicky's not really ready for people like you. He has this macho front, but he doesn't know how to handle a professional woman with balls."

"You're welcome. I guess." Balls? I adored those vulnerable male bits, but I preferred not to think of myself in those terms. Truth was, Nicky Russo played a large part in my personal anxieties. "But I mean it. N. O."

"I hear you," he said, sighing. Then he snapped back to the moment. "So where do things stand otherwise?"

I'd come for an after-the-fact green light of the day's shoot, but already I was thinking about Hannah Klein. "David, I'm going to find out in about an hour whether Steve and I are ever going to have a baby. But truthfully I don't think I'm pregnant. I think it's over." It hurt to say it. He knew about Steve and me—I'd written some language on maternity leave into my contract—and I think he was mildly rooting for us. Or maybe not.

"Could be it's all for the best," he declared. He'd sat back down, picked up a pencil off his desk to distract himself, and was whirling it pensively, one of his few habits that made me crazy. "Maybe you were destined to make movies, not kids."

I listened to his tone of voice, knowing he often hid his real feelings with safe, sympathy-card sentiments. He rose to eloquence only when nothing much was at stake. He'd even sent me flowers and a mea-culpa note twice as a make-up after we'd had a disagreement over costs and scheduling. And one of those times, I should have sent *him* flowers. Sometimes I wondered why we worked so well together. The truth was, we operated on very different wavelengths.

Some history to illustrate. Over the past eight years, before I teamed up with David, I'd done three "highly praised" documentaries. But getting to that point meant busting my behind for years and years at the lower end of the professional food chain. After NYU, I toiled as a script supervisor on PBS documentaries, about as close to grunt work as it comes. Eventually I got a fling as a production assistant, assembling crews, but then the money dried up. (Thank you, Jesse Helms.) Whereupon I decided to try capitalism, working for three years as an AD on the soaps: first *Guiding Light,* then *As the World Turns,* then *Search for Tomorrow.* I can still hear the horrible music. Then a connection got me a slot at A&E as a line producer. Eight months later the series got canceled, which was when I decided the time had come to take my career into my own hands. I hocked every last credit card, went to Japan, and made a documentary. The result: I was an "overnight" success. Men started addressing me by my name.

My first film was about the impact of Zen on Japanese business. As part of my research, I shaved my head and lived three months at a Kyoto temple, eating bean curd three meals a day, after which I had enough credibility to land long interviews with Tokyo CEOs. I then sold the edited footage to A&E. When it became a critical hit, they financed a second film, about the many gods of India and how they impact everything about the place. There, I also got caught up in the mystical sensuality of ragas, Indian classical music, and took up the violin (one of my major professional mistakes). Next I moved on to Mexico's southern Yucatan to film a day in the life of a Maya village for the Discovery Channel. They wanted me to add some footage from Guatemala, but I scouted the country and decided it was too scary. Instead, I spent several months in Haiti filming voodoo rituals, again for A&E. *And met Steve.*

Then one day I checked my bank account and realized that, financially speaking, I was a "flop d'estime." I was doing the kind of work that does more for your reputation than your retirement plan. I decided to go more mainstream and see what happened. But to do that I needed a commercial partner, a backer.

Ironically enough, when I first teamed up with David, he had bottom-line problems too, but from the opposite direction. He was busy disproving the adage that nobody ever lost money underestimating the taste of the American public. He knew something was wrong, but what?

Apparently, when he started out, somebody told him cable audiences possessed an insatiable appetite for bare-skin-and-jiggle. Hey, he figured, that stuff he could grind out in his sleep. His first, and last, epic in the skin genre was *Wet T-Shirt Weekend,* whose title says it all. He explained the economics to me once, still baffled why the picture hadn't worked. He'd assumed all you had to do was find a bunch of nineteen-year-olds who looked like they're sixteen, go nonunion someplace down South with a beach, and take care the wardrobe trailer has nothing but string bikinis. "Cost only a million-eight to make," he declared with pride, "but every penny is on the screen."

He insisted I watch it, perplexed that it was universally regarded as a turkey. It was a painful experience, so much so I actually began to wonder if his heart was really in it. (The great schlockmeisters secretly think they're Fellini; they're operating at the top of their form, not consciously pandering.)

Chastened financially, he decided to move into low-budget action-adventure. His efforts, most notably *Virtual Cop,* had car chases, blue-screen explosions, buckets of fake blood. Somebody died creatively in every scene.

They did business in Asia and Southern Europe, but he was dumbfounded when nobody at HBO or Showtime would return his calls. It gnawed at his self-esteem.

That was the moment we found each other. He'd just concluded he needed somebody with a quality reputation to give

Applecore an image makeover, and I'd realized I needed somebody who knew more than I did about the mechanics of making and distributing independent films.

We were an odd couple. I finally shook hands on the partnership after he caved in and agreed I could do anything I wanted, so long as it looked mainstream enough to get picked up by Time-Warner or somebody else legit. Well, quasi-legit. We both agreed on no more bikinis and no more films about places that required cholera shots. It was something of a compromise on both our parts.

Thus far, though, we were getting along. Maybe luck was part of it, but *Baby Love* was still on schedule and on budget. And I already had a deal nearly in the bag with Lifetime, the women's channel, that would just about cover the costs. Everything after that would be gravy. Again, hope hope. Maybe not the theatrical release I'd been praying for, but good enough—so he had to smile and not give me a hard time about the money I'd just spent. Had to, right?

I took a deep breath.

"David, I did a little extra shooting this morning that's kind of . . . outside the plan. But it's really important. Want to hear about it?"

"What! I thought you were finished with principal photography." He looked disoriented, the deer in the headlights. Hints of extra crew time always had that effect on him. "You're saying this wasn't in the budget?"

"Just listen first, okay?" Like a politician, I avoided giving him a direct answer. I told him about the interview with Carly and the reason for it.

"Nice of you to share the news with me." His eyes narrowed. "I think we've got some big-time communication issues here."

"Look, don't worry. I'll figure out how to save some money somewhere else."

"Morgy, before we continue this unnerving conversation, we've got to have a serious review of the matter of cash flow." He frowned, then went back to whirling the pencil, his hair backlighted from the wide window, his eyes focused on its stubby eraser as though he'd just discovered a new strain of bacteria. "So let me break some news regarding the current budget."

He put down the pencil, adjusted its location on his desk, and looked up. "I didn't want to have to upset you, since the picture seems to be going so well, but we've drawn down almost all our cash. I actually think that's why Nicky was here today, sniffing around, wanting to see a rough cut. He's got a keen nose for indy cash-flow trouble."

"What are you saying?" It was unsettling to see David turning so serious. "Are we—?"

"I'm saying we can cover the payroll here, all our fixed nut, even Nicky's vig, for maybe six more weeks, if you and I don't pay ourselves. Of course, if we can get an advance on some kind of cable deal, that would tide us over more comfortably till this thing is in the can. But right now we're sailing pretty close on the wind. I've bet Applecore on your picture, Morgan. We can't screw this up."

I swallowed hard. I knew we were working on the edge, but I didn't know the edge was down to six weeks.

"David, I'm all but ready for postproduction. I'm just thinking I may need one more interview. Just a one-day shoot. I'm *going* to make this picture work. You'll see."

He sighed. "All right, if you think it's essential, get the footage. Maybe I can even shake another fifty out of Nicky, if I string him along about the distribution deal—don't look so alarmed, I won't go through with it. Anyway, I can tell he's impressed with the picture so far. Happy now?"

No, I wasn't happy. What was I going to do if Hannah Klein had bad news? Adoption? I finally was facing the fact

I'd possibly been making a movie about myself all this time. Like Yeats, penning his own tombstone. "Cast a cold eye, on life, on death . . ."

So why not give him the whole story?

"David, if it turns out Steve and I can't have a baby, I've begun thinking about trying to adopt." There it was. More pain. "Maybe I'm about to become the heroine of my own picture."

He stared at me incredulously.

"Morgy, you of all people should know by now that adopting would take up all your energy, like a giant sponge. Come on. I've seen your dailies. I got it, about how hard it is. You telling me now *you* didn't get it?"

He was right. Righter than he realized. But then I thought again about Carly Grove, who'd found Kevin in no time at all, with zero hassles. The only troubling part was that it was all so mysterious. . . .

After I left David's office, I remembered I hadn't actually had lunch, so I grabbed two hot dogs with sauerkraut (okay, it was junk, but I secretly loved kosher franks) and a Diet Pepsi to go, from one of the striped-umbrella vendors, then hailed a cab clutching the grungy brown bag.

I was heading for Hannah Klein's office on the Upper West Side. And now I had another clock ticking in addition to the biological one. The big money clock in the sky was suddenly on final countdown.

Three

It took only a few minutes for Hannah Klein's assistant, Lori, to run the pregnancy test that confirmed my suspicions and settled my future. Steve's and my final attempt, another intrauterine insemination (IUI, med-speak for an expensive "turkey baster") with the last of his deposit, had failed. The end. The bitter end.

"Morgan," Hannah declared, staring over her desk, her raspy New York voice boring through me like a drill, "given how this has all turned out, maybe you ought to just start considering adoption—if having a child still means that much to you."

Hannah Klein was pushing seventy, a chain smoker who should have been dead a decade ago, and she unfailingly spoke the truth. Her gaze carried only synthetic solace, but I was probably her fifteenth patient of the day and maybe she was running low on empathy. Oddly, though, sitting there in her office, miserable, I felt strangely liberated. I adored the woman, a child of the Holocaust, with layers of steel like a samurai sword, but I also loved the thought of never again having to go through the humiliation of cowering in her straight-backed office chair, like a so-so student on probation waiting to receive my failing grade.

It was now time to come to grips with what I'd known in my heart for a long time. God had made me a theoretically functional reproductive machine that just wouldn't kick over.

Translation: no cysts, fibroids, polyps, no ovulatory abnormalities. My uterus and Fallopian tubes were just fine, Steve's sperm counts were okay, but no baby was swimming into life inside me.

Sometimes, however, reality asks too much. It's not easy getting your mind around the idea that some part of your life is over, finally over. The baby part. To admit that it's time to move on to Plan B, whatever that is. Such realizations can take a while, especially if you've been living with high-level hope, no matter how irrational.

"I frankly don't know what else we can do," she went on, projecting through my abyss of gloom. She was shuffling papers on her ash-strewn desk, white hair in a bun, fine-tuned grit in her voice. Upper West Side, a fifty-year fixture. She never wore perfume, but to me she always smelled faintly of roses mixed with smoke. Earthy. "Aside from trying in vitro."

We'd already discussed that, but it was definitely the bottom level of Hell. Besides, I was running out of money, and spirit. And now, with Steve gone, the whole idea seemed moot anyway.

"So," she concluded, "barring that, we've done everything possible, run every test there is, both on you and on your . . ."

"Steve," I inserted into her pause. She seemed to deliberately block his name at crucial moments. Maybe she thought I could have done better. Maybe a nice solid dentist who owned a suit instead of some freelance photo jock who showed up for his sperm counts wearing khaki safari shirts. Well, let her deal with it.

". . . and I can't find anything. Sometimes, the body just won't cooperate. We may never know why. You've got to face that. But still, adoption is always an option."

Adoption. All along I'd told myself I didn't have the courage, or the heart. Making movies is a full-time job, not leaving time to go filling out forms and jumping through hoops for years and years. And to cap it off, I was just two years short of the big four-oh and financially struggling—hardly an adoption agency's profile of "ideal."

But now, now I'd just discovered Carly Grove and the miracle of Children of Light. So maybe there really could be a way to adopt a beautiful child with no hassles. Maybe it would simplify everything to the point I could actually pull it off. Could this be my Plan B? Then what if Steve came back? Could we be a family finally?

I wasn't used to being that lucky. And I still wanted Hannah Klein's thoughts, a reality test, which was why I pressed her on the point.

"Truthfully, do you think adopting is really a workable idea for somebody like me? Would I—?"

"Morgan, I know you're making a film about the realities of the adoption process. We both realize it's not easy." She must have seen something needful in my eyes, because she continued on, adding detail, letting the well-known facts convey the bad news. "As you're well aware, finding a young, healthy, American baby nowadays is all but impossible. At the very least it can take years." She was fiddling with some papers on her desk, avoiding my eyes. Then she stubbed out her cigarette in a gesture that seemed intended to gain time. "And even if you're willing to take a baby that's foreign-born, there still can be plenty of heartbreak. That's just how it is."

"I'd always thought so too," I said. "It's actually the underlying motif of my picture. But today I had an incredible experience. I filmed an interview of a single woman, early forties, who just adopted a baby boy. It took less than three months and he's blond and blue-eyed and perfect. I saw him, I held him, and I can assure you he's as American as peach cobbler. The way she tells it, the whole adoption process was a snap. Zero hassles and red tape."

"That's most exceptional." She peered at me dubiously. "Actually more like impossible. Frankly, I don't believe it. This child must have been kidnapped or something. How old, exactly, was he when she got him?"

"I don't know. Just a few weeks, I think."

Her eyes bored in. "This woman, whoever she is, was very, very lucky. *If* what she says is true."

"The organization that got the baby for her is called Children of Light," I went on. "That's all I know, really. I think it's up the Hudson somewhere, past the Cloisters. Have you ever heard of them?"

Dr. Hannah Klein, I knew, was pushing three score and ten, had traveled the world, seen virtually everything worth seeing. In younger years she was reputed to have had torrid liaisons with every notable European writer on the West Side. Her list of conquests read like an old *New Yorker* masthead. If only I looked half that great at her age. But whatever else, she was unflappable. Good news or bad, she took it and gave it with grace. Until this moment. Her eyes registered undisguised dismay.

"You can't mean it. Not that place. All that so-called New Age . . . Are you really sure you want to get involved in something like that?"

I found myself deeply confused. Were we talking about the same thing? Then I remembered Carly *had* said something about an infertility clinic.

"Frankly, nobody knows the first thing about that man," Hannah raged on. "All you get is hearsay. He's supposedly one of those alternative-medicine types, and a few people claim he's had some success, but it's all anecdotal. My own opinion is, it's what real physicians call the 'placebo effect.' If a patient believes hard enough something will happen, some of the time it actually might. For God's sake, I'm not even sure he's board-certified. Do yourself a favor and stay away. Oftentimes, people like that do more harm than good." Then her look turned inquisitive. "Did you say he's providing children for adoption now? That's peculiar. When did he start that?"

Was I hearing some kind of professional jealousy slipping out? Hannah Klein was definitely Old School to the core.

"He who?" I was trying to remember the name of the doctor Carly had mentioned. "You mean—"

"He says his name is . . . what? Goddard? Yes, Alex Goddard. He's—"

My pager chirped, interrupting her, and she paused, clearly annoyed. I looked down to see a number I knew well. It had to be Lou Crenshaw, our aforementioned security guard. He'd been off today, but there was only one reason he would page me: some kind of news from Lenox Hill.

Maybe it was good news about Sarah! My hopes soared. Or maybe it was bad. Please, dear God.

"I'm sorry, Dr. Klein. I've got to go. Right now. It could be a medical emergency."

She nodded, then slid open the top drawer of her desk and handed me a list of adoption agencies. "All right, here, take this and look it over. I've dealt with some of them, letters of reference for patients like you." She must have realized the insensitivity of that last quip, because she took my hand and squeezed it, the closest we'd ever come to intimacy. "Let me know if I can help you, Morgan. Really."

Grasping the lifeless paper, I ached for Steve all over again. Times like this, you need some support. I finally glanced down at the list as I headed out. Sure enough, Children of Light was nowhere to be seen.

Why not? I wondered. They'd found Kevin, a lovely blond baby boy, for Carly, a single woman, in no time at all. They sounded like miracle-makers, and if there was ever a moment for miracles, this was it. Shouldn't they at least have been given a footnote?

I wanted to stalk right back and demand to know the real reason she was so upset, but I truly didn't want to waste a moment.

Lou had paged me from a pay phone—he didn't actually have a cell phone of his own—and I recognized the number as belonging to the phone next to the Lenox Hill Hospital's third-floor nurses' station. When I tried it, however, it was busy, so I decided to just get in my car and drive there as fast as I could.

And as I battled the traffic down Broadway, I realized that by diverting my mind from my own trivial misery to the genuine tragedy of Sarah, I was actually getting my perspective back. That was one of the many things Sarah had done for me over the years.

All right. Sarah and Lou, who figure so largely in this, deserve a full-dress introduction, so obviously I should start by admitting I'd known them all my life. Lou was my mother's half brother, three years younger than she was, who came along after my grandfather widowed my grandmother in a freak tractor rollover and she remarried a lifelong bachelor neighbor. (I have old snapshots of them, and I can tell you they all were cheerless, beady-eyed American Gothics.) I'd arranged for David to hire Lou eight months earlier, not too long after I came to Applecore. At that time he'd just taken early retirement from the FBI, because of an event that shook us all up pretty seriously.

For some time now, Lou's been a rumpled, Willy Loman figure, like a traveling salesman on the skids, shirts frayed at the collars, face tinted from a truckload of Early Times. Over the past fifteen years I'd watched his waist size travel from about thirty-three inches to thirty-seven, and I'd guess it's been at least a decade since a barber asked him if he needed any off the top. Natalie Rose, his spirited, wiry wife of thirty-seven years, succumbed to ovarian cancer seven years ago last September, and I know for a fact she was the one who bought his shirts, provided him with general maintenance.

My first memories of him were when he was a county sheriff in a little burg called Coleman, smack in the middle of Texas, some fifty-five long, dusty miles from the ranch where I grew up. When I was about fourteen, I remember he gave up on that and moved to Dallas, there to enter training for the FBI. He eventually ended up in New Orleans, and then, after Natalie Rose passed away and he more or less fell apart, he got transferred to New York, considered the elephant graveyard of an FBI career.

Probably the reason I saw him as much as I did as a kid was because of my cousin Sarah, his and Rose's only child. She was six years younger than me, a lot when you're kids, but we were very special to each other, had a kind of bonding that I've never really known with anybody since. We spent a lot of time staying at each other's house, me the almost-grown-up, and truthfully, I loved her helplessly, like a little sister. I always wanted to think she needed me, which can be the most affirming feeling in the world. I do know I needed her.

She was now lying in a coma, and the way she got there was the tragedy of my life, and Lou's. To begin with, though, let me say Sarah was a pretty blonde from the start, with sunshiny hair that defined her as perpetually optimistic—and who wouldn't be, given the heads she always turned. (I was—am—blond too, though with eyes more gray than her turquoise blues, but for me blond's always been, on balance, an affliction: Sexist film producers assume, damnit, that you're a failed showgirl, or worse. I've actually dyed it brunette from time to time in hopes of being taken more seriously.) Sarah and I had always had our own special chemistry, like a composite of opposites to make a complete, whole human being. Whereas I was the rational, left-brained slave of the concrete, she was a right-brained dweller in a world of what-might-be. For years and years, she seemed to live in a dream universe of her own making, one of imagination and fanciful states.

Once, when she was five, Lou hid in his woodworking shop for a month and made an elaborate cutaway dollhouse to give her at Christmas. But when I offered to help her find little dolls that would fit into it, she declared she only wanted angels to live there. So we spent the rest of the winter—I dropped everything—hunting down Christmas tree ornaments that looked like heavenly creatures. She'd swathe them in tinsel and sit them in balls of cotton she said were little clouds.

I always felt that just being around her opened my life to new dimensions, but her dream existence constantly drove Lou and Rose to distraction. I think it was one of the reasons he never got as close to her as he wanted, and his feelings about that were deep frustration, and hurt. He loved her so much, but he could never really find a common wavelength.

Finally she came down to earth enough to start college, and eventually she graduated from SMU in biology, then enrolled at Columbia for premed. By then she was interested in the workings of the brain, in altered states. I didn't know if it was just more pursuit of fantasy, but at least she was going about it professionally.

Anyway, when Lou got transferred to New York, he was actually delighted, since it gave him a chance to be closer to her. We all managed to get together for family reunions pretty often, though Lou and Sarah were talking past each other half the time.

Then tragedy struck. She was just finishing her master's, and had been accepted by Cornell Medical—Lou was bursting with pride—when he suggested they use her Christmas break to drive back down to Texas together, there to visit Rose's grave. (I think he really wanted to show off his budding doctor-to-be to the family.) Sarah was driving when they crossed the state line into Louisiana and were sideswiped by a huge Mack eighteen-wheeler, which was in the process of jackknifing across a frozen patch of interstate. They were thrown into the path of an oncoming car, and when the blood and snow were cleared, a six-year-old girl in the other vehicle was dead.

The result was Sarah decided she'd taken a human life. Her own minor facial cuts—which Lou immediately had repaired with plastic surgery—somehow evolved into a major disfigurement of her soul. All her mental eccentricities, which had been locked up somewhere when she started college, came back like a rush of demons loosed from some Pandora's box deep in her psyche. She dropped out of school, and before long she was in the throes of a full-scale mental meltdown. She disappeared, and in the following two years Lou got exactly one card from her, postmarked in San Francisco with no return address. He carried it with him at all times and we both studied it often, puzzling over the New Age astrological symbol on the front. The brief note announced she'd acquired "Divine Energy" and was living on a new plane of consciousness.

Then eight months ago, the State Department notified Lou she was missing in Guatemala. She'd overstayed her visa and nobody knew where she was.

So how did her "new plane of consciousness" land her in Central America? Was that part of the fantasy world she'd now returned to? Lou still worked downtown at 26 Federal Plaza, but he immediately took a leave of absence and, though he spoke not a syllable of Spanish, plunged down there to look for her.

He was there a month, following false leads, till he finally ran into a Reverend Ben Jackson, late of a self-styled Protestant ministry in Mississippi, who was one of the ardent new Evangelicals swarming over Central America. The man mentioned that some chicle harvesters in the northwest Peten Department of Guatemala had found a young woman in an old dugout canoe on the Guatemala side of the wide Usumacinta River, near a tributary called the Rio Tigre, lodged in amongst overhanging trees. She'd been struck on the head and presumably set adrift somewhere upriver, left for dead. She was now in a coma, resting at Jackson's "Jesus es el Hombre" clinic, also located deep in the northwest Peten rain forest. He had no idea who she was.

Lou rented a car and drove there, almost a day on unpaved roads. It was Sarah.

Thus she was no longer missing; she was now the apparent victim of an attempted murder. However, rather than being helpful, the local *policía* appeared annoyed she'd been found, thereby reopening the matter. A blond gringa was out hiking somewhere she had no business being in the first place and tripped and hit her head on something. Where's the crime?

Lou brought her back to New York, using a medevac plane supplied by the State Department, which, wanting no more CIA-type scandals of American nationals being murdered in Guatemala, cooperated with great dispatch.

After that, he needed a job that would afford him time flexibility, so he could be at her bedside as much as possible. David was looking for a security head, and I realized it would be a perfect match. Since we didn't really need a full-time person, Lou could spend a lot of hours at Lenox Hill, watching over Sarah.

She was just lying there now, no sign of consciousness, her body being kept alive with IV. I'd go by to visit her as much as I could, and almost as bad as seeing the comatose Sarah was seeing the grief in Lou's eyes. He would sit there at the hospital every day, sometimes several hours a day, fingering an old engraved locket that carried her high-school graduation picture, just rubbing it through his fingers like a rosary. We always made allowances when he wanted to take time off during one of our shooting schedules, figuring maybe he was helping her. . . .

As I turned east, to go crosstown, I thought again about Sarah's condition. She and I looked a lot alike, dense blond hair for one thing, but to see her now you'd scarcely know it, since hers had been clipped down to nothing by the hospital. Her cheekbones, however, were still strong, a quality now exaggerated by her emaciated state, and her eyes, which I had not seen in years, were a deep languid, turquoise blue. But seeing her lying there inert, being kept alive with tubes and liquids, wearing pressure pants to help circulate blood through her legs, you'd scarcely realize she'd been a strikingly beautiful woman before the accident.

What's worse, from what I knew, the horrific brain traumas that bring on a coma don't automatically go away when you regain consciousness. If the coma is the result of a head injury, and if it lasts more than a few days, the chances of regaining all your mental functions are up for grabs. Lou once said there's a scale of eight stages to full recovery. People who have short comas can sometimes come out of them and go through those stages quickly—from initial eye movement to full mental faculties. Others, who've been under for months or longer can require years to come back. Sometimes they can only blink their eyes to answer questions; sometimes they babble on incessantly. They can talk sense, or they can talk nonsense, incoherent fantasies, even strings of numbers. The brain is a complex, unpredictable thing. . . .

I always thought about this as I took the elevator up to Lenox Hill's third floor. The room where they kept Sarah was painted a pale, sterile blue, and made even more depressing by stark fluorescent lights. Everything was chrome and baked-on enamel, including the instruments whose CRT screens reported her bodily functions. None of the instruments, however, had ever shown the brain activity associated with consciousness.

Lou was there when I walked in. He had a kind of wildness in his eyes, maybe what you get when you mix hope with despair. We hugged each other and he said, "She had a moment, Morgy. She knew me. I'm sure she did."

Then he told me in detail what had happened. A nurse passing Sarah's room had happened to notice an unexpected flickering on one of her monitors. She'd immediately informed the nurses' station, where instructions included Lou's home number.

He'd grabbed a cab and raced there. When he got to her room, he pushed his way past the Caribbean nurses and bent over her, the first time he had hoped a conversation with her would be anything but a monologue.

"Honey, can you hear me?"

There was no sign, save the faint flicker of an eyelid.

It was enough. His own pulse rocketed.

"Where's the damned doctor?"

While the physician was being summoned, he had a chance to study her. Yes, there definitely was some movement behind her eyelids. And her regular breathing had become less measured, as though she were fighting to overcome her autonomic nervous system and challenge life on her own.

Finally an overworked Pakistani intern arrived. He proceeded to fiddle with the monitors, doing something Lou did not understand. Then without warning—and certainly attributable to nothing the physician did—Sarah opened her eyes.

Lou, who had not seen those eyes for several years, caught himself feasting on their rich, aquatic blue. He looked into them, but they did not look back. They were focused on infinity, adrift in a lost sea of their own making. They stared at him a moment, then vanished again behind her eyelids.

He told me all this and then his voice trailed off, his despair returning. . . .

"Lou, it's a start. Whatever happens is bound to be slow. But this could be the beginning. . . ."

We both knew what I was saying was perilously close to wishful thinking, but nobody in the room was under oath. For the moment, though, she was back in her coma, as though nothing had changed.

I waited around until eight o'clock, when I finally convinced myself that being there was not doing anybody any good. Lou, I later learned, stayed on till well past eleven, when they finally had to send security to evict him.

Okay, I've been holding out on the most important detail. The truth is, I hardly knew what to make of it. At one point when I was bending over Sarah's seemingly unconscious face, her eyes had clicked open for just a fleeting moment, startling me the way those horror movies do when the "undead" suddenly come alive. Lou was in his chair and didn't see it, didn't notice me jump.

The last thing I wanted to do was tell him about it, and I was still shivering as I shoved my key into the Toyota's ignition and headed for home. She'd looked directly into my eyes, a flicker of recognition, and then came the fear. She sort of moved her mouth, trying to speak, but all that came was a silent scream, after which her eyes went blank as death and closed again.

She knew me, I was sure of it, but she had looked through me and seen a reminder of some horror now locked deep in her soul.

Four

Lou took the next few days off to spend by Sarah's side, but nothing more happened. I repeatedly called him at the hospital to check on her, though it was becoming clear her brush with consciousness had only been an interlude. Finally, I decided to show Carly's rushes to David (he loved them) and try to concentrate on postproduction for the rest of the week and the weekend, anything to make me not have to dwell on Sarah's ghostlike, soundless cry of anguish.

Postproduction. When you're shooting a picture, you have to make all kinds of compromises; but in post, with luck and skill, you can transform that raw footage into art. You mix and cut the takes till the performances are taut; you loop in rerecorded dialogue where necessary to get just the right reading of a line; the Foley guys give you clear sound effects where the production sound is muddy; and you balance the hues of reds and blues, darks and lights till you get just the right color tone.

All of the polishing that came with post still lay ahead. The first step was to go through the rough cut and "spot" the film, marking places where the sound effects or dialogue would need to be replaced with rerecorded studio sound—which meant several days, maybe weeks, of looping to edit out background noise and make the dialogue sound rich and crisp. For some of it, the actors would have to come back in and lip-synch themselves, which they always hate.

It was daunting, to have to work back and forth between production sound tracks and loop tracks, blending alternate takes. You had to figure on only doing about ten minutes of film a day, and then, after all that, you had to get the "opticals" right, the fade-outs and dissolves and, finally, the credit sequences.

Normally, once I started post, I would have exactly ten weeks to accomplish all that before the executive producer, David, got his hands on my picture. That was the prerogative that was part of the standard director's contract. Now, though, I figured that was out the window. With the money going fast, I had to produce a rough cut and get the picture sold to cable in six weeks, period.

But first things first. I deeply needed at least one more interview—Carly's was too much of a happy one-note—which was why I needed to shoot Paula Marks. It was now on for Thursday, today.

The appointment had taken all weekend, including a Sunday brunch, to set up, but by that time I was sure this second mother would be perfect. She was a tall, willowy woman, forty-three, who had let her hair start going to gray. Honesty, it was right there in her pale brown eyes. She wrote children's books, had never married—she now believed she never would—and had decided to adopt a child because she had a lot of extra love she felt was going to waste. Different from Carly Grove, maybe, but not in the matter of strength, and fearless independence.

We arrived around ten A.M. to discover her apartment was in one of those sprawling prewar West Side monoliths, thick plaster walls and a rabbit's warren of halls and foyers, legacy of an age before "lofts" and open spaces. Terribly cramped for shooting. But Paula agreed to let the blue-jeaned crew move her old, overstuffed couch out of the living room, along with the piles of books that lined the walls.

Another issue was makeup. At first Paula insisted she didn't want any. Never wore it, it was deceitful, and she didn't want to appear on camera looking like Barbie. (Small chance of that, I thought. A little war paint now and then might help your chances of landing a father for this child.) Eventually Arlene persuaded her that cameras lie and the only way to look like yourself is to enhance those qualities that make you you. It was a thin argument, but Arlene came from a long line of apparel proprietors who could unload sunlamps in the Sahara.

Paula's adopted daughter Rachel, who was a year and a half old, was running around the apartment, blond tresses flowing, dragging a doll she had named Angie. Except the name came out "Ann-gee." She was immediately adopted by the crew, and Erica, the production manager, was soon teaching her how to play patty-cake. Then Rachel wanted to demonstrate her new skills at eating spaghetti. In five minutes she was covered head to toe in Ragu tomato sauce.

When the Panaflex was finally rolling, the story Paula spun out was almost identical to the one told by Carly Grove. She'd spent hours with all the legal services recommended by NYSAC, New York Singles Adopting Children, listening to them describe a scenario of delays and paperwork and heartache. It could be done, but it could take years. Look, she'd declared, I'll cash in my IRA, do anything, just give me some hope. Okay, they'd replied, tighten your belt, scare up sixty big ones, and go to see Children of Light. We hear stories. . . .

Soon after she called them, the skies had opened. A New Age physician and teacher there, a man with striking eyes named Alex Goddard, had made it happen. Rachel was hers in just four months, no paperwork.

Sure, she declared, Children of Light was expensive, but Alex Goddard was a deeply spiritual man who really took the time to get to know you, even practically begged you to come to his clinic-commune and go through his course of mind-body fertility treatment. But when she insisted she just wanted to adopt, he obligingly found Rachel for her. How could she be anything but grateful? She was so happy, she wanted everybody in the world to know about him.

As she bubbled on, I found my attention wandering to Rachel, who'd just escaped from the crew keeping her in the kitchen and was running through the living room, singing a song from *Sesame Street.* Something about the way she moved was very evocative.

Where've I seen her before? Then it dawned on me. Her walk made me think of Kevin. Actually, everything about her reminded me of Kevin. Were all kids starting to look the same? God, I wanted them both.

Yeah, I thought, daydreaming of holding her, she's Kevin all over again, clear as day. She's a dead ringer to be his older sister. It feels very strange.

Or maybe I was just seeing things. To some extent all babies looked alike, right? That is, until you have one of your own.

I had to swallow hard, to try to collect my thoughts. Carly and Paula scarcely even knew each other. If Rachel really was Kevin's sister, they'd never know anything about it.

Incredible . . . it was just too big a coincidence.

But still . . . and what about the film footage? Show close-ups of the kids, and anybody not legally blind was going to see the similarity. . . .

Why would somebody give up *two* children for adoption? I found myself wondering. Giving up one was tragic enough.

"Cut." I waved at everybody. "Take ten. We need to recharge here, take a break and stretch."

Paula was caught off guard, in the middle of a sentence, and she let her voice trail off, puzzled.

"Hey, I'm sorry Rachel came barging in," Paula finally said. "Guess she broke everybody's concentration, huh?"

"Yeah, well, sometimes we all need to lean back and take a fresh run at things." I called to Rachel, who came trotting over, spaghetti sauce still on her face, and picked her up. I felt at a loss about what to do. Tell Paula her daughter had a younger brother in the Village, and she might fall apart. "I was actually curious about something. Do you know anything about Rachel's birth mother?"

"I don't want to know. It would disrupt my life. And my peace of mind." Her eyes acquired a kind of sadness mingled with anxiety. "I'm reconciled to the fact she probably got into some kind of trouble, may not have exactly been Nobel Prize material, but I'm a big believer in nurture over nature. That's why I write books for kids. So I think Rachel's going to end up being a lot more like me than like her real mother."

Brave words. But I'll bet you anything the story of Rachel's mother is a lot more complicated than you imagine.

I glanced at my watch, the hour pushing four-thirty. Time to call it a wrap. Besides, if we shot any more today, the crew would end up on overtime, and David was getting increasingly nervous about my extra costs.

I also needed a little downtime to reflect.

"Look, I think I've got enough footage to work with for now. Let me just get the release signed, take this film downtown, and get it processed. Maybe we can come back for another shoot when I figure out exactly where this is going."

"Anytime. Just give me some notice and I'll try to have the place cleaned up more next time."

"Don't worry. I like it to look real. Just sign the release and I'll take it from there." I was about to set Rachel back on the floor when something caught in my sweater. Looking down, I realized it was a tiny charm bracelet, with two little medallions on it. One was a little red plastic likeness of Po-

cahontas, the Disney character, and the other was a silver
face of a cat, long and stylized. And on the back, those curious lines and dots again, only these were arranged differ-
ently from those on the one Carly's boy Kevin had.

"Paula, what's this? This cat. Where'd you get it?"

"Oh, that." She smiled. "She was wearing it when I got
her, on a little silk cord around her waist, under her diaper.
They told me it was a gift from her real mother, a keepsake.
Sort of breaks your heart, but the way they said it, you want
to keep it forever. . . ."

At that moment Erica was just plugging the phone back
in, and the second she did, the old, black Panasonic cordless
began to ring.

"Hang on a sec," Paula said. "Let me get that. My agent
is supposed—" She'd picked up the phone and was plopping
back onto the couch. "Hi."

Then her look turned blank. "No, of course not." She fell
into an uncomfortable pause, looking around at everybody.
Then she continued. "Nobody's contacted me." She halted
again, her face white, and stared directly at me. I abruptly
sensed that I was the topic of the conversation. "Sure I'm
sure. . . . Yes, I remember signing. . . . Don't worry. I'd have
no reason to. . . . Okay, sure, I'll let you know."

She clicked off the phone and looked up with startled
eyes. "It was somebody who said they worked for Children
of Light. She wanted to know if you'd contacted me." Her
face collapsed. "You. She asked me specifically about *you*.
By name. How did—?"

"I have no idea." My hands were growing cold. Had Carly
told them about me? Why would she do that? "Anyway, you
handled it okay."

Which made me wonder. If Children of Light was such a
perfect organization, why was Paula so frightened she im-

mediately felt compelled to lie, to swear she hadn't broken their rules?

"Right." Her composure was slowly coming back. "Look, now that I think about it, why should they care? It doesn't make any sense. They got their money." She turned to me. "Let me have that release."

She seized the paper and endorsed it with a flourish.

My pulse was still in overdrive, but I hugged her, then signaled the crew that shooting was over for the day.

"Okay, everybody. Time to wrap."

The gang immediately began striking the lights and rolling up electrical cords. They would take the equipment back downtown and deliver the film to the lab, while I would head home. It had been a long day and lots of thinking was needed. Besides, it was starting to rain, a dismal spatter against Paula's grimy windows, as the gray spring afternoon had begun darkening toward sullen evening.

"Listen, I enjoyed this." Paula had taken Rachel in her arms and was stroking her blond hair. "I really love talking about her. She's changed my life."

I gave her another hug. "You're great. And you're going to be wonderful in the film." If I used her. The whole thing was getting unnerving. "You have no idea how much you've helped." Then I said good-bye to Rachel, who responded with a perfect "Bye, bye" through her haze of spaghetti sauce.

Okay, get the superintendent. Crank up the freight elevator. Get out of here.

Scott Ventri, key grip, took charge of handling the gear, dictating which equipment got loaded on first. I watched long enough to make sure everything was going okay, and then I joined Arlene, old friend and queen of outrageous makeup, on the other elevator.

"You notice it?" she whispered. The door had just closed.

"Notice what?" I knew full well what she was talking about. But it just felt too bizarre.

"Those kids could almost be twins. That little boy last week, and this girl. They look just alike. It's spooky."

"Guess their parents couldn't figure out what was causing those pregnancies. So they just kept having more babies." I decided to try to insert some humor, deflect the conversation. "Maybe we should tell Paula and Carly."

"Very dumb." Arlene bit at a long, red, false fingernail, a perennial habit for as long as I'd known her. "We should mind our own business, that's what we should do."

"Works for me. But it also proves we were smart not to shoot any footage of the kids. The whole world would realize something's funny." Then I had an idea. "Want to come downtown to my place after we unload? Have some deep thoughts over what all this means?"

First the kids, then the call. What was this guy Alex Goddard, whoever he was, up to? Definitely time to talk to somebody . . .

"Gee, I'd love to," Arlene was saying, "but I can't. I gotta go out to Kew Gardens for my mom and dad's anniversary tonight. Their thirty-fifth, can you believe? Of course, I was a very late baby." She blinked her dark, languid eyes, as though rehearsing the line for a downtown club.

"A miracle of modern fertility science, right?" Shit. Arlene, I need you.

"Right." She giggled, then seemed to study the flashing lights on the elevator's control panel. "God, those kids, they're too good to be true. I'd love to have one like that." She impatiently pounded the number one a couple of times, perhaps hoping to speed our creaky descent. "I can get bonked every night of the week, but I can't get a serious boyfriend. New York's clubs aren't exactly brimming with the vine-covered-cottage-and-picket-fence type. And as for the pickings at work, given the kind of pictures David makes, forget it. Last thing I need is some twenty-year-old pothead who thinks with his wang."

"I'm afraid I'm not helping you much with this one." I'd cast *Baby Love* mostly with Off-Broadway unknowns. The actress Mary Gregg was a veteran of Joseph Papp's original Public Theater, the experimental enterprise downtown. The few male parts all went to guys who were either gay or married.

"Oy, what can you do, right? If it happens, it happens." Arlene watched the door begin to stutter open as we bumped onto the lobby level. Then she zeroed in on me. "You really want a kid too, don't you? I mean, that's why you did this script, right? Which, by the way, is great. I mean the script."

"I think most women do, down deep."

She smiled. "Well, if I ever have one, it's going to be the old-fashioned way. It's a heck of a lot cheaper than adopting." She was heading out, into the front foyer. "Not to mention more fun getting there."

On that I definitely had to agree.

The lobby's prewar look was gray and dismal, and as we emerged onto the street, the rain had turned into a steady downpour. Lou was off again today, down at the hospital with Sarah, so I'd engaged a doorman from a new co-op across the street to keep an eye on our vans. A crisp twenty had extracted his solemn promise to do just that. At the moment, however, he was nowhere to be seen. Proving, I suppose, David's theory that we needed our own security guy at all location shoots.

Lou, I thought, I hope you're finally getting through to her.

"No limo, but at least we get first call on the vans," Arlene observed, her voice not hiding the sarcasm. "Just once I'd like to work for somebody who had serious VIP transportation."

"David would walk before he'd get a limo."

We were headed down the street, me digging out my keys, when I noticed the man standing in the rain. He was just behind our lead van, a three-year-old gray Ford, waiting for us.

My first thought was he must be connected to Nicky Russo, David's wiseguy banker, here to bust my chops over the Teamster issue. Screw him. Just my luck he'd send somebody the very day Lou was not on hand. But then I realized I'd guessed wrong. The man was more Hispanic than Italian. He also was short, solidly built, late fifties maybe, with intense eyes and gray hair that circled his balding pate like the dirty snow around a volcano's rim. As he moved toward us, I thought I detected something military in his bearing, not so much the crispness of a soldier but rather the authoritative swagger of an officer. Well, maybe a retired officer.

"The paper on your windshield says you are filming a movie," came a voice with a definite Spanish accent. No greetings, no hiya, how're you doin'? Just the blunt statement. Then, having established what was already clear to all at hand, he continued. "It says the title is *Baby Love*. Why are you making this movie here?"

That was it. I glanced at Arlene, who'd turned white as a sheet. You get a lot of onlookers around a location shoot, but not too many who challenge your right to exist, which was exactly what was coming through in his menacing tone.

I handed Arlene the keys. "Here, go ahead and open up. I'll handle this."

Then I turned back to him. "What you saw in the windshield of the vans is a New York City Film Board permit. That's all the information we are required to provide. If you read it, you know everything I'm obliged to tell you." I returned his stare. "However, if people ask nicely, I'm happy to answer their questions."

"Are you making this movie about a person in this building? Your other films have been documentaries."

God help me, I thought. Is this what my fans are like?

Then it hit me. I don't know how I'd missed the connection, but now it just leapt out. First the phone call, then this hood. Somebody was tracking me.

"I'm scouting locations," I lied, feeling a chill go through me. "We're second unit for an action film, shooting some prep footage for the producers. Does the name Arnold Schwarzenegger mean anything to you?"

"Then why is the film about babies?"

"That's meant to be a joke. Remember the movie *Twins*? It's a joke title. Do you understand?"

At that moment, Paul Nulty came barging out the door with a huge klieg light, followed by several other members of the crew carrying sound gear. Our cordial tête-à-tête was about to be disrupted.

My new Hispanic friend saw them and abruptly drew up. That was when I noticed the shoulder holster under his jacket, containing some sort of snub-nosed pistol.

Jesus, I thought, this must be what some kind of hired killer looks like. That gun's not a prop.

"I think you are lying." He closed his jacket and, ignoring my crew, bored in relentlessly on me, his eyes dead and merciless. "That is a big mistake."

It was the first time in my life I'd ever stood next to a man who had a gun and was deeply ticked at me. He'd *wanted* me to see his piece, just to make sure I took him seriously. He wasn't threatening me, per se. Rather he was letting me know how strongly he cared about what I was doing.

Well, damn him, but I still was scared. I might have managed to bluff Nicky Russo, but he was a guy who operated by an age-old set of Sicilian rules. *This* thug didn't strike me as the rule-book type.

Hand shaking, I pulled out my cell phone, flicked it open, and punched in 911.

"Listen, if you're threatening me with a gun, I'm calling the cops. Whatever problem you have with the New York film industry, you can explain it to them."

New York's police emergency number was still ringing as he abruptly turned and strode away.

I clicked the phone shut and moved to get out of the way as a trolley loaded with more gear was rolled past me down the sidewalk. Unfortunately, I also took my eyes off him for a second, and when I looked up again, he seemed to have disappeared into the rain, though I did notice somebody who could have been him get into a long black car well down the block and speed off toward Broadway.

"What did that creep want?" Arlene asked, coming back with the keys.

I was only slowly returning to reality, and it took me a few moments to form a coherent answer through all the adrenaline surging into my brain.

"I . . . I don't know. But I think I'd better warn everybody to keep an eye out for strangers. He's . . . he's wound a little tight, to put it mildly." I was still shaking, which she fortunately failed to notice. At that point, there seemed no great reason to spook her with mention of the gun.

"Boy, he wasn't just some homeless junkie," she said. "He looked like a heavy in one of David's old action pictures. All he needed was a Mack-10."

"Right." Jesus, Arlene, I think he might have *had* one. "So let's get moving."

As I watched the vans being loaded, slowly calming down, I kept thinking about him. He was undoubtedly connected to the phone call, but why would anybody be so worried about what I was doing? I couldn't think of any serious reason.

Half an hour later we were all headed downtown. Along the rain-swept streets the "All Beef" hot-dog vendors cowered under their red-and-yellow striped umbrellas, while departing office workers, briefcases perched above their heads as makeshift protection, scurried along the edges of buildings searching for cabs. While Arlene continued to chat nonstop, I tried to do a little mental processing. And my mind kept drifting back to the sight of little Rachel, and Kevin. What perfect kids. The way she was running . . .

Hey, wait a minute. How could they be siblings? Brother and sister? Rachel was almost exactly half a year older than Kevin. Biology didn't work that way. No way could they be related, but still . . . they looked *so* alike.

I realized Arlene hadn't put it together about the ages. The brother/sister theory made absolutely no sense. Those kids were *born six months apart.*

If that wasn't strange enough, why did they both have those tiny cat medallions with the lines and dots on the back? Which were actually kind of creepy, more like sacred amulets than little toys.

Talk to Lou. He might have some insights.

No, better yet, go to the source. Children of Light. Call Alex Goddard's adoption agency or clinic or whatever it is and make an appointment.

Five

I was feeling a bit off center that evening, but I explained it away as mental overload, the rain, and the implied threats. That diagnosis got revised the next morning when I awoke with a mind-numbing headache, chills alternating with a mild fever, and my chest feeling like it was caught in a compactor. It was a so-called common cold, but there was nothing common about my misery, which was truly exceptional.

I made a cup of Echinacea tea and then washed down 2000 mg of Vitamin C with some aging orange juice from my fridge, after which I took a couple of Tylenol, put on yesterday's jeans, and headed uptown to work. I also treated myself to a cab.

When I settled into the cluttered corner room that was my office, I told myself this was not a day to make any big decisions. Just stick to matters that required nothing more than autopilot.

The first thing I did was call Lou to check on Sarah (no change), and then I told him about my Hispanic visitor. He made concerned sounds and promised to accompany me on any further location shoots.

Next I pulled out my date book and punched in a phone number I'd scribbled in the back. I'd gotten it when I was winding up my interview with Carly Grove.

"Children of Light," said an unctuous voice. "This is Ramala."

I hesitated a moment before giving my name. They already knew who I was; Ramala or somebody had called Paula Marks and asked about me. *Me*. What would she do when she heard it was yours truly in the flesh?

I tried to take a deep breath, working around the feeling my lungs were on fire, and identified myself.

Ramala received the information as though she'd never heard of me. Maybe she hadn't. Then I asked for an appointment with Alex Goddard. As soon as it was convenient.

"He leaves his Saturdays open," she said, more of the smiley voice, "so I could make a special appointment for you tomorrow. Would ten A.M. be all right?"

Her accent was the kind of Delhi colonial-ruling-class you associate with expensive silk saris and ruby bracelets, yet at the same time her voice had an overlay of that melodious, touchy-feely unctuousness you hear on relaxation tapes. I half expected her to next say, inhale deeply and feel the love flowing through the universe. In any case, she couldn't have sounded more open and forthcoming.

I had to remind myself immediately that it wasn't true. Given the inquisitive phone call to Paula Marks, Children of Light was an organization that deeply cherished its privacy. Presumably they had a reason, and that reason didn't necessarily have to be sinister, but still, I had every reason to think they were upset about me and it made me paranoid. And now Alex Goddard immediately had time for a "special appointment."

"Ten o'clock will be fine," I said, just barely croaking the words out of my chest.

She gave me directions for reaching the Riverdale clinic, called Quetzal Manor, and hung up. I felt so miserable I could barely remember afterward what she'd said, but fortunately I'd taken notes.

Quetzal Manor. An odd choice for a name, I'd thought.

Some kind of bird sacred to the Maya Indians of Central America. But then Paula had mentioned at one point that he was very interested in indigenous Third World herbs and remedies. So maybe it fit.

But still, one big puzzle kept coming back to haunt: How do you produce perfectly healthy siblings six months apart? (I actually called Carly and Paula back to verify the ages.) The more I thought about Kevin and Rachel, the more I realized they were so unmistakably related.

Puzzling over that, I began to wonder if maybe I was on the verge of uncovering a blockbuster documentary. Could we be talking something approaching science fiction here? Making documentaries, you're always on the lookout for the unexpected, the fresh. So how about an organization that could obtain beautiful Caucasian babies seemingly at will, including peas-in-a-pod born a few months apart? I was already framing a pitch to David in my mind.

Anyway, the rest of the day, while I was busy battling my cold with antihistamines and lots of hot soup, I mounted a major phone inquiry just to make sure all the rules on adoption hadn't somehow changed when I wasn't looking. They hadn't. First off, to get a child in three or four months, you'd almost certainly have to go with foreign adoption. China was everybody's flavor of the month, because they favored older parents and also because the one-child-per-family policy there had ended up producing a wide-scale abandonment of girls (who were all those precious boys going to marry? I often found myself wondering). However, the shifting politics there made the process very unreliable. A few months? Don't even think about it.

Pressing on, I satisfied myself that the country-specific organizations that found babies in the emerging parts of the world all still worked the same. Cradle of Hope specialized in orphaned Russian kids. Children and Families, Inc., provided adoptions for Equadorian children. International Adoption Assistance, Inc., handled Brazilian orphans. But they all were still fussy, and they could take ages. How about a brand-new healthy baby in just a few months? I'd ask. Some kind of new fast track? The question was always taken as a joke. . . .

I would be driving up to Quetzal Manor in my old Toyota, and I dearly wished Steve could somehow materialize and be with me. In his absence, however, I convinced Lou to come along. I figured the change of scene would do him good, and I also wanted the security of having him with me, after the threatening phone call to Paula and the Hispanic thug who'd accosted me outside her apartment building. Besides, it'd just be a couple of hours.

The next morning, as we trekked up Riverside Drive, then the Henry Hudson Parkway, the sky was a flawless blue and the wide Hudson seemed like an ardent highway leading into the heart of America. Still in elevated spirits over Sarah's momentary brush with consciousness, Lou had noticeably less of a hangover than was usual most mornings. Maybe he was looking forward to a little mental R&R. For my own part, I felt my curiosity growing. I'd gone to a lot of appointments over the years, but rarely did I suspect the person I was going to see already knew more about me than I knew about them.

After we crossed the Henry Hudson Bridge, we left the highway and headed down a service road that led toward the river. Then there was an imposing gate, open, and a tree-shrouded driveway. Finally the place loomed in front of us.

The physical appearance of Quetzal Manor was a study in European grandeur, translated with a few extra frills from the New World. Carly had told me it had once been a Carmelite convent, dating from sometime in the middle of the last century, and it was a monument to Church authority, with endless arches of cut stone, turrets, gargoyles. As we were motoring to the end of the long cobblestone drive, I felt as if I was approaching some Gothic movie set. Given its hovering sense of regal authority, the place could easily have been a castle, but it seemed more like a brooding homage to medieval torture. Let me just say it was truly magisterial, yet also more than a little creepy.

As we parked under a huge oak tree in front, I surveyed the facade, trying to marshal my strength. Enough of my cold still lingered that I didn't feel as if my mind was working on all cylinders, and for a moment I merely sat looking, trying to breathe.

"Want me to go in with you?" Lou asked finally. He was examining the building suspiciously, like a detective surveying a crime scene.

I wanted him with me and then again I didn't. I longed for the company, a protector, but I didn't want the complications, more things to explain inside. Finally I made a snap decision.

"Why don't you take a stroll around the grounds?" I suggested. "Commune with nature. The fresh air will do you good. This can't take long. Mainly I just want to get some literature and try to gain a feeling for the place."

That wasn't entirely, or even partly, true. What I really wanted to find out was threefold: How did they manage to get beautiful healthy Caucasian babies for two single women in just a few months; how could those babies be only six months apart in age and still obviously be siblings; and (this was where my feelings got complicated) could they get a baby for me the same way, never mind how they did it. It was the third thing that actually bothered me the most, since I was far from sure I wanted to be a part of whatever was going on.

Lou just shrugged and leaned back in his seat. "Take as

long as you like. I'll just wait here in the car. I'm not the nature type."

That was certainly the case.

I walked across the cobblestones to an arched entryway that had no door. I wondered at this—most convents are like a fortress—and then I realized the front door had been removed, leaving only its ancient hinges still bolted into the stones. Perhaps it was intended to be a symbol of openness, inviting you in.

There was no sign of anybody—the saccharine-voiced Ramala was not on hand to greet me—so I just headed on down a wide hallway, past a table of brochures. The place had been decorated with expensive good taste: tapestries all over the stone walls, perfect Persian rugs, classic church statuary—all of it calling forth powerful feelings from deep in the psyche.

Then I entered a vast interior courtyard, where a central fountain splashed cheerily in the midday light. The courtyard was circled with a picturesque gallery of cells, all with massive wooden doors, most likely rooms once inhabited by chaste sisters.

The place did seem to be a clinic-commune now, just as Paula had said. Not nuns this time around, but rather New Age acolytes whose tastes ran more to secular music than to religious chants, as witness the cacophony of sounds that wafted out from several of the cells. Only it wasn't any kind of conventional music; it seemed a mixture of Japanese flute, North Indian ragas, African drumming. I liked the ragas, even recognized my favorite, "Bhairavi."

Then I spotted something that riveted my attention. At the back of the courtyard, just past a final wooden door, stood a huge South Indian bronze statue, about five feet high, of the Dancing Shiva. It appeared to be presiding over the archway that led out into a dense natural garden behind the building.

I walked across the cobblestones to examine and admire it. It seemed an odd item to find here in the courtyard of a once-cloistered convent. I was so enthralled I failed to hear the door behind me open.

"Do you find my Shiva interesting, Ms. James?" said a soothing voice, just barely audible above the chirps of birds. I think I caught a breath in my phlegm-locked chest, but then I turned to see a tall man dressed in casual chinos and a dark sweater. He was trim, looked to be in his early sixties, with a mane of salt-and-pepper hair and lean features more craggy than handsome. But his eyes were everything, telling you he owned the space around him, owned, in fact, the air he breathed. It had to be Alex Goddard.

"Yes," I answered almost before I thought. "It just seems to be a little out of place here."

I wondered if he was going to introduce himself. Then I realized that when you're used to being the master of a private domain, you probably never think to bother with such trivial formalities. Everybody knows who you are.

"Well," he said, his voice disarmingly benign, "I suppose I must beg to differ. May I suggest you consider this Shiva for a moment and try to imagine he's a real god?"

"He is a real god," I said, immediately feeling patronized. Nothing makes me angry faster. "In India, he's—"

"Yes," he said, "I know you did a film about India—which I found quite extraordinary, by the way—but why wouldn't the Shiva fit right in here? You see, he's a very modern, universal figure. He incorporates everything that exists in the contemporary world. Space, time, matter, and energy. As well as all of human psychology and wisdom."

"I'm aware of that," I said, sensing my pique increase. We were not getting off to a great start.

"Yes, well." He seemed not to hear me. Instead he started putting on the leather jacket he'd had slung over his shoulder. "Notice that Shiva has four arms, and he's dancing with one foot raised. He's also standing inside that great circle of flame, a sort of halo encompassing his whole body. That circle stands for the great, all-embracing material universe, all of it. Dark and light, good and evil. He knows and controls everything."

Hey, I realized, this guy's got some kind of identity thing going with this ancient Indian god.

He continued as he zipped up the jacket. "Shiva has four arms because—"

"Let *me* tell *you*," I said, interrupting him. He looked startled, clearly not accustomed to a woman meeting him on his own ground. "He has four hands because he has a lot to do. That little drum in his upper right summons things into existence. And there in his upper left he holds a fire that destroys."

Goddard was examining me curiously, but I just stared back and continued.

"His lower right hand is held up in a kind of benediction, as if to say, 'Find your peace within,' and the lower left points down at his feet, where one foot is planted on the back of that repulsive little dwarf there, the human ego. Crush the ego and be free. The other foot is lifted to signify spiritual freedom."

"You seem to know the Shiva well." He broke into a grudging smile, as though we'd just met. Chalk up round one as a draw. "I'm glad you came, Ms. James. I'm a great admirer of your work and I especially wanted to provide your orientation personally. It's a genuine pleasure to meet you at last."

At last? I took his proffered hand and stared. All the questions I'd been brooding over for the past week sort of disappeared into a memory file somewhere. Instead all I could do was focus in on him.

Meeting Carly and Paula's miracle worker in the flesh made me recall something Aldous Huxley once observed. He declared that the kind of man, and they are almost always men, who can control others with his mind needs to have certain qualities the rest of us can only envy. Of course he has to be intelligent and have a range of knowledge that can be used to impress people, but most of all, he has to have a will of iron, an unswerving tenacity of purpose, and an uncompromising self-confidence about who he is, what he wants. This means a slightly remote manner, a glittering eye, and a sympathetic gaze that bores in deeply on you one minute, then seems off in another realm, focused on infinity, the next. Perhaps most importantly of all, his voice must be that of a Pied Piper, a soft yet penetrating instrument that acts directly on the unconscious of his listeners.

Even though he was doing a casual number with me, my first impression of Alex Goddard was that he perfectly embodied all those qualities. I also sensed a false note. What was it? Maybe he was being just a little too casual.

"If you're here about doing a film," he began, "please be aware we do not encourage publicity. If you've come because of your infertility, as Ramala said you mentioned in your call, then I welcome you with open arms."

Well, he knew how to cut to the chase. And after his phone call to try to intimidate Paula Marks, I was well aware he didn't "encourage publicity." But now I also realized he wouldn't be overly interested in my new idea of someday doing a documentary on this place. But then a lot of people say no at first and then come around.

"I was actually interested in neither," I said, feeling my sinuses about to close down permanently. "I was actually hoping to find out about your adoption service, how it works."

"Ah," he said, his eyes shifting from intense scrutiny to somewhere lost in the ozone, "that's not something I handle personally. In any case, you first must come and participate in our program. Then, if we fail to achieve your objectives, we can take the adoption matter under consideration."

"I think I'd like to hear about it anyway." I took a deep breath, again groping for air. "For instance, where and how you get the children you place."

"I see," he said calmly, as though my question were about the weather. Then he secured his coat tighter. "I'm thinking, how would you like to take a short walk? Down to the river. We could get to know each other better."

I just nodded, not looking forward to the harsh wind that would assault my inflamed sinuses. But maybe I was getting somewhere.

As we started out through the stone archway and into the rear garden, which seemed to extend for acres, he continued.

"You seem to have a lot of questions about what I'm doing here. So let me try and put my efforts into perspective. As I like to point out to women when they first come here, we in the West are making do with only half the world's medical knowledge. We ignore all of the East. There's also the wisdom of the indigenous peoples here in the Western Hemisphere, the Native Americans. Who are we to say they don't have a lot to teach?" He smiled, as though embarrassed to be passing along such a commonplace. "For example, Western medical practice, virtually until this century, consisted mainly of using leeches to drain away 'humors' in the blood. At the same time, the indigenous peoples of this continent knew more about the curative powers of plants, even drugs, than Europe ever dreamed of. Yet they were deemed savages."

I wasn't sure where he was leading, but the supreme self-confidence with which he spoke had the effect of sweeping me along. The engaging eyes, the voice, the well-used designer jacket, it all worked. He was good, very good.

"So you see," he went on, "what I've tried to achieve here at Quetzal Manor is to integrate the knowledge of East and West, ancient and modern."

"So what, exactly, do you—?"

"Well, first let me explain that I studied in the Far East for over a decade, until I understood how to control the energy flows in the body, your Chi. Then I moved to Central America, where I learned all that is currently known about Native American practices and medicines. I still have a special place there, where I carry out pharmacological research on the rare plants of that area, studying their effects on human fertility, on the origins of life. I have no time to waste on disease and degeneration."

We were well into his Eden-like rear garden now, which had lots of herbs and was also part orchard. There were apple trees and other fruit trees I couldn't readily identify, all just starting to show their first buds. When we came to the end, there was a cobblestone path leading west. In what seemed only a few moments, we'd reached a line of bluffs overlooking the Hudson. The early spring wind was cutting into my face, causing my nostrils to feel on fire.

As we stood gazing down at the rippling waters of the Hudson below, where a lone sailboat was caught in the breeze, the moment took on a timelessness, feeling as though it could have been any place, any century.

"Incidentally," he went on, turning slightly to me, "are you familiar with the name Asklepios?"

I had to shake my head no. It sounded vaguely familiar, but . . .

"He was the ancient Greek god of medicine. The physicians who revered him held that sickness could be cured using drugs and potions that came from outside the body, since they believed that's where disease originated. Now, of course, billion-dollar industries thrive by enhancing our arsenal of antibiotics."

I listened to this, wondering where he was headed. Then he told me.

"There was, however, another school of healing at that time, those who honored the daughter of Asklepios. She was Hygeia, their goddess of health. The Hygeians believed that wellness originated from properly governing your own body. For them, the greatest service of the physician was to learn how we can work *with* our bodies. Their ideal was healing from within rather than intervention from without."

Again he was studying me, as though trying to determine whether I was going along with what he was saying.

"Unfortunately," he continued, "the Hygeian school more or less died out in the West. However, it lives on in other places. For example, primitive peoples have no manufactured, synthetic drugs, so they use natural herbs to enhance their own immune system and stay healthy."

He turned to study the river, dropping into silence.

"Maybe I'm missing something," I declared finally. His hypnotic voice had drawn me in, in spite of myself. "How does this relate to infertility?"

He turned back and caught me with his shining eyes. They seemed to be giving off heat of their own. "Just as the body is intended to heal itself, so is a woman's womb meant to create life. If she's childless, the reason more often than not is that her body is out of harmony with itself. What I do here is seek out each woman's unique energy flows and attempt to restore them, using Eastern practices and Hygeian herbal therapies."

"Does it always succeed?" I abruptly wondered if his techniques might work for me. Face it, Western medicine had completely struck out. The problem was, the guy was just a little *too* smooth.

"Not always. Some women's bodies are naturally unresponsive, just as all organizms are subject to random . . . irregularities. In those cases, I try to provide her a child by other means."

"You mean adoption," I suggested.

"By whatever means seems appropriate," he replied cryptically.

"Well, there's something I'd like to understand. Last week I met a woman who had adopted a baby boy through Children of Light. She got him in three months. Such a thing is, according to what I can find out, totally unheard of. So how did you manage that?"

He stared down at the river. "I thought I'd explained that adoptions are not what we primarily do here. They're provided only as a last resort, in the few cases where my regimen of Hygeian therapies fails."

"But in those cases, where do you find—?"

"As I've said, before we talk about adoption, first we need to satisfy ourselves that no other options are possible." Then his eyes clicked into me. "If you could come back next Saturday to begin your tests and receive an orientation, I could give you an opinion about your chances of bearing a child. It will require a thorough examination, but I can usually tell with a good degree of certainty whether my program can help someone or not. It's really important, though, that you stay at least . . ." He was staring at me. "Mind if I do something that might relieve some of the symptoms of that cold?"

He reached out and touched my temples with his long, lean fingers. Then he placed his thumbs just above my eyebrows and pressed very hard. After a long moment, he slowly moved the pressure down to the bridge of my nose, then across under my eyes. Finally he put the heel of his hands just above my ears and pressed again. After a couple of seconds he stepped away and continued talking as though nothing had happened.

"After I give you a full examination, we can discuss our next step." With that he turned, ready to head back. "Now if you'll excuse me, I've got a lot of research data to organize."

I guess he assumed his juggernaut of arcane medical theory had rolled over me sufficiently that he could move on to other matters. I sensed he really wanted me to come back, but he was careful to wind down our mutual interview with a take-it-or-leave-it air. All the same, I felt intrigued as we moved back through the gardens and then into the courtyard. A baby. Maybe he *could* make it happen for Steve and me. In spite of myself, I felt a moment of hope.

"Thank you for coming," he said by way of farewell, just brushing my hand, then turned and disappeared through one of the ancient wooden doors along the veranda, leaving me alone.

Well, I thought, the calm voice and casual outfit are probably just part of his bedside manner, but you can't be near Alex Goddard and not feel a definite sense of carefully controlled power. But is his power being used for good?

This was the man whose staff was trying to deny me interviews with mothers who'd adopted through Children of Light. And what about the Hispanic hood with the gun? Did Alex Goddard send him? If not, his appearance at Paula's building was one hell of a coincidence. So why should I trust . . .

That was when I noticed it. My lingering cold had miraculously vanished, inflamed sinuses and all. I was breathing normally, and even my chest felt cleared.

My God, I thought, what did he do? Hypnotize me? It was as though a week's healing had passed through my body.

I had an epiphany, a moment that galvanizes your resolve. I *had* to do a documentary about this man, to find out what he was really up to. He'd mentioned he had a place in Central America. Was that the source of his special techniques, some kind of ancient MesoAmerican medical practices he'd discovered?

He claimed he didn't want any publicity, but that's always just an opening move. When somebody says that, what they really mean is they don't want any *bad* publicity; they just want to have final say about what you produce. There're ways to handle the problem.

I liberated a brochure from the hall table on my way out, thinking I would study it soon. Very closely. I had a nose for a good story, and this one felt right.

When I got back to the car, Lou was nowhere to be seen. He'd given me the impression he intended merely to sit there and doze while I went inside, but now he was gone.

Then he appeared, emerging from the forest of trees. Actually, there was another building opposite the stone drive that I hadn't noticed at first. Hmmm, I thought, I wonder what that's all about. For some reason Alex Goddard hadn't offered me a tour; he'd taken me for a stroll in the opposite direction. . . .

"That was fast," Lou said, settling into the car. "You get what you came for?"

The answer to that was both yes and no. In a sense I'd gotten considerably more than I bargained for.

"He wants me to come back," I said. "And I think I might do it. There's a lot more going on with Alex Goddard than you'd know from just looking at this place. The trick is to stay in control when you're around him."

I tossed the brochure into Lou's lap as I started the engine. He took it and immediately began looking through it.

Lou, I knew, was a man always interested in facts and figures. As we headed toward the Parkway he was pouring through the brochure with intense interest, even as I tried to give him a brief reprise of Alex Goddard's medical philosophy.

"It says here his patients come from all over the United States and Europe," he noted, finally interrupting me.

I found nothing odd in that, and went back to rambling on about Quetzal Manor. Give the place its due, it was placid and tranquil and smacked of the benign spirituality Goddard claimed to put so much stock in. Still, I found it unsettling.

However, Lou, as usual, chose to see matters his own way. He'd been studying the fine print at the back of the brochure, mumbling to himself, and then he emitted a grunt of discovery.

"Ah, here's what I was looking for," he declared. "You know, as a registered New York State adoption agency, this outfit has got to divulge the number of babies they placed during their last yearly reporting period."

"According to him, he only resorts to adoption if he can't cure your infertility with his special mind-body regimen," I reminded him. "Your energy flows—"

"No shit," Lou observed, then went on. "Well, then I guess his mind-body, energy flows, whatever, bullshit must fail a lot. Because last year the number was just under two hundred. So at sixty thou a pop, like it says here, we're talking about twelve million smackeroos gross in a year. Not a bad way to fail, huh?"

I caught myself emitting a soft whistle as he read out the number. There was *definitely* a lot more going on with Alex Goddard than met the eye.

"So what's he do with all that dough?" Lou mused. "Better question still, where in the hell did he find two hundred fresh, orphaned babies, all listed here as Caucasian? And get this: The ages reported at final processing are all just a couple of months, give or take."

Good questions, I thought. Maybe that's the reason he doesn't want publicity; it sounds a little too commercial for a mind-body guru.

My other thought was, with so many babies somehow available, why was Alex Goddard so reluctant to even discuss adoption with me?

The answer, I was sure, lay in the fact he already knew more about me than I knew about him. He knew I was making a film about adoption (how did he come by that knowledge? I kept wondering) and he was concerned he might be mentioned in it. I kept asking myself, why?

On our drive back down the Henry Hudson Parkway, I decided I was definitely looking at a documentary in the making. I just had to decide whether to do it with or without his cooperation.

Six

After I dropped off Lou at his space in Soho, where he was house-sitting for an estate now in the courts, I decided to head on home. The more I thought about Alex Goddard, the more I felt frustrated and even a little angry that I'd completely failed to find out any of the things I'd wanted to learn about him. I replayed our interview in my mind, got nowhere, and then decided to push away thoughts of Quetzal Manor for a while and dwell on something else: Sarah, my film, anything.

It was Saturday, and unfortunately I had no plans for the evening. Translation: no Steve. Back to where I started. How many million stories in the naked city, and I was just so many million plus one. It's not a jungle out there, it's a desert.

The truth was, after Steve took off, I hadn't really been trying all that hard to pick myself up off the canvas and look around. Besides, I didn't want some other guy, I wanted *him*. Added to that, I somehow felt that when you're on the short countdown for forty, you shouldn't have to be going out on blind dates, wondering whether that buttoned-down MBA sitting across from you in some trendy Italian restaurant thinks you're a blimp (even though you skipped lunch), telling yourself he's presentable, doesn't seem like a serial killer, has a job, only mentioned his mother once, and could qualify as an acceptable life's mate. There's no spark, but he's probably quite nice. You wanly remember that old Barney's ad jingle, "Select, don't settle," but at this stage of life you're ready to admit you've flunked out in Love 101 and should just go with Like.

Which was one of the reasons I missed Steve so deeply. He was a lover, but he was also a best friend. And I was running low on those.

Every woman needs a best pal. After my former best, Betsy, married Joel Aimes, Off-Broadway's latest contribution to Dreamworks, and moved to the Coast with him, I was noticing a lot of empty evenings. In the old days, we could talk for hours. It was funny, since we were actually very different. Betsy, who had forgotten more about clothes and makeup than most women would ever know, hung around the garment-center showrooms and always came away with samples of next season's couture, usually for a song. I envied her that, since I usually just pretended not to care and pulled on another pair of jeans every morning. But she shared my love of Asian music.

Anyway, now she was gone and I could tell we weren't working hard enough at staying in touch. She and Joel had just moved to a new apartment and I didn't even have her latest phone number. . . .

Which brought me back to Steve. I'd often wondered why we were so alike, and I'd finally decided it was because we both started from the same place spiritually. In his case, that place was a crummy childhood in New Haven—which he didn't want to talk about much because, I gathered, it was as lonely and deprived as my own, or at least as depressing. His father had owned a small candy store and had wanted all his four children to become "professionals." The oldest had become a lawyer, the next a teacher. When Steve's turn came, he was told he should become a doctor, or at the very least, a dentist.

Didn't happen. He'd managed four years of premed at

Yale, but then he rebelled, cashed in his med-school scholarship, and went to Paris to study photography. The result was he'd done what he wanted, been reasonably successful at it, and his father had never forgiven him. I think he was still striving for the old man's approval, even after all the years, but I doubted he'd ever get it. Steve was a guy still coming to grips with things that couldn't be changed, but in the meantime he lived in worlds that were as different from his own past as he could find. He deliberately avoided middle-class comforts, and was never happier than when he was in some miserable speck on the map where you couldn't drink the water. Whatever else it was, it wasn't New Haven. . . .

Thinking about him at that moment, I had an almost irresistible desire to reach for my cell phone and call him. God, I missed him. Did he miss me the same way? I wanted so much to hear him say it.

I had a contact number for him in Belize City, an old, Brit-like hotel called the Bellevue, where they still served high tea, but I always seemed to call when he was out somewhere in the rain forest, shooting.

Do it. Don't be a wuss.

But then I got cold feet. Did I want him to think I was chasing after him? I didn't want to sound needy . . . though that was exactly what I felt like at the moment.

Finally I decided to just invent a phone conversation, recreating one from times past, one where we both felt secure enough to be flip. It was something I did more than I'd like to admit. Usually there'd be eight rings at his Park Slope loft and then a harried voice. Yes. Steve, talk to me. . . .

"Yo. This is not a recording. I am just in a transcendent plane. And if that's you, Murray, I'll have the contact sheets there by six. Patience is a virtue."

"Honey, it's me. Get out of the darkroom. Get a life."

"Oh, hi, baby." Finally tuning in. "I'm working. In a quest for unrelenting pictorial truth. But mainly I'm thinking of you."

"You're printing, right? Darling, it's lunch hour. Don't you feel guilty, working all the time?"

The truth was, it was one of the reasons I respected him so much. He even did his own contacts. His fervor matched my drive. It's what made us perfect mates.

"I've got tons of guilt. But I'm trying to get past it. Become a full human person. Go back to the dawn of man. Paint my face and dance in a thunderstorm." He'd pause, as though starting to get oriented. "Hey, look at the time. Christ. I've got a print shoot on Thirty-eighth Street at three."

He was chasing a bit of fashion work to supplement his on-again, off-again magazine assignments.

"Love," I said in my reverie, "can you come over tonight? I promise to make it worth your while. It involves a bubble bath, champagne, roses everywhere, sensuous ragas on the CD. And maybe some crispy oysters or something, sent in later on, just to keep us going."

Then I'd listen to the tone of his voice, knowing he'd say yes but putting more stock in *how* he said it. Still, he always gave his lines a good read.

"Then why don't we aim for about nine?" I'd go on, blissful. "That ought to give me a chance to get organized. And don't bring anything except your luscious self." The fantasy was coming together in my mind. Thinking back, I realized how much I missed him, all over again. . . .

That was when the phone on the armrest beside me rang for real. For a moment I was so startled I almost hit the brakes. Then I clicked it on, my mind still buzzing about Steve, and also, in spite of my resolve, about the curious runaround I'd just gotten from Alex Goddard.

"Listen, there was a message on my machine when I came

in. I've got to go up to the hospital. Right now." Lou's voice was brimming with hope and exuberance. "They said Sarah was stirring. She's opened her eyes and started talking. They said she's not making much sense, but . . . oh, God."

"That's wonderful." I felt my heart expanding with life. For some reason, I had a flash of memory of her climbing up into the rickety little tree house—well, more like a platform—I'd helped her build in my thirteenth summer, no boys invited to assist. A year later that part had seemed terminally dumb. "I'll meet you there."

I was almost home, but I screeched the car around and headed east. Racing over, though, I tried not to wish for too much. I kept remembering all the stages to a complete recovery and telling myself that whatever had happened, it was only the first step on a very long, very scary journey. . . .

I hadn't realized how scary till I walked into the room. Lou, who had gotten there just minutes before I did, was sitting by her side, holding her hand, his gaze transfixed on her. She was propped up slightly in her bed, two pillows fluffed behind her head, staring dreamily at the ceiling. Three attentive middle-aged nurses were standing around the sides of her bed, their eyes wide, as though Sarah were a ghost. I very quickly realized why. She was spinning out a fantasy that could only come from a deranged mind. Had she regained consciousness only to talk madness?

"Lou, does she recognize you?" I asked.

He just shook his head sadly, never taking his eyes off her face. She was weaving in and out of reality, pausing, stuttering, uncertain of her incoherent brain. Once, when she'd fallen off a swing and got knocked out for a brief moment, she came to talking nonsense. Now she seemed exactly the same way.

"Lights . . . so bright," she mumbled, starting up again to recount what seemed to be a faraway fantasy, ". . . like now.

Why . . . why are there lights here?" Her lips were moving but her eyes were still fixed in a stare. Then, with that last, odd question, her gaze began to dart about the room, looking for someone who wasn't present. She settled on me for a moment, and I felt a chill from her plaintive vulnerability. When I tried to look back as benignly and lovingly as possible, I couldn't help noticing how drawn her cheeks were, doubtless from the constant IV feeding, and again my heart went out. "I'm scared," she went on, "but—"

"I'm here, honey," Lou declared, bending over her, his eyes pained. "Do you know who I am?"

"The jade face . . . a mask," she babbled on, still ignoring him. "All the colors. It's so . . . so beautiful."

Her hallucination didn't relate to anything I could understand. She clearly was off in another world, like when she was a kid, weaving the lights of the room now into some kind of dream. I touched Lou's shoulder and asked permission to turn off the overhead fluorescents, but he just shrugged me off, his attention focused entirely on her.

His eyes had grown puzzled, as though he wanted to believe she was returning to rationality but his common sense was telling him it wasn't true.

I was having a different reaction. What she was saying was random babblings, all right, but I was beginning to think she was reliving something she had actually seen.

However, she wasn't through.

"I want to pray, but . . . the white tunnel . . . is coming." She shuddered, then almost tried to smile. "Take me . . ."

She was gone, her eyelids fluttering uncontrollably.

"Honey, talk to me," Lou pleaded. He was crying, something I'd never seen him do, something I was not even aware he was capable of. What he really was trying to say was, "Come back."

It wasn't happening. She stared blankly at the ceiling for

a moment, then slowly closed her eyes, a shutter descending over her soul.

"She'll be okay," I whispered to him, almost believing it. Her brain had undergone a physical trauma, enough to cause a coma, but some kind of mental trauma must have preceded it. Was she now trying to exorcise that as part of her path to recovery?

The nurses in the room stirred, perhaps not sure what to do. The overhead lights were still dazzlingly bright, and I moved to shut them off, leaving only a night-light behind the bed. Perhaps the lights had brought her awake, but I was convinced what she'd just gone through had tired her to the point that she would not revive again that day.

Then one of the Caribbean nurses came over and placed her hand on Lou's shoulder. She had an experienced face, full of self-confidence. Something about her inspired trust.

"I wouldn't let this upset you too much," she said, a lovely lilt in her voice. "What just happened may or may not mean anything. When patients first come out of a coma, they can sometimes talk just fine, and yet not make any sense. They ramble on about things they dreamed of like they were real." Then she smiled. "But it's a good first step. She could wake up perfectly fine tomorrow. Just don't pay any attention to what she says for a while. She's dreaming now."

Lou grunted as though he believed her. I nodded in sympathy, though no one seemed to notice.

I also thought that although what Sarah had said was bizarre, it sounded like something more than a dream. Or had she gone back to her child-state where imaginary worlds were real for her?

Then in the dim glare of her bed light, Lou took a wrinkled blue booklet out of his inner pocket and stared at it. I had to stare at it a moment before I realized it was a passport.

"What—?"

"The American consulate in Merida, Mexico, sent it up to 26 Federal Plaza yesterday, because my name and office address are penciled on the inside cover as an emergency contact. The police down there said somebody, some gringo tourist fly-fishing way down on the Usumacinta River, near where the Rio Tigre comes in from Guatemala, snagged this floating in a plastic bag. He turned it in to the Mexican authorities there, and it ended up with our people." He opened the passport and stared at it. "The photo and ID page is ripped out, but it's definitely Sarah's." He handed it over. "Guy I know downtown dropped it off last night. I'm not sure if it has anything to tell us, but now, I was hoping it might help jog her memory."

I took it, the cover so waterlogged its color was almost gone. However, it must have been kept dry in the plastic bag for at least some of its trip from wherever, since much of the damage seemed recent.

Lou shook his head, staring wistfully at me. "I still don't know how she got down there. She was in California. Remember that postcard? If she'd come back East, she'd have got in touch. Wouldn't she?" His eyes pleaded for my agreement.

I didn't know what to say, so I just shrugged. I wanted to be sympathetic, but I refused to lie outright. He took my ambivalence as assent as he pulled out the locket containing her picture, his talisman. He fingered it for a moment, staring into space, and then he looked down and opened it, as if seeing her high school picture, from a time when she was well, would somehow ease his mind.

"This whole thing doesn't sound like her," he went on. "Know what I think? She was being held down there against her will."

My heart went out to him, and I reached over and took the locket for a moment, feeling the strong "S R C" engraved on its heart-shaped face. "Lou, she's going to come out of it. And when she does, she'll probably explain everything. She's going to be okay any day now, I've got a hunch. A gut feeling."

I had a gut feeling, all right, but not that she was going to be fine. My real fear was she was going to wake up a fantasy-bound child again.

Then I handed the locket back. He'd seemed to turn anxious without it. He took the silver heart and just stared down at it. In the silence that settled over us, I decided to take a closer look at the passport. I supposed Lou had already gone through it, but maybe he'd missed something.

As I flipped through the waterlogged pages, I came across a smudgy imprint, caked with a thin layer of dried river clay, that was almost too dim to be noticed.

"Lou, did you see this?" I held it under the light and beckoned him over. "Can you read it?"

"Probably not without my specs." He took it and squinted helplessly. "My eyes aren't getting any better."

I took it back and rubbed at the page, cleaning it. It was hard to make out, but it looked like "Delegacíon de Migracíon, Aeropuerto Internacional, Guatemala, C.A."

"I think this is a Guatemalan tourist entry visa." I raised the passport up to backlight the page. "And see that faint bit there in the center? That's probably her entry date. Written in by hand."

He took it and squinted again. "I can't read the damned thing, but you're right. There's some numbers, or something, scribbled in."

I took it and rubbed the page till I could read it clearly. "It's March eleventh. And it was last year."

"Hot damn, let me see that." He seized it back and squinted for a long moment, lifting the page even closer to the light. "You're right." He held it for a second more, then turned to me. "This is finally the thing I needed. Now I'm damned well going to find out what she was doing down there."

"How do you think you can do that?" I just looked at him, my mind not quite taking in what he'd just said.

"The airlines." He almost grinned. "If they can keep track of everybody's damned frequent-flyer miles for years and years, they undoubtedly got flight manifests stored away somewhere too. So my first step is to find out where she flew from."

"But we don't know which—"

"Doesn't matter." He squinted again at the passport. "Now we know for sure she showed up at the airport in Guatemala City on that date there. I know somebody downtown, smooth black guy named John Williams, the FBI's best computer nerd, who could bend a rule for me and do a little B&E in cyberspace. He owes me a couple. So, if she was on a manifest for a scheduled flight into Guatemala City that day, he'll find it. Then we'll know where she left from, who else was on the plane." He tapped the passport confidently with his forefinger. "Maybe she was traveling with some scumbag I ought to look up and get to know better."

"Well, good luck."

In a way I was wondering if we weren't both now grasping for a miracle: me half-hoping for a baby through some New Age process of "centering," Lou trying to reclaim Sarah from her mental abyss with his gruff love. But then again, miracles have been known to happen.

Seven

"Quetzal Manor could have the makings of a great documentary," I was explaining to David Roth. "I just need some more information-gathering first, to get a better feeling for what Alex Goddard is up to. So going back up there will be two birds with one stone. I'll learn more about him, and he might even be able to tell me why I haven't been able to get pregnant."

He was frowning, his usual skeptical self. "How long—?"

"It's just for the weekend, or maybe a little . . . I'm not sure exactly. I guess it depends on what kinds of tests he's going to run. But the thing is, I have to do it *now,* while he and I are still clicking. An 'iron is hot' kind of moment. The only possible problem might be if I have to push back my schedule for looping dialogue for *Baby Love* and then somebody's out of town."

"You check with the sound studio to warn them about possible rescheduling?" He wanted to appear to be fuming. But since he'd invited me down to his Tribeca loft at least once every three months, now that I'd finally shown up, he also had a small gleam in his eye. What did *that* mean?

"Yes, but I've already spotted most of the work print, and I've made tentative dates for people to come in. In a week and a half. Everything's still on schedule."

He leaned back on his white couch, as though trying to regroup. It was Saturday morning and I'd already made the appointment to see Alex Goddard. I was going. I probably should have run it by David first, but damnit, it was *my* life.

Truthfully, though, I'd been dreading telling him all week, so to try and make him as congenial as possible, I'd arranged to see him at home and relaxed. It seemed to be working, more or less.

"Okay, okay, sometimes I guess it's best to just go with your gut," he said, beginning to calm down. He'd offered to whip up some brunch when I first arrived, and now I was feeling sorry I'd turned him down. I really *did* like him. But, alas, only as a friend. "Before I cave in totally, though, do me a favor and tell me some more about this . . . documentary? What, exactly, makes you think it's—"

"Everything." Whereupon I laid on him the full story of Carly and Paula, the children, and my encounter with Alex Goddard. The only thing I left out was the story of the Hispanic hood, since I didn't think he could handle it.

"This Quetzal Manor sounds like a funny operation," he declared solemnly when I'd finished. "I say the less you have to do with a place like that, the better. Who knows what's going on."

"But, David, that's what makes it so interesting. The fact that it *is* a 'funny' operation. I really can see a documentary here, after *Baby Love* is in the can. But I'll never have a chance if I don't get to know this guy while I've got a good excuse. That's how my business works."

"So you're going to go back up there and . . . Is this like going undercover or something?"

"Well . . ." What was I going to say? I was actually half beginning to believe that Alex Goddard might be able to figure out why Steve and I couldn't conceive. It was certainly worth a few days of my life, documentary or no documentary. "Look, I really want to find out what's going on. For a lot of reasons."

He sighed and sipped at his coffee.

"Morgy, this has got to be quick. Nicky Russo called again. The thing I've learned about loan sharks, they keep your books better than you do. He knows exactly how much money we've got left and how long we can last. He's licking his chops, getting ready to eat us whole."

"What did you tell him?" The very thought of Nicky gave me a chill. If we missed so much as a week on the juice, he'd have the legal right to just seize my negative. When you're desperate, you sign those kinds of loans.

"I told him something I haven't even told you yet." He smiled a wicked grin. "I know you've been schmoozing Lifetime about a cable deal, but before we put the ink to that, I want to finish some new talks I've started with Orion, their distribution people."

I think I stopped breathing for a second or two. Was there a chance for a theatrical release for *Baby Love,* not just a cable deal?

"When . . . You've actually *met* with them? How—?"

"Late yesterday." He was still grinning. "I ran into Jerry Reiner at Morton's and pitched the picture. Actually, I heard he was in town, so I wore a tie and ambushed him at lunch. He wants to see a rough cut as soon as we've got something ready."

"David, you're an angel." I was ecstatic. It was more than I'd dared hope for.

"So stay focused, for chrissake, and finish your picture. We're *this* close to saving our collective asses, so don't blow it. I've gone over all the schedules pretty carefully, and I'd guess we can spare a day or two, but if you drag this out, I'm going to read you your contract, the fine print about due diligence, and then finish up the final cut myself. I mean it. Don't make me do that."

"Don't you even *think* about that." Never! "This is *my* picture."

"Just business. If it's a choice between doing what I gotta do, or having Nicky Russo chew me a new asshole and become the silent partner in Applecore, guess what it's gonna be."

"David, you know I would never let that happen." I walked over and gave him the sweetest hug I knew how, still filled with joy. "And thanks so much for trying to get us a theatrical. You don't know how much that means to me."

"Hey, don't try the charm bit on me. I'm serious. I'll cut you a weekend's slack, but then it's back to the salt mines. Either this picture's in the can inside of six weeks, or we're both going to be looking for new employment. So go the hell up there, do whatever it is you're going to do, and then get this damned picture finished. There'll be plenty of time after that to worry about our next project. With luck we might even have the money for it."

With that ultimatum still ringing in my ears, I took my leave of David Roth and headed north, up the Henry Hudson Parkway. My life was getting too roller-coaster for words. . . .

As I drove, I tried not to dwell on the practical aspects of what was coming. It was hard to imagine what tests Alex Goddard could perform that hadn't already been done by Hannah Klein. Just thinking back over that dismal sequence made me feel baby-despondent all over again.

When I first mentioned I was thinking about trying to get pregnant, she looked me over, perhaps mentally calculating my age and my prospects, and then made a light suggestion.

"Why don't I give you a prescription for Clomid. Clomiphene citrate enhances ovulation, and it might be a good idea in your case. You're still young, Morgan, but you're no longer in the first blush of youth."

I took it for six months, but nothing happened. That was the beginning of my pregnancy depression.

By that time, she'd decided I definitely had a problem, so she began what she called an "infertility workup." The main thing was to check my Fallopian tubes for blockages and look for ovulatory abnormalities. But everything turned out to be fine. Depression City.

"Well," she said, "maybe your body just *thinks* you've released an ovum. We need to do an ultrasound scan to make doubly sure an ovarian follicle has ruptured when it's scheduled to and dropped an egg."

It turned out, however, that all those hormonal stop-and-go signals were working just fine. In the meantime, Steve and I were doing it like bunnies and still no pregnancy.

Okay, she then declared, the problem may be with your Fallopian tubes after all. Time to test for abnormalities. "This is not going to be fun. First we have to dilate your cervix, after which we inject a dye and follow it with X rays as it moves through the uterus and is ejected out of your Fallopian tubes. We'll know right away if there's any kind of blockage. If there is something, we can go in and fix it."

"Sort of check out my pipes," I said, trying to come to grips with the procedure. I was increasingly sinking into despondency.

She did it all, and for a while she suspected there might be some kind of anatomical problem. Which brought us to the next escalation of invasiveness.

"We've got to go in and take a close-up look at everything," she said. "It's a procedure called laparoscopy. I'll have to make a small incision near your navel and insert a tiny optical device. In your case, I want to combine it with what's called a hysteroscopy, which will allow me to see directly inside your uterus for polyps and fibroids."

But again everything looked fine. I began to wonder what

had happened to everybody's mother's warning you could get pregnant just letting some pimply guy put his hand in your pants.

Prior to all this, I should add, Steve had provided samples of sperm to be tested for number and vigor. (Both were just fine.) Then, toward the end of all the indignities, he actually paid to have some kind of test performed involving a hamster egg, to see if his sperm was lively enough to penetrate it. No wonder he finally went over the edge.

Now I was reduced to Alex Goddard. I'd brought a complete set of my medical test records, as Ramala had requested on the phone. I'd also brought a deep curiosity about what exactly he could do that hadn't already been done. I further wondered how I was going to talk Steve into coming back long enough to share in the project. As I motored up the driveway to Quetzal Manor, I told myself he loved me still, wanted a baby as much as I did . . . Well, let me be safe and say almost as much. The problem was, he was so demoralized about the whole thing. And then what? What if nothing happened?

I started to park my car where I had the last time, then noticed the place actually had a parking lot. It was located off to the left side of the driveway, near the second, modern building, and was more or less hidden in amongst the trees. The lot was filled with a lot of late-model but inexpensive cars, basic working-girl transportation, and it seemed a better bet for long-term parking.

The front lobby, which had been empty the first time I was there, was now a minimalist reception area, a long metal desk rolled in from somewhere. I had the odd feeling it was there just for me. The woman behind the desk introduced herself as Ramala, the same person I'd talked to twice on the phone. She looked to be about my age, with long dark hair and quick Asian eyes, punctuated by a professional smile.

She knew my name, used it the minute she saw me, and then abruptly handed me a twenty-page "application" to complete.

"It's not just a formality," she explained, businesslike and earnest. "Dr. Goddard feels it's essential that he come to know you as a person. He'll read this carefully, believe me."

She ushered me to a chair that had a retractable table for writing, then gave me a ballpoint pen.

The document turned out to be the most prying, nosy thing I'd ever filled out. The pages demanded what amounted to a mini life history. One of the things that struck me as most strange was the part asking for a ten-year employment and residential history. If you've moved around as much as I have, worked freelance a lot, you'll understand how difficult it can be to reconstruct all those dates and places, but I did my best.

There were, of course, plenty of health questions too. One page even asked whether there was anything out of the ordinary about my own birth: Was the delivery difficult, a cesarean, a breach baby? It was, as noted, a *life* history.

"Why does he need all this information?" I asked finally, feeling the onset of carpal tunnel syndrome in my right wrist. "I brought all my medical records."

Ramala gave me a kindly smile, full of sympathy.

"He must know you as a person. Then everything is possible. When I came here, I had given up on ever having a child, but I surrendered myself to him and now my husband and I have twin boys, three years old. That's why I stayed to help him. His program can work miracles, but you must give him your trust."

Well, I thought, I might as well go with the flow and see where it leads.

When I'd finished the form, she took it back, along with the pen, then ushered me into the wide central courtyard where I'd met Alex Goddard the first time. He was nowhere to be seen, but in the bright late-morning sunshine there was a line of about twenty women, from late twenties to early forties, all dressed in white pajamalike outfits of the kind you see in judo classes, doing coordinated, slow-motion Tai Chi–like exercises. They were intent, their eyes fixed on the fringes of infinity.

These must be some of his acolytes, I thought, the ones I heard in their nuns' cells the first time I was here. What on earth does all this orientalism have to do with fertility? I then found myself wondering. I've studied the Far East enough to do "penetrating" documentaries about it, and I still can't get pregnant.

I took one look at them—none of them looked at me—and my heart went out. They were so sincere, so sure of what they were doing. For somebody who's always questioning everything, like me, it was touching, and maybe a little daunting too.

Without a word, Ramala led me past them and on to an entryway at the far end of the courtyard, past the giant Dancing Shiva. The door was huge and ornate, decorated with beaten-copper filigree—much like one I'd seen in a Mogul palace in Northern India. Definitely awe-inspiring.

She pushed open the door without ceremony and there he was, dressed in white and looking for all the world like the miracle worker he claimed to be. He seemed to be meditating in his chair, but the moment I entered, his deep eyes snapped open.

"Did you bring your records?" he asked, not getting up. While I was producing them from my briefcase, Ramala discreetly disappeared.

"Please have a seat." He gestured me toward a wide chair.

The room was a sterile baby blue, nothing to see. No diplomas, no photos, nothing.

Except for another, smaller bronze statue of the Dancing Shiva, poised on a silver-inlaid table. I also noticed that his own flowing hair seemed to match that of the bronze figure.

Yes, I thought, I was right. That's who he thinks he is. And he has complete power over the people around him. How many chances do you get to do a documentary about somebody like this? I should have brought a Betacam for some video.

He studied my test records as a jeweler might examine a diamond, his serious eyes boring in as he flipped through the pages. The rest of his face, however, betrayed no particular interest. I finally felt compelled to break the awkward silence.

"As you can see, I've had every test known to science. And none of them found anything wrong."

He just nodded, saying nothing, and kept on reading.

After a long, awkward silence, I decided to try and open things up a bit.

"Tell me, do you have any children of your own?"

The question seemed to be one he didn't get asked too often, because he stopped cold.

"All those who come here are my children," he replied, putting aside my records, dismissively finished with them.

"Well"—I pointed to them—"what do you think?"

"I haven't examined you yet," he said, looking up and smiling, indeed beaming with confidence. "Nothing in those records tells me anything about what may be your problem. I look for different things than do most physicians."

He fiddled with something beneath his desk, and the room was abruptly filled with the sound of a hypnotic drone. Perhaps its frequency matched one in my brain, because I instantly felt relaxed and full of hope. Much better than Muzak. Then he rose and came over.

Is he going to do my exam right here? I wondered. Where's all the ob/gyn paraphernalia? The humiliating stirrups?

Standing in front of me, he gently placed his hands on my heart, then bent over and seemed to be listening to my chest. His touch was warm, then cold, then warm, but the overall effect was to send a sense of well-being through my entire body.

"You're not breathing normally," he said after a moment of unnerving silence. "I feel no harmony."

How did he know that? But he was right. I felt the way I had the first time I tried to sit in Zen meditation in Kyoto. As then, my body was relaxing but my wayward brain was still coursing.

"I'll try," I said, attempting to go along. What I really was feeling was the overwhelming sense of his presence, drawing me to him.

Next he moved around behind me and cradled my head in his hands, placing his long fingertips on my forehead, sort of the same way he'd done when I was standing with him on the windy heath, nursing a killer cold. All the while, the drone seemed to be increasing to a piercing, overwhelming volume, as though a powerful electrical force were growing in the room, sending me into an alpha state of relaxation.

"What are you doing? Is this how you do an exam for—?"

"The medical tests you had showed there's nothing wrong with your uterus or your Fallopian tubes, nothing that should inhibit conception. There's no need to pursue that any further. But the mind and the body are a single entity that must be harmonized, must work as one. Although each individual has different energy flows, I think my regimen here could be very helpful to you. Already I can tell your problem is a self-inflicted trauma that has negated the natural condition wherein your mind and body work in unison."

"What 'trauma'?" I asked.

He didn't answer the question. Instead he began massaging my temples.

"Breathe deeply. And do it slowly, very slowly."

As I did, I felt a kind of dizziness gradually coming over me, the hypnotic drone seeming to take over my consciousness. Instead of growing slower, my breathing was actually becoming more rapid, as though I'd started to hyperventilate. But I no longer had any control over it. My autonomic nervous system had been handed over to him, as dizziness and a sense of disorientation settled over me. The room around me began to swirl, and I felt my conscious mind, my will, slipping out of my grasp. It was the very thing I'd vowed not to let happen.

The same thing had occurred once before, after I broke my collarbone in the Pacific surf that slammed a Mexican beach south of Puerto Villarta. When a kindly Mexican doctor was later binding on a harness to immobilize my shoulder, the pain was such that I momentarily passed out while sitting on a stool in his office. I didn't fall over or collapse; it just seemed as though my mind, fleeing the incredible pain, drifted away in a haze of sensation.

Now the pastel blue walls of the room slowly faded to white, and then I was somewhere else, a universe away, surrounded by blank nothingness. I tried to focus on the bronze Shiva directly across, but the ring of fire around him had become actual flames. The only reality left was the powerful touch of Alex Goddard's hands and a drone that could have been the music of the spheres.

Eight

Sometime thereafter, in a reverie, I felt myself in a magical forest whose lush vines reminded me of Kerala in India. It was a verdant, hazy paradise, another Eden. A child was with me, a child of my own, and I felt jubilation. I watched the child as she grew and became a resplendent orchid.

But with childbearing came pain, and I seemed to be feeling that pain as I took up the flower and held it, joy flowing through me.

Then Alex Goddard drifted into my dream, still all in white, and he was gentle and caring as he again moved his hands over me, leaving numbness in their wake. I thought I heard his voice talking of the miracle that he would make for me. A miracle baby, a beautiful flower of a child. I asked him how such a thing would happen. A miracle, he whispered back. It will be a miracle, just for you. When he said it, the orchid turned into the silver face of a cat, a vaguely familiar image, smiling benignly, then transmuted back into a blossom.

Then he drifted out of my dream much as he had come, a wisp of white, leaving me holding the gorgeous flower against my breasts, which had begun to swell and spill out milk the color of gold. . . .

A wet coolness washed across my face, and—as I faintly heard the sounds of Bach's *Well-Tempered Clavier,* Glenn Gould's piano notes crisp and clear—I opened my eyes to see Ramala massaging my brow with a damp cloth. She smiled kindly and lovingly as she saw my eyes open, then widen with astonishment.

"What—?"

"Hey, how're you doing? Don't be alarmed. He's taking great care of you."

"What . . . Where am I?" I lifted my head off the pillow and tried to look around. I half expected Steve to be there, but of course he wasn't.

"You're here. At Quetzal Manor." She reached and did something and the music slowly faded away. "Don't worry. You'll be fine. I think the doctor was trying to release your Chi, and when he did, it was too strong for you."

"What day is it?" I felt completely disoriented, my bearings gone.

"Sunday. It's Sunday morning." She reached and touched my brow as though giving me a blessing. Like, it's okay, really.

At that moment, Alex Goddard strolled in, dressed again in white.

Just as in the dream, I thought.

"So, how's the patient?" He walked over—eyes benign and caring—and lifted my wrist, absently taking my pulse while he inserted a digital thermometer in my ear. For a flashback moment he merged into, then emerged from, my dream. "You're looking fine. I have to say, though, you had quite a time yesterday."

"All I remember is passing out in your office," I mumbled, glancing around at the gray plastic thermometer. And that strange dream, you telling me I would have a miracle baby.

"You had an unusual reaction," he went on. "You remember I spoke to you about mind-body harmony. You see what can happen when I redirect the flows of energy, Chi, from your body to your mind." He smiled and settled my wrist back onto the bed. "Don't worry. I have a lot of hope for you. You're going to do fine."

He looked satisfied as he consulted the thermometer, then jotted down my temperature on a chart. He's already started a medical record, I thought. Why?

"I'm . . . I'm wondering if this really is working out," I said. It was dawning on me that I was getting into Alex Goddard's world a lot deeper and a lot faster than I'd expected. I'd come planning to be an observer and now *I* was the one being observed. That was exactly *not* how I'd intended it. Maybe, I thought, if I back off and make a new run, I can keep us on equal footing. "Perhaps I ought to just go back to the city for a few days and—"

"I'd assumed you came to begin the program." He looked at me, a quick sadness flooding his eyes. "You struck me as a person who would follow through."

"I need to think this over" I really feel terrible, I thought, trying to rise up. *What* did he do to me? "Maybe I'm just not right for your 'program'?" The idea of a documentary had momentarily retreated far into the depths of my mind.

"On the contrary." He smiled. "We've shown that you're very responsive."

"Maybe that's it. Maybe I'm *too* responsive." I rose and slipped my feet off the bed. The motion brought a piercing pain in my abdomen. "OUCH! What's . . ." I felt my pelvis, only to find it was very sensitive.

Pulling aside my bed shift, I gazed in disbelief at my lower abdomen. There were red spots just above my pale blue panties.

Alex Goddard modestly averted his eyes. "I didn't want to say anything," he explained to the wall above my head, "but you were in pretty delicate shape there for a while. Mild convulsions, and I think your digestive system had gone into shock. The stomach is a center of energy, because it's constantly active. So I gave you some shots of muscle relaxant. Nothing serious. It's an unusual treatment, but I've found it works. It . . . modulates the energy flows. I also took a blood sample for some tests, but the results were all normal."

He then asked me about my menstrual cycle, exact days, saying he wanted to make sure it wasn't just routine cramps. "The seizure you had passed almost as soon as it came, but you might actually have been hallucinating a bit. You had a slight fever all night."

"Well . . ." Something like that *had* happened to me years ago in rural Japan, when I stupidly ate some unwashed greens and my stomach went into shock. At one point a local doctor, Chinese, was trying acupuncture, which also left me sore.

"Nothing to be worried about," he continued. "But if you're the least bit concerned, maybe we ought to do a quick sonogram, take a sound picture. Ease your mind that everything's okay."

"That doesn't really seem necessary," I said. For a clinic specializing in "energy flows" and "mind-body" programs, there was a lot of modern equipment. Odd.

"Won't do a bit of harm." He nodded at Ramala, who also seemed to think it was a good idea. "Come on, help me walk her down to the lab." He turned back. "It's totally noninvasive. You'll see for yourself that you're fine."

Before I could protest, I found myself walking, with some dizziness, down the hallway. This part of Quetzal Manor, which I had not seen before, was a sterile, high-tech clinic. I realized I was in a different building from the old convent, probably the new one I'd noticed across the parking lot, the one he hadn't bothered to mention that first day. But all I could focus on were the blue walls and the new white tiles of the floor.

The sonogram was as he described it, quick and noninvasive. He rubbed the ultrasound wand over my abdomen, watching the picture on a CRT screen, which showed my insides, a jumble of organs that he seemed to find extremely informative.

"Look." He pointed. "Those lines there are your Fallopian tubes, and that's your uterus." He pushed a button to record a digital image. "Seems like whatever was upsetting your stomach is gone. Obviously nothing's wrong here."

"Good," I said, "because I really need to take a few days and think this over."

"You should stay," he said, reaching to touch my hand. "I think the worst is well behind us. From here on, we can work together. In fact, what I actually wish you would do is come with me to my clinic in Central America. It's truly a place of miracles."

I assumed he was referring to the "special place" he'd mentioned during our first interview. If Quetzal Manor was on the exotic side, I thought, what must *that* place be like? A documentary that took in the totality of who and what he was could be—

"In fact," he went on, "I just learned I have to be going there later today. A quick trip to catch up on some things. So this would be an ideal time for you to come. We could go together."

Well, I thought, I'd love to see what else he's up to, but this whole scene is getting out of control. When I first met Alex Goddard, we had a power balance, but now he's definitely calling the shots.

"I don't think I'm ready for that kind of commitment yet."

"As you wish." He smiled with understanding. "But let me just say this. It's not going to be easy, but nothing I've seen so far suggests there's any physical reason why you can't have a child. We just need to get you in touch with the energy centers in your body. Rightness flows from that."

"You really think so?" In spite of myself I felt my hopes rising, even though I had definite mixed feelings about his kind of "holistic" medicine.

"I'm virtually certain. But whether you want to continue with the program or not is a decision you'll have to make for yourself."

"Well, maybe when I'm feeling better we can talk some more about it." I definitely needed to reconsider my game plan. "For now, I think I'd better just get my things and—"

"As you wish." He sighed. "Your clothes are in your room. There's a closet in the corner by the window."

I shot a glance at him. "Does my Blue Cross cover this?"

"On the house." A dismissive wave of his hand, and another kindly smile.

I was still feeling shaky as I moved back down the vacant hallway, but I refused to let either of them help me. Instead I left him to oversee Ramala as she shut down the equipment.

Oddly, the place still seemed vacant except for me, though there was a large white door that appeared to lead to another wing. What was in there? I wondered. The questions kept piling up.

It soon turned out I was wrong about the clinic being empty. When I reached the door to the room where I'd been, I thought I heard a shuffling sound inside. I pushed it open gingerly and saw the room was dark. It hadn't been when I left. The shuffling noise—I realized it was somebody closing the venetian blinds—immediately stopped.

I began feeling along the wall for the light switch.

"Please leave it off," said a spacey female voice. "It's nice when it's dark."

As my eyes became accustomed to the eerie half-light, I finally made out a figure. It was a short woman, childlike but probably mid-twenties.

"What are you doing in here?"

"I just wanted to, like, be with you." She'd done her dark hair in multiple braids, with a red glass bead at the end of each. "You're special. We all know it. That's why he brought you over here, to this building. To be near them."

"What do you mean, 'special'?" I asked, heading for the closet and my black jeans. Then I wondered. Near who?

Now she was reaching into a fanny pack she had around her waist and taking out a baggie filled with plastic vials. "These are herbs I've started growing here. I picked them for you. If you'll—"

"Slow down," I said, lifting my jeans off the hanger and starting to struggle into them. Finally I took the baggie, moved to the window, and tilted up the blind. Inside it were clear plastic medicine bottles containing various gray and green powders and flakes.

My God, what's she trying to give me? And why?

"Listen," she went on, insistent. "Take those. Put two teaspoons of each in water you've boiled and drink it. Every day for a week. They'll make you strong. Then you'll be—"

"Hey, I'm going to be just fine, really." I set them aside and studied her, still a ghostlike figure in the semidark. There was a wildness in her eyes that was very disturbing.

At that moment, Alex Goddard appeared in the doorway. He clicked on the light, looking puzzled.

"Couldn't find the switch?" Then he glanced around. "Tara, did you get lost? I thought you were doing your meditation. It's Sunday. Afterwards, though, you can weed the north herb boxes if you want."

She nodded silently, then grabbed the baggie and glided out, her brown eyes filled with both reverence and what seemed like fear.

"Who was that?" I asked, staring after her, feeling unsettled by the whole experience. "She seemed pretty intense."

"Tara's been pretty intense for some time, perhaps for

much of her life," he declared with a note of sadness as he closed the door behind her. "I've not been able to do anything for her, but I've let her stay on here since she has nowhere else to go. She loves the gardens, so I've let her work out there. It seems to improve her self-esteem, a kind of benign therapy, her own natural path toward centering."

Well, I thought, she certainly could use some "centering."

"Look, Dr. Goddard, let me get my things, and then I've got to be going. I can't start on anything right now. Not the way I'm feeling. And visiting your other clinic is completely out of the question, at least for the moment."

"I have great hopes for you," he said again, placing a gentle hand on my shoulder. "I'm sorry we can't begin to work together immediately. But do promise me you'll reconsider and come back soon."

"Maybe when I'm feeling better." Keep the option open, I told myself. For a lot of reasons.

"In that case, Ramala can show you out. I've arranged for her to give you some herbal extracts from the rain forest that could well start you on the road to motherhood. Whether you decide to come back or not, I know they'll help you."

And he was gone, a wisp of white moving out the doorway. It was only then that I realized I'd again been too preoccupied to ask him about Kevin and Rachel, the beautiful siblings born six months apart. Instead all I had left was a memory of those penetrating eyes. And the power, the absolute power.

Nine

After giving me a small bag with two bottles, Ramala led me out, and I discovered I really had been in a different building, the one situated across the long-term parking lot and all but hidden in the trees. It was new, one-story, and probably larger than it appeared from the front. Again I wondered what went on in there, since it seemed so empty.

Check it out and soon, I told myself as I slipped my key into the ignition. You've got to find out a lot more about this place.

On the drive back to the city, my main thought was that I'd lost a day of my life. It'd just sort of slipped away. But that wasn't all. I also began to meditate on the fact that Alex Goddard could have an immense influence over my body (or was it my mind?) with a simple touch. Give him his due, he could definitely make things happen. First my cold and now this. Perhaps he *could* give me a child, if I got "centered," whatever that meant. But why should I trust him?

And there was another problem. For a baby I'd need Steve, the man I loved, the guy who'd promised to be with me through thick and thin. Did he really mean it? He'd have to fly in, which meant a serious piece of change for the airfare. Finally, could he face another chance of failure? My spirits sank at the prospect of having to ask him. Were we both just going to be humiliated one more time?

He'd made his home base in Belize, that little Rhode Island

of a country abutting big, bad Guatemala. He liked the fact they used English, more or less, as the official language and they hadn't gotten around to murdering two hundred thousand Maya, the way Guatemala had. In a romantic moment, I'd programmed his Belize hotel number into the memory of my cell phone—the telephones down there are amazingly good, maybe the Brit legacy—though I'd never actually tried it. (I'd called him from home about half a dozen times, but he was rarely there.) Well, I thought, the time has come. Maybe it was the sensual feelings released by all the Chi flowing around, but for some reason I found myself feeling very lonely. He hadn't called recently, though. . . .

It took ten rings, but eventually the hotel answered. A moment later, they were trying his room. I guess I was half afraid a woman might pick up, but it was him and there were no hushed tones or cryptic monosyllables. I heaved a minor sigh of reassurance.

"Baby, I can't believe it's you," he declared. "I've actually been trying to reach you for a day now."

"You finally get around to missing me?" It was so good to hear his voice, full of life and energy.

"All the time. Never didn't. You've just got to understand it's crazy down here. All last week I was in Honduras, haggling over permits. Don't ask." He paused. "So, when are you coming down? They've got a national park here that's a pure chunk of rain forest, jaguars everywhere." He laughed. "But forget that. If you come down, we'll never get out of the hotel. Just room service all day."

"No immediate plans," I said, immediately wondering how I could swing it. "But you never know."

I wasn't entirely sure how to approach Steve anymore. There was something about the abrupt way he took off that left things up in the air. A tiny sliver of uneasiness was slipping into my head-over-heels trust, the camel's nose under the tent.

"First the good news," I declared. "David's talking to Orion about a theatrical release for *Baby Love*."

Steve knew how deeply I longed for a theatrical—it would be my first—and he enthused appropriately. But he also knew I wouldn't call him early Sunday morning just to tell him that. There was only one other thing that would inspire such an unsocialized act.

"Uh, should I be asking how the other baby project is going?" he said.

For a moment I wasn't sure what to say, since I didn't really even know myself.

"Still a work in progress," I said finally. Then; "Honey, I've just been to see a doctor who's . . . well, he's a little unconventional. And nervous-making. But everything else has failed."

Whereupon I gave him a quick, cell-phone summary of what I'd just been through at Quetzal Manor.

"So are you going to go back eventually?" He sounded uneasy. "For the full 'program'?"

He had a way of zeroing in on essentials. The truth was, my baby hopes and my sense of self-preservation were at war with each other. . . .

"Morgy, are you there?"

"I'm here. And I guess the answer is, I'm still trying to decide. Like I said, he's into Eastern medicine and Native American . . . I'm not sure what. But if I need you, are you still in the project?"

"What do you mean?"

"Darlin', don't play dumb. You know exactly what I mean. Could you come back if I needed you? Really needed you?"

There was a long pause, wherein the milliseconds dragged by like hours. Trees were gliding past, throwing shadows on my windshield, and I still felt vaguely dizzy. I also had a residual ache in my abdomen where Alex Goddard had given me those damned muscle-relaxant shots. *Why* was I even considering going back?

Finally: "You're not making this easy, you know. Down here, without our . . . project on the front burner every day, I've been reassessing . . . well, a lot of things. If we had a baby, it would turn our lives upside down. I mean, it's not like we just bought a sheepdog and chipped in on the grooming. This is a human life we're talking about. Are we really prepared to do justice to a child?"

There it was. I didn't know whether I wanted to burst into tears, or strangle the man.

"Well, why don't you just think about it," I told him. "This doesn't sound like a conversation we should be having on a cell phone." Blast him. "If that's the way you feel now, then I might just have a baby on my own." How, I wasn't sure. I'd been so certain we were a couple, I'd not given it any real thought. "Or then again, I might just go ahead and adopt, with or without you."

"Look, I'm not saying I *won't* do it. I'm just saying it's not a trivial thing." He paused. "So where does that leave us?"

Translation: second thoughts.

"I don't know where that leaves us, Steve. In the shit, I guess. But I'd still like to know if I can count on you, or am I going to have to go to a sperm bank or something?"

"Jesus. Let me think about this, okay? Do I have to answer you now?"

"No. But I'm not going to wait forever either."

"All right." Then he paused. "Morgy, I miss you. I really do. I just need some time to think about our next step. Are you sure you're okay? You sound a little out of it."

"Thanks for asking. I've just got a lot on my mind."

Turmoil, dismay, and hope, all tossed together, that was what I had on my mind. I really didn't need mixed signals from Steve at the moment.

A few more awkward pleasantries and I clicked off the phone, wiped the streaks from my cheeks, and abruptly sensed Alex Goddard's face floating through my psyche. Why was that? Then I looked down at the bottles on the seat beside me, the "herbal extracts" Ramala had given me on the way out. What, I wondered, should I do about them? For that matter, what were they anyway? And what did they have to do with "centering"? If I started on his homeopathic treatments, what would I be getting into? Then I lectured myself: *Never* take something when you don't know what it is.

Hannah Klein. That's who I should ask.

I was so focused, I pushed the number I had stored for her in my phone memory before I remembered it was Sunday. Instead of getting her office, I got an answering service.

"Do you want to leave the doctor a message?" a southern-sounding voice enquired.

Without thinking, I heard myself declaring, "No, this is an emergency."

What am I saying? I asked myself. But before I could take it back, Hannah was on the line.

I know how intruded on I feel when an actor calls me at home on Sunday to bitch. Better make this good, I told myself.

"I was at an infertility clinic yesterday and passed out," I began. "And now I have some herbs to take, but I'm . . . well, I'm not sure about them."

"What 'clinic'?" she asked. There was no reprimand for calling her on Sunday morning.

When I told her about Alex Goddard, she said little, but she did not sound impressed. Looming there between us like the dead elephant on the living room floor was the fact that she'd specifically warned me not to go near him. And after what had just happened, there was a good case she might be right.

"Can I buy you brunch?" I finally asked, hoping to lure her back onto my case. "I'd really like to show you these herbs he gave me and get your opinion."

"I was just headed out to Zabar's to get something," she said, somewhat icily. Well, I suppose she thought she had good reason. "I'll get some bagels and meet you at my office."

Sunday traffic on upper Broadway was light, and I lucked out and found a parking space roughly two blocks from her building. It was one of the low-overhead "professional" types with a single small elevator and no doorman. When I got there, the lobby was empty.

Her suite was on the third floor, and I rang the bell before I realized the door was open. She was back in her office, behind the reception area, taking off her coat, when I marched in.

While she was unwrapping her sesame bagels, smoked sturgeon, and cream cheese with chives, she got an earful. My feeling was I'd better talk fast, and I did. I told her everything I could think of about what had happened to me at Quetzal Manor. I didn't expect her to make sense of it from my secondhand account, but I wanted to set the background for my next move.

"When I was leaving, his assistant gave me these two bottles of gel-caps. She said they're special herbal extracts he makes from plants in the rain forest. Do you think I ought to take them?"

I suspected I already knew the answer. Given her previously voiced views on Alex Goddard, I doubted she would endorse any potions he might dispense. But plant medicine has a long history. At least she might know if they presented any real danger.

She was schmearing cream cheese on the bagels, but she put down the plastic knife, took the two bottles, and examined them skeptically.

"These are not 'herbal extracts,' " she declared, giving her first analysis before even opening them. "They're both manufactured drugs. The gel-caps have names on them. It's a Latin American pharmaceutical company."

Then she opened the first bottle, took out one of the caps, crushed it between her fingers, and sniffed.

"Uh-huh, just what I thought." Then she touched a pinch of the white powder to her tongue. "Right." She made a face and wiped her tongue with a tissue. "Except it's much stronger than the usual version. I can tell you right now that this drug, in this potency, is illegal in the U.S."

What was it? I wondered. Cocaine? And how could she tell its potency with just a taste? Then I reminded myself why I'd come to her in the first place: She'd been around the track many, many times.

"It's gonadotropin," she said, glaring at me. Like, *you damned fool.* "I'm virtually certain. The trade name here in the U.S. is Pergonal, though that's not what this is. This is a much stronger concoction, and I can see some impurities." She settled the bottle onto her desk with what seemed almost a shudder. "This is the pharmaceutical equivalent of hundred-and-ninety-proof moonshine."

"What is it? What's it supposed it do?" Jesus, I thought, what's he giving me?

"It's a hormone extracted from the urine of menopausal women. It triggers a greater than normal egg production and release. It's sometimes prescribed together with Lupron, which causes your body to release a similar hormone. Look, if you want to try Pergonal, the real version, I'll write you a prescription, though I honestly don't think it's going to do you the slightest bit of good."

I couldn't believe what I was hearing. I'd almost been considering giving Alex Goddard the benefit of the doubt, at least till I found out more about him, and now he hands me *this*.

Now we both were looking at the other bottle.

"What do you think *that* is?" I asked, pointing.

She broke the plastic seal, opened it, and looked in. It too was a white powder sealed in gel-caps, and she gave one a sniff, then the taste test.

"I have no idea."

She set the bottle back on her desk, and I stared at it, terrified of what it might be. Finally I got up my courage and reached for it. A white sticker had been wrapped around it, with directions for taking . . . whatever it was . . . written on it. Then I happened to notice that one corner showed the edge of another label, one beneath the hand-applied first one. I lifted a letter opener off her desk and managed to get it under the outer label. With a little scraping and tugging, I got it off.

"Does this mean anything to you?" I asked her, handing it back. "It's in Spanish, but the contents seem to be HMG Massone."

"I don't believe it," she said, taking the bottle as though lifting a cobra. I even got the distinct feeling she didn't want to leave any fingerprints on it. "That's an even more powerful drug to stimulate ovarian follicles and induce superovulation. It's highly illegal in this country. Anybody who gives these drugs in combination to a patient is flirting with an ethics charge, or worse."

I think I gasped. *What* was he trying to put into my body?

She settled the bottle back on the desk, her eyes growing narrow. "Since you say his 'nurse' or assistant or whatever she was gave you this, I suppose there's always the chance she made an innocent mistake. But still, what's he doing with this stuff at all? They manufacture it down in Mexico, and also, I've heard, somewhere in Central America, but it's not approved in the U.S. Anybody who dispenses this to a patient is putting their license at risk." She paused to give me one of those looks. "Assuming Alex Goddard even has a medical license. These 'alternative medicine' types sometimes claim they answer to a higher power, they're board-certified by God."

"I don't for a minute think it was an 'innocent mistake.' " I was beginning to feel terribly betrayed and violated. I also was getting mad as hell, my fingertips tingling. "But why would he give me these drugs at all? Did he somehow—?"

"I think you'd better ask *him,*" she said, passing me a bagel piled high with cream cheese and sturgeon.

She bit into her own bagel and for a while we both just chewed in silence. I, however, had just lost all my appetite. Alex Goddard, who might well be my last chance for a baby, had just dispensed massive doses of illegal drugs to me. Which, my longtime ob/gyn was warning me, were both unnecessary and unethical.

"What do you think I should do?" I asked finally, breaking the silence but barely able to get my voice out.

She didn't say anything. She'd finished her bagel, and now she'd begun wrapping up the container of cream cheese, folding the wax paper back over the remaining sturgeon. I thought her silent treatment was her way of telling me my brunch consultation was over. She clearly was exasperated with me.

"Let me tell you a story," she said finally, as she carefully began putting the leftover sturgeon back into the Zabar's bag. "When I was eight years old, all the Jews in our Polish ghetto were starving because the Nazis refused to give us food stamps. So my father bribed a Nazi officer to let him go out into the countryside to try to buy some eggs and flour, anything, just so we could eat. The farmer came that Saturday morning in a horse-drawn wagon to pick up my father. At the last minute, I asked to go with him and he let me. That night the Nazis liquidated our entire ghetto, almost five thousand people. No one else in my family survived. Not my mother, not my two sisters, not anyone."

Her voice had become totally dispassionate, matter-of-fact, as though repression of the horror was the only way a sane person could deal with it. She could just as easily have been describing a country outing as she continued. I did notice, however, that her East European accent had suddenly become very prominent, as though she was returning there in her thoughts.

"When we learned what had happened, my father asked the farmer we were visiting to go to a certain rural doctor we knew and beg him to give us some poison, so we could commit suicide before the Nazis got us too. The doctor, however, told him he had only enough poison for his own family. He did, however, give him a prescription for us. But when my father begged that farmer to go to a pharmacy and get the poison, he and his entire family refused. Instead, they hid us in their barn for over a year, even though they knew it meant a firing squad if the Nazis found us." She glared at me. "Do you understand what I'm saying? They told us that if we wanted to do something foolish because we were desperate, we would have to do it without their help."

It was the first time I ever knew her real story. I was stunned.

"What, exactly, are you driving at?" I think I already knew. The long, trusting relationship we'd shared was now teetering on the brink. By going to see Alex Goddard—even if it was partly a research trip to check him out—I had disappointed her terribly. She'd lost respect for me. She thought *I* was desperate and about to embark on something foolish.

"I'm saying do whatever you want." She got up and lifted her coat off the corner rack. "But get those drugs out of here. I don't want them anywhere near this office. I tried everything legal there was to get you pregnant. If that wasn't good enough for you and now you want to go to some quack, that's your affair. Let me just warn you that combining gonadotropin and HMG Massone at these dosages is like putting your ovaries on steroids; you get massive egg production for a couple of cycles, but the long-term damage could be severe. I strongly advise you against it, but if you insist and then start having complications, I would appreciate not being involved."

Translation: If you start fooling around with Alex Goddard, don't ever come back.

It felt like a dagger in my chest. What was I going to do? One thought: Okay, so these drugs aren't the way, but *you* couldn't help me get pregnant. All I did was spend twenty thousand dollars on futile procedures. Not to mention the heartbreak.

"You know," I said finally, maybe a little sharply, "I think we ought to be working together, not at cross-purposes."

"You're welcome to think what you like," she bristled. "But I have to tell you I don't appreciate your tone."

I guess I'd really ticked her off, and it hurt to do it. Then, finally, her own rejection of *me* was sinking in.

"So that's *it?* You're telling me if I try anything except exactly what you want me to, then just don't ever come back."

"I've said all I intend to." She was resolutely ushering me toward the door, her eyes abruptly blank.

Well, I told myself, going from anger to despair, then back to anger, whatever else I might think about Alex Goddard, at least he doesn't kick people out because of their problems, even a sad soul like Tara.

Still, what about these illegal drugs? There I was, caught in the middle—between an honorable woman who had failed, and Alex Goddard, who'd just lived up to my worst suspicions. Heading down in the elevator, alone, I could still hear Hannah Klein's rejection, and warning, ringing in my ears. Maybe she had just confirmed that still, small voice of rationality lecturing me from the back of my mind.

I marched out onto the empty Sunday streets of upper Broadway, and when I got to the corner, I stood for a long moment looking up at the pitiless blue of the sky. The sun was there, but in my soul I felt all the light was gone.

Finally I opened the first bottle and then, one by one, I began taking out the gel-caps and dropping them into the rainwater grate there at my feet, watching them bounce like the metal sphere in an old pinball machine before disappearing into the darkness below. When both bottles were empty, I tossed them into the wire trash basket I'd been standing next to.

The next time I saw Alex Goddard, he was going to have a hell of a lot of explaining to do. Beginning with why he'd given me a glimmer of hope, only to then cruelly snatch it back. I found myself hating him with all my being.

Ten

I headed on back downtown, planning to take a bath, change clothes, and then recalibrate my game plan. Maybe, I thought, I ought to just go up to the editing room at Applecore, try some rote work to help tranquilize my thoughts.

But first things first. About halfway there, at Thirty-eighth Street, I pulled over and double-parked by a Korean deli, and surveyed the flowers they had out front, an array of multicolored blooms that virtually blocked entry to the doorway of the tiny grocery. Azaleas, chrysanthemums, birds-of-paradise, but I wanted the pink roses. At ten dollars a bunch, they seemed the right touch. I dug out a twenty and picked two.

Still standing on the street, I pulled them to me and inhaled deeply. As far back as I could remember, I'd always loved the scent of roses. I'd never really thought myself pretty, the natural-blond, often-dyed-brown hair notwithstanding, but just having roses around somehow made me feel that way. I wanted to be engulfed in them, especially any time confusion threatened to get the upper hand.

Five minutes later and I was at Twenty-first Street. I'd arrived. My refuge, my one-bedroom cocoon. Time to collapse into a hot bath, wonder why Alex Goddard had given me illegal drugs, and contemplate roses.

I was looking for a parking space when my cell phone rang. No, don't bother, I told myself. Enough intrusion for one day. Then I remembered I'd sprung for the caller-ID feature, and I glanced down at the little liquid crystal slot. It was a number I happened to know, Lou's place downtown. One eye still on the street, I reached over and picked it up.

"Finally got you," he boomed. "Where the heck are you?"

"I just got home from—"

"Yeah, I know where you been. Dave told me." He paused, as though he was holding off on some important announcement. "Hang on a sec. There's somebody here might like to speak to you."

I thought about Lou's makeshift digs, lots of "heirloom"—worn-out—family furniture he'd lugged along with him. Sarah and I used to play on the couch, and it still had a dim mauve stain where I'd once dumped a glass of "grape" Kool-Aid on her head when she was six. Whatever else, definitely not a Soho look.

Then I heard a whispery voice.

"Hi, Morgy."

It was a tentative utterance I'd heard only once before, when she was waking up after falling off a playground swing. She'd been knocked out cold for a moment and I'd been frantic, wetting a handkerchief in the nearby fountain and desperately rubbing it over her face. When she came to, she'd gazed up into my eyes and greeted me as though we'd just met.

My God!

Before I could recover and say anything, Lou came back on. "We're practicing eating chicken-noodle soup. And we're trying to do a little talking. Why don't you come on down? She asked about you earlier this morning, said, 'Where's Morgy?' "

"Lou! This is incredible!"

"You gotta believe in miracles, right? Just come on down."

"Is she . . . God, you've got it." My hopes went into orbit as I clicked off the phone and revved my engine.

I could have swamped him with a lot of questions then and there, but I immediately decided I wanted to see her first, with my own eyes. I still couldn't quite believe it was true. On the other hand, a weekend partial recovery was not totally beyond the realm of medical possibility. With a coma, so little is understood that anything's possible. Lou was right. This was definitely a weekend of the unexpected.

I'd been close to the deaths of people near to me, both my parents for starters, but I'd never been close to the restoration of life. It's hard to explain the rush of joy when you think somebody is gone for good and then they pop up again, like they'd never been lost. And with Sarah that feeling was especially jarring. It was almost as though some part of me had come back alive.

The fact is, since Sarah and I were both only children, we'd identified a lot with each other. True, we'd traveled our separate paths, each looking, perhaps, for something to fill the lonely void in our lives that a sibling might have taken. As a child of the dusty, empty plains of West Texas, I didn't see other kids very much during the summer, and I made up reasons why she and I should visit each other as often as possible.

Once, when I was plowing, turning over oat stubble—yes, my dad warily let me do that if I asked—I unearthed a rabbit nest full of little baby cottontails. Sarah was coming to visit the next day, and I rescued the infants so we could play nursery. We fed them milk with little eyedroppers, and before long Sarah decided she was actually a reincarnated mother rabbit. That was when she became a vegetarian, and she remained so—by her account—till she finished college. It was just another of those magic moments of childhood I ended up sharing with her.

I also sometimes wondered, as you might have guessed, what it would've been like to be born a boy. I was definitely a tomboy, had a real collie (my own version of Lassie), liked to climb trees and dig holes in the hardscrabble West Texas earth. Maybe that was why I felt so at home—free associating now—when I filmed my documentary of the Maya village in Mexico's Yucatan. It was hot and dry and lay under a pitiless sun, a blazing white bone in the sky that seared the spare landscape. None of my crew could understand how anybody could bear to live in such a place, but to me it seemed perfectly natural, almost like home.

Thoughts of which now made me sad. I only wish my parents had lived long enough to see that documentary. Maybe then they'd have understood how terribly lonely I'd been as a child, a loneliness I shared so deeply with Sarah. Would we ever be together again?

On my hurried trip downtown, I kept wondering what I was about to encounter. Was it going to be the fantasy-bound Sarah of her girlhood, perhaps the same Sarah who'd spun out some stuttering vision of a jade mask? Or would all that be past and would she again be the ambitious, sparkling pre-med student she'd become when she was in college?

Getting to Soho took only about ten minutes, scant time to think. Lou's place was in what had once been a garment factory sweatshop. He'd rented it from another agent at the bureau, who had inherited it from a cousin, a well-known downtown artist, lately dead of AIDS. Lou paid virtually no rent, was there mainly to keep out squatters, and couldn't care less that he was living in one of New York's trendiest sections. All he knew was that there was plenty of room, and free parking on the street for his old Buick.

I'd been down many times before. Inside, the space was still inhabited spiritually by the dead artist, with acrylic paint spattered on walls and graffiti I didn't fully understand in the bathroom. The place seemed to be a broom-free area, with layers of the past littered on the floor like an archaeological excavation. And the old Kool-Aid-stained furniture, fitting right in.

What always struck me, though, was the number of photos of Sarah. They were everywhere in the open space, on tables, the desk, several on the walls. Mostly they were old, several blown up and cropped from snapshots, grainy. The space felt like a shrine to her memory.

When Lou let me in, I was greeted by a spectral face, a wheelchair, and a valiant attempt at smiling normalcy. Maybe Lou thought it was real, was progress, but I was immediately on guard.

It was Sarah's eyes that caught me. They pierced into my soul and we seemed to click, just like always, only this time it was as though all our life together passed between us. I had the sense she was trying to tell me something with her eyes that went beyond words, that she was trying to reach out to me, perhaps to recapture that shared understanding we'd had years ago.

Lou introduced me to a Mrs. Reilly, a kindly, Irish-looking practical nurse who was part of the outpatient package the hospital provided. She wore a white uniform and was around sixty, with short-bobbed gray hair and an air of total authority. She'd just finished feeding Sarah a bowl of soup, and was brushing out her cropped blond hair, what there was of it.

Mrs. Reilly glanced at me, but never broke the rhythm of her strokes. "She's tired now, but she's already stronger than she was."

Then Lou spoke up. "They called me early yesterday morning. But by the time I got around to trying to reach you, you'd vanished. So I rang Dave and he told me where you were, up there with that crackpot." He was grinning. No, make that beaming like the famous cat. "By last night, she was walking with some help, so they said she might as well be here. Like I said, it's a miracle."

"You brought her home just this morning?" I couldn't believe the hospital would discharge her so soon, but this was the HMO Age of medical cost-cutting.

"Only been here a couple of hours." He pointed to a shiny set of parallel steel railings in the corner. "That's for physical therapy. Right now she can only walk with somebody on either side holding her, but in a few days, I figure . . ." His voice trailed off, as though he didn't want to tempt fortune. Then he turned toward Sarah. "In a few days, right, honey?"

She nodded, then finally spoke directly to me. "Morgy, I want some clothes. Please. I hate these horrible hospital things. I never want to see them again."

I noticed that she'd started crying, a line of tears down each emaciated cheek. Was it something to do with seeing me? I wondered. Then she began trying to struggle out of the blue bed shift she was wearing, though she didn't have the strength.

"I'll get you something great, Sar, don't worry." I reached to stay her hand. It was, I thought, extraordinarily cold, even though the loft itself was warm as toast. What kind of clothes should I buy for her? I found myself wondering. Blouses with buttons? Pullovers? What could she manage? Maybe I'd bring some items from home first and let her try them out. We used to be about the same size, though now she was all skin and bones.

I moved a chair next to her, took her other hand, and leaned as close as I dared. I desperately wanted to put my arms around her, but I wasn't sure how she would respond to my touch. Her eyes, however, were clear and had never looked a deeper blue. "Sar, what's the matter? Why're you crying?

You should be happy. Your dad's right here and he loves you and we're going to take wonderful care of you."

"Who? Him?" she asked, looking straight at Lou, her blue eyes like an unblinking camera's lens.

The plaintive question took my breath away. Hadn't they been talking for two days?

"Don't pay any attention when she says things like that," Mrs. Reilly declared, her voice just above a whisper. "She's still not quite herself. She drifts in and out."

She seemed to be drifting in and out at the moment, though it was mostly out.

Then she looked directly at me, only now her eyes were losing their laserlike focus, were starting to seem glazed. "Who're you?" She reached out and touched my unwashed hair, running her hands through the tangled strands.

Next she stared off, terrified, her eyes full of fear.

"The smoke," she whispered. "The knife. I'm next."

Abruptly she was off again in the reverie that had enfolded her that first time in the hospital. Or at least that was what I guessed.

"What are you talking about?" I felt like shaking her, except I was too shook-up myself.

She turned back, and for a moment she just stared glassy-eyed, first at me, next at Lou, and finally at Mrs. Reilly. Then she reached for a glass of orange juice on the table beside her. She looked at it as though it were some potion, then slowly drank it off, not pausing once. Outside, a faint police siren could be heard, and I was afraid it was distracting her. Anyway, something told me her momentary seance was played out. Her face had grown calm and rested, though I could barely repress a tremble.

"Whatever you think," I said finally, slipping an arm around her shoulder, "we're both right here. And we love you and we want to help you get better."

She didn't say anything more, just closed her eyes and drifted away. But it wasn't back into a coma, since her breathing was growing heavier. I wanted to grab her and yell at her and demand that she come back to us, but I was fearful of what effect it might have.

"What the hell was she talking about?" Lou asked finally, his voice quavering.

"I don't know," I said, as puzzled as he was.

That was when Mrs. Reilly spoke up. She was the only one not upset.

"When they come out of a coma, sometimes they're not right for a while." She patted Sarah's hand, then gave it a solicitous squeeze. "I once had a man wake up and start talking about magic trips through the air, about how he was a dual citizen of the earth and the sea. He was talking like a lunatic. One day he would know his family, and the next he would look at them and start screaming they'd come to kill him. You just never know how these things will go at first. But she'll be herself before long." She lifted Sarah's limp hand up to her cheek, then kissed it. "You're going to be all right, dear. I've seen enough like you to know."

"Then what do you make of what she just said?" Lou asked her, having given up on me. "Earlier this morning she was fine. Knew who I was, everything. Then the minute Morgan comes in, she starts making up that loony jabber."

The sanguine Mrs. Reilly just shrugged, as if it didn't really matter.

For my own part, I didn't necessarily like him implying my arrival had caused her to relapse into her dreamworld of terror. It seemed to me that whenever I showed up, she started trying to tell me what was really eating away at her soul.

Well, I told myself finally, maybe she's regressed back to when we were kids, when we only had each other to share our secrets with. What if we've rebonded in some new, special way? It would be natural, actually. She's trying to reach out to me, like long ago.

Now she appeared to be dozing off, exhausted, her head tipping downward toward her blue hospital shift. Mrs. Reilly took that as a hint, and slowly began wheeling her toward the bedroom, leaving me alone with Lou.

I glanced over at him, thinking more and more that I had to do something, track down what had happened to her. I wanted to do it for me, but even more for him. I'd never seen him so despondent. Maybe it was the thing scholars call the curse of rising expectations. Back when she was hardly more than a vegetable, he was overjoyed by a flickering eyelid. Now that she was talking, he wanted all of her back. Instead, though, it seemed as if she had returned to us for a moment, only to be snatched away again. I could tell it was killing him.

"Look, I'm sorry that when I showed up, she started going off the deep end." I wanted desperately to help, but at that moment I felt powerless. "Maybe I should just stay away for a while."

"Nah, she loves having you here. Don't worry. But anyway, Dave said something about you taking a couple of days off. Maybe I can use that time to be here with her and settle her down." Then he grimly took out her locket and rubbed its worn silver in his fingers, his eyes brimming with his heartache. "This is all just so damned confusing."

Was he telling me, indirectly, that I should go away and leave them alone? First Hannah Klein rejects me, and now *et tu,* Lou? Maybe, I thought, he's taking out his despair on me, blaming me for her relapse. Truthfully, I guess I was blaming myself a bit too.

"Listen, I'm going to go home now and leave you two alone," I said. "But why don't you see if you can get her to talk some more? Without me around, maybe she'll make more sense."

"If she wants to say something, I'll listen." He gave me a strong, absent embrace, his eyes still despondent. "But no way am I gonna start pushing her."

I edged into the bedroom, unsure if I really should, to say good-bye to Sarah and to give her one last hug. Her eyes were open again and she just stared at me for a second, then whispered a word I couldn't quite make out. It might have sounded like "Babylon," but that made no sense at all. Finally she covered her eyes with her hands and turned away, gone from me, leaving me more alone than I'd ever felt.

Eleven

Heading home, finally, I told myself to try to calm down. I was determined to help Sarah get over her trauma, though truthfully I was too tired to really think straight at that moment. So instead I decided to let everything rest for a few hours and try for some distance. In fact, I began imagining myself in a hot bath, gazing at my now-wilting roses. Home Sweet Home.

Mine was a standard one-bedroom in a building that had been turned into a co-op five years earlier, the owner offering the individual apartments to the tenants. I'd stayed a renter, however, passing up the "low" insider price, $138,000, because I didn't really have the money, and when I did have it someday I would want something bigger. I wished I had more space—a real dining room and a bigger bathroom would do for starters, along with some place for more bookcases. And if a baby should someday miraculously come along . . .

I'd often thought you could tell a lot about somebody from where and how they lived; it's revealing as a Rorschach test. What, I often wondered, did my apartment say about me?

A decorator might conclude I'd done up the place with love, then lazily let it go. They'd decide I cared about nice things, but once those nice things were there, I neglected them. It would be true.

I'd covered the walls of the living room with pale blue cloth, then hung a lot of framed pictures and old movie posters. Okay, I like movies. For me even the posters are art. My couch was an off-white, more like dirt-colored actually, and covered with pillows for the "feminine" touch. I'd hoped you'd have to look twice to realize it was actually a storage cabinet in disguise, with drawers along the bottom of the front. The floor was polished hardwood, rugs from India here and there, in sore need of a vacuuming, and even a couple of deceased insects that'd been there for over a week. That sort of said it, I thought glumly. I'm a workaholic slob.

The bedroom revealed even more about me. The bed was a brass four-poster, queen-size, partly covered by an heirloom quilt. It hadn't been made in a week. (Who has the time?) The room itself was long and divided into areas for work and sleep. Opposite the bed itself was an antique English desk, on which sat my old Macintosh, and next to that was my file cabinet, the indispensable part of the "home office" the IRS loves to hate. On top of it was a stack of marked-up scripts, notes scribbled all over them in six different colors. You never realize movies are so complicated till you see a breakdown sheet. Camera angles and voice-overs and . . .

Next to the bed was a violin case and three books about Indian ragas. What was that about? somebody might wonder. Some kind of Indian music nut? I was, albeit a very minimally talented nut.

The kitchen was the New York efficiency kind, painted a glossy tan, the color of aerosol olive oil. The cabinets contained mostly packages of pasta, instant soup, and coffee filters. Not even any real food. I live on deli takeout these days. An inventory of my fridge at this moment would clock two cartons of "fresh squeezed" orange juice, a half quart of spoiling milk, a bag of coffee beans, plastic containers of wilting veggies from the corner salad bar, and three bottles of New York seltzer. That was it.

God help me, I thought, my mind-state turning even more

morose. This is my life. I had become that retrograde Woman of the Nineties: works ninety hours a week, makes ninety thou a year, weighs ninety pounds, and thinks (pardon my French) Cooking and Fucking are provinces in northern China. Well, the ninety-pounds part of that obscene quip didn't fit—and it wasn't the nineties anymore, anyway.

In any case, was my apartment a place to raise a child? No earthly way. Like Carly, I'd have to spring for some decent space, preferably with a washing machine. . . .

A parking slot was open right in front of my building, a minor miracle on this day of uncertain events. As I was pulling in, I glanced over to see a man walking past, not catching the face but sensing something familiar in the walk. He was in the process of unbuttoning a Federal Express uniform, peeling away the top to reveal a dark suit. He certainly seemed to be in a big hurry, carrying an unmarked shopping bag. Maybe, I thought, his shift was over and he was meeting his wife, or a friend.

I wondered if he'd left a package for me, and told myself to check with the super. Not the usual delivery guy—did they come on Sunday now?—and also . . .

Where was the truck? They always parked right here by the building.

I was still so upset over Sarah, I couldn't immediately process those illogical observations, so I just grabbed my pink roses, dripping from the bottom of their paper wrapping, and opened the car door. It was definitely good to be home. I loved my Chelsea neighborhood, where you got to know the locals, running into them in the delis, the little restaurants, the dry cleaners. Just like a small town. If you worked at home, the way I sometimes did, you even got to know the mailman and the delivery guys for UPS and FedEx. . . .

Hey! That guy. I finally placed the walk, a kind of a strut. He was the slimeball who'd been outside Paula Marks's building last week, carrying a gun and threatening me. What's *he* doing here?

My pulse went off the charts. Was he one of Nicky Russo's wiseguy crew after all? Had he come back, with his pistol, to pay me a return engagement?

My God.

Chill out, I told myself, take a deep breath. He's leaving. Just try and find out who he is.

Roses in one hand, held up awkwardly around my face, I slowly ambled down the street after him. I didn't have to go far. Within about a hundred feet, he unlocked a long black Lincoln Towncar, stepped out of the FedEx camouflage, tossed it onto the seat along with the bag he was carrying, pulled the cap off his bald head, got in, and sped away.

The license plate looked different from the usual, but I got what I needed: DL and a string of numbers.

Uh-oh, I thought. Was he leaving a package bomb for me?

I turned back and let myself into the outer lobby, glancing around as I did. There were no parcels anywhere, just blank, brown tile.

My apartment was 3A. The name on the bell was M. James. As I stepped through the inner lobby—still no package—a rumpled face appeared in the doorway just to my left. The sign on it, flaking, said SUPER.

"Oh, hi." The voice was Patrick Mooney, our superintendent, who did not normally emerge to greet those arriving. But there had been complaints from the building's managing agent that he could never be found for emergencies, so he probably wanted to appear available, even on Sundays. His voice was slurred from some midday medicinal Irish whisky. "Thought you were home. FedEx guy was here earlier looking for you."

Oh, boy. "Did he leave a package?"

"He had something with him, if that's what you mean. Like a bag of some kind."

"And you let him go up?" I couldn't believe what I was hearing. I felt a rush of dismay.

"Said he had to. Needed a signature." Patrick Mooney then shrugged and reached for the doorjamb to steady himself, his whisky breath wafting across the hall. Great security.

I stepped into the elevator as the door was clanking shut, and watched as he rubbed his eyes and eased his own door closed.

Now I was really puzzled. If the FedEx guy came "earlier," why was he just now leaving? A lot of scary theories went through my mind as I pushed the button for the third floor.

I took a deep breath as the elevator opened, but again I saw no packages. So far so good. Getting off, I set down my roses on the hall carpet and fumbled for my key. When I inserted it, the lock felt a little rough, causing me to think for an instant I'd used the wrong key, but then it responded.

What had caused that? I wondered. Had the guy been fiddling with my door, wiring a bomb? Using one hand I pushed it open, again holding my breath and standing aside, but it opened okay. I exhaled, then reached back to drag in the flowers.

But if he didn't leave a package, *what was he doing here?* Casing out where I lived? Planting a bug in the elevator? And why was he here so long?

The place was dark when I stepped in, the drapes drawn. I relocked the door, then surveyed the gloom. No explosions, so I guessed he didn't plan to kill me. Yet. Here I was, home, safe and sound. I just stood a minute, still uneasy.

Then I remembered the flowers, my dripping bouquet, and headed for the kitchen. Deal with them, and then maybe get a bottle of white wine out of the fridge and sip some in the bath.

After my unnerving sequence with Sarah, thoughts of going to the office had zero appeal. Time to lighten up, way up.

Preoccupied, not looking around, I stuffed the roses into a vase by the sink, and then I thought again about the white wine and opened the refrigerator. I'd still not bothered to turn on any lights, but the kitchen and its ancient fridge were dimly illuminated by the tiny window just across. I wasn't sure where I'd put the bottle, since I'd had to rearrange things to make room for the dup of Carly's interview. (I was also planning to take home a safety dup of Paula's interview sometime later in the week.)

Why was I doing that? Taking home copies? It was a sign of deep compulsion. You couldn't really make a professional-quality second negative from a first positive—by that time it would be third-generation—but I'd brought it anyway. Now and then I just have a raw instinct that keeping a safety backup around is a good idea. But the canister had ended up devouring the entire lower shelf of the fridge.

I opened the white door and peered in. The light was out, and for a moment I stared numbly at the dark, half-filled shelves. The only thing that struck me as odd was that I could see the pure white of the empty bottom shelf.

For a second I could only stand and stare, but then I backed away, trying to figure out what was wrong, and stumbled over something. I regained my balance and flipped on the overhead light.

"What!"

The floor around me was littered with bottles, my old toaster, my tiny microwave. It was a total shambles.

I recoiled, stumbling again, this time over cans strewn across the linoleum. My kitchen, it was slowly sinking in, had been completely trashed.

I felt a visceral wave of nausea. It's the scariest thing in the world, having your space invaded, like a form of psychic rape. I sagged against the refrigerator as I gazed around. The cabinets had been emptied out, a hasty and haphazard search. Quick and extremely dirty, as glass containers of condiments, including an old bottle of dill pickles, were shattered and their contents smeared into the floor.

"I don't believe this." I marched back into the living room and reached for the lights. This room too had been turned upside down. The TV, stereo, VCR, all had been swept onto the rug. But they were still there. That guy, that animal, who did this wasn't a thief. He'd been looking for something.

My breath now coming in pulses, I edged into the bedroom and switched on the light. The bed was the way I'd left it, the covers thrown back and the pillows in a pile. The clock radio was there, and so was the old Mac, still on the table in the far corner, my "workstation." Again nothing seemed to be missing.

I headed back to the kitchen, where the refrigerator door was still open. I gazed at the interior a moment, still puzzled, trying to figure out what wasn't right. . . .

Shit! Shit! Shit! That's what was wrong. The field of white bottom shelf was empty. Totally empty. The film canister of Paula's interview was gone.

For a moment I just leaned against the kitchen counter, barely pushing aside an impulse to throw up in the sink. Think, I told myself, get a grip and think. . . .

It was the film he'd wanted. And he'd wanted it badly enough to pick the lock, then rip my home apart looking for it.

I pulled at a tangle of hair, feeling my mind in chaos, and tried to reason out the situation. Why? Why would he steal a positive that couldn't be used for anything?

Finally the real truth of what had happened hit me like a fist in the chest. My Home Sweet Home had been violated.

Seething, I went into the living room and reached for the phone, the only thing not on the floor.

My first instinct was to call David, but then I decided he'd just go into a tizzy of hysteria and be no support at all. So instead I called Lou, praying I wouldn't wake Sarah. In an unsteady voice, I tried to tell him what had happened.

He seemed puzzled to hear from me again so soon, but then he quickly turned FBI, concerned for my safety.

"Guy sounds like a professional," he declared. "Probably got in with an electric picker, like the Edge. Any asshole can buy one for a hundred and thirty bucks. It'll rake cylinders at a hundred times a second. Pro like that, you can be sure there'll be no prints."

"But why would . . . ?" My voice was still a croak. "I mean, my God, all for a lousy reel of film?"

"Fucker wants you to know he's in town. So *how* he did it's as important as what he did. It's a time-proven scare tactic." He paused. "Morgan, I don't like this one bit. There could be more before this is over."

"Think I should call the cops?"

"Damned right you should," he said, slowly and sadly, "but to tell you the truth, they ain't gonna do all that much. Somebody messed up your apartment and lifted a third-hand copy of a woman talking. They'll say it sounds more like malicious mischief than a crime. Then they'll write it up and that'll be the last you'll hear from them."

"Well," I said, my anger welling up, "maybe I don't feel quite so laissez-faire. Tell me, you know anybody who can run a plate for you on a Sunday?"

"You got the prick's license number?" he exclaimed. "Why the hell didn't you say so?"

"Honestly, it sort of slipped my mind. I'm having a little trouble thinking straight right now."

Fortunately my short-term memory is pretty good, even when I'm stressed, so I spewed it out.

"Don't go anywhere," he declared. "I'll get back to you in five minutes."

I hung up the phone and lay down, flat out on the carpet, trying a breathing exercise to calm down. The problem was, it wasn't working. Having had some experience with being robbed—I once got completely cleaned out when I had a ground-floor apartment down in the Village—I know you go through certain Kubler-Ross-like stages of anger, denial, depression, acceptance. You also go through a predictable series of recriminations: I should have had window bars and gates; I should have had a different lock; I should have had *two* different locks. In the instance just recalled, I'm virtually certain an apartment painter duplicated a set of my keys on his lunch break and then passed them on to a second-story artist. No way to prove that, mind you, but it had to be what happened. I also suspect he checked my appointments calendar to see when I was going to be out of town.

But in this case the lock was definitely picked. Nobody had a set of my keys except the super, and Steve. So the guy with the Spanish accent knew how to slip through doors and he had no financial interest in my old VCR. He only had an interest in my film. What had he said there on the sidewalk outside Paula Marks's apartment? Something about how making this picture was a big mistake?

I jumped as the phone erupted by my ear.

"The name Colonel Jose Alvino Ramos Grijalva mean anything to you?" Lou asked.

"How could it? I'm not sure I can even pronounce it."

"Well, Colonel Ramos declares himself to be a military attaché at the Guatemalan Consulate here. You've got a big shot in the Guatemalan Army rummaging through your apartment. This is even worse than I thought. Those guys are killers."

"Jesus." I was still coming to grips with the horrifying fact he'd been in my apartment, in my *only* refuge. "Think I could bring charges against him ?"

"Well, let's consider this a minute. Probably no prints, no credible witness. You'd have a damned hard time proving anything." He sighed. "Truth is, I doubt you could even get a restraining order, given what little you've got to work with."

"The bastard." I sat a moment, feeling the logical, left side of my brain just shut down. My mind went back to its most primitive level, running on adrenaline. "Look, I need to check out something. I'll call you in the morning."

"Well, *be careful,*" he said warily. "And for God's sake don't go running off anyplace alone. I'm telling you you're not safe. Always be around people."

"I'll keep it in mind." With that I gently hung up the phone and exhaled.

Think. Some colonel from Guatemala just broke into my apartment looking for what I might know about Children of Light, where I've been going to see about having a baby. So why is he so interested in what I'm doing?

I remembered Alex Goddard wanted me to go to a "clinic" he had somewhere in Central America. Ten to one that clinic was in Guatemala. That was what this whole thing was about. And now he'd just gone back there; at least that was what he'd said.

Guatemala was a long way off, but his other operation was right up the river. I hadn't seen all of it this morning, but that was about to change. A lot of things were about to change. It was time to start getting the playing field level again.

Twelve

I arranged with Patrick Mooney to have his sister in Queens, a full-figured woman named Rosalyn, come in and finish the job of reconstructing my wrecked home. She arrived an hour and a half later, and was hard at work when I left. I also agonized over the police-report issue, but finally decided to forgo the bother. Lou was right: It would be a two-hour ordeal of futility. Besides, I had better things to do with my time. I was going to return the favor of an information-gathering expedition.

Alex Goddard had said he'd be absent from Quetzal Manor—who knows for how long—and this time around I was going to do the place right, the next step in my undercover research. The first, and main, thing I wanted to do was explore the new high-tech clinic that sat nestled in the woods across from the old building. Everything about it was the exact opposite of a "Manor." Not a shred of New Age "spirituality," just a lot of digital equipment and ultrasound and . . . what else? Chief among my questions: What was behind that big, white door?

Maybe I was being impulsive, but I was completely wired and the truth was, I wasn't going to sleep till I knew a lot more than I did. And if I went late tonight, Sunday, I probably wouldn't have to deal with Ramala.

I called Roger Drexel, my unshaven cameraman, and asked him to come up and meet me at Applecore. It was

Sunday and he was watching the third quarter of a Knicks game and into his second six-pack, but he agreed. After all, I was his current boss.

All I really wanted was his Betacam and some metal tape, which would be broadcast quality. (I'd wanted to do it yesterday, but now the time had definitely come.) We met at the office, and he unlocked the room with the camera gear and loaded in a fresh tape. With any luck, he made it home for the end of the game.

I then had a sinful cheeseburger and fries at a Greek diner two blocks down the avenue. It was my idea of a courage-bolstering indulgence.

My watch read six thirty-five and daylight was waning when I revved my old Toyota and started my northbound trek back to Quetzal Manor. When I was passing the George Washington Bridge, the first drifting flakes of a freak late-season snowstorm began pelting my windshield. Good, I thought, turning on my wipers, the less visibility, the better. At least I believed that till the road started getting slippery and I had to throttle back. It was only then I realized I'd been pushing eighty on the speedometer, passing a lot of cars. Lou's warning not to go anywhere alone was still filed in the back of my mind, but I kept trying not to think about it. Sometimes there are things you've just got to do.

The highway grew more treacherous the farther north I went, but the traffic was thinning out and by the time I reached the turnoff to Quetzal Manor, total darkness had set in, in addition to which the paving was covered with at least an inch of sparkling-new pristine snow.

As I eased up the roadway, my headlights made the trees around me glisten with their light dusting of white, like frosting on the tips of a buzz cut. I switched off my lights as I made the last turn in the road, but not before catching a glimpse of Quetzal Manor, and I must confess to feeling a shudder, of both anger and apprehension, run through me as I watched its magisterial turrets disappear into the snowy dark.

I parked my car at the back of the lot and retrieved the flashlight I'd brought, a yellow plastic two-battery model. I hadn't realized there'd be snow when I left home, so I was just wearing some old sneakers, but they'd do. I then sat there in the dark for a long minute, listening to the silence and thinking. The first thing was to find out if anybody was guarding the place. The next was to get some video of the new building.

I grabbed the bag carrying the Betacam, tested my flashlight against the floorboard, and then headed up the snowy driveway. I marched straight through the open arch that was the front door, and I was again in the drafty hallway where I'd met Ramala Saturday morning. It was empty and dark now, no lights anywhere, not even out in the courtyard beyond. The stony quiet—no music, no chants—felt unnatural, but it also suggested that Alex Goddard's adoring acolytes were safely tucked away. Early to bed . . . you know the rest. So maybe I really *had* come at the right time.

A chilly wind was blowing in from the far end of the hallway, and I felt like I'd just entered a dank tomb, but I tightened my coat and pressed on. When I got to the end and looked out, the snowy courtyard was like a picture postcard. And completely empty.

All right, I thought, move on to what you came for.

But when I turned and headed back down the hallway, toward the entry arch, I caught a glimpse of a furtive form, dark and shadowy, lurking just outside. Shit! I froze in my tracks, but then the figure stepped inside, wearing something that made me think of Little Red Riding Hood, like a tiny ghost in a cowl.

It was Tara, Alex Goddard's spacey waif, who was moving so oddly, I thought for a moment she might be sleepwalking.

She wasn't, of course. She'd just been out strolling around the driveway in the snow. I soon realized she lived her life in something resembling a trance, as though she were a permanent denizen of the spirit world. For her it was a natural condition.

"It's so beautiful like this," she mumbled dreamily, as though we'd been in the middle of a lifelong conversation. "I just love it." Her voice was barely above a whisper, but in the silence it seemed to ricochet off the stone walls. "I want to take them out, show them God's paintbrush. Will you help me?"

"Take who out?" I asked, immediately deciding to go with the moment.

Finally she looked directly at me and realized whom she'd been talking to.

"You were here before. I tried to give you herbs to help you, but then he came and . . ." Her voice trailed off as she walked back through the portico and out again into the drifting snow. Then she held up her hands, as though attempting to capture the flakes as keepsakes. "I so want to show them. They've never seen it before." She glanced back at me. "Come on. Let's do it."

As I followed her out into the drifting white and across the parking lot, the accumulation of snow was growing denser, enough now to start covering the cars, but still, something told me the flurry was going to be short-lived. I took a long, misty breath of the moist air and clicked open the case holding the Betacam, readying myself to take it out the minute we got inside.

Well, I thought, maybe I've gotten lucky. She was headed for the new clinic, which was exactly where I wanted to go. It was nestled in the trees, up a winding pathway, and as I slogged along I could feel the snow melting through my sneakers.

When we got to the front door, large and made of glass, she just pushed it open.

"We never lock anything," she declared, glancing back. "It's one of our rules."

The hallway was dark, silent, and empty except for the two of us. Still, I felt a tinge of caution as we entered. At some level this was trespassing.

"Come on," she said, casually flipping a switch on the right-hand wall and causing the overhead fluorescents to blink on. "He's away now, and everybody's in bed. But I'll bet they're still awake in here. It's a perfect time."

I didn't feel anything was perfect, but I did know I wanted to learn what was behind the door I'd seen when I was leaving. It was at the end of the hallway, wide and steel and painted hospital white. And, sure enough, that was exactly where Tara was heading.

She just kept talking nonstop, in her dreamy, little-girl voice. "We've got to try and make them understand it's okay. That it'll be just for a minute."

She shoved open the door without knocking, and my ears were greeted by the faint strains of Beethoven's "Moonlight Sonata," one of my favorites. For an instant I was caught up in the music, a poignant moment drawing me in.

The room itself was spacious, with a row of white bassinets along one side and subdued lighting provided by small fluorescent bulbs along the walls. It was, I immediately realized, a no-frills nursery. Alongside the bassinets were tables with formula and boxes of Pampers and Handi-Wipes. Two short women of undefinable nationality—they looked vaguely Asian—were in attendance, and at the moment one was facing away and bouncing a baby on her shoulder. Her infant looked like a boy—or was that just my imagination?—

and I felt my heart go out. The light was dim, but I could tell he was a gorgeous sandy-haired kid, plump and peachy, so sublime in his tender vulnerability as he gazed around with eyes full of trust. He was staring directly back at me and before I could stop myself, I gave him a little wave and wrinkled my nose. He stared at me a second, then responded with a tiny smile. Hey, I thought, I've got the touch.

"Come on," Tara said, ignoring the women, "let me show you. They're all so beautiful."

By then my eyes were adjusting to the subdued light, and as we walked down the middle of the long room, I confirmed my assumption that the bassinets next to the tables all contained infants. I'm no expert on babies, but I'd guess they were all around six weeks old, maybe a couple of months at most.

This is the nest, I thought. Ground zero. Kevin and Rachel were both probably in this room at one time too. . . .

"Aren't they wonderful?" Tara was saying, still in her squeaky, spaced-out voice.

I was opening the Betacam bag when the first woman, the one holding and lightly bouncing her little boy, absently put her hand under his quilt, then spoke to the other in deeply accented English.

"He's wet again."

It was the first words either of them had uttered. Then she turned to me in exasperation, assuming, I suppose, that I was one of Alex Goddard's flock. "And I just changed him." Again the accent, but I still couldn't identify it. She made a face, then carried him over to a plywood changing table in the center of the room.

I felt a great baby-yearning as I moved over beside her, but she was behaving like a typical hourly wage-earner, glumly going about her job, and I just stood there a moment, vainly wanting to hold him, then turned back to Tara.

"Where do all these children come from?"

"Ramala says they're orphans or abandoned or something. From overseas or wherever." She sighed. "They're so perfect."

She was completely zombied-out. It felt like talking to a marshmallow on downers.

"But how, exactly, do—?"

"People bring them here." She seemed uninterested in the question, just plunging on as she wandered on down the line of bassinets.

I'd finally come to my senses enough to take out the Betacam, though the light wasn't actually enough to really work with, certainly not broadcast quality.

She stopped and picked up one of the infants out of its bassinet, then turned back to me, her eyes turning soft as she hugged it the way she might a small puppy. "Isn't this one cute? I'd so love to have him."

Was she on some kind of drug that suppressed curiosity? I found myself wondering as I panned the camera around the room. There must have been at least twenty bassinets, all just alike, wicker with a white lace hood. A couple of the babies were sniffling, and the one Tara had picked up now began crying outright, much to her annoyance. The room itself smelled like baby powder.

"And then what happens?" I asked finally, zooming in on one of the women.

"What happens when?" Now Tara was twirling in a circle, humming futilely to the shrieking child. "You mean, after they come here?"

"Right." God, getting answers from her was making me crazy.

"The girls here take them to their new mothers." Her eyes had turned even more dreamy as she lightly bounced the bawling bundle she was holding one last time, after which she returned it to its bassinet. Then she gazed around the room. "It's so sad to see them leave."

Did Paula and Carly get their babies that way? I found myself wondering. Probably, but it was one more thing I'd neglected to ask.

"Come on," Tara continued. "Let's take some of them out. He makes the nurses try and speak English around the children, but they don't really know much. Maybe you could figure out a way to, like, explain—"

"Tara, I don't think taking any of these babies out into the snow is a very hot idea. Not tonight. Maybe in the morning." Stall her, I thought. She's completely out of it. Then I looked at the woman changing the baby. Sure enough, I was right. It was a boy.

"But I want to." Tara turned crestfallen. "To show them how beautiful—"

"Well, I don't speak whatever language they're speaking," I said, cutting cut her off. "I'm not even sure I could make it sound reasonable in English. So you'll have to do it without my help."

Then I turned to the woman who'd been changing the baby.

"Do you know where this child came from?" Why not take a shot?

She just stared at me, alarmed, then turned away. Nothing. She clearly wasn't going to tell me anything, even if she could. She and the others were just cheap hired help, probably illegal immigrants without a green card and scared to death for their jobs. They weren't going to be doing an indepth tell-all to anybody.

I thought about the situation for a moment, and decided I'd seen what I came to see. This was pay dirt. Alex Goddard was running a full-scale adoption mill, just as Lou had suspected. He was collecting beautiful white babies from "overseas or wherever," and selling them here at sixty thousand a pop.

Which went a long way toward explaining why he didn't want Children of Light to be featured in my film. And the Guatemalan colonel who'd just trashed my home was almost certainly in on the operation. Alex Goddard might be a New Age miracle worker rediscovering ancient Native American herbal cures, but he also was running a very efficient money machine.

Still, the big question kept coming back: Where did he get all the babies? To extract any more information about that from Quetzal Manor, I'd have to break into an office somewhere, and I wasn't quite up to that yet. I didn't have the nerve of Colonel Jose Alvino Ramos.

"Tell you what, Tara, I think I'm out of here." I was returning the Betacam to its bag. Nothing I'd shot was remotely broadcast quality, but I did have proof of what was going on. My "undercover" investigation was making some headway.

"Okay." She sighed, her expression increasingly glazed.

I took one last look around the room, at the row of bassinets, then gave her a parting pat and headed for the exit.

"Look," I said, turning back as I reached the door. "Don't say anything to anybody about me being here tonight, okay? Can we just let it be our secret?"

"Sure, whatever." She shrugged absently. Like, why not.

"And Tara, do yourself a favor. Get out of this place."

"But there's nowhere else I can go," she said, sadness in her eyes. As I slowly closed the door, the last thing I heard was the sound of the Beethoven sonata dying away.

What a day . . . and night. As I walked down the hallway carrying the camera bag, I tried to process my new information. I'd just seen some of the most incredibly lovable babies ever. That part of it was a beautiful experience, one that pulled at my heartstrings more strongly than I'd ever imagined something like that could. The part that troubled me was, the babies were so alike, so fair, and . . . they all could have been perfect siblings for Kevin and Rachel.

No, I told myself, surely that was my imagination. Though they did look amazingly related. . . .

As I moved across the parking lot, I thought I saw a movement in the shadows just inside the entry archway, a quick change in the pattern of dark. Was it Ramala or one of the girls, I wondered, or was it just my paranoia?

Keep walking, I told myself. Lose yourself in the snow. The only way they can stop you from exposing this racket now is to kill you.

When I got back to my car, I gazed up at the imposing turrets of Quetzal Manor one last time, wishing there was enough light to film them, and collected my thoughts. Was the story about the babies being orphans or abandoned children or "whatever" really true? I didn't believe it, not for a minute.

But as Carly Grove said, Alex Goddard could "make it happen." The problem for me was, he wouldn't tell me where he got the children, and nobody I'd talked to so far seemed to want to know, not really.

I wanted to know.

Thirteen

In moments I was heading down the snowy drive, south toward my home (which had been hopefully put back together). I pushed the pace, mesmerized by the snow, and tried to decide what to do next. The thug Ramos had stolen some second-generation interview footage from me, but now I had a tape of something a lot more interesting.

When I pulled into my street, the time was just past eleven and I was thinking about calling Lou, or Steve, or both. But then I saw something odd. A woman was walking down the steps from the lobby of my building, a woman I recognized from somewhere.

Her hair was tangled and she was wearing black jeans and a black sweater. It took a second before I finally processed the fact it was Carly Grove. And she seemed frantic. I assumed she'd come in a cab, but she had my home phone number, so why would she come over if I didn't answer? New Yorkers don't just drop in. A social no-no.

Maybe the reason had something to do with how she looked. I felt like I was seeing a specter.

"Thank God you're here," she blurted out, striding up. She was actually shaking, and I could tell she'd been crying. Nothing like the gutsy woman I'd seen a few days earlier. "I kept getting your machine, but I thought maybe you were hiding."

I looked at her, and forgot all about my own issues. It was

hard to remember ever seeing a human being in such distress, except for Sarah.

"Why would I be hiding?" I was taking out the Betacam bag and closing my car door, hoping to seem normal and professional.

"They called me about six o'clock tonight. Children of Light." She could barely get the words out. "They'd seen my interview with you. How did they get it?"

I looked down at the snowy—make that slushy—street and felt a chill go through me, followed immediately by anger. Ramos, that *bastard*.

"They . . . Somebody took a copy this morning." Stated like that, it sounded pretty lame. "I'm so sorry—"

"He threatened Kevin. He actually said if I signed a release to let you use the film, my child would 'meet with an accident.' And then he said something about you, that your own—"

"Who? Who called you? Did he tell you his—?"

"He wouldn't give a name. Just some man. He had a foreign accent." She threw her arms around me, and I hugged her back as best I could.

"Where's Kevin now?" I was so concerned about Carly that I'd repressed the information that he'd also mentioned me.

"Marcy was there, so I told her to take him with her. To her mother's place in the Bronx, where she lives." Carly was still trembling as she loosened her grip on me. "I called a car service to drive them up."

"Well, come on in. Let's talk." Truthfully, I wasn't sure how much I wanted to tell her about what I'd just seen at Quetzal Manor. It would probably just distress her more. Where *had* Kevin come from? Did I really want to delegitimize him in her eyes?

As I led her through the lobby, hoping to appear composed, Patrick Mooney greeted us, announcing that his sister, Rosalyn, had been gone for an hour and that she appreciated my memorable tip.

The place looked like nothing had happened, and Carly immediately collapsed onto my "earth-tone" couch. I hadn't told her my apartment had been tossed along with the robbery and, thanks to Rosalyn, I didn't need to. In fact, it actually looked cleaner than it had in months. Maybe, I thought, I should reprioritize my life and hire her more often.

Then I got a glass of water for Carly and sat down next to her.

"I'm really sorry," I began, deeply meaning it. "If I'd known all this was going to happen, I'd never——"

"It's not your fault." She took a long drink. I hadn't bothered with ice, and I immediately felt I'd been inhospitable. Kind of a vagrant, minor concern, considering. Then she went on. "I guess I knew down deep I shouldn't have given you that interview. But I wanted the world to know about Kevin. Now, though . . . should I call the police or something?"

The short answer to that was yes, but my mind was already skipping on to a different topic.

"Carly, do you know where Kevin came from? *Really* came from? Did you ever actually try to find out?"

She sighed and took another sip.

"I told you I don't care. When they brought him, all pink and helpless, I just——"

"Who brought him?" I interrupted.

"Well, I'd been up there the day before, signing all the papers. I was supposed to go up that day, but then somebody called and said one of the girls who was staying in the clinic or whatever it is was bringing him to me. So don't come."

"You're saying one of the girls——?"

"Yeah." She looked wistful for a moment, as though remembering. "Then she just showed up, looked like some blond college dropout. I guess a little more fanfare would've been nice, but Marcy was there to help me and that was it. That's the last contact I ever had with Children of Light." She shuddered involuntarily. "Till now."

Well, I thought, the last thing I'm going to do is tell her about what I just saw. She's the ideal customer for Alex Goddard: She truly doesn't want to know details.

"Carly, there's not much I can do about what's already happened, but I can try to keep you from getting into any more trouble. Why don't you call them in the morning and tell them you've yelled at me and rescinded your permission for Applecore to use the film? And say I've promised I won't. You've threatened to sue me or something. That should get you off the hook."

"You really think so?" Her look brightened slightly.

"Yes, it's *me* they're worried about, not you. I represent some threat to them, because of the film I'm making. Just bail out and you'll be okay."

"Thanks. I did get the feeling that's all they really want." She took another drink of water. "But if they wanted to scare me, they're doing a hell of a good job."

"Well, then, why not take Kevin and go away for a couple of weeks? On a vacation someplace? And while you're doing that, I'm going to have a one-on-one with Alex Goddard. I've got a little leverage now."

She looked at me. "What . . . what are you going to do?"

I couldn't tell her about my videotape of his baby cache without explaining a lot more about Children of Light than I thought she wanted to hear.

"Don't you think the less you know the better?" I said, taking her hand. "I've caused you enough trouble already."

"No, I caused myself trouble." She was getting up. "Can I use your bathroom?"

"Sure." I pointed the way.

While she was gone, I went to the kitchen and surveyed it, checking the cabinets. Again, the place was cleaner than it had been in ages. The look of it momentarily bucked me up.

When Carly came back, she hugged me and then announced she wanted to go check on Kevin.

"I'll do what you said about calling them," she concluded, reaching for her bag. "I think you're right. That ought to get them off my case. At least for the moment. As for the long run—"

"Carly," I said, taking her hand again, "we'll get through this. Just trust me."

We hugged one more time and then she was gone. I took the moment to double-lock the door, and then collapsed on the couch. What should be my next move? I closed my eyes and tried to review all the insidious things that had happened in the last twenty-four hours. The illegal drugs, the break-in and theft of my film, the suspicious nursery of Children of Light, the threats to Carly . . .

Then it finally came back that she'd mentioned Ramos saying something about *me*. By now I was getting used to being threatened by the man, so one more time was hardly news. But I wished I'd asked her the specifics.

That was when I roused myself and reached for the phone. The time was pushing eleven, but I still wanted to check in on Sarah, see how she was doing. Had she come back to reality after I left?

I was listening to the phone ring, my mind drifting to thoughts of how to gently ask Lou about her, when I realized nobody was picking up.

What's going on? I wondered, immediately coming alert. Mrs. Reilly had probably gone home for the day, but no way would Lou be in bed before midnight. He always had trouble settling into sleep.

Maybe, I then hoped, I'd just dialed the wrong number. But when I tried again, still no answer.

I clicked off the phone and felt a wave of concern. If Colonel Jose Alvino Ramos could find out I was making a movie, and then find out where I lived, he sure as hell could locate my extended family. Was *that* what he'd meant when he mentioned me to Carly?

I grabbed the set of Lou's keys I had stored in my bedroom's desk drawer and flew out the door.

The streets were plastered with a grimy veneer of city snow, melting fast, but I pushed the limits of safety and ran a couple of lights since the traffic was spotty. There was a parking space just across the street from Lou's building, and as I pulled in I looked over at his windows.

Through the curtains I could tell a dim light was on, probably coming from Sarah's bedroom. The front room, however, was dark.

My pulse was pounding as I raced up the steps to the street door. I thought about pushing his bell, but I didn't have the patience. Instead I just fumbled with the key set till I found the biggest one and shoved it into the lock.

The building had no lobby, just a row of stairs leading up to the next floor, with Lou's own door set off to the left. I shoved his Medeco key into the deadlock and pushed it open. The room was pitch-dark.

"Who . . ." said a startled voice, and I knew it was Lou, somewhere in the direction of the couch.

I clicked on the light switch and saw him lying on the floor, leaning against the couch, blood everywhere, his eyes in shock.

"My God! What happened?"

"I'm afraid to move. The phone was ringing and I figured

it was you, but I didn't dare get up. Knowing you, you'd come over if I didn't answer." He was holding his side as he looked at me. "Morgy, she's gone."

At first what he said didn't sink in as I bent over him. The right side of his shirt, just above his belt, was soaked in blood. Taking care, I unbuttoned it and saw an open cut that looked as though he'd been stabbed with a knife. It also appeared to be reasonably superficial, as though a thin blade had pierced through a couple of layers of tread on his ample spare tire. But it was bleeding still, enough to make it look worse than it probably was. However, if it'd happened to me, I'd doubtless be in shock too.

I got up, went to the bathroom, and pulled two towels off the rack, then doused water over one and came back.

"Don't move. I'm going to pull your shirt away and try to clean you up, see how bad it is."

He just groaned and stared at the ceiling.

As I was swabbing his side, what he'd said finally registered.

"Did you say . . . *Sarah!*"

I dropped the towels and ran into the bedroom.

It was empty, the bed rumpled and beige sheets on the floor.

"No." I turned and, feeling a hit of nausea, hurried back to his side. "What happened? Did—?"

"Fat Hispanic guy. Spic bastard. He had a couple of young punks with him. Mrs. Reilly had just left and I went to the door, thinking it was probably you ringing my bell. He flashed a knife and they shoved their way in. Then one of his thugs went into the bedroom and carried her out. When I tried to stop them, the SOB knifed me. I guess I . . . swooned, 'cause the next thing I remember is waking up here on the floor."

It sounded garbled, and probably didn't occur as quickly

as he thought. But I knew immediately what had happened. Ramos—of course that's who it was—had come to take Sarah. It was his one *sure* way to stop me from mentioning Children of Light in my film. She was a hostage. My first instinct was to kill him.

"What else can you remember?" I was already dialing 911. Time to get an ambulance. And after that, the cops.

After about ten rings I got somebody and, following an explanation that was longer than it needed to be, a woman with a southern accent told me the medics would be there in fifteen minutes. I took another look at Lou and ordered them to hurry, then hung up. I was going to call the police next, but first I needed to hear exactly what had happened, before he got quarantined in some emergency room.

His eyes were glazing over again, as shock and blood loss started to catch up with him. Clearly he would pull through, but right now, sitting there in a pool of blood, he could have been at death's door.

"Look . . . at that." He was pointing, his rationality beginning to fail. For a second I didn't realize what he meant, but then I saw a fax lying beside the phone. I picked it up. The time on it was 9:08 P.M. and it was from somebody named John Williams. Then I remembered. Wasn't that the FBI computer whiz he'd talked about the other day at the hospital, after we'd deconstructed Sarah's waterlogged passport?

There was no message, just a sheet with a date—two years old—and a list of names accompanied by numbers and a capital letter. Then I noticed the letterhead of Aviateca, the Guatemalan national airline, and it dawned on me I was looking at a flight manifest.

I scanned down the page, and then I saw it.
Sarah Crenshaw, 3B.

Williams found her, I thought. And she was traveling First Class.

What caught my eye next was the name of the person sitting in 3A, the seat right next to hers. *A. Godford.* Probably a computer misprint. Or maybe it was the name he used when he traveled. So if it *was* him, which it surely was, the bastard didn't even try to hide it.

I just stood there, thinking. Maybe you get one big-time coincidence in life, and if so, this must be mine. Sarah and I had both found Alex Goddard. Or he'd found us. Other women came and went through Quetzal Manor, but we were different. She'd escaped from him, half dead, but now he'd sent Ramos to bring her back. It was the one way he could be sure to keep me under his control. But again, why? Was it just to stop my film, or was there more to the story?

"Morgy," Lou groaned, "that son of a bitch took her tonight. I just know it."

That was my conclusion precisely, though I hadn't been planning to say it to him, at least not yet.

"How can you be so sure?"

"Something they said. I didn't quite catch it, but it sounded like, 'He wants you back.' Then some word. It sounded like 'Babylon' or something."

I stared at him a second, trying to remember where I'd heard that before. Then it clicked in. That was the last thing Sarah had said, she'd whispered that word, when I was putting her to bed. What could she have been talking about?

He wheezed, and I went back to him and pressed the towel against his side. The bleeding was about stemmed, but he was definitely due for a hospital stay. A siren was sounding down the street. Probably the ambulance. Thank God, I thought. Now it's time to call the police.

Then I noticed he was crying. What was that about?

"Morgy, they didn't actually kidnap her. You see, she—"

"What?" I guess I was trying to take it in. "What do you mean?"

"Know what she said? Sarah?" He choked for a second, then continued. "She said, 'Yes, I want to go back.' "

Fourteen

Before I could ask him what the hell he was talking about, the medics were ringing the doorbell. They strode in with a gurney, also rolling a portable plasma IV, young guys who looked like they'd be more at home at a Garden hockey game, followed immediately by two uniformed policemen, actually policewomen, one short and heavy, with reddish hair, the other a wiry young Hispanic. (I found out that ambulances called out for stabbing or gunshot wounds automatically get a cop escort.) In less than three minutes, Lou was in the blue-and-white ambulance and on his way to St. Vincent's emergency room.

I rode in the backseat of the squad car as we followed them and tried to explain what little I knew of what had happened. It turned out to be an education in the mindless sticking points of the law.

Long story short: The fact that I hadn't reported the burglary of my apartment that very same day immediately cast doubt on my seriousness as a truth-seeking citizen; I had no proof the unreported burglary of my apartment (if, indeed, such had actually occurred) was by some Guatemalan military attaché named Jose Alvino Ramos; since Lou had never seen Colonel Ramos before tonight, he couldn't possibly identify him as that burglar either; accusing diplomats of a crime without ironclad proof was frowned on downtown; and when I stupidly repeated what Lou had said about Sarah's last words (well, he was going to tell them sooner or later, it would just come bubbling out at some point), the whole case that she was kidnapped went into revision mode.

By the time we got to the hospital, I was getting questions that seemed to imply that maybe it was all a domestic affair—like most of their calls: some spaced-out chick who'd run away once and got brought back and then, still unstable and crazy, decided to knife her own dad and disappear again. Now he was understandably covering for her. Happened more than you'd think.

I kept stressing that Lou was former FBI and not the sort to invent such a whopper, but this was listened to in skeptical silence. If it was a kidnapping, they then wondered aloud, what was the motive and where were the demands of the perpetrators? I was ready to start yelling at them by the time we parked in the Seventh Avenue driveway of the emergency room at St. Vincent's.

They next made me cool my heels in the waiting room while they went back to interrogate Lou. They were with him for almost an hour, then came back to where I was and asked me to read and sign the report they'd written.

A troubled girl, who had emerged from a coma and apparently was suffering bouts of nonrationality, had disappeared, and her father had been stabbed, but not seriously. He was the only witness to the incident and claimed she'd been kidnapped. However, the girl had run away once previously, and there was no physical evidence she'd been taken against her will; in fact, her father admitted she had declared just the opposite. The whole incident would be investigated further after he came downtown and made a complete statement.

"I'm not going to sign this." I handed it back, fuming.

"Is there anything here that's not factually correct?" The

Hispanic cop was looking me straight in the eye, her expression cold as Alaska.

The question made me seethe. Sarah was probably already on her way out of the country, and here I was trying to reason with two women who practically thought *she* was the criminal. But I knew a lost cause when I saw one.

"Forget about it. I want to see Lou."

An intern was coming out and I snagged him, announced I was next of kin to a patient, and demanded to be taken through the official door and into the back. At that moment, the stout cop's radio crackled. They were being summoned to a Christopher Street gay bar where somebody had just been knifed in a back room. She looked at me, as though to say, "This sounds like a real crime," and then they hurried out for their squad car. Christ!

The intern, a young black guy, led me past a row of gurneys and into a private room at the rear of the huge space. Lou was bandaged all around his chest and hooked up to an IV and a monitor. He looked better, but I wasn't sure he'd be ready for what I was about to tell him.

"Hey, how're you feeling?" I asked as I walked in, trying to seem upbeat.

"Fucking cops." He was boiling, his face actually red. "Where do they get them these days? McDonald's rejects?"

"Easy, don't get your blood pressure up." I reached over and touched his brow. It felt like he had a mild temperature. "Let's all just calm down and try to think rationally."

"Yeah, I'm thinking rationally. You saw that fax I got from Williams."

"You think that was Alex Goddard seated next to her, right?"

"Who else? When she was in her moonbeam phase, she must have heard about him and gone up there and ended up in his clutches. But why did she let him take her down to—?"

"He told me he has a clinic in Central America. He called it 'a place of miracles.' And then Colonel Ramos shows up, part of the Guatemalan diplomatic corps. Put two and two together. That's got to be where they're taking her."

"Who knows, but I'm going to get the boys downtown to put out a missing-persons APB nationwide. Gerry'll do it for me if I ask. Fuck New York's Finest. They ain't gonna do crap anyway."

I listened, wondering how to impress my bright idea upon him. The chances were Ramos was taking Sarah back to Guatemala. Probably right this minute. For some kind of unfinished business. Or just to hold her there as an insurance policy that Children of Light would never be mentioned in my picture.

"I seriously doubt a missing-persons alert is going to do any good, Lou, because I seriously doubt she's going to be walking the streets of this country. That bastard Ramos is taking her where he knows he can hide her."

"You mean . . . Jesus." He stared at me as though the idea had never crossed his mind. I think he'd just repressed it. "What are we going to—?"

"The only thing we *can* do. I'm going down there. I'm going to go straight down there and locate Alex Goddard."

"That's an exceptionally lousy thought process." His voice seemed to be coming from a great distance.

"Why? Give me one good reason why. You think the police down there are going to bring charges against a colonel?" I really could have used some encouragement. "It's the only way—"

"Morgan, you've always been high-strung." He sighed, and then winced. "Ever since you were a kid. I worried about you then and I'm worried about you now. I don't want you to go down there and get into trouble. Because believe me, that's a seriously wrong place to get crossways with the pricks who make the rules. You don't know your way around that Third World craphole. Wouldn't be that hard to end up a statistic. We can alert the embassy. Have them start looking for her."

"Listen, there's a lot more going on between Alex Goddard and me than you know." This was definitely not the time to tell him about the babies, or about Carly and the threats. "Trust me. I'm going down there. In the morning, if I can. Who knows? Sarah and Ramos might even be on the same plane."

As I was finishing that pronouncement, two nurses came in rolling a gurney and announced that his room was ready. Then they gave him a sedative.

Was I being irrational? The thing was, though, what would *you* do? I was absolutely sure Ramos had taken her. So it was obvious that was where he would go next. He was a "diplomat," apparently, so he could easily fudge the passport formalities.

As the nurses were helping Lou onto the gurney, I stood there holding his hand and thinking about what lay ahead. Steve was in Belize and maybe not even reachable, but I decided to start by giving him a call the minute I got home.

Then a middle-aged WASP, with dark hair, slightly balding, strode in the room. The photo ID on his chest read "Dr. M. Summers."

"So, how's the patient?" he enquired cheerily, ignoring me as he immediately began checking the chart at the foot of Lou's bed.

"Felt better," Lou said, not being taken in by his pro forma cheer.

"Well, we're going to make sure you get a good night's rest." Dr. Summers finished with the chart and started taking his pulse. "What's left of it."

"How long am I going to be in here, Doc?" Lou asked, flinching as the nurses removed the IV stuck in his arm.

"A couple of days. For observation. To make sure there're no complications." He smiled again. "You're a lucky man, Mr. . . . Crenshaw. Just a superficial cut. But we don't want you out playing handball for a few days." He turned and gave me a conspiratorial wink, then glanced back. "Okay, up we go."

"Can I come with him?" I asked, not optimistic but hoping.

The doctor looked genuinely contrite. "I'm really sorry, but he's going to be fine and visiting hours are long past. You can call in the morning. And you can come up anytime after two P.M. tomorrow. Let's let him get some rest now."

I walked around and took Lou's hand, hot and fevered, feeling so agitated.

"Don't think about anything tonight, okay? Worrying won't help. Just get some sleep. I'm going to find her, I promise you."

"Don't—" He mumbled some words, but I think the sedative the nurses had given him was seriously starting to kick in.

"Look, you can call down to 26 Federal Plaza tomorrow. See what they can do. In the meantime, let me follow my nose."

He tried to answer, but he was too far gone. I then watched wistfully as he disappeared down the sterile alley of beds.

After I stopped by the desk and helped them fill out the insurance forms, I caught a cab downtown to retrieve my Toyota. The time was now two-fifteen in the morning, but I still had plenty to do. When I got home, the first thing I did after I walked in the door was grab a phone book and call American Airlines. They had a flight, in the morning at nine-thirty. I gave them my credit card specifics and made a reservation.

I no longer thought that Alex Goddard's Children of Light and its Guatemalan accomplices were merely doing something shady. My hunch now was that it was completely illegal. They were getting hundreds of white babies in some way that couldn't bear the light of day, and they were prepared to do whatever it took to prevent me from highlighting them in my film. And with the Army involved, and now Sarah taken, their game was beginning to feel more and more like kidnapping. They certainly knew how.

Sarah had become a pawn, and all because of me. I almost wondered if I'd been unconsciously led to him by her, though that was impossible. Whatever had happened, the remorse I now felt was overpowering. It was, in fact, an intensified version of the guilt that had dogged me for the past fifteen years, the horrible feeling I'd somehow let her down, not done enough for her. I could have flown back for her high school graduation, but I was cramming for grad school finals and didn't take the time. Things like that, which, looking back, seemed terribly selfish. And now I'd brought this on her. God.

Okay, I thought, glancing at the clock, time to start making it up to her. Screw up your courage and wake Steve.

The problem was, Lou had been right about one thing. It'd been years since I'd been to Guatemala, and I wasn't sure I knew beans about how things operated down there these days. I was high on motivation and only so-so in the area of modus operandi. I needed Steve's help in plying the tricky waters of that part of the planet. He was busy, but this was definitely "us against the world" time, so maybe he could drive over to Guatemala City and help.

I picked up the phone again and punched in the number of his hotel in Belize City, which seemed to be embedded permanently in my brain. That wonderful accent at the desk, mon, and then they were ringing his room. I had no reason on earth to assume he would be there, but . . .

The click, the voice, it was him.

"Sorry to call so late, love. You said you missed me, so I've decided to find out if it's true. Your coming attraction is about to arrive."

I guess I was trying to keep it flip. After our talk that morning, I wasn't entirely sure where we stood anymore.

"Who . . . Morgy, is that you? God, it's two . . . Are you okay?" Then he started coming around, processing what I'd said. "You're coming . . . Honey, that's great."

As I noted before, he always knew how to give a good reading, sound sincere, no matter what the occasion.

"Actually, I've just made a plane reservation, and I'm going to be in Guatemala City tomorrow, just after noon." I hesitated, then thought, why beat around the bush? "Care to meet me there?"

"That's terrific," he declared, coming fully awake. "But why don't you just come to Belize City? Can't you get a flight? It's actually not nearly as wild here as the travel books—"

"Well, I've . . . Look, I'd rather not talk about this on the phone. But do you think you could get free and drive over? I really could use your help. I've got a situation."

"Well . . ." He paused. "I could be there by late tomorrow, assuming my rented Jeep still operates after last week and the roads haven't totally disintegrated. Where're you going to be staying?"

"I don't know. Got any suggestions? I want to keep out of the limelight."

"Then try the Camino Real. It's like a Holiday Inn with plastic palm trees. Definitely low maintenance and low profile. Hang on, I'll get you the number."

Which he did, though I could hear him stumbling around the room in the dark. Then he continued.

"But listen, here's the bad news. I've got to be back here day after tomorrow. I just got a special permit to do some night shooting in the jaguar preserve down by Victoria Peak—you remember the rain forest I told you about?—but it's only good for one night, and I hear rumors there's an off-season hurricane forming in the Caribbean, which means I've got to stick to schedule. After that, though, I'm free again."

"We'll work it out." I was thrilled he would just drop everything and come. Maybe we were over the rough spot about the baby.

He didn't bring that up and I didn't either. Instead we killed a few minutes, and then I let him go back to sleep. I wanted to say I love you, but I didn't want to push my luck.

After that I called the hotel he'd recommended. The exchange was more Spanish than English, but they had a room. Apparently lots of rooms.

Next I rang Paula Marks, even though it was terribly late. She must have had the phones off, but I left a message telling her to be careful, with a postscript that I'd explain everything later. Just stick close to home.

Finally I called David's voice mail up at Applecore. I told him I had a personal crisis and was going to Guatemala City. I'd try to be back by the end of the week, hell or high water, but no guarantees. And if he touched so much as a frame of my work print while I was gone, I'd personally strangle him.

I don't remember much of what happened next. I basically went on autopilot. It's as though I dropped into a trance, totally focused. I packed my passport, a good business suit, the tailored blue one, and also a set of mix-and-match separates, easy to roll and cram in. Finally a couple of pairs of good (clean) jeans, a few toiletries, and then, thinking ahead,

I also threw in my yellow plastic flashlight. I almost always overpack, but not this time.

Oh, and one other thing. For airplane reading I grabbed a Lonely Planet guide to Central America that Steve had left behind—I guess he figured he was at the stage of life to start writing them, not reading them—that turned out to be very helpful, particularly the map of Guatemala City and the northern Peten rain forest. I then collapsed and—images of Sarah's emaciated face haunting my consciousness—caught a couple of hours' sleep.

The next thing I knew, it was 9:20 A.M. and I was settling into window seat 29F on American Airlines Flight 377—next to a two-hundred-pound executive busy ripping articles out of the business section of *El Diario*—headed for Guatemala City.

Fifteen

For once in my life, I took my time getting off an airplane. But the instant I felt that first burst of humid tropical air against my face, like a gush from a sauna, I found myself wondering what Sarah had felt the moment her feet first touched the ground of Guatemala. In fact, I'd decided to try to think like her, to better understand why she might want to come back. Truthfully I didn't have a clue.

But first things first. Not knowing whether I was being stalked by Ramos or his proxies, I decided the idea was to see and not be seen—which actually was easier than I'd expected, at least during the initial pell-mell stages. Turned out the self-centeredness of Homo sapiens blossoms under those circumstances. Ignore thy neighbor, goes the credo. I just buried myself in the crush.

When I got to *"Inmigracion,"* I labored through the "formalities" (as all countries love to call the suspicious looks you get from their airport bureaucrats) along with all the other gringo passengers on AA Flight 377, paranoid I might be arrested on the spot for some spurious reason. The purpose of my visit, I declared, was tourism. Just a nod at my passport and a stamp, which looked exactly like the one in Sarah's. I stared at it and felt a renewed sense of purpose. In fact, the photo in my passport looked more than a little like her. Maybe, I thought, I'm getting carried away with the identity issue, but there it was.

As I emerged through the wide glass doors of the arrival area, which fronted out onto the steps leading down to the parking lots and the humidity, I spotted a black Land Rover with tinted windows right in front. Uh-oh. That was, Steve once told me, a vehicle much favored by the notorious Guatemalan G-2 military secret police, who had retired the cup for murderous human-rights abuses over the past two decades.

Then two middle-aged men with Latin mustaches and nondescript brown shirts began getting out through the door on the far side. They next walked around to the terminal side of the car and glanced up the steps in my direction, as though looking for somebody. It was a quick survey, after which they turned back and nodded to the vehicle before it sped away.

What's that about? Am I imagining things already?

By the time I reached the bottom of the steps, I was being beseiged by clamoring cabbies, so it was difficult to keep an eye on the two men, who were now walking off to the side of the main commotion, toward a shady grove of palms at the end of the arrival drive, lighting cigarettes.

Get out of here. Whether you're fantasizing or not, the thing to do is grab an unsuspecting cab and *get going*.

I strolled toward the other end of the long row of concrete steps till I reached an area where cabs were parked, more drivers lurking in wait. They all looked the same way most cabbies in Third World lands look: shabby clothes, with beat-up cars, an expression in their eyes somewhere between aggression and desperation.

Just pick one whose car looks like it might actually make it to downtown.

I spotted a dark blue Chevy that seemed clean and well maintained, its driver young and full of male hormones as he beckoned me to his vehicle, all the while undressing me with his eyes. Yep, he was definitely my guy.

I ambled by his car, acting as though I was ignoring the innuendos of his pitch. Then I bolted for the back door, opened it myself since he was too startled to help, threw in my carry-ons, piled in behind them, and yelled, "Let's go. *Rapido.*"

As we sped away, I realized his greatest surprise was that I hadn't raised the subject of price. At that point, it was the last thing on my mind. I looked back to see the two guys from the black Land Rover, together with two others, heading for a car that had been double-parked right in front.

Had I been right after all?

We made a high-speed turn onto the highway, and I immediately ordered the driver to take a service road that led off toward a cluster of gas stations and parking lots with falling-down barbed-wire fences. I figured I had about half a minute of lead time, whatever was going on.

We dodged massive potholes and the loose gravel flew, but then we reached a ramshackle gas station and I ordered him to pull in. Then I watched the line of traffic speeding by on the main highway for several minutes. Nobody pulled off. Good.

My driver finally got around to asking where I wanted to go, and as calmly as I could, I told him.

"The Palacio Nacional."

"*Sí.*"

With that he gunned his engine and spun out. Jesus!

"*Mas despacio, por favor.*"

"Okay," he said, showing off his English as he donned his sunglasses. "I go more slow. No problem."

The initial destination was part of my new plan, hatched while I was on the plane. When I was reading my guidebook and filling out my entry card, I'd had a bright idea. I knew exactly how I wanted to begin.

Heading into town, the time now the middle of the afternoon, I leaned back in the seat and tried to absorb the view, to get a feeling for where I was. We first traveled through the suburban fringes, the heavily guarded, luxurious mansions of the landholding and military elite, the one percent of Guatemala who own ninety-nine percent of the country. Iron fences and wide expanses of lawn, protected by Uzi-toting security guards, guarded whimsical architectural conceits topped by silver satellite dishes. A twenty-foot wall shielded their delicate eyes from the city's largest shanty-town, makeshift hovels of bamboo and rusted tin, with no signs of water or drains or toilets. Guatemala City: as Steve had put it once, a million doomed citizens, the rich and the poor, trapped together side by side in the most "modern" capital in Central America.

Why on *earth* had Sarah decided to come here? Even if she did travel with the mesmerizing Alex Goddard, it was hard to imagine a place less spiritual. Couldn't she feel that this was all wrong? One of us had to be missing something major.

Fifteen minutes later I was passing through the fetid atmosphere of downtown, which seemed to be another world, Guatemala City's twin soul. It was an urban hodgepodge of Burger King, McDonald's, discount electronics emporia, an eye-numbing profusion of plastic signs, filthy parking lots, rattletrap buses and taxis, stalled traffic. Exhaust fumes thickened the air, and everywhere you looked teenage "guards" in uniforms loitered in front of stores and banks with sawed-off shotguns, boys so green and scared-looking you'd think twice about letting one of them park your car. But there they were, weapons at the ready, nervously monitoring passersby. Who were they defending all the wealth from? The ragged street children, with swollen bellies and skin disease, vending single cigarettes from open packs? Or the hordes of widows and orphans, beneficiaries of the Army's Mayan "pacification" program, who now begged for centavos or plaintively hawked half-rotten fruit from the safety of the shadows?

My bright-idea destination was a government office in the Palacio Nacional, right in the center of town, where I hoped I could find Sarah's old landing card, the record of when tourists arrived and departed. When I'd filled mine out on the plane, I'd realized you were supposed to put down where you'd be staying in Guatemala. I figured the best way to locate her this time was to find out where she went last time. . . .

As my cab pulled up in front, a black Land Rover was parked in a *"Prohibido Estacionarse"* zone by the front steps. To my eyes it looked like the same one I'd seen at the airport. Shit.

But nobody was around, so I decided maybe I was just being paranoid again.

The Palacio turned out to be a mixture of Moorish and faux Greek architecture, with a facade of light green imitation stone that gave off the impression of a large, rococo wedding cake. I took a long look, paid off the driver—who had turned out to be very nice—and headed in. It was, after all, a public building, open to tourist gringos.

Nobody in the lobby appeared to take any particular notice of me, so after going through their very serious security, uniforms and guns everywhere, I checked the directory.

It turned out the president, cabinet ministers, and high military officers all kept offices there, but it didn't take long to find the bureau I was looking for. Going down the marble-floored hallway on the third floor, I passed by the Sala de Recepcíon, a vast wood-paneled room of enormous chandeliers, stained-glass windows, and a massive coat of arms. Quite a place, but not my destination. At the far end of the hallway, I found the door I wanted, went in, and tried out the Spanish question I'd been practicing in the cab. Not necessary: English worked fine.

"Señora, the records for that time were only kept on paper," a Ladino woman declared, shrugging, her nails colored a brash mauve, her hair a burst of red, "but you are welcome to look." She'd been on the phone, chatting in rapid-fire Spanish, but she quickly hung up and got out her glasses.

"Thanks."

The welcome mat was obviously a little thin. The woman was trying to be friendly, but very quickly her nervousness began to come through. "We're always glad to accommodate Americans searching for friends or relatives," she went on, attempting a smile. "Some of your American press has been printing distortions, that the Guatemalan Army conspired with the CIA to cover up murders. It's a total lie."

Right. Maybe you ought to see some of the photos Steve has of the "Army-pacified" Maya villages up in the mountains.

The search took an hour and a half of leafing through dusty boxes, which chafed my hands raw, but then . . . voilà.

There it was. The crucial piece of information Lou had missed. A hastily scribbled-in landing card for an American, with the name Sarah Crenshaw. I stared at it a moment, feeling a glow of success. Was it an omen?

It was definitely her. She'd even dotted an "i" with a smiley face, one of her personal trademarks.

Then I looked down the form. What I wanted was the address she'd put down as a destination in Guatemala.

The answer: "Niños del Mundo, Peten Department."

My hopes sank. Great. That was like saying your address

is Children of the World, lost somewhere in the state of Montana.

The home address was equally vague. Just "New York." So much for the high level of curiosity at *"Inmigracion."*

However, the carbon copy of the landing card, which you're supposed to surrender when you leave, was not stapled to it, the way it was on all the others in the box. Naturally, since she'd left in a medevac plane, half dead.

"What does this mean?" I got up and walked over to the woman's desk, carrying the card. Mainly I just wanted to get a rise out of her. "The carbon copy is missing. Does that mean she could still be here?"

Red alert. She glanced at the arrival date a moment and her eyes froze. Then, doubtless with visions of another CIA scandal looming in her consciousness, she brusquely announced that the office was getting ready to close for the day.

"You'll have to pursue any further inquiries through the American embassy, Mrs. James, which handles all matters concerning U.S. nationals."

"Well, thanks for all your help." I was finally getting the police-state runaround I'd expected all along. I guess I needed her to care, and it was obvious she didn't.

Okay . . . I'd planned to go to the embassy anyway. Maybe *they* could tell me about this place she'd put on her landing card. Could it be the local name for Alex Goddard's clinic?

As I picked up my things, I thought again about the prospect of showing my face on the streets of Guatemala City. Would there be more loitering men in grungy brown shirts waiting to watch my every move? More black Land Rovers? As I marched back out through the ornate lobby, I decided not to let my imagination get too active. It was now late afternoon, but I was making progress. I also was thinking about Steve, wondering if he'd gotten into town yet. Probably not for another couple of hours, but just thinking about seeing him again, and having him for support, was boosting my energy.

A short cab ride later I arrived at the embassy of the all-powerful United States of America, a two-block-long concrete fortress on Reforma Avenue guarded by Yank Marines with heavy automatic weapons. When I explained myself to the PR people manning the reception desk, including my brush with Guatemalan bureaucracy, they told me to check with the Internal Security section.

"In fact, if you're looking for an American national, this is where you should have come in the first place," said a very efficient-appearing young woman, with a business suit and dark, close-cropped hair. "A phone call from here works wonders at the Palacio Nacional."

I had no proof Sarah was in Guatemala yet, and if she was, it would doubtless be under a different name. What's more, telling them my suspicion that she'd been kidnapped by a high official and brought here would definitely brand me as a conspiracy theorist. So for now, all I could really hope to get from them was an address for Alex Goddard's clinic, someplace to start. Where and what was "Niños del Mundo"? Apparently the woman hadn't fully understood that.

Moments later a thirtyish male attaché showed up, looking very harried. He also could have been president of the local Young Republicans, with a cute haircut and preppie tie, knotted perfectly.

"Hi, I'm Mel Olberg. How can I . . ."

I told him I wanted to see someone who was responsible for the records of missing American tourists. I also sensed he was edgy and trying to get it over with fast; all the while he kept checking his watch, only half listening.

"Gee, I really wish you'd come earlier," he said. "Monday

afternoons are a little nuts around here, weekly reports due and all, and it's getting late." When he glanced at his watch again, making sure I noticed, I found myself wanting to yell at the guy. "I mean it's been two years since this woman you're looking for filled out a landing card. We might have something in the files, but . . . would it be possible for you to come back tomorrow?"

"No, it will not be possible," I lied. "I've got a plane back to New York tomorrow." I felt my frustration rising. I wanted to just grab him and shake him.

My first thought was to tell him I make documentary films and maybe he'd like to end up in one about how my country's Guatemala City embassy didn't care about its citizens. But then I decided to go in a different, probably more productive, direction.

"Just for five minutes," I declared, reaching for feigned helplessness.

"Well, let me call upstairs," he muttered, realizing, I suppose, that the best way to get rid of me was to kick me up the chain of command, "and see if Mr. Morton can take a moment to meet with you."

It worked. The next thing I knew, I was in the office of a good-looking diplomat named Barry Morton—gray temples, tailored suit, rugged face of a sixty-year-old soap-opera heartthrob who plays tennis and keeps a mistress. Chief Information Officer.

"Actually, I do remember her, vaguely," Morton declared, flashing me his professional smile. "The Crenshaw girl was an unfortunate case. To begin with, anybody who overstays their visa that long gets us in a lot of hot water with the locals. They always tend to blame us, Ms. . . ."

"James. My name's Morgan James."

"Ms. James." Another of those smiles. "Frankly, I don't know what to tell you, though." He shrugged, exuding helplessness. "It's hard to keep track of every American tourist who comes and goes through this country. Some of the hippie types end up in a mountain village somewhere, gone native. In this instance, as I recall, we got her out on a medevac."

"Her landing card gave her destination as someplace called 'Niños del Mundo,' up to the Peten. That ring a bell? Any idea how I could find it?"

"Niños del Mundo?" He glanced up quickly. "That's a new one on me." He'd been fiddling with a stack of papers on his desk, giving me only half his attention, but he abruptly stopped. "You try the phone book?"

"Like I said, it's in the Peten." I was getting the definite sense he wanted to get rid of me as soon as possible. The whole scene was feeling tense and off. "My understanding is that's mostly rain forest. Do they even have phones up there?"

"Not many," he said, his tone starting to definitely acquire an "I have better things to do" edge.

That was when he focused in on me, his look turning protective.

"Let me speak candidly, Ms. James, strictly off the record. Down here people have been known to 'disappear' just for asking too many questions. Curiosity killed the cat, and all that. Between us, this place is still a police state in many regards. You want my advice, let sleeping dogs lie. Just forget about this Crenshaw girl. She's out of the country now, so . . . Let me put it like this: People who go poking around here are just asking for trouble."

I felt a ring of sincerity in his voice. Maybe a little too much sincerity. Why was he so worried for me?

"That may be true, but I'm still going to see what I can find out. My heart is pure. Why should anybody care?"

"Do what you think best," he said with a sigh, "but I've

told you everything we know. Which, I'm afraid, is actually very little."

"By the way." Try one more thing on him, I thought, see what he'll say. "Since you're so concerned about Sarah, you'll be relieved to know she's regained consciousness and started to talk." There seemed no point in telling him any more. The rest was all still speculation.

That stopped him cold. "What . . . what has she said?" His eyes appeared startled in the glaring light of the office fluorescents. At long last I had his undivided attention.

"You're busy." I smiled at him. "I don't want to bore you with details. But it's just going to be a matter of time before she remembers exactly what happened down here."

"She hasn't talked about it yet?" He was fiddling with an ornate letter opener, an onyx jaguar head on the handle.

"She's getting there." I stared back at him, trying to read his mood. "We may soon find out who was behind whatever happened to her." Then I tried a long shot. "Maybe official-dom here had something to do with it."

"Let me tell you something." He sighed again, seeming to regain his composure. "The sovereign state of Guatemala definitely plays by its own rules. Whenever foreigners down here meet with foul play, lower-level officials have developed a consensus over the years that sometimes it's better not be too industrious. Nobody's ever sure of what, or who, they might turn up."

The meeting was definitely ending, and once again I had more questions than answers. Something about Barry Morton felt wrong, but I couldn't quite get a grip on what it was. One thing I was certain of: He knew more than he was telling me. Why was that?

As I was exiting through his outer office, headed for the swarming streets below, I waved good-bye to his secretary, a stout, fiftyish Ladino matron with defiantly black-dyed hair, a hard look mitigated somewhat by the Zircon trim on her thick glasses and a small silver pendant nestled on her ample, low-cut sweater. It was the pendant that caught my eye, being the silver face of a cat, most likely the local jaguar. Looked just like the ones I'd seen you-know-where. I was staring so hard I almost stumbled over a chair. Yes. It was definitely like those I remembered from Kevin and Rachel.

The only difference was, when she bent over to reach for her stapler, the medallion twisted around and the back, I could see, flashed blank silver, no engraving of lines and dots.

So where did she get it? I started to ask her, but decided I'd just get more BS runaround. Then I had another thought: Maybe she handled a lot of things that never made it to Barry Morton's desk, the "don't waste the boss's valuable time" kind of secretary. Maybe *she's* the one I really should have been talking to, the kind of woman who takes care of everything while the high-paid senior supervisor is at long lunches.

She looked at me, and our eyes met and held for a second. Had she been listening in on my chat with Morton? Did she know something I ought to know?

By then, however, thoughts of Steve were weighing in. I hadn't seen him in three and a half months and I was realizing that was about my limit. I wanted to recapture the lost time. Our being together was going to make everything turn out right.

Clinging to that thought, I grabbed a cab and headed for my hotel and a much-overdue hot bath.

Sixteen

"Come here," he said.

Whoosh. There he was. He strode through the door, tan safari shirt, smelling like a man who'd just driven hundreds of miles through Central America in an open Jeep. I wanted to undress him with my teeth and lick off the sweat. Brown eyes, skin tan as leather, he threw his arms around me and I felt the weight of the world slip away. He was here. I was wearing a robe, fresh from the tub, but it was gone in a second. Steve, I gotta say, knew a thing or two about the bedroom.

As we wound ourselves together for the next two hours, I had a refresher course in how much I'd missed him, soul *and* body. His taste, his skin, his touch. Finally, we were both so exhausted we just lay there bathed in sweat, spooned together on the sagging bed. I hadn't felt so good in years. It was like another world.

"God, I've missed you," I said, again, holding him closer. The air-conditioning was beginning to lose ground against the late sun, but I didn't care. After my solo nightmare of the last two days, I was remembering what it was like to be a couple again.

The Camino Real, by the way, turned out to be an American-style hideaway with budget shag carpeting and flaking blue walls. In a way, though, the downtrodden decor actually made it more romantic, like we'd sneaked off to a garish hot-sheet motel for a twilight rendezvous.

I finally dragged myself up and got us a bottle of water. Then, leaning against the rickety headboard, I recounted an abbreviated version of what had happened yesterday after we'd first talked—the theft of my film, and then Lou being assaulted and Sarah taken, apparently willingly, to be brought (I strongly suspected) back here. What I held out on were the details about a certain Colonel Jose Alvino Ramos, my belief that he was behind the crimes and in league with Alex Goddard and stalking me. I was afraid our room was bugged.

"Morgy, we'll get through this," he said, reaching over to stroke my hair. "If somebody brought her back down here, we'll find her. And I apologize for being such a shit on the phone, about the baby. I'd just had a local lab lose three rolls of high-speed Kodachrome and I was seriously frosted at the world. We can keep trying if you want to."

"Just hold me." I put down my glass and I reached around and ran my finger across his chest. It was so lovely to be this close to somebody you wanted so much. I loved his earnest brown eyes and his soft skin. I loved *him*. Just having him with me made such a difference.

The unexpected part was, I'd asked him to come and help me, but now that he was here, I was starting to feel uneasy about luring him into my personal nightmare. Was that really fair?

Also, I was getting hints he had problems of his own. The photo book, I gathered, was not coming together the way he'd hoped. He'd mumbled something about finding himself torn between a heartstrings essay about the children (his specialty; you've probably seen his work, whether you know it or not), a devastating portrayal of the latest crop of sleazy politicos, or a nature valentine to the vanishing rain forest. But whenever he agonized about his work, I knew enough to keep my mouth shut and just listen. He didn't want bright ideas; he just wanted me to clam up and be there for him.

Anyway, I knew he'd think his way through the problem. He had a deceptive air of vulnerability that always disappeared in a crunch. He was the master of ad hoc solutions. . . .

At that moment, he reached for his watch, studied it, and abruptly bolted straight up. "Hey, I almost forgot my surprise. I hope you're still up for it. Did you know this is our anniversary? It was on this very day I first watched you dive into that grungy swimming pool at the Oloffson in Port-au-Prince."

"My God, you're right. I'm humiliated." I hugged him contritely, feeling like a self-centered twit. I guess I was too focused on Sarah. (I screw up a lot on birthdays too, always with an excuse.) "I don't even have a present for you. I've been so—"

"That's okay." He grinned, then stood up and headed for the shower. "Not the first time. But I've got one for both of us. We'll make it a gift to each other. It'll help start you thinking like a *guatemalteco* insider."

"What? You sneak. What did you get?"

"A trip back into the void of prehistoric time," he yelled over his shoulder. "I am the possessor of a little-known secret about this town. I called from Belize City this morning and made dinner reservations for us downtown. You'll see."

God, I loved this man. But the last thing on my mind at that moment was food.

"Honey, I don't know if I'm really—"

"Hey, don't wimp out on me. If we're going to do this place, at least we can do it in style. Besides, you can't live on smog alone. You gotta eat."

He had a point. Starving myself wasn't going to help find Sarah any sooner. And there were details I wanted to tell him that I didn't want to broadcast in the room. What if Colonel Ramos had long ears to match his long arm?

"Come on," he pressed. "Just put on the slinkiest thing

you've got and get ready to go native. It'll help you put this part of the world into perspective."

Alas, I had nothing particularly "slinky," though fortunately I'd packed a silk blouse I could loosen and tie with a scarf around the waist. Don't laugh, it worked. I even brushed on some serious eye shadow, which normally I don't bother with much.

I tried not to let him know how concerned I was as we walked down the driveway of the hotel and hailed a cab, while I furtively searched the shadows. Seeing the streets after dark made me sad all over again for Sarah. I still wanted to see and feel Guatemala the way she had, but when I got close to the realities of the place, it made me uneasy.

It turned out the marvel he'd discovered was called Siriaco's, a wonderful old place with a patio and garden in back—both roofed by glittering tropical stars—which were down a stone pathway from the main dining room and bar. It appeared to be where a lot of VIPs, the ruling oligarchy, dined. It was romantic and perfect.

When we arrived, his special anniversary surprise was already being laid out on a low stone table, attended by Mayan women all in traditional dress: the colorful *huipil* blouses of their villages, red and blue skirts, immense jade earrings.

"They've reconstructed a kingly feast from old documents," he explained, beaming at my amazement. "Cuisine of the ancient rain forest. We're going to have a banquet of authentic *guatemalteco* chow from aeons ago."

And the meal was definitely fit for royalty. Soon we were working our way through a long-forgotten medley of piquant flavors that swept through my senses as though I were in another world. There was pit-roasted deer, steamed fish, baked wild turkey. One calabash bowl set forth coriander-flavored kidney beans; another had half a dozen varieties of green legumes all in a rich turtle broth; a third offered vanilla-seasoned sweet potatoes; others had various forest tubers steamed with chiles. We even had a delicious honey wine, like heavenly nectar, served in red clay bowls, that made me want to have sex right on the table. There with Steve, the unexpected juxtaposition of spices and flavors made every bite, every aroma, a new sensual experience. (Let me say right here he's a cooking fanatic, whereas I've been known to burn water. I think it's the new division of labor in post-feminist America.) Finally the Mayan waitresses brought out cups of a chocolate dessert drink from ancient times, cocoa beans roasted, ground, and boiled with sugarcane. The whole event was pure heaven.

Except for the occasional unwanted intrusions. Various dark-eyed, low-cut Ladino divorcées, about half a dozen in all, hanging out at the bar with heavy perfume and too much jewelry, kept coming over purportedly to marvel over our private feast (or was it Steve's big brown eyes). He returned their attentions with his polite and perfect Spanish, but I despised them. In any case, they were shameless. Not remembering quite enough Español, however, the best I could do was just to put my hand on his and give them the evil eye. It seemed to work, though what I really wanted to do was hold up a cross the way you do to ward off vampires. . . .

"Hey, check out Orion," he said, finally leaning back, an easy, delicious finger aimed at that sprawling constellation. I looked up at the canopy of stars, and sure enough, the hunter and his sword dominated the starry sky above like a stalwart centurion, guarding us. "I always know I'm in the tropics when it's right overhead."

"Honey, this has been wonderful," I declared. "Thank you so much." I moved around and kissed him. "It's exactly the attitude adjustment I needed."

"Well"—he smiled back—"now I guess we've got some

organizing to do. So tell me everything you left out back there at the hotel. I know you were holding off."

I was feeling increasingly hyper, probably from the high-octane chocolate, but I proceeded to recount all my findings about Alex Goddard and Quetzal Manor. Then I moved on to Colonel Ramos and how he'd threatened Carly and me about my film. Finally, I told him my deep belief that Colonel Ramos and a couple of his goons were obviously the ones who'd roughed up Lou and taken Sarah.

"Bad scene," he said when I finally paused for breath. He was toying with his cup and running his fingers through his sandy hair, in that "deep thought" mode of his. "Way I see it, this just sounds like a classic case of selling kids. To me, that's right up there with murder and grand larceny."

"Well, I also firmly believe it's all tied in with Alex Goddard's clinic here, or whatever it is. The place Sarah called Niños del Mundo on her landing card. I'll bet you anything that's where Ramos has taken her."

"You know," he said, his brow a perfect furrow, eyes narrowed, "about the babies you saw, there've been press stories over the last few years about Americans being attacked in Guatemala on suspicion of trying to kidnap Maya children out in the villages, to put up for adoption. But I've never seen any proof of it. I've always thought it just might have been dumb gringos who don't know the culture. They go poking around out in the countryside and stupidly say the wrong thing. Maybe using schoolbook Spanish nobody out there really understands. But now this makes me wonder if—"

"Love, those babies I saw up at Quetzal Manor are not kidnapped Indian children, trust me. They're Caucasian as vanilla snow cones. Try again."

"I get your point," he said quickly. "But let me relate the facts of life down here. When you've got some Guatemalan colonel behind something, you'd better think twice about how many rocks you turn over."

"Funny, but that's exactly what some guy at the embassy named Barry Morton said to me."

"And you'd better listen. This is the country that turned the word 'disappear' into a new kind of verb. People get 'disappeared.' I actually knew some of them, back in the late eighties. One dark night an Army truck rolls into a village, and when the torture and . . . other things are over with, a few Maya are never heard from again." He looked at me. "You saw my pictures of that village in the Huehuetenango Department, Tzalala, where the Army mutilated and murdered half the—"

"I know all about that." It was chilling to recall his gruesome photos. "But I'm going to track down Alex Goddard's clinic, no matter what. That's where they've taken Sarah, I'm sure of it. I just may need some help finding it."

He grimaced. "Damn, I've got to head back to Belize by noon tomorrow." Then his look brightened. "But, hey, I finish my shoot Wednesday, so I can drive back here on Thursday. Then on Friday maybe we could—"

"Come on, love, I can't just sit around till the end of the week. What am I going to do till then?" The very thought made me itchy. "I need to find out if Niños del Mundo, the place Sarah put on her original landing card, is for real. Her card said it's somewhere in the Peten, the rain forest. If I could find somebody who—"

"Okay, look." He was thinking aloud. "How about this? There's a guy here in town who owes me a favor. A big one. He screwed me out of twenty grand in the U.S. We were going to start a travel magazine—I think I told you about that—but then he took my money and split the country. He ended up down here and went to work for the CIA—till they sacked him. After that he leased a helicopter and started some kind of bullshit tourist hustle. He sure as hell knows what's going on. Name's Alan Dupre. The prick. Maybe I could give him a call and we could get together for a late drink. He's got an easy number these days: 4-MAYAN."

"How's he going to help?"

"Trust me. He's our guy."

I leaned back and closed my eyes, my imagination drifting. In that brief moment, my mind floated back to yesterday afternoon at Lou's loft, and Sarah. Her hallucinations still haunted me. What had happened to her in the rain forest? And why would she say she wanted to go back?

Then I snapped back. "All right. Try and ring him if you think he can help. Right now I need all I can get."

He got up and worked his way to the phone, past the crowded bar, while I tried to contemplate the night sky. I looked up again, hoping to see Orion, but now a dark cloud had moved in, leaving nothing but deepening blackness. He'd said there was a storm brewing, part of an out-of-season hurricane developing in the Caribbean, so I guessed this was the first harbinger.

"Tonight's out, but tomorrow's okay." He was striding back. "Crack of dawn. Which for him is roughly about noon. We'll have a quick get-together and then I've got to run. Really. But if this guy doesn't know what's going on down here, nobody does. He's probably laid half those hot *tomatillos* there at the bar. The man has his sources, if you get my meaning."

"Then let's go back to the glorious Camino Real." I took his hand. "We'll split the check. At the moment, even that seems romantic."

"I'm still thinking about—"

"Don't. Don't think." I touched his lips, soft and moist, then kissed him. An impulsive but deeply felt act. "We've all had enough thinking for one day."

Seventeen

Alan Dupre didn't ring till almost ten-thirty the next morning, and I had the feeling even that was a stretch. He then offered to meet us in the Parque Concordia, right downtown. As I watched him ambling toward our bench, my first impression was: Why'd we bother?

The man appeared to be in his early forties, puffy-eyed and pink-cheeked, with discount aviator shades, looking like a glad-handing tourist just down to Central America for a weekend of unchaperoned bacchanals. The flowered sport shirt, worn outside the belt, gave him the aura of a tout insufficiently attired without a can of Coors in hand.

How can this be progress? I'm down here hoping to find Sarah, and I end up in a trash-filled park meeting some expat operator.

Steve had explained that the main benefit of Alan Dupre's CIA gig was that he did learn how to fly a helicopter. With that skill he'd ended up starting a tourist agency in Guatemala City using an old Bell he leased: "Mayan Pyramids from the Air." Mainly, though, he was a self-styled bon vivant who knew people.

"Steve the brave." On came Dupre's mirthless smile as he approached, a jaunty spring entering his step.

"Alan, any friend of yours has got to be brave." Steve just stared at him.

Dupre had the kind of empty grin that looked like it'd

been rehearsed in his high school bathroom mirror. It was thin, kind of forked and dangerous, and this morning its plaster quality undermined any attempts at honesty. Maybe dealing with complaining tourists every day of your life did that to you.

"You called, I came." He was now shifting from foot to foot. "Guess it finally had to happen. What's the phrase? You can run but you can't hide? Surprise us both and pretend you're happy to see me."

Steve looked like he was not entirely prepared for this moment. He used the awkward pause that followed to introduce me. Dupre shook hands like he was fearful of germs, then turned back.

"Jesus, man, I'm still working on the money, honest to God. But do I get a last cigarette before the firing squad?"

"Hey, Alan, ease up." Steve was deadpan. "Good to see you again. I mean it. Love that Waikiki shirt, by the way. Never knew you had such progressive taste."

"This is actually my incognito attire. For secret missions. It's my objective today to look like some cruise-ship jerk." He glanced around nervously. "So how'm I doing?"

"I'd say your years of training in undercover work have paid off."

I listened, remembering Steve had explained that Alan Dupre's career as a CIA information-gatherer was hampered by his propensity to drink too much tequila and then brag about his occupation, hoping to impress whatever woman he had in his sights at the moment.

"So bring me up to date." Steve was trying to hide his total contempt. "Why'd you get out of the spook business? Langley couldn't find a 'new mission' for you after the Evil Empire dissolved?"

Dupre's face turned pensive. "Man, you don't get it, do you? Langley's still got plenty on its mind. Nothing has changed. Most people don't realize the U.S. isn't run by the folks they vote for. There's a permanent government that doesn't appear on *Larry King,* and I was part of it. The Central Intelligence Agency of the U.S. of A. will go on doing exactly what it's always done, guiding events in Third World toilets like this through whatever means are necessary to protect America's strategic concerns. Keeping the world safe for Microsoft and Ronald McDonald." He paused and glanced at me, as though slightly embarrassed. Then he continued. "What I'm saying is, all those Beltway turkeys with the briar pipes and gigabyte computers, sitting around wringing their hands, worried the Company needs a new mission, never really grasped its old mission."

"You're right," Steve said, going along with the *shtick,* the applause lines Dupre had doubtless used in a thousand bars. "I'm getting slow. What Langley needs nowadays is a new cover story."

"Couldn't have phrased it better." Dupre smiled, again too easily. "They're—"

"Actually," Steve said, cutting him off impatiently, all the while gazing up at the gathering dark clouds as though they were a hovering adversary, "the truth of the matter is, we called you to discuss a favor. A small helping hand." He seemed to be searching for a sales point. "For old times' sake."

"For old times' sake?" Dupre appeared to be having trouble with the concept.

"Yeah. All we want is to hear a little talk of the town." He gazed out over the square, Uzi-toting police still strolling by. "You know, local information of the kind that doesn't make the papers."

"Right," I said. "For starters, how could a gringa sort of melt into the Peten rain forest, disappear for months and months, and then end up in a coma?" I'd decided to feel him out before going for the bigger questions.

"People disappear down here all the time, and nobody in their right mind goes around inquiring why." Dupre seemed genuinely astonished that anyone would find such a thing unusual. He also was fingering a cigarette pack in his breast pocket, clearly nervous about the quick turn our conversation had taken. "Whatever's your problem in Guatemala, just forget about it. Drink some *cerveza,* take a few snapshots of the picturesque natives, and then move on to a civilized place. This is a land of mystery, lady, and the people who matter like it that way. There are those here who take their privacy very seriously."

Just like Alex Goddard's Children of Light, I thought. Or Niños del Mundo, or whatever it's called. It was chilling to hear Alan Dupre backing away so quickly from my question. The guy seemed truly scared under all the bluster. I also observed that his eyes were curiously small, out of proportion to his face. I hadn't noticed it at first.

"Well," I went on, determined to push him, "an old landing card for the person I'm looking for said her destination was a place called Niños del Mundo, up in the Peten. I assume that's somewhere in the northern rain forest, right? So I guess what I want to know is, does that name stir up any connections?"

He looked around, then extracted a Gauloise from a blue pack and lit it with a wooden match, flicking the tip with his fingernail. He inhaled, taking his time. "Well, maybe I've heard a little something about a place some people call by that name." He drew again on the cigarette. "And the story might include a female American *tourista* or two—about one a year, actually—who've sort of melted into the forest never to be seen more. I'm not exactly sure where it is, though. Or even if what you hear is true. But who cares? Come on, guys, this is Guatemala, for chrissake. Shit happens. Get a life."

"The embassy, or the CIA, or anybody ever carry out an inquiry?" I felt my energy rising. "A woman every year or so? I went by Reforma Avenue yesterday and nobody there seems to have ever heard of any of this."

"No kidding." He snorted. "Whatever happened, *that* place, our caring embassy, ain't gonna do zip—don't faint at the news—and there's no way the Company's going to pull their old-time Yankee number, roll in with the beige sunglasses, and yell, 'Okay, you peons, we're here to take names and kick butt. What happened to our national?' They've recently acquired a habit of taking local situations at face value. Makes for a lot better tables at the tony supper clubs in town."

This guy liked to talk, I realized, but he had no interest in going beyond glib one-liners. I glanced at Steve, and I could tell he was having the same thoughts.

"Tell you what," Steve said finally, "how about this? Tell us whatever you know about how to find this place, and maybe we can adjust the terms on the money you screwed me out of. I might settle for something less on the dollar and let bygones be bygones."

"Hey, man, you'll get your money. I'm good for it." Dupre sighed and drew on his Gauloise. "It's just that things are a little tight right now, you know." He paused. "Matter of fact, I was hoping you might be able to spare a couple of bills for a week or so. But I guess . . ." His voice trailed off.

Alan Dupre knew something I needed to know, or might know it. Steve had definitely found the right guy in that regard. But he clearly was cautious to the point of paralysis as he kept furtively glancing around. What was he so fearful of, and what could I do to convince him to help me?

I stood gazing at the dark sky for a long moment, and

then I had an off-the-wall idea, a long shot, the all-or-nothing take you go for when the sun is dying and the unions are looking at overtime.

"You do tourist flights, right?" I started, still working on the idea. "So how about pretending I'm an eco nut? A lover of the rain forest. You can tell whoever you're so afraid of that you're taking me up into the wilds to show me jaguars or something. A regular tour. Just cruising around, taking in the sights. Totally innocent. And then if we accidentally scouted a little, maybe we could find the place."

"Jesus, you're serious about this, aren't you?" Dupre nervously crushed out his cigarette, staring at me glassy-eyed.

"Never been more."

He extracted another Gauloise.

"Okay, a counteroffer, Miss . . ."

"James. Morgan James."

"Right, Miss James. I'm beginning to think you've got no realistic sense of proportion about this part of the world. You—"

"Fools rush in, right?"

"My point precisely. But if Steve here means what he says, well, maybe there's a little room to negotiate. Maybe I *could* take you on a quick sightseeing trip. And just for laughs I could kind of inadvertently stray over the area I think you might find productive. Assuming we can locate it. But here're my terms. I do it and Steverino and me are square. Consider it a twenty-thousand-dollar cruise."

"Fine with me." Steve didn't even blink, and I loved him all over again, right on the spot. Though the truth was, I knew he'd never planned on seeing a penny of the money again anyway.

"And you think this place is Niños del Mundo?" I was trying not to get my hopes up too much, but still . . .

Dupre lit his new cigarette. "You didn't hear this from

me, okay? You heard it from the embassy or some other damned place. But that's one name for it. Another is 'Jungle Disneyland.' Actually, I think the local name is Baalum, the old Maya word for jaguar. But everybody acts like it's a state secret, so all you get are rumors."

"Well, assuming we find it, then how could I get in? I mean actually in." I was squinting at him, feeling my body tense. What was it Lou had said about a word he'd heard when they were taking Sarah? It sounded like "Babylon"? I also thought that was what she'd whispered to me. Could it be the word was actually Baalum? The gloomy morning skies abruptly flooded with the brilliant white light of hope. I glanced back at Steve, and our eyes locked for a long moment.

"Morgy, for chrissake, what are you saying?" Steve took my hand. "Don't you realize this is Guatemala? Don't even *think* about it."

"We're just talking now, okay?" I squeezed his hand, then looked back at Dupre. "I was just wondering. Once we've found it, could I get a sneak look-see? Assuming I wanted to?"

"Well, I'll tell you one thing, Miss Morgan James." Dupre was fingering his new cigarette, oblivious to my reaction. "Give no serious thought to just driving up. The Army'd be all over your butt in the time it takes to cock an AK-47." He glanced up at the sky again, though now a dense bank of dark clouds had swallowed what remained of the sun. A pre-rain gloom was enveloping the park, which was starting to empty out, the hawkers and loiterers headed home to wait out the weather. "But if we do find it, then as long as we're there, I might be able to drop you off for a quick glance somehow, say, if we did it around twilight time . . . that is, if that's what you want. But it's ten minutes tops, and that's my final offer. Frankly, I think you'd be ill-advised in the extreme to do it, but . . . in any case, it's got to be a low-profile enterprise all the way. We screw this up and we could easily swell the ranks of the 'disappeared.' "

"But you think you could actually locate it?"

"What I hear, the place is on a tributary of the Usumacinta River, a latrine they call the Rio Tigre. Way up in the north-west. Low-level Army types, you meet them in bars from time to time, like to BS about it. I've got a rough idea where it might be, though you don't know whether to believe a bunch of kid recruits after half-a-dozen beers."

Then my mind clicked. The Rio Tigre? Didn't that have something to do with where Lou said Sarah was found? That was *definitely* where I wanted to go.

"Morgy, have you lost your senses?" Steve had placed his hand on my shoulder. "If the Army's involved in something down here, you don't want to know about it. Don't lose sight of the fact those goons knocked off two hundred thousand villagers since the freedom-loving days of the Gipper, for fear they might be Commies, with the CIA practically flying in the ammo. This whole damned country's just one big mass grave. Yet another unclaimed corpse or two won't make a hell of a lot of difference."

"Steve, I'll bet you anything that's where she is." Saying it, I had a vision of all the things that had happened to me, and to Sarah, because of Alex Goddard. I couldn't wait to confront the bastard. "He's brought her back."

Steve just glared at me for a long moment, despairing.

"Christ, you make me nuts. Okay, look, how about this? At least let me come with you. That way we'll face the un-known together."

Though I had a lump-in-the-throat moment, I didn't say anything, just stood there glorying in the feeling of being together. It was so wonderful to have him with me and so difficult to think about pressing on without him.

There was a long, awkward pause, and then he glanced at his watch. "Blast, I've got to hit the road if I'm going to get back in time to set up for tonight's shoot. I just pray I can beat the rain." Then he pulled me around and circled me fully in his arms. "Please, Morgy, I really don't like the sound of this. I'll move heaven and earth to get back here by Friday night, and if you still want to check out this 'Baalum' place, then we'll figure out a way to do it together."

"Just *you* stay safe." I hugged him back. "Nothing I do is going to mean much if I don't have you. Don't worry. I'll be okay."

Alan Dupre had abruptly taken an even deeper interest in the darkening sky. I got the feeling he was uncomfortable being around two people capable of caring.

"It's only for a couple of days," Steve went on. "We'll both be okay if we just stick together."

"Right," I said, and kissed him harder than I ever had.

Five minutes later, my heart and my head still at war with each other, I was alone in the virtually empty park with my brand-new best friend. Watching Steve's Jeep blend into the smoggy haze of the avenue made me feel like half of me had just disappeared into another dimension.

"So that's that," I declared finally, turning back and taking a deep breath. I had to find Sarah before something else truly horrible happened to her. And the one thing I was determined to do was keep Steve as safely distant from my search as I could, even though it meant I was going to be terribly lonely for the next few days. "When can we leave?"

"Hey, get real." Dupre choked, whirling around. "We can't go today. Case you hadn't noticed, there's a storm coming. If you really want to go . . . and I mean *really* want to, then maybe in a day or so. Preferably when Steve—"

"I don't want to drag him into this," I said evenly. Truthfully, I was sounding braver than I felt. But then I remem-

bered once going down into the four-hundred-year-old sub-
terranean harem quarters of the Red Fort in Agra, seemingly
miles underground and pitch black, with nothing but a flashlight, surrounded by screaming bats and knee-deep in guano,
for no better reason than I was determined to see how the
women there once lived. So how much scarier could this be?

"Well, I say no way," Dupre told me. "Not today. Correc-
tion, make that no fucking way." He had removed his aviator
shades and was cleaning them with a dirty hanky. "Besides,
I don't think you have any business going up there in the
first place. If you're not scared shitless, you ought to be."

"Alan, I think *you're* the one who's afraid to go."

He almost reached for another cigarette, but then stopped
himself. "I will definitely plead guilty to a deep-seated disquiet about the people who rule this placid paradise. But if
it'll square things with Steve, then I'll take you up to have a
quick look, for my sins. But it's got to be after the weather
clears."

I finally realized he was already thinking about his next
loan. Steve, beware.

"Tomorrow then?" I wasn't going to blink, because the
Peten was where Sarah had ended up the first time and I
was sure that was where Ramos had taken her now. Baalum.

Dupre stared at the sky a moment longer, then caved.
"Maybe we can shoot for tomorrow late. *If* I can convince
myself this storm has done its worst." He looked back at me.
"But I gotta tell you one thing, Ms. Morgan James. We blunder in up there and end up getting ourselves 'disappeared,' we
won't even get our pictures in the papers. You'd better tell your
immediate loved ones where you're going, and it wouldn't be
the worst time in the world to think about making a will."

The way he said it, I was sure for once he meant every
word.

Eighteen

When I got back to the Camino Real, the time was early afternoon and the bed was freshly made, with all signs and scents of my and Steve's torrid reunion long gone. I tried to push aside thoughts of how much I was already missing him and focus on what I was getting myself into. I must admit I was having serious qualms about going up to the Peten, the part of Guatemala where Sarah had been left for dead, with my brand-new tour director, the flaky Alan Dupre. I'd never been in a helicopter before, much less one flying over a stormy rain forest. On the other hand, if that was where they'd taken Sarah, the sooner I got there, the better.

Sitting there in the room, I found myself feeling right at home: Everything about it was so familiar to an expert on budget travel like me. Off-brand carpet the color of decaying vegetation, the usual two double beds (one totally unused, except as a suitcase shelf), the TV suspended over the dresser and bolted to the wall. Funny, but it was the first time I'd noticed half the things in the room.

Okay, I told myself, the thing to do first is call St. Vincent's and check on Lou. Also, I wanted to tell him what was happening. I just hoped he wouldn't launch into a lecture about the recklessness of what I was planning. I needed support, not male advice.

I got the desk to give me the local AT&T contact number,

then rang right through to St. Vincent's. The next thing I knew, they were calling his room.

"Hi. How's the patient?"

"Morgan, what the hell are you up to? I've been trying to reach you. I finally called David and he said you'd left a message; something about Central America. Why the hell—?"

"I was trying to explain that to you Sunday night, but you were pretty far gone."

"Well, I ain't that far gone now, so I'm telling you to—"

"By the way," I interrupted, hoping to change the subject, "how're you feeling?"

"I guess I'll live. They let me get up and go to the bathroom now. They're saying I can probably go home tomorrow."

"That's encouraging." Thank God he was going to be okay.

"I also had a talk with Gerry, downtown. *He* believes Sarah was kidnapped, even if New York's Finest don't, so that means the FBI has jurisdiction. We're gonna get some action. They're trying to get a photo of that colonel, so maybe I can ID the bastard. But the consulate's giving us a lot of shit about it."

"Well, I'm tracking something down here. Between the two of us, I think we'll find her."

"So, what the hell are you doing?"

I told him about finding the name of a destination on Sarah's old landing card, and about meeting a guy who was going to take me there as soon as the weather cleared.

"And you think she could be there now?" He didn't sound hopeful.

"There're reasons to check it out." I didn't want to elaborate. "Maybe we'll get lucky."

I was attempting to say as little as possible, fearing the

phone was tapped. In that spirit, I decided to get off the line as quickly as possible.

"Lou, you get lots of rest, and I'll try and call you tomorrow."

With a final warning to watch out for myself, he took down my hotel number and hung up. Truthfully, he was sounding pretty tired and weak, not nearly his old self.

Well, he had a right to be. But at least there were no complications.

My next call was going to be to David Roth, to check in on things at Applecore, but first I wanted to order up some *huevos rancheros,* get some breakfast protein. I was becoming energized by the prospect of progress, and being that way always makes me ravenous. It's probably a primal female response that has a Latin name.

I checked out the number for room service, and was literally reaching for the black phone when it rang of its own accord. Startled, I picked up the receiver, wondering who had my number.

"Hello." It was a man's voice that sounded vaguely familiar. "Thought I'd check in and see how things are going with your search."

"Hi," I answered back after a pause, trying to place his intonation.

"Oh, sorry. Barry Morton. Remember me? Fortress America. You came by the office yesterday."

"How . . . ?" Why was he calling me? "How did you get this—?"

"You must have accidentally put the wrong hotel on your landing card as your address in Guatemala City." He hesitated a second, then said, "But I had my secretary call around and . . . well, it happens all the time."

"I see." It did have the ring of logic. And I *had* put down a different hotel. A safety measure. "Do you always take this much . . . interest in your fellow citizens?"

"Only when they come to see me personally." He chuckled. "So how's it going?"

"Well, thanks for calling," I said. "Everything's moving along."

"Good, good." There was another pause, then, "Incidentally, you having any luck finding that Niños del Mundo place you were looking for?"

I hesitated, wondering why he would ask and also unsure what to say.

"Not yet," I volunteered. My God, it finally dawned on me. The guy was *tracking* me. He wanted to know what I knew. "You come up with anything at your end?"

"I've been busy, a string of meetings, but I still think you might want to check out the phone book." It was the second time he'd made the suggestion. He was practically ordering me to do it. Why? "You never know. I'm afraid that's about the best I can do."

"Maybe I will," I said. "I've been a little busy too."

The phone call was feeling stranger and stranger. He was sending me to see something, probably in hopes it would make me go away. It was actually more unnerving than if he'd done nothing at all.

"Well, in any case, I hope you have a good visit," he declared diplomatically. Another pause. "Planning to be here long?"

"I'm not sure yet." Why did he want to know *that?*

"I see. Whatever happens, I hope you find what you're looking for. Best of luck."

He hung up, leaving me with the feeling he already knew the answer to every question he'd asked. The guys at the airport, and now the embassy—I was the best-known tourist in the country.

Okay, maybe I should just play along and see what happens. In any case, I'd just lost my appetite for fried eggs with hot sauce, but I had a definite interest in the phone book.

And there they were. Niños del Mundo. Complete with an address, way out the Boulevar R. Aguilar Batres.

Well, why not see where it leads you? Sarah's card said the place was in the Peten, but who knows?

I got up off the bed and went into the bathroom for a shampoo and shower. Despite the fact that Barry Morton wanted me to see this Niños del Mundo place, whatever it was, I didn't want to show up looking and smelling like some bedraggled tourist. I'd wear my tailored blue suit, which, along with the dark blue heels, ought to make me look adequately businesslike.

The shower was wonderful, purging away the soot of the park, and I was wrapping my hair in a large beige towel when the phone jangled again. I tucked in the edge to secure it and walked over. Maybe it was Lou ringing back.

No such luck. The caller was none other than my brandnew partner Alan Dupre. I was not thrilled to hear his voice. Was he about to get cold feet and back out?

"Morgan, listen," he said, not wasting time on niceties, "there's been a small change of plans. I've—"

"Alan, don't do this to me." You shit. "You *agreed*— "

"No, why I'm calling is, we've got to go ahead and go up today, storm or no, God help us. You happy now?"

What? After that neurotic song-and-dance he'd just given me in the park? I should have been overjoyed, but something about the whole thing immediately felt synthetic. I paused a long moment, trying to think the situation through. What was going on?

The answer to that was clear as day. I was being set up. Somebody wanted me out of town, and they'd just found a way.

Or was I being paranoid again? Had the weather cleared? I reached over and pushed aside a curtain. Nope, it looked as threatening as ever.

No question. This was definitely a setup.

On the other hand, why not *use* whoever had put him up to this? This told me for sure I was on the trail of Sarah, and the sooner I got going, the better. Aside from calling New York and then checking out the local Niños del Mundo that Barry Morton wanted me to see so badly, I had no other pressing plans. . . .

"Alan, I thought you declared no 'effing' way were you going to go today," I said, testing him. "Why the sudden revision in scheduling?"

"Yeah, well, something heavy's come up for tomorrow. I'm afraid it's gotta be now or forget it for at least a week."

Unrefined bullshit. But somebody knew how badly I wanted to go.

"Look, there's something I need to check out first. I just learned about a place here in town I want to at least see. It's also called Niños del Mundo."

"No shit." He paused. "Okay, we'll talk about it. Get the address and maybe we can cruise by if there's time. Thing is, we don't have all that much leeway here."

"One last question." I thought I'd give him a final shot at the truth. "Just tell me honestly why it has to be today. The *real* story."

"Like I said, everything's changed." He wasn't budging. "So if we're doing this, I've got to pick you up now and get us on our merry way."

He was too cheerful by half, which definitely told me he was lying.

"All right, but I really need to make at least one phone call first." I wanted Steve to know where I was. "And if I walk out of here with a bag, I've got to let the desk know I'm not skipping on the bill."

"Forget the phone call. No time. Do it after we get back. Just be out front in exactly nineteen minutes. This is not a dry run. The train is leaving. I'm outta here now."

There was a click and he was gone.

I sat there a moment staring at the floor. What was I getting into?

Well, there's one way to find out. Play their game and beat them. There's no better way to get inside what's going on.

The first thing I did was call Steve's hotel in Belize City. Of course he wasn't there, but I left a long message to the effect that I was taking a "sightseeing" trip up to the Peten with Alan Dupre today because of unforeseen new circumstances. The reasons were complicated, but I'd watch out for myself and therefore he shouldn't worry.

That out of the way, I looked around the room. It was a disaster, but I quickly began cramming things into the small folding backpack I always took on trips. Then I rang the kitchen and told them to make up a quadruple egg sandwich (quatro huevos, por favor) to go, along with a large bottle of distilled water.

By the time I got to the reception desk and explained I wasn't actually checking out for good, Alan Dupre was already waiting outside in his battered green Jeep, cleaning his scratchy shades and leaning on the horn.

Let him wait. I wrote out a long note to Steve, on the chance he might come looking for me. Then with deliberate slowness, I wandered out to where Alan's Jeep was parked and tossed my backpack behind the seat.

"First things first." I climbed in and handed him the address of Niños del Mundo I'd copied onto some hotel stationery. "This is where we've got to go."

He stared at it a moment, puzzling, and then seemed to figure out where it was.

"Upscale part of this beautiful oasis." He shifted into gear. "But it's more or less on the way." He glanced up nervously at the sky. "We just don't have all day."

Off we headed toward the suburbs, through a ganglia of downtown streets laced with pizza joints and frying-meat vendors, till we eventually ended up on a tree-lined avenue that looked as genteel as Oyster Bay. When we got to the address, I told him to park across the way, and just sat a moment staring.

The building itself was a windowless compound surrounded by trees and a high wall of white stucco, with a guardhouse and wide iron gate (not unusual for Guatemala) protecting a long walkway. The whole thing looked like a fortress, except the view through the gate was a pastoral vista of neat flower beds and a pristine lawn. The guardhouse itself had a dozing teenager, undoubtedly with an Uzi resting across his lap.

"Okay, Alan," I said, "time to get with the program. How's your Spanish?"

"Depends on who I'm trying to BS." He shrugged and began cleaning his sunglasses again.

"Well, why don't you see if you can talk us past that guard."

He stared at the entrance a moment. "Be a waste of our precious time. Tell you right now, kids like that only answer to one boss, the *jefe,* the big guy, whoever he is. That's how they retain their employment. A joint locked down this tight don't give Sunday tours."

"Well, I think he's asleep. So I'm going to be creative and see if there's a back entrance of some kind. Maybe a service area that'll give me some idea of what's going on here."

"Do what you want, but make it fast," he said, leaning back in the seat. "And try not to get shot."

I carefully got out and walked down the empty street a way, then followed the stucco wall/fence—the building covered an entire city block—until I came across an alley entrance, with another large iron gate, padlocked shut.

I peered up the driveway, shrouded in overhanging trees, but there was nothing in the parking lot except a couple of Army Jeeps. And a black Land Rover.

Well, Barry Morton really wanted me to see this. But why? Is there a connection to the place in the Peten? And what are the Army vehicles all about?

I sighed and made my way back to the street. When I reached the Jeep, Alan was gone, but then I realized he was over talking to the young guard, offering him a cigarette. A few moments later he waved good-bye and casually ambled back.

"Okay." He settled in and hit the ignition. "Here's the official deal. This place is some kind of hospice for unwed mothers. They also take in orphans, or so he thinks. According to him, no American women have ever had anything to do with the place, which is probably why I'd never heard of it." He glanced at me as we sped off. "You happy now? Debriefing young Army dudes is a speciality of mine, so I think that's probably the straight scoop."

"Did you ask if it's connected with something in the Peten?" I was still hoping. In any case, whatever it was, I was collecting more pieces of the puzzle.

"Hey, give me a break." He shifted up, gaining speed. "I know when to push, and this wasn't the precise moment. The kid was itchy enough as it was. Like, who the fuck are you, gringo, and what are you doing here? I got all I could get without a cold *cerveza*." He glanced over. "You ask me, a little gratitude wouldn't be entirely out of place."

"Okay. *Muchas gracias, amigo.* Happy now?"

"Ecstatic."

The Jeep was open and I checked out the sky, which was growing darker and more threatening by the minute. The promised foul weather still seemed to be just that, promised, but it was definitely on the way. Alan Dupre must really be scared. Finally I leaned back in the torn plastic seat and closed my eyes.

Was this Niños del Mundo the Latin branch of Children of Light? The place where Alex Goddard's babies came from? Considering the interest Colonel Ramos had in my movie, the Army Jeeps could be a tip-off. Also, there seemed to be an even chance that Barry Morton was involved somehow. But it was all still guesswork. And anyway, this wasn't the place Sarah had put on her landing card. That Niños del Mundo was somewhere up north, hidden in the rain forest.

Ready or not, Sar, hang on.

Nineteen

"What did he say?" I asked, not quite catching the burst of rapid-fire Spanish from the cockpit. The explosion of expletives had included the word *navegación*. Something about malfunction.

God help us.

Alan Dupre's helicopter reminded me of the disintegrating taxis on Guatemala City's potholed streets. The vibration in the passenger compartment was so violent it made my teeth chatter. My stomach felt like it was in a cocktail shaker, and the deafening roar could have been the voice of Hell.

I was staring out the smudgy plastic window, where less than three hundred meters below I could just make out the top of the Peten rain forest of northwest Guatemala sweeping by beneath us. So this was what it looked like. Dense and impenetrable, it was a yawning, deciduous carpet enveloping the earth as far as the eye could see—if something ten stories high could be called carpet. I'd been in the forests of India's Kerala and seen some of the denser growth in southern Mexico, but this was like another planet.

The main problem was, a violent downpour, the leading edge of the hurricane, was now sweeping across the Yucatan, stirring up the treetops of the jungles below. The rain, which had begun in earnest about ten minutes after we got airborne, had been steadily increasing to the point it was now almost blinding.

This was the risk I'd chosen to take, but let me admit right here: The weather had me seriously scared, my fingernails digging into the armrests and my pulse erratic. And *now* was there something else? We'd only been in the air for thirty-five minutes, and already we had some kind of mechanical issue looming? What was left to go wrong?

"Some of the lights went out or something." Dupre tried a shrug. "I'm not sure. No big deal, though. This old bird always gets the job done." His pilot, Lieutenant Villatoro, formerly of the Guatemalan Army, had just shouted the new development back to the cabin. "Probably nothing. Don't worry about it."

Don't worry about it! His "tourist" helicopter was a Guatemalan candidate for the Air & Space Museum, an old Bell UH-1D patched together with chicle and corn *masa*. Surely the storm was pushing it far beyond its stress limits.

"Right, but what exactly—?"

"Sounds like the nav station." He clicked open his seat belt. "Something . . . Who knows? If you'd be happier, I'll go up and look."

I felt my palms go cold. "Doesn't seem too much to ask, considering."

The world down below us was a hostile melange of towering trees, all straining for the sky, while the ground itself was a dark tangle of ferns, lianas, strangler vines, creepers— among which lurked Olympic scorpions and some of the Earth's most poisonous snakes. If we had to set down here—I didn't even want to think about it. To lower a helicopter into the waves of flickering green below us would be to confront the hereafter.

"It's just the lights, like he said." Dupre yelled back from the cockpit's door, letting a tone of "I *told* you to chill out" seep through. He was peering past the opening, at the long

line of instruments. He followed his announcement with a
sigh as he moved back into the main cabin. "Relax."

I wasn't relaxed, and from the way his eyes were shifting
and his Gauloise cigarettes were being chain-smoked, he was
on the verge of a nervous breakdown. In his case it wasn't
just the weather. He was fidgeting like a trapped animal,
giving me the distinct sense he was doing someone's invisible
bidding and was terrified he might fail.

"Well, why don't you try and fix it?" Was he trying to
act calm just to impress me? "Can't you bang on the panel
or something?"

"Okay, okay, let me see what I can do. *Jesus!*" He edged
back into the cockpit, next to Villatoro. The wind was shaking us so badly that, even bent over, he was having trouble
keeping his balance. Then he halfheartedly slammed the dark
instrument readouts with the heel of his open hand. When
the effort produced no immediate electronic miracle, he settled into the copilot's seat.

"Que pasa?" he yelled at Villatoro, his voice barely audible over the roar of the engine and the plastering of rain on
the fuselage. Then he looked out the windscreen, at the torrent slamming against it, and rubbed at his chin.

"No sé, mi comandante," the Guatemalan shouted back.
I sensed he was hoping to sound efficient and unperturbed.
Dupre claimed his pilot had personally checked out the Bell
and prepped it. Now, though . . . *"Mira.* Like I said, the
lights. On the nav station. Maybe the electrical—"

"How about the backup battery?" Dupre was just barely
keeping his cool.

Villatoro scratched his chin. "I'll tell you the truth. The
backup is *muerto.* I tested it before we left, but I couldn't
find any replacements in *Provisiones.* I figure, no problem,
but now, *amigo* . . ."

I felt another wave of dismay, right into my churning stomach.

"Well, keep your heading north." Dupre's voice was coming from a place of extreme pain. "And if you sight the Rio Tigre, then Baalum or whatever should be more or less due west, according to what I'm assuming. Just keep your eyes open." He paused. "Problem is, with all this rain, the river's going to be tough to make out."

I redoubled my efforts to peer out the window, searching, my breath coming in bursts. Still nothing. Dear God, what now?

Finally Dupre headed back, bracing himself against the firewall as he crouched and passed through the door into the main cabin. When he settled into the seat across from me, he was glaring at me as though everything was my fault. "You know." He was yelling again. "I'm beginning to think maybe we ought to try to find a clearing and just sit out this crap till morning." He leaned over and peered down through the Bell's spattered side windows at the dense tangle of growth below. After a moment he got up and once more moved the toward the cockpit, still with the same troubled look. This time, however, he was beaming as he shouted back.

"There may be a God after all. I think we just intersected the Rio Tigre. We can bear due west now, along the river. We could be getting close, if it's where I think it is."

I turned and stared down again, barely making out the thread of the stream through the rain. *Yes!* Maybe there's hope. Still, below us the windblown treetops were a solid mass of pastel sparkles, a dancing sea of hungry green . . . But then I thought I saw something. Hey! It might even be a clearing. I quickly unbuckled and made my way up to the cockpit, hanging on to anything I could grasp.

"Alan, look," I yelled, and pointed off to the side, out

through the rain-obscured windscreen. "I think we just passed over something. Back there. See?"

"Where?" He squinted.

"You can still just make it out." I twisted and kept pointing. I was biting my lip, trying to hold together. "There ... it looks like some kind of clearing. Maybe ... I don't know, but what if we just set down there and let this storm blow over?"

He ordered Villatoro to bank and go back for a look. A few moments later it was obvious there *was* an opening in the trees.

"Yeah, let's check it out." He then said something to Villatoro and we started easing toward it, definitely a wide opening. The billowing ocean of trees below us seemed to be parting like the Red Sea as we settled in. There had to be solid ground down there somewhere. Had to be.

"What's ..." I was pointing. "There, over to the side, it's a kind of hill or something. It's—"

"Where?" Dupre squinted again, his voice starting to crack. Then he focused in. "Yeah, maybe there's something there. Hard to tell what it is, though. But I guess we're about to find out."

He gestured to the lieutenant, barking an order in quick Spanish. While the Bell kept moving lower through the opening, Dupre flicked on the landing lights, and appeared to be muttering a prayer of thanks.

I was staring out, growing ever more puzzled. A "hill" was there, all right. The problem was, it was definitely man-made, topped by a stone building. I could just make it out in the glare of the lights.

"What do you think that is?"

"What do I think?" Dupre studied the scene for a moment longer, and then his face melted into the first smile I'd seen since we left. "I think we are lucky beyond belief. God help us, we may have found it. That could be the damned pyramid or whatever's supposed to be up here." He leaned back. "Yeah, congratulations. Look at that damned thing. Either this is the place, or we're about to become the archaeologists of the year. Cover of *Time*. The Nobel frigging Prize."

At that moment I almost wanted to hug Alan Dupre, but not quite. Instead, I moved farther into the cockpit, trying to get a look out the windscreen. By then we had lowered well through the opening in the trees, the helicopter's controls fighting against the blowing rain, and it felt as though we'd begun descending into the ocean's depths in a diving bell, surrounded by thrashing, wind-whipped branches.

Now, though, I was staring at the ghostly rise of the pyramid, emerging out of the rain.

"It looks brand new."

"Yeah, the whole place is 'Jungle Disneyland,' remember? Except this deal ain't about Mickey Mouse, believe me. There's plenty of Army hanging out around here."

Lieutenant Villatoro took us ever lower, gently guiding the chopper's descent, and now we were only a few feet above the ground. There certainly was no mistaking what was around us, even with the blowing rain. The pyramid loomed over one side of a large plaza, a big paved area that was mostly obscured from the skies since the swaying trees arched over and covered it from aerial view.

"Okay, we're about to touch down." Dupre was clawing at his pocket, yearning for a cigarette. "So if you still want to get out, move over by the door. I'll disengage the main rotor once we're on the ground."

As we settled in, the rotor began to cause surface effect, throwing a spray off the paving stones, which now glistened under the cold beam of the landing lights. And looming above us, off to the right, was a stepped pyramid in the classic Mayan style. We all lapsed into silence as the Bell's skids thumped onto the stones. The ex-Army pilot, Villatoro, kept glancing over at the pyramid as though he didn't want to admit even seeing it. Did he know something Alan and I didn't?

This was the moment I'd been bracing for. I was increasingly convinced somebody wanted me to see this place, whatever it was, but now what should I do?

Well, the first thing was to dip my toe in the water, do a quick reconnoiter on the ground. If this really was Baalum, Dupre's Maya Disneyland, could it also be part of Alex Goddard's clinic of "miracles," the location Sarah called Niños del Mundo? If I knew that for sure, then I could start figuring how to find out if she was here—as I suspected—and get her out of his clutches. Maybe the see-no-evil embassy might even be prodded into helping an American citizen for a change.

"I'm getting out, to look around a little, but not till you turn off the engine. I want to be able to use my ears."

"All right, but don't take all day. This kind of weather, I want to keep it warm." He turned to Villatoro and shouted the order. In the sheets of pounding rain, I figured that no one could have heard us come in. That, at least, was positive.

When the rpm's of the engine had died away, I clicked open the Bell's wide door, slid it back, and looked around. In the glare of the landing lights I realized at once that the stones were old, weathered, and worn, but the grout that sealed them was white and brand new. The plaza was free of moss, clean as the day it was done—which did not appear to be all that long ago. Above me, the pyramid, continuous recessed tiers of glistening stones, towered into the dim skyline of trees.

I stepped out onto the pavement, holding my breath. The plaza was almost football-field in size, reminding me of an Italian piazza. Around me the rain was lessening slightly, and as my eyes adjusted . . . my God. There wasn't just a pyramid here; through the sparkle of raindrops at the edge of the helicopter's lights I could see what looked like a wide cobblestone walkway leading into the dense growth just off the edge of the square, probably toward the south, away from the river, connecting the plaza with distant groups of small, thatch-roofed houses, set in clusters. . . .

Could Alex Goddard's "miracle" clinic be in some collection of primitive huts? It made no sense.

But I decided to try to get a closer look. I'd walked about thirty feet away from the helicopter, across the slippery paving, when I saw a flash of lightning in the southeast, followed by a boom of thunder that echoed over the square.

At least I thought it was thunder. Or maybe the Army was holding heavy artillery practice somewhere nearby. Abruptly the rain turned into a renewed torrent, and the next thing I heard was the helicopter's engine start up again. Then I sensed the main rotor engage, a sudden "whoom, whoom, whoom" quickly spiraling upward in frequency.

Hey! I told him not to—!

When I looked back at the Bell's open door, Dupre was standing there, frantically searching the dark as he heaved out my tan backback and what looked like a rolled-up sleeping bag, both splashing down onto the rain-soaked paving.

What! For a moment I thought the thunder, or whatever it was, must have completely freaked him. Then what was actually happening hit me with a horrifying impact.

"Alan, *wait!*"

I started dashing back, but now the main rotor was creating a powerful downdraft, throwing the rain into me like a monsoon. By the time I managed to fight my way through the spray, the rotor was on full power and Alan Dupre and his Bell were already lifting off. I reached up, and just managed to brush one greasy skid as he churned away straight upward into the rainy night.

"You shit!" I yelled up, but my final farewell was lost in

the whine of the engine. My God, I thought, watching him disappear, I've just been abandoned hundreds of miles deep in a Central American rain forest.

Then it all sank in. Whoever had gotten to him was playing a rough game. They didn't want me just to see Baalum, they wanted me delivered here. Probably to secure me in the same place Sarah was. Colonel Ramos, or whoever had frightened Dupre into bringing me, had wanted us both. So what now? Were we both going to be "disappeared"? Staring around at the pyramid and the empty square, I could feel my heart pounding.

Then I tripped over the rolled sleeping bag and sank to my knees there in the middle of the rain-swept plaza, soaked to the skin and so angry I was actually trembling. Up above me, Alan Dupre, king of two-timers, had switched off his landing lights, and a few moments later the hum of the Bell was swallowed by the night sounds of the forest—the high-pitched din of crickets, the piercing call of night birds, the basso groan of frogs celebrating the storm.

And something else, an eerie sense of the unnatural. I can't explain it. Even the night songs of the birds felt ominous, the primeval forest reasserting its will. It was haunting, like nature's mockery of my desolation. I pounded the sleeping bag and felt . . . shit, how did I let this happen?

Get a grip. I finally stood up and looked around. Maybe when God wants to do you up right, She gives you what you want. You used Alan Dupre just like you intended: He got you here. But there's more to the plan of whoever's holding his puppet strings. So the thing now is, don't let yourself be manipulated any more. Get off your soggy butt and start taking control of the situation. . . .

That was when I sighted a white form at the south, forested edge of the plaza. What! I ducked down, sure it was somebody lurking there, waiting to try to beat me to death as they had Sarah. Did Ramos intend to just murder me immediately?

But there was no getting away. If I could see them, they surely could see me. And where would I escape to anyway?

I dug my yellow plastic flashlight out of my backpack and, my hand shaking, flicked it on. The beam, however, was just swallowed up in the rain. All right. I strapped on the pack and, taking a deep breath, threw the rolled sleeping bag over my shoulder and headed across the slippery paving toward the white, which now glistened in the periodic sheets of distant lightning.

Meet them straight on. Try and bluff.

When I got closer, though, I realized what I was seeing was actually just the skin of a jaguar, bleached white, the head still on, fearsome teeth bared, which had been hung beside the paved pathway. Thank God.

But then, playing my light over it, I thought, *Bad sign. My first encounter at Baalum is with a spooky, dead cat.* It felt like a chilling omen of . . . I wasn't sure what.

I studied it a moment longer with my flashlight, shivering, then turned and headed quickly across the plaza toward the pyramid, now barely visible in the rain. If there were jaguars, or God knows what else, around, I figured I'd be safer up at the top.

When I reached the base and shined my light up the steps, I saw they were steeper than I'd thought, but they also looked to be part of some meticulous restoration and brand-new, probably safe to climb. And there at the top was a stone hut, complete with what appeared to be a roof. Good. If there hadn't been anything taller than it around, I think I might have just climbed a tree.

On the way up I began trying to digest what the place really was. The pyramid was "fake". . . or was it? A hundred years ago the eccentric Brit archaeologist Sir Arthur Evans whimsically "reconstructed" the Palace of Minos on Crete with his own money, and it's still a tourist highlight. So why couldn't somebody do the same with a reclaimed Mayan pyramid in Central America? Still, this was different, had the feel of being somebody's crazed obsession.

As I topped the steps, I realized the building that crowned the pyramid was also a "restoration" like everything else, including a decorated wooden lintel above the door that looked to be newly lacquered. Bizarre.

I moved through the door and unloaded my gear, then extracted my water bottle, now half-empty, for a pull. Finally I unrolled Alan Dupre's sleeping bag on the (dry) stone floor, removed and spread out my wet clothes, peed off the edge, then took a new pair of underpants, jeans, and shirt out of my backpack, donned them, and uneasily crawled in. I was shivering—whether from the soaking rain or from fright, I didn't know—and my teeth were trying to chatter. Was I hidden away enough to be safe? I didn't know. All I did know was, I was in something deeper than I'd ever been in my life, and I had no idea how I was going to get out. And I was both scared to death and angry as hell.

Sarah was here, though, I was certain. Like a sixth sense, I could feel her presence, out there somewhere in the rain. For a moment I was tempted to just plunge into the storm looking for her, but a split second's reflection told me that was the stupidest thing I could do. Instead, I should try and get some rest, till the storm cleared, and keep periodic watch on the plaza in case somebody showed up. Then, the minute there was light, I'd hit the ground and go find her.

I suppose nothing ever happens the way you plan. My mind was racing and my nerves were in the red, but I was so exhausted from the teeth-rattling trip in the Bell I couldn't really stay alert very long. In spite of myself, I eventually drifted off into a dreamless doze, a victim of the narcotic song of wind in the giant Cebia trees and the insistent drumming of forest rain on the roof.

Twenty

I awoke as a sliver of sun flashed through the stone door-way of the room and forest birds erupted around me in celebration. As I pulled myself up and moved over to the opening, a quick tropical glare burned into my face. My God, the dawn was electric; it was the purest blue I'd ever seen, a swath of artist's cobalt. An azure radiance from the sky glistened off the rain forest leaves around me. Had I dreamed the stormy, haunted world of the night before?

When I looked down, everywhere below me was a bank of dense, pastel mist. Was the plaza really there or had I imagined it? I felt like the top of the pyramid was floating on a cloud.

"Babylon." That was what Sarah had called this place. Ancient and mysterious. I took a breath of the morning air and wondered what would draw her back here. Was Baalum the ultimate escape from her other life? Even so . . . why would she want to return after somebody had tried to murder her? What was waiting down there in the fog?

Turning back, I noticed that the room's inside walls were embossed with rows and rows of classic Mayan glyphs, like little cartoon faces, all molded in newly set plaster. To my groggy sight they seemed playful, harmless little caricatures, though next to them were raised bas-reliefs of warriors in battle dress. It was both sublimely austere and eerie, even creepy.

I knelt down and rolled my sleeping bag, trying to clear my head. Then I stuffed my still-moist clothes into my backpack and thought about the river, the Rio Tigre, down somewhere at the back of the pyramid. And I felt my pulse rate edging up. The first thing I wanted to do was see it in the light of day. It had been Sarah's way out, the only thing I knew for sure she'd touched.

Get going and do it.

I headed through the rear door and down the back steps. When I reached the ground, the dense forest closed in around me, but I was certain the river lay dead ahead, through the tangle of trees. As I moved down a path that grew ever steeper, the canopy up above thickened, arching over me till it blotted out the pure blue of the sky. And the air was filled with nature sounds—birdcalls, trills, songs, and clacks, all mingled with the hum and buzz of insects. Then suddenly, from somewhere up in the canopy, a pack of screeching spider monkeys began flinging rotten mangos down in my direction. I also thought I heard the asthmatic, territorial roar of a giant howler monkey, the lord of the upper jungle. And what about snakes? I kept an eye on the vines and tendrils alongside the path, expecting any moment to stumble across a deadly fer-de-lance, a little red-and-black operator whose poison heads straight for your nervous system.

On the other hand, the birds, the forest birds, were everywhere, scarlet macaws and keel-billed toucans and darting flocks of Amazon parrots, brilliant and iridescent, their sweeping tails a psychedelic rainbow of green, yellow, red. Then the next thing I knew, the path I was on abruptly opened onto a mossy expanse of pea-soup green, surely the Rio Tigre, and . . .

My God, those dark-brown bumps scattered everywhere . . . they're the eyes and snouts of . . . yes, *crocodiles,* lurking there in wait, hoping I'm dumb enough to wade in.

Forget what Alan Dupre said. This is definitely not "Disneyland."

Then I glanced upstream and caught sight of a string of mahogany dugout canoes tied along the shore. They were huge, about fifteen feet long and three feet wide, and clearly designed to be crocodile-resistant. They . . .

Wait a minute. Lou said Sarah was found in a dugout canoe that had drifted all the way down the Rio Tigre to where it joins the Usumacinta. One more clue she might have been here. Maybe I was closing in. Yes!

I glared back at the crocodiles' unblinking reptile eyes and tried to get my mind around the fact Sarah could have stood right where I was standing, or been set adrift from here in a coma, to float downstream. Seeing that vision, I felt unbidden tears trailing down my cheeks. And the questions I had kept piling up. Was this the location of Alex Goddard's "miracle" clinic? Why was Baalum such a high-security secret? What was the connection between this place and Sarah's ravaged mind and body? I wanted to know all of it, and by God I would.

This was the farthest I'd ever been from "civilization," though I was trying not to let that fact sink in too deeply. The water was green and full of small aquatic creations, but I managed to find a reasonably un-mossy spot and—still keeping an eye on the leering crocodiles—splashed my face. It felt good, even if it was filthy. . . .

Okay, I'd seen enough of the river. I raised up and stretched. Time to go.

My hopes at war with my nerves, I turned my back on the scummy, fetid Rio Tigre and headed back up the jungle trail toward the plaza.

When I got there, I was struck all over again by the vision of the pyramid. Something like it might have been here originally, but in any case it had been completely redone, with newly cut yellowish stones and white lime plaster, an exotic castle nestled in the green lap of the rain forest, rising above the square like a haunting presence. It must have been well over a hundred feet high, a stone wedding cake with a dozen steep tiers between the ground and the platform at the top, which also was square and roughly fifteen feet on the side.

Standing there gazing at it, I think I'd never felt more disoriented. Sarah, Sarah, how could we both end up here, at the last outpost of the known world? But seeing is believing. I took a deep breath, then turned down the pathway toward the thatch-roofed huts.

Through the mist it was gradually becoming clear that Baalum actually was a village, and a sizable one. The walkway led past a string of clearings, each with clusters of one-room huts built in the ancient, classical style, with walls of mud over rows of vertical saplings, their roofs and porches peaked with yellow-green thatch weathering to browns and grays. The structures, outlined starkly against the towering green arbor of the forest above, were grouped around paved patios. It all was neat and meticulous, like a jungle Brigadoon. Although the effects of the storm were everywhere—blown thatch and bamboo—I still felt as if I'd fallen into a time warp where clocks had gone backward. What . . .

Then I began to catch the outlines of people, as though they had materialized out of the pale fog. All pure Maya, short and brown, shiny black hair, they appeared to be just going about their daily lives. I was approaching a workshop area where, under a wide thatch shade, men with chipped-flint adzes were carving bowls, plows, various implements from mahogany and other rain forest woods. Next to them, potters were fashioning brown clay jugs. They all were wearing white loincloths and a large square cotton cloth knotted around their shoulders, their hair tied back in dense ponytails. It must have been how the Maya looked a thousand years ago.

Their earnestness reminded me of the villagers I once filmed in the Yucatan for the Discovery Channel—with one big difference: There I was the big-shot gringo; here I felt like a powerless time traveler. The sense of being lost in another age was as compelling as the "colonial" mock-up at Williamsburg, but this was real and it was decidedly spooky.

Finally one of the men looked up and noticed me. Our eyes locked for an instant—it seemed like forever—and then he reached over and, in a way that seemed breathless, shook the man next to him, gesturing toward me. Together they gazed back as though viewing a phantom, their brown faces intent, and then they turned and called out to the others, alerting them.

What are they going to do with me? I wondered with a sudden chill. A stranger here in their hideaway midst. Would they just turn on me?

Find some women. Get *off* the street.

I turned and headed as fast as I could down the cobblestone central path, till I saw a cluster of females on a whitewashed stone porch, long hair falling over their shoulders as they bent to their tasks beneath the thatch overhangs. Some were stirring rugged clay pots of corn soaking in lime; others were grinding the softened maize to tortilla thinness on wide granite platters. Behind them was another group that appeared to be part of a sewing commune, young wives busy at their back-strap looms, layering thread after thread of dyed cotton. None of them was wearing a *huipil*—the traditional multicolored blouse I'd remembered from the waitresses in the restaurant. Instead, they all had on a kind of handloom-woven white shift I'd never seen before.

Talk to them. Let them know you're no threat to anybody.

As I moved down the hard clay pathway toward them, two looked up and took notice. Their first reaction seemed to be alarm, as they tensed and stared. But then I tried a smile and it seemed to work. Their looks turned to puzzlement, then embarrassed grins, as though they wanted to be friendly but weren't sure how to acknowledge my presence.

When I reached the porch, several reached out to touch me. One older woman, short and wizened and extremely brown, even tried to stroke my hair.

What was going on? I was taken aback, but I also was determined to get through to them. Why not just ask them point-blank if Sarah's here? Is there any chance they understand Spanish?

"Buenos dias." I smiled and nodded. *"Dispénseme. Quiero descubrir . . . esta una gringa de los Estados Unidos aqui?"*

They all returned uncomprehending looks, then glanced quickly at each other in confusion. Or at least that was how I read their faces.

"Sarah," I said, pronouncing the name slowly. "Sarah Crenshaw."

"Sara," one voiced, then others. They backed away and immediately began a heated dispute, which eventually involved all the women. Well, one thing was for sure: They damned well knew who I was asking about. But why were they so upset? Next, several of them grew testy, pointing at me as they continued to argue.

Finally the two I'd first approached turned and began urging me to leave, gesturing at me with their hands as though sweeping me out of the compound. Yes, there was no mistaking. I was being dismissed. And I detected an odd nervousness as they glanced around, seemingly worried somebody might catch me there with them. I got the feeling they'd finally decided they didn't want me anywhere near them, since they kept pointing down the thoroughfare in the direction of the pyramid.

I've blown it, I thought. They must have figured out I'm here to get her and decided they no longer want to have anything to do with me. What did that mean?

And now what do I do? As I retreated back out to the main walkway, I felt a growing sense of defeat. Then, looking down it, I realized I'd literally been going in a circle. It was actually a large oval that curved back to the main square and the pyramid, where I'd started from.

God, what a nightmare. I obviously had to rethink my game plan, find a way to communicate. And on top of that, I was dying of thirst.

I fished out the almost-empty plastic container from my backpack, then walked across the square and settled myself on the first step leading up the steep front. As I drew on the bottle, my mind still swirling, I happened to notice an upright stone slab off to the side, like a tall, thin tombstone, with a bas-relief of a Maya warrior on it, next to some kind of two-headed serpent god—probably Kukulkan, one of the few Maya dieties I knew. And then, down the side, were rows of lines and dots. I studied them a minute before realizing it was the classical Mayan number system, telling precisely when things happened to the ruler shown there: born on such and such a date, assumed the kingship, won great battles, etc., all carefully dated as career high-points. I knew that dots represented single years, horizontal lines the number five. The Maya loved numbers and numerology, so . . .

That was when I glanced up to see a group of women approaching slowly across the square, with a bunch of the men watching from the forest arbors beyond, and they were huddled around something they were carrying. Whatever it was, they seemed to be delivering it to me. Then I realized they were the same ones who'd just kicked me out of their compound. What next? Are they coming to drive me from the plaza too? Should I try and forcibly search all the huts?

But then they set down their load—it turned out to be a crude bamboo-and-thatch palanquin—and stepped aside as they beckoned me forward.

For a moment I just stared, disbelieving. I felt like I was seeing someone I didn't want to recognize, perhaps because that someone looked so much like me.

"Morgy, they told me a new one was here, and I hoped it was you." Sarah was swinging her skinny legs off the side, her voice bright. Her face was drawn, but her hair was neat and her eyes were radiant. "Isn't Baalum the most wonderful place you've ever seen?"

She was wearing a white shift that reminded me of the blue hospital smock she'd had on the last time I saw her, except here it seemed more like something that had a special significance, like the robes of an acolyte. Her shoes were soft brown slippers that looked brand-new, and around her waist was a braided leather band. As I stared at her, I wondered if she was really as transformed as she looked. She was undeniably stronger than two days ago, in spite of what that bastard Alex Goddard and his Guatemalan Army cronies had done to her to get her here. But still, she had to be half dead. Thank God Lou couldn't see her now.

"Sar, oh, Sar." I rushed over and threw my arms around her. She'd been freshly bathed and perfumed—a fragrance like chocolate—but she felt like a bag of bones. "Are you okay?"

"I was afraid Baalum was all just a dream." She hugged me back, then started rising to her feet. God, could she walk? "But now I remember everything."

"Sar, I've come to take you home." I grasped her hand, warm and soft, to help her stand—though it wasn't necessary. "You're not safe—"

"No, it's wonderful now" Then she turned and said something to one of the women. It took me a moment to realize she was speaking their language; I guessed it was Kekchi Maya.

I was stunned. How did she learn it? Finally she looked back at me and switched to English again. "I didn't understand before. I was . . . sick so much."

"Sar, come on." I slipped my arm around her. "We're going to get you out of here."

I'd never felt so helpless. Alan Dupre had said there was a road, but it was controlled by the Army. Right now, I didn't even know where it was. Maybe I could find a phone, or radio. Call the embassy. There must be something. Alex Goddard has to be here somewhere, but he's not going to stop me. I'll strangle him if he tries.

I hugged her again, the feel of her skin-and-bones frame making my soul ache. But most hurtful of all, I wasn't sure she would want to leave.

"Sar, can you understand me?" I tried to catch her deep blue eyes. "I'm taking you home. Your father's very worried about you."

Mention of Lou seemed to finally get through to her. She turned and examined me with a quizzical look, and then her eyes hardened.

"Morgy, he was never there for me." Her voice was filled with certainty, and pain. "But when I went to see Dr. Goddard, he let me come here for the ceremony. It's so spiritual. After—"

"Sar, come *on*." What did she mean by "ceremony"? Whatever it was, I had to get her out of this place. Immediately. "We've—"

"Are you here for the ceremony?" Her face flooded with renewed joy. "It's two days from now. Maybe he'll let you—"

"She should be resting." It was a harsh voice, directly behind us.

I recoiled, then whirled around. Three men were standing there, two of them young privates in uniforms of the Guatemalan Army and carrying AK-47 assault rifles, the ones with the long, ominous curved clip Steve called *cuerno de cabrio,* the "horn of the goat."

The third was in a black sweatshirt and black jeans, his long salt-and-pepper hair tied back in a ponytail.

"They should have known better than to bring her out here," Alex Goddard said. "Not in her condition."

The bastard. It was all coming together in my mind. He'd tried to kill her once before, and now he was going to finish the job. But he'd have to kill me first.

"I'm here to take her home." I marched up to him. "You're not about to get away with kidnapping. I'm going to get the embassy to—"

"She's here for important medical reasons." He met my eyes. "I hope you'll allow me the opportunity to help her."

"What do you mean, 'help'?"

"I'll explain if you'll give me a chance." He revolved and delivered some brusque orders in Kekchi Maya to the women, who nodded apologetically and began helping Sarah back onto the palanquin. After he admonished her in the same language, he then said something in quick Spanish to the two young Army privates, who gave him a firm salute, turned, and walked over to pick the palanquin up, to carry it for the women. The sense of authority he exuded reminded me of that first morning we met at Quetzal Manor. His eyes flashed from benign to demanding to benign in an instant.

"No, damn it, *alto!*" I strode over, shoved the soldiers aside, and took her hand. "Sar, honey, don't you understand what's going on? Something terrible happened to you when you were here before. I'm so worried—"

"But he says I need to stay, Morgy." She drew back. "It's best. He's helping me."

As I watched the two privates carry her away, down the cobblestone pathway, AK-47's swung over their shoulders, I felt my helplessness become complete. The Army here was under his control, just like everything else.

How was I going to tell Lou about this, that Sarah had been brainwashed? Whatever Alex Goddard had done to her had turned her into some kind of "Moonie," ready to denounce her own father. So now did I have two battles to wage: one with Alex Goddard and one with her?

Then he walked over to me.

"I'm not going to ask how you got here, though I assume it wasn't easy." He smiled, like a kindly priest, and put his hand on my shoulder. "But however you did it, I'm glad you decided to come. It's important for you to be here. She needs you now."

Twenty-one

"Cut the crap." I pulled away, still in shock from seeing Sarah so addled. I wanted more than anything else in the world just to slug him. "Why did you bring her here? Think about your answer. Kidnapping is a serious crime in the States."

"I've been very concerned about her." He looked up at the groves of Cebia trees around the square, a quiet glance, as though to inhale the misty morning air. My legal threat had gone right past him—probably because here *he* was the only law. "But now she's receiving the treatment she needs. I expect she'll be fine before long."

"Treatment?" I was caught off guard. Okay, let's start getting things straight. "When she was here before, somebody tried to beat her to death. How—?"

"What happened then was beyond my control." He motioned me to join him as he settled onto the first step of the pyramid, sadness in his eyes. We were alone in the square now, and I felt like I'd become his personal prisoner, trapped. "Sarah was . . . is very dear to me. I care for her deeply."

"You cared so much for her she ended up in a coma, over on the Mexican border." I didn't sit. Instead I just bored in, hoping to stare him down, but his eyes had grown distant, that little trick he had of alternating between intimacy and remoteness. Again it reminded me of that first morning we'd met, looking out over the bluffs of the Hudson.

"If you'll let me, I'd like to try and tell you something of the circumstances surrounding that tragedy." He was gazing off in the direction the women had gone. "You see, when Sarah first appeared at Quetzal Manor in New York, she was a very troubled young woman. She declared she was a person of pure spirit and she wanted to have a baby without so much as touching a man, some procedure that would produce a divine child created of cosmic energy."

Cosmic energy. I had a flashback, hearing the words, to the time when she'd just turned six and we'd been sent by my mother to the hayloft to track down nests secreted there by rogue chicken hens. When we came across a cache of eggs, she asked if baby chicks came out of them. I assured her they did, and then she asked if human babies came from eggs too. My biology was pretty thin, but I told her I supposed they did, sort of, but then the eggs were probably hatched, or something, before babies were born. She thought about that a moment, scrunching up her face, then declared "No!" and bitterly began smashing the eggs. Babies and all living things came from another world, she declared, a special place *we* could not see. They came directly from God. . . .

That was why she would seek out someone like Alex Goddard. For her, he must have seemed a messenger of the Unseen. Who better to create a child for her? The ironic part was, I'd found him for almost the same reason, seeking a miracle when all else had failed. Were Sarah and I even more alike than I'd realized?

"So I began trying to work with her." He was turning back to me. "But then I discovered she'd been born with an abnormality of the uterus. It has a medical name, but suffice to say it's very rare, and afflicts only about one woman in twenty thousand. Even after my diagnosis, though, she refused to give up. She was a person of enormous tenacity."

God, I thought. Why didn't she come home to *us,* to Lou

and me? We loved her. I felt my guilt go out to her all over again.

"She next declared she wanted to come here to Baalum, to the place of miracles. I told her that, yes, miracles can sometimes transpire here, but only at a great price. We would need to have an agreement and she would have to keep it no matter what."

"What do you mean, an agree—?"

"Truthfully, though," he went on, ignoring me, "I immediately regretted the offer, since I realized she was far too unstable for this . . . environment. Finally I forbade her to come, but just before my next scheduled trip she found out and booked herself on the same flight. There was literally nothing I could do to stop her."

"She put Niños del Mundo on her landing card." I was growing sick to my stomach at the rehearsed way he was recounting her story. "That's this place, right? Baalum."

"My clinic here is known by that name. The village itself is called Baalum." He was easily meeting my eye, holding his own in our battle of wills. "Sarah was, I have to say, a very impressionable young person. Once here, she forgot all about her purpose for coming. She should have stayed up the hill there"—he was pointing off to the south—"where I could care for her, but instead she moved down here, into the compounds. Then she discovered a hallucinogenic substance they have here, began using it heavily, and I think it tipped her into a form of dementia."

So, she *was* doing drugs, something I'd always secretly feared. Well, maybe she was still having flashbacks of some kind; maybe that explained why she was off in another world when she came out of her coma.

"What . . . kind of 'hallucinogenic substance'?"

He sighed, then shrugged and answered. "Here in the rain forest there's an ugly three-pound toad, the Bufo marinus—

you'll see them around, near sunset—that has glands down its back that excrete a milky white poison."

I knew about them. They were migrating north now, even into Florida. They were huge and looked like Jabba the Hutt in *Star Wars*. I hate toads of all varieties, but the thought of those monsters made me shudder.

"My God, isn't their toxin lethal?" Was Sarah trying to destroy herself? Was that why her mind was so blitzed? "I've heard—"

"Yes, it can kill you, but it can also—if processed correctly, with fermented honey—give you truly supernatural visions. The classical Maya used it for ceremonial purposes. I'd managed to reconstruct how they prepared it, and—something I now deeply regret—I showed the shamans here how to replicate the procedure. At the time it was just a minor part of my research into traditional pharmacology, but she heard about it and persuaded them to give her a vial. Then more and more."

That did sound like Sarah. Always out on the edge, testing new realities. But then I thought a moment about what he'd *actually* said. Some of the people here in his "place of miracles" were doing heavy drugs, and she'd got caught up in it.

"But why didn't you stop her?" You unfeeling bastard.

"I tried, believe me. But I'm afraid she was far past listening to me. By then she was learning the Kekchi Maya dialect, becoming totally immersed in their world. She began having episodes of complete nonrationality, and then one day she told the women in her compound she was going over to Palenque, the Maya ruins in Mexico. It's where the classical Maya held their last kingship ceremony. Before anyone realized she was serious, she stole one of their *cayucos,* their mahogany dugout canoes, and headed down the Rio Tigre." His eyes had turned completely dark, the way he used to blank them out. "She just went missing. Everyone here was devastated. We all loved her."

I stood there weighing his story. It didn't ring true. I supposed she was capable of something that crazy, but would she have actually done it? I didn't think so.

Then I remembered something else he'd said.

"You said you proposed an 'agreement.' What was that about?"

He stared at me. "It's nothing that need concern us. Suffice to say I kept my part. Anyway, it's over and past now."

Why wouldn't he tell me? Did she make some bargain with the Devil?

"But regarding Sarah," he went on, "I only just learned she'd been found and brought to New York in a coma. Wanting to do what I could, I immediately called the hospital and, out of professional courtesy, they told me she'd shown early stages of coming out of it, but she appeared to be hallucinating. It was exactly what I'd feared. . . ." His voice trailed off. "I hope I did the right thing, but when I learned she'd been released, I arranged for her to be brought back here, where perhaps I can do something for her."

"What?"

"In rare cases, the hallucinogen she took permanently alters critical synapses in the brain. I'm fearful she may have abused it to the extent something like that could have occurred. No one in the U.S. would have the slightest idea what to do, but I think I may know of an herbal antidote they turned to in ancient times that can repair at least part of the damage. I also knew that getting her back here through normal channels would be impossible."

"So you had Colonel Ramos and a bunch of his Guatemalan thugs just break in and take her?" I didn't know which part of the story horrified, and angered, me the most.

"I have the misfortune to know him reasonably well, and

I explained it was very important to me, and he agreed to assist. I honestly didn't know where else to turn. I understand there may have been some violence, for which I apologize, but these people have their own way of doing things." He rose and came over and put his hand on my shoulder. "I hope you'll understand."

The son of a bitch was coming on oily and contrite, when he'd just subcontracted an outright kidnapping. I wanted to kill him.

Finally I walked away, trying to get a grip on my anger.

"You know, that bastard also broke into my apartment and stole a reel of a picture I'm shooting." I turned back. "I've also got a strong feeling he's the one who just threatened one of the women I filmed."

"Well, if that happened, then let me say welcome to the paranoid harassment of the Guatemalan high command." He sighed against the morning sound of birds chirping all around us. "Unfortunately, I gather they've assumed you're documenting the operations of Children of Light in some way, doing a movie." His eyes drifted off into space, as though seeking a refuge. "You see, my project up here in the Peten is to carry out pharmaceutical research with as few distractions as possible. But in Guatemala City, I have what is, in effect, a hospice for girls in trouble—which is also called Niños del Mundo, by the way—that's connected with my U.S. adoption service, Children of Light. However, any time Niños del Mundo takes in an orphaned or abandoned infant and tries to provide it with a loving home through adoption in the States, the government here always threatens to hold up the paperwork if I don't give a bribe, what they call an 'expediting fee.' So if you were to probe too deeply . . . Let me just say it's not something they'd care to see lead off *60 Minutes.*"

It sounded like more BS, but I couldn't prove that. Yet.

"Well, why don't you just clear that up, and then I'll take Sarah and—"

"But I've only now initiated her treatment. Surely you want to give it a chance."

I looked out at the rain forest. This was the place she'd come to once, and—though I'd never admit it to Alex Goddard—it was the place she'd announced she wanted to return to. But something devastating had happened to her mind here. What should I do?

The fact was, I didn't trust Alex Goddard any farther than I could throw him. I had to get Sarah and get us both out of here as soon as possible, though that meant I'd have to neutralize him *and* the Army, and then use my limited American dollars to try to buy our way back to Guatemala City.

"But come." He turned his gaze toward the south. "Let me show you the thing I'm proudest of here. It's just up there." He was pointing toward a dense section of the rain forest, in the opposite direction from the river and up a steep incline.

I couldn't see anything but trees, but then I still had the feeling I'd stepped through the looking glass and found Sarah trapped there. The next thing I knew, we were on an uphill forest trail, headed due south.

"I think it's time you told me what's going on back there in the village," I said. What was it about this place that had seized such a claim on Sarah's mind?

"Baalum is difficult to explain to someone encountering it for the first time." He paused. "Much of it is so—"

"I think I can handle it."

"You have every right to know, but I don't really know where to start."

"How about the beginning?" Why was he being so ambiguous?

"Very well." He was taking out a pair of gray sunglasses,

as though to gain time. "It actually goes back about ten years ago, when I was prospecting for rain-forest plants up here in the Peten and accidentally stumbled across this isolated village, which clearly had been here since classical times. I immediately noticed a huge mound of dirt everybody said was haunted by 'the Old Ones,' and I knew right away it had to be a buried pyramid. They're more common down here than you'd think. So I struck a bargain with the village elders and acquired the site. But after I unearthed it and began the restoration, I became inspired with a vision. One day I found myself offering to restore anything else they could find—which eventually included, by the way, a magnificent old steam bath—in exchange for which they would help me by undertaking a grand experiment, a return to their traditional way of life."

"So you deliberately closed them off to the modern world?" It told me Alex Goddard could control a Mayan village just as he controlled everything else he touched. It also confirmed he had a weakness for the grandiose gesture. Would a time come when I could exploit that?

"I told them that together we would try to recreate the time of their glory, and perhaps in so doing we could also rediscover its long-lost spirit, and wisdom. On the practical side, they would help me by bringing me the rare plants I needed to try and rediscover the lost Native American pharmacologies, and in return I would build them a clinic where families can come for modern pediatric and public-health services. So Baalum became a project we share together. I call it a miracle."

That still didn't begin to explain why it felt so eerie. Something else was going on just under the surface. What was he *really* doing here?

Then the path uphill abruptly opened onto a clearing in which sat a large two-story building, its color a dazzling white, most likely plaster over cinder block, with a thatch roof and a wide, ornate mahogany door at the front. The building was nestled in a grove of trees whose vines and tendrils had embraced it so thoroughly, there was no telling how far it extended back into the forest. There also was a parking lot, paved and fed by a well-maintained gravel road leading south.

Seeing it, I felt an immediate wave of relief. Even better, the lot itself contained half-a-dozen well-worn pickup trucks, while sunburned Maya men were lounging in the shade of a nearby tree and smoking cigarettes. They were not from Baalum. They wore machine-made clothes and they were speaking Spanish, unlike the men in loincloths down in the village.

Yes! That's how I can get us out of here. A few dollars . . .

Parked there also was a tan Humvee, the ultimate all-road vehicle, which I assumed belonged to Alex Goddard. Maybe I should just try to steal it.

As we passed through the door and into the vestibule of the building, I glimpsed a cluster of Maya women and children crowded into a brilliantly lit reception area. Goddard smiled and waved at them, and several nodded back, timorously and with enormous reverence. They were being attended by a dark-eyed, attractive Maya woman in a blue uniform—the name lettered on her blouse was Marcelina—who was holding a tray of vials and hypodermic needles. She was pure *indigena,* all of five feet tall, with broad cheekbones and deep-set penetrating eyes. Unlike the other women in the room, however, there was no air of resignation about her. She was full of authority, a palpable inner fire.

"One of my most successful programs here"—he nodded a greeting to her—"is to provide free vaccinations and general health resources for the villages in this part of the Peten Department."

"I thought USAID already had public-health projects in Guatemala." The sight deeply depressed me. They all looked so poignant, the women with their shabby *huipils* and lined faces, the children even more disheartening, sad waifs with runny noses and watery eyes.

Which confirmed again that they'd come in the pickups parked outside, driven here by the men.

I had six hundred cash in dollars. I could just *buy* one of those worn-out junkers for that.

Alex Goddard glanced around, as though reluctant to respond in the presence of all the Maya.

"You saw those 'security guards' down there just now. They're nothing but boys with guns, 'recruits' kidnapped by the government on market day and pressed into the Army. They're all around here. The powers that be in Guatemala City are very threatened by what I'm achieving, so they've got these Army kids hanging around, keeping an eye on me. They also hate the fact I can provide health services better than they can. But to answer your question, most of the AID money gets soaked up by the bureaucracy in Guatemala City, so the people up here have learned to rely on me. The Army, however, despises me and everything I'm doing."

What a load of BS. You just admitted you had an inside track with Colonel Alvino Ramos. Anybody can see Children of Light or Niños del Mundo, or whatever the hell other aliases you use, is thick as thieves with the Guatemalan Armed Forces. Don't insult my intelligence. It just makes me furious.

I turned to Marcelina. She'd begun passing out hard-sugar candies to the mesmerized children, showing them how to remove the cellophane before putting them into their mouths. Though she was pure Maya, she looked educated. I instinctively liked her. Maybe *she* could tell me what was really going on here.

"Do you speak English?"

"Yes." She was gazing at me with a blend of curiosity and concern. "If—"

"I've got a procedure scheduled shortly," Goddard interjected, urging me on down the tiled hallway. "But I need to take a moment and recharge. Come with me and we can talk some more."

Near the end of the hall, we entered a spacious, country-style kitchen. He walked over and opened the refrigerator.

"Care for a little something to eat?" He looked back, speckled white hair swinging across his shoulders as his ponytail came loose. "I had Marcelina whip up some gazpacho last night and I see there's some left. It's my own secret recipe, special herbs from around here. It's good *and* good for you."

"I'm not hungry." It wasn't true. I was growing ravenous. But I was repressing the feeling because of everything else that was going on. His "village" was holding back its secrets, and now his clinic of "miracles" also felt suspiciously wrong. I'd seen plenty of rural public-health operations in developing countries, and *this* setup was far too big and fancy. The whole thing didn't begin to compute.

"As you like." He gave an absent shrug.

I looked around and noticed that just off the kitchen was another space, which was, I realized, his private dining room. There was a rustic table in the center that looked like it had been carved from the trunk of a large Cebia tree. I walked in, and moments later he followed carrying a tray with two calabash bowls of gazpacho and some crusty bread.

"In case you change your mind and decide to join me." He placed a bowl opposite where he was planning to sit. "Like I said, there're unusual herbs around here with flavors you've never dreamed of."

He began eating, while behind him I glimpsed Marcelina

moving down the hall, carrying more trays of vaccine and headed out toward the vestibule again. I had to find a way to talk to her.

As I settled into the rickety chair that faced my plate, I glanced down and saw a red lumpy mixture with a spray of undefinable green specks across the top like a scattering of jungle stars. No way.

When I looked up again, he was swabbing his lips with a white napkin, his penetrating eyes boring in.

"Now," he said, "it's time we started concentrating on *you*. Got you going with your program."

Twenty-two

"My program?" I stared back at him, feeling a jolt. With my thoughts completely focused on Sarah, the last thing on my mind was my own baby.

"Now that you're here"—he smiled—"there's no reason we shouldn't proceed. This is, after all, a place of miracles."

Right. You let Sarah destroy her mind and now you want me to . . .

Don't even *think* about it.

"I have to tell you, I'm not overly impressed thus far with your 'program,' " I said. "First I passed out in your clinic, and then my doctor in New York told me those drugs Ramala gave me are highly illegal, and for good reason."

"What is 'legal' is more often than not the judgment of medical reactionaries." He dismissed the issue with a wave of his hand. "My work has moved far beyond anything the FDA has ever dreamed of." Then his look turned grave. "I hope you'll give me a chance to try to help you. I've been giving your case a lot of thought since our first examination, about what we should do. But first let me ask you . . . do you have a partner who could come here soon?"

Okay, maybe the thing to do was appear to play along for a while, move under his radar, and *then* get Sarah and split.

"It's a possibility."

He smiled again. "Excellent. If this person can come here

to the clinic for a . . . deposit, then we could put you on a fast-track schedule."

"One thing at a time. First I'd like to know exactly what it is you have in mind." Would his "program" include stringing me out on the toad drug, the way he'd done with Sarah?

"Of course." He leaned forward in his chair. "I believe that, given your history, an in-vitro procedure would have the highest chance of success. You undoubtedly know how it works. We remove a number of eggs by aspiration and grade them for maturity and viability, after which we fertilize them to begin embryos growing. Then we pick the most promising for implantation."

"In vitro is invasive and dangerous and there's a lot that can go wrong." I genuinely hated the idea.

"To some extent." He examined his watch for a moment, then looked up. "But let me just say this. Since any reproductive therapy, particularly in vitro, is strongly dependent on the factor of timing, I've developed experimental compounds down here that can regulate egg maturities very precisely. It minimizes a lot of uncertainties, which is why we're so lucky you're . . ." He paused. "Look, the first thing we need to do is put you on a strict regimen of diet and spiritual discipline, using my system for regulating your Chi, your energy flows. Then, if you respond, we can start thinking about the procedure. And should you eventually decide you want to go ahead and you can have your partner come here, we could possibly have everything done in just a few days."

"Well, you can forget about me taking any 'experimental compounds.'" How long could I stall him?

"Morgan, there's more to this." His look grew pained. "It's awkward to bring it up, but your presence here creates no small difficulty for me. I told you certain people in the military high command have concerns about the film you're making. And then the next thing they know, you show up here. It's just going to heighten their paranoia. But if I can convince them you're here for fertility treatment . . . In any case, it's important that nothing you, or I, do is at odds with that presumption. I hope it's true, but even if you chose to forgo it, I still need to put you on my normal regimen. You understand."

That's baloney. Somebody had me brought to Baalum. Whoever did it knows full well why I'm here. The problem is, I still don't know what they really want.

"Well, you can say I've come to take Sarah home," I told him. "That seems reason enough."

"The other story is simpler to explain." He took a last bite of gazpacho, then rested his pewter spoon on the table. "Take my word for it."

"And what if I don't choose to go along with this charade?"

"We would both be in jeopardy. They're entirely capable of . . . things I'd rather not have to elaborate on."

I sat there, feeling a chill envelop the room. *How* was I going to get out of this place?

"By the way, a while ago Sarah mentioned something about a 'ceremony.' What's that—?"

"It's a special time here." His gaze shifted to the ceiling. "In fact, it's supposed to take place in three days, but the Army has informed me it has to be two days from now. That's the day they rotate the troops here, so there'll be double strength."

"But why do they need—"

"Things can get a bit frenzied." He smiled, though he seemed to be embarrassed. "However, the people will love the fact you're here to share it with them."

Did he say "frenzied"? My mind immediately flashed on the Aztec rituals of ripping out beating hearts. But the Maya didn't go to that extreme, at least so far as I knew. Once again, though, I had the feeling I was only hearing what he wanted me to know, not the whole truth. It felt like a chess game where I didn't know the location of all the pieces or how they could move.

"Tell you what." He was getting up, turning toward the hall. "Why don't you let me show you around the clinic? In fact, I'm scheduled to perform an in vitro this morning for a childless couple here. You're free to see it. Perhaps that could help you make your own decision."

"Well . . . do you have a phone? I need to make some calls." Would he let me call out? That would be a first test of what his intentions were. It was all getting so insidious. I had Sarah to worry about, and the Army, and now some kind of "ceremony" that he'd managed to stay cannily vague about. I only knew I wanted the whole world to know where I was.

"Of course," he said. "You're welcome to use my office." He was pointing down the hall. "It's right this way."

Yes! Maybe I'm not completely his prisoner yet. I still have privileges. But I'd damned well better use them while I can.

I walked out and felt a breeze, and then I studied the far end of the hallway, at the opposite end from the entrance, and noticed huge slatted windows. As we walked in their direction, I realized there was a stairway on one side, at the end of the hall, leading up to the second story of the building.

"What's up there?"

"Hygenic nursery rooms." He glanced at the stairs. "Unlike U.S. practice, new mothers here aren't sent home after a day or two. Women and their newborns are encouraged to stay here at the clinic for at least a week. It's actually very much a part of their tradition, a period of bonding. You're welcome to visit with them later if you like."

I intended to. In fact, I found myself looking around and

trying to memorize everything about the place. A two-story building, a marble stair, a nursery upstairs, downstairs rooms along either side of the hallway (what was in them?), and an office I was about to see. Could the clinic be locked down? What were the escape routes? How closely was the Army watching? The time would come, I was sure, when I'd need every scrap of intelligence I could collect.

When we reached the end of the hall, the fresh cool wind still blowing against my face, he stopped in front of a large, ornate wooden door with a brass knob in the very center. There was no sign of a lock, just a sense of great gravity about its purpose.

"The phone's in here." He pushed the door and it slowly swung inward on hinges that must have required ball bearings.

It was indeed an office, dimly lighted by the moving screen-savers of two computers, each on a separate desk. He flicked on the overhead lights and I noticed that one computer was hooked to a fax machine, the other to a separate printer. An impressive assembly of data-management technology for out here in the rain forest.

Then I focused on the central desk, on which sat an open, briefcase-looking box containing a mini-console labeled Magellan World Phone. A small satellite dish was bolted down next to it.

"It uplinks to the Inmarsat Series 3 geostationary satellites." He indicated the dish. "But it works like a regular phone. The international codes all apply." Then he turned to leave. "I should be ready for the procedure in a few minutes."

I picked up the handset and flicked it on. Three green diodes flashed, then two yellow ones, after which a white light came on and I heard a continuous hum, a dial tone.

Hooray. But was his satellite phone tapped? Why would

he let me just call out? Was this a feint in our game of cat-and-mouse, just to lull me into believing everything here was safe and benign? Remembering Sarah's drug experience, I already knew that couldn't be true. For now, though, I had to get an SOS out while I had the chance.

I'd long since memorized the number of Steve's hotel in Belize City, and if I could reach him, he could go the embassy in Guatemala City and . . . I wasn't sure what. I still hoped to get out of here on my own, but if that failed . . . maybe some of those sturdy Marines . . .

When I dialed the Belize number, however, the phone just rang and rang.

Come on. Somebody *please* pick up.

Then they did. Thank goodness. But when I asked for Steve . . .

"So sorry, mon," came the proud Caribbean voice, "but Mr. Abrams check out Monday. Early in the morning."

"Right, I know that. But he came back last night, didn't he?"

"No, mon. He say he be coming back, to hold his room, but—"

"He didn't come back?" I felt my palms go icy. *Who* was going to know where Sarah and I were? "What do you mean?"

"He not coming back here, mon." The man paused and mumbled something to another clerk, then came back on. "Nobody seen him since. You want leave a message, that's okay. But I don't know when—"

"No." I didn't know what to say. The implication was only gradually sinking in. "No message. Thanks anyway. I'll try back later."

"Any time, mon. No problem."

I hung up, trying to stay calm. Steve, where *are* you?

Okay, I told myself, you don't actually *know* something's

wrong. It could be anything. Still, it was very worrying. Steve, my one and only . . .

I was staring at the phone, wondering what my next move should be.

Whatever else, I've got to try to reach Lou, tell him I've found Sarah. But then what? He certainly wasn't going to be any help in getting us out. If he blundered his way down here, there was a real chance he'd misread the delicacy of the situation and end up getting us all "disappeared" by the Army. But still, I had to tell him about her.

I picked up the handset again, keyed in the U.S. country code, and tried the number for his place in Soho. He'd said he was going to be released from St. Vincent's today, so maybe he was home by now.

The familiar ring jangled half a dozen times and then . . .

"Crenshaw residence." It was the Irish tones of Mrs. Reilly, Sarah's day nurse. Hallelujah. I guessed she was there now taking care of Lou.

"Uh, this is Morgan James. Mr. Crenshaw's niece. Remember? I came by. Is he home yet? I need to talk to him."

"He's resting, dear. I was just about to go out and get some things, milk and soup and the like."

"So . . . dare I ask? How is he?"

"He's weak, but I think he's going to be fine. If people will just let him be."

"Look, I hate to bother him, but it's really an emergency. I'm calling from Guatemala."

"Oh. I truly don't know if he's awake, dear. He was napping a while ago."

"Could you . . . could you go and see? Please. And take the phone?"

"Just a minute." She sounded reluctant, but I could hear her movements as she shuffled across the loft. I listened, wondering how long Alex Goddard was going to be away, and then a moment later . . .

"Yeah." There was a rustle as Lou got a grip on his cordless. "Morgan, is that you? Where the hell are you now?"

It took me a second to even find my voice, I was so thrilled to hear him. He sounded just like always.

"Hey, how's it going, champ?" I said. Come on, Lou. *Get well*. Fight.

"I started having these migraines, but they gave me some medicine—"

"Listen." I cut him off, and immediately felt guilty I'd been so impatient. "I'm up in northern Guatemala and I've found Sarah."

"Oh, my God." That was followed by a long silence, probably an emotional meltdown. "Is she all right?"

What was I going to say? That she'd been brainwashed or worse by Alex Goddard? That we were both in his clutches, cut off from the world, and in deep, deep trouble?

"She's able to stand," I said.

I don't remember what white lies I eventually managed to tell him. I think it was something like, "She's being treated for a post-coma syndrome by a medical specialist. I've found out that when she was in Guatemala before, she was given some very bad drugs, and someone here who knows about them is trying to reverse some of the damage."

"Alex Goddard, right?" There was no BS-ing Lou for very long. "That bastard."

"Lou, I'm going to get her out of here and back home as soon as possible. Everything's going to be all right. Don't worry. It's really too complicated to try and explain over the phone."

"Yeah, well, I'm coming. Soon as I'm up. I'm gonna take that son of a bitch by the—"

"Don't. Don't you go anywhere. I'm *handling* it, okay?"

I heard him grunt, whether from pain or frustration I couldn't be sure. "Lou, listen, I'm going to try and phone you every day. If I miss a day, then you should call the embassy down here. Tell them you're FBI. That might get their attention. The place where I am, where Sarah is, is named Baalum. It's a . . . kind of village. In the northern Peten Department. I don't know if the U.S. has any clout up here, but that's where they should come looking."

I got him to write it down, and then eased him off the line as gently as I could and hung up. I would have loved for him to be here, but I wanted to try to get Sarah out by stealth if I could. And stealth was scarcely Lou's style.

My calls were one for two, and there still wasn't anybody to help me. The time had come to try David. I was having the glimmerings of a new strategy.

It was lunchtime in New York, but on Wednesdays he usually just had a sandwich at his desk. Maybe I could catch him.

"Hello," declared the British female voice he'd put on his machine, hoping it would sound like he had a classy secretary. "You've reached the office of David Roth, president of Applecore Productions. We're sorry Mr. Roth is not available at this time to—"

"David," I barked into the phone. "If you're there, *pick up.* This is Morgan. I've got to talk to you."

While the announcement kept running, noises erupted outside in the hall, voices and a clicking sound, as though something was being rolled along the tile floor. Shit. Was Alex Goddard about to walk in? My mouth went dry. Come on, David, I know you're there, hiding—*Variety* with a tuna salad on rye, extra pickle. Dr. Brown's Cel-Ray soda.

"David, damnit, pick up." I said it quieter this time, but I could feel my heart pounding. "This is an emergency."

"Morgy, don't!" He yelled as I heard the receiver being

lifted. "Jesus, I just walked in from the deli. Listen, thank God it's you. Drop whatever the hell you're not doing and get your butt in here. Jerry Reiner called, you know, the Orion distribution deal—and he wants a rough cut of *Baby Love* yesterday so he can pitch it to the suits on the fifth floor. We could be staring at financial success here. I hope you can handle the vulgarity of that."

"David, you're not going to believe where I am," I began, working out my game plan as I went along, trying to sound cool and control my racing pulse. "I'm in northern Guatemala, at a place that would make a terrific feature. It's like a Maya theme park, deep in the rain forest. But it's real. I want you to contact the embassy and get them to grease the way for my crew to come here. This is too good to pass up." I thought about the costs and then added, "At least one camera and sound."

One sure way to get Sarah out was to blow the place open to the world.

"What's . . . Where are you again?"

I gave him a glowing trailer of the Williamsburg-like qualities of Baalum—a beautiful, exciting recreation of times gone by that out-Disneyed Disney. The cable channels would be bidding for the footage.

"Hey, look, all things in time." He wasn't buying. "I'm talking an actual deal here. You know, money? Fuck the jungle wonderland. You've got exactly one more day down there on the Tarzan set, or wherever the hell it is, and then I'm gonna start finishing final cut on this damned picture myself. Don't make me have to do that, Morgy. This is not a drill. Nicky Russo came by again yesterday. He's fully prepared to call our note and impound your original negative. It's here, under lock and key, but we've *got* to get this project in the can and sold."

"You touch a frame of my movie and I won't be responsible for my actions." God, he was missing my SOS. "David, do one thing for me, please. I can't tell you how important it is. I haven't explained everything. This situation is . . . It's very threatening. I need you to at least call the embassy down here and see if they'll send somebody. The Army's all over the place and—"

A loud noise intervened, followed by complete, absolute silence. The diodes on the panel all began flashing yellow.

"Shit!" Had Alex Goddard been listening in and decided to cut me off before I could get word to the embassy?

I slammed the box and went for the usual maneuver: I cut the connection and tried again, but nothing. Again, and still nothing.

My hands were trembling. I'd just lost contact with the outside world. I was completely isolated in the middle of nowhere.

How convenient. Alex Goddard let me tell a couple of people I was physically okay, and then he blocked the line.

I exhaled, settled into the padded chair next to the computers, and tried to think. David, David, why wouldn't you *listen?* He was so excited he'd completely ignored my distress signal. Nobody was going to come and help me get out of here.

I gazed around the room, wondering what to do next. Was there another phone, a radio, a box of flares, for godsake?

That was when I spotted the outlines of another door—why hadn't I noticed it sooner?—this one steel, there on the left. Alex Goddard might walk in any second now, but I had to try to learn everything I could as fast as I could. What was going on besides what was going on?

Alert for any new sounds from outside, I quickly went over and tried the knob.

It was locked tight.

Figured. Now I really wanted to know what was in there.

When I glanced around the office, I noticed a ring of keys on the desk. Could he have forgotten them?

More important, would I blow everything if he caught me snooping? In spite of his attempt at a cool veneer, he might go ballistic.

I made a snap decision. Take the chance and give them a try.

My hands were so moist I had trouble holding the slippery keys, but finally I managed to shove in the first one. It went in, but nothing would turn.

Come *on.* I managed to wiggle the next one in, my hand trembling now, but again the knob wouldn't budge. Footsteps outside marched up to the door and I stopped breathing, but then they moved on.

Hurry. I was rapidly losing hope when the fifth one slipped in and the knob turned. Yes!

Taking a deep breath and working on a story in case Alex Goddard walked in, I clicked the lock and eased the door inward just enough to look inside.

Hello, what's this? The space was a fully equipped medical research lab. The lights were off, but like the office, it was illuminated by the glow of several CRT screens stationed above a long lab bench. There also was a large machine, probably a gas chromatograph, with its own screen, flanked by rows of test tubes. Finally, there was a large electronic microscope complete with video screen.

One nonmedical thing stood out, though: There in the middle of the workbench was a two-foot-high bronze Dancing Shiva presiding over whatever was going on. It was breathtakingly beautiful.

So . . . what was The Lord of the Dance giving his blessing to? Time to try and find out.

Now clanking noises were filtering in from out in the hall,

along with the pounding of heavy boots, and my pulse jumped again. Was the Army coming to drag me away?

Just go in. Do it.

The CRT screens were attached to black metal containers, their doors closed, that all were connected to a power supply, doubtless to maintain some temperature. It looked like Goddard was incubating something in a carefully controlled environment. The whole arrangement was very carefully organized and laid out.

Finally I noticed a row of large steel jugs, six in all, near the back and covered with a sheet of black plastic, thin like a wrap. What could they be? Some kind of special gas for use in the lab?

Voices in Spanish drifted in from the hallway. A woman and a man were arguing about something.

Okay, get out of here. Come back and check this out when nobody's around.

I stepped back into the office, clicked off the thumb latch on the door so it wouldn't lock, and closed it. I realized I was pouring sweat.

What next? Well, see if the phone's working again and try calling the Camino Real and see if Steve's come back there for some reason, maybe a change in plans. It would be a long shot, but still . . .

My hand was shaking as I opened up the phone case. Thank God, the diodes were all quiet. Maybe . . .

The steel door I'd closed only moments before swung open and Alex Goddard walked through. Did he realize I'd left it unlocked? How did he get in there? Was there another door?

He'd changed clothes and was wearing a pale blue surgical gown. I shut the phone case, as though just finishing with it. Could he tell I'd turned myself into a nervous wreck? I tried to smile and look normal, but my shirt was soaking.

"Ah, I see you're finished," he said, not seeming to notice.

"Good. As I said, I've got an in-vitro procedure scheduled now for one of the couples here in the village. You're welcome to observe. It might help you decide what you want to do in your own case." He was moving across the room. "You can watch on the closed circuit."

He reached up and snapped on a monitor bolted to the wall in the corner.

"Oh, just one small word of forewarning." He was turning back. "Down here I've made certain . . . cosmetic changes in the procedure to keep patients' anxiety levels as low as possible. It wouldn't be appropriate in your case, but . . . well, you'll see."

Before I had time to wonder what he meant, he disappeared back through the steel door with a reassuring smile.

Twenty-three

The monitor's picture was in color, but the predominant hue was brown. Where was this? The OR had to be somewhere in the clinic, but still . . .

The space looked flawlessly sterile, obviously an operating theater, but it was certainly like none other on earth. The walls were not white or pale blue; they had the shade of stone and were decorated with Maya picture writing and bas-reliefs. It was as though a sacred chapel had been converted into a surgery. I guessed this was what he meant by "cosmetic changes." A door was visible on the right side of the screen, and moments later Alex Goddard strode through, coming in from the hallway.

So, it must be right next door. God, the place looked ancient and haunted.

I watched as he walked over to a basin and scrubbed his hands, then donned a white surgical mask. Next he flipped various switches on the walls. Finally he put on a second mask that glistened like some green crystaline material.

What was that for? Then it hit me. A "jade" mask . . .

That was something Sarah had mentioned in her ramblings. So she must have seen this too. Which meant . . . not everything she described was just some drug-induced hallucination. The mask part was very real. . . .

Now Marcelina was rolling a steel operating table, bearing a dark-haired Maya woman, through the doorway. The patient looked like all the others down in Baalum, except that she had a strange expression on her face. She appeared to be tense and very afraid, as her eyes kept darting around the room, then to the "jade" mask Alex Goddard was wearing— most likely papier-mâché covered with shiny green granules.

When she was in position, he walked to the corner and flipped another switch, whereupon there started the deep droning of a chant, probably from speakers in the walls, that sounded like Kekchi Maya.

He bent over her and said something in the same language, after which Marcelina placed a rubber mask over her nose and mouth. Her eyes still frightened, the patient uttered a few words, perhaps a final prayer, then inhaled deeply. As her eyelids fluttered, he turned and opened what appeared to be some kind of stone tableau, covered by its own bas-relief. It was, I finally realized, merely painted fiberglass—that was what the whole room was—and inside were CRT monitors designed to display various vital life functions. As Marcelina helped him, he began attaching sensors to the patient's body.

When the woman's eyes had fully closed, he removed his green mask and tossed it into a box.

It's all fake. The room, everything. Just like Baalum. But now he's got Sarah's mind caught in his thrall. I've got to make her understand nothing here is real.

Marcelina was carefully watching the screens, her apprehension obvious as she fiddled uncertainly with the knobs.

"Oxygen steady." Her voice was small and uneasy. "EKG stable."

He immediately stripped away the sheet that had been covering the patient. Beneath it was an open-sided gown colored in brilliant stripes of red and blue. He pulled it back with absent precision, then turned to Marcelina.

"Shave her and scrub her."

With the woman now under sedation, Marcelina put on

her own surgical garb: She pulled a blue plastic cap over her hair, then secured a white OR mask over her face. While she was finishing the preparations, he turned and walked to the far side of the room, where he abruptly seemed to disappear through the wall.

What . . . There must be a panel there, a camouflaged door.

He was gone for a moment, then reappeared carrying a long metal tube that looked to be emitting white vapor. He next opened yet another ersatz stone cabinet to reveal a microscope with a CRT screen above it. He took out three glass ampules from the tube—frozen embryos, undoubtedly—and placed them in a container. When he switched on the microscope, its CRT screen showed him whatever he needed to know. Interesting. In surgery, he was coldly efficient, no "human touch." Here he was the "scientist" Alex Goddard.

Next, Marcelina activated an ultrasound scanner and began running the wand over the woman's stomach. The screen above the table showed her uterus and her Fallopian tubes with flickering clarity.

He'd been readying the embryos, and now he walked over and carefully inserted a needle into the woman's abdomen—ouch—his eyes on the ultrasound scan, which indicated the precise location of the needle's tip.

I watched as the screen showed the needle on its way to its destination, a thin, hard line amidst the pulsing gray mass of her uterus. Seconds later all three embryos had been implanted with such flawless precision it was scary.

Did I want to undergo this deeply invasive procedure at the hands of Alex Goddard? The very thought left a dull ache in my stomach.

While Marcelina bandaged her and began preparing her for return to wherever she'd been, he turned off the systems, then closed their "stone" cabinets.

I thought back to some of the "hallucinations" Sarah had poured out. She'd mentioned the green mask, and she'd also relived some sinister event that seemed to her like disappearing down a long white tunnel. Was that her own anesthesia? Did he perform an in vitro on her too?

I jumped as I heard the "bump, thump, bump" sound of the operating table being rolled out of the OR and back down the hall. For some reason I thought of the sound of fate knocking on the door, like death coming to take Don Giovanni. Did Alex Goddard have plans to take *me*, only with drugs and medical sleight of hand? It wasn't going to happen.

I switched off the monitor and turned to stare at the computers. Why were they here in this "place of miracles"? What did they hold? Maybe *that* was where I should be. . . .

That was the moment when the heavy office door swung open and Marcelina appeared.

"Your room is ready now." Her English was heavily accented but sure. "He sent me to show you. And I can wash any of your things if you like."

My room? Whoa! Since when had I checked in?

"Marcelina, we need to talk. What happened to Sarah the last time she was here? Was she operated on like that woman just now?"

I also planned to ask her about all the bizarre trappings surrounding the procedure. Why was the woman so sucked in by his phony Mardi Gras mysticism? Had Sarah fallen for it too?

"*Sara* was one of the special ones. You are surely blessed too. You resemble her a lot." She looked at me, affection in her dark eyes, then turned and headed out the door. "But come, let me take you up."

Of course I resembled her; she was my cousin. But so

what? I didn't like the odd way she'd said it. And what about my question?

Watching her walk away, clearly nervous, I realized this was the moment I'd been dreading—when I had to make a decision about how far to play along with Alex Goddard. Steve couldn't be reached, yet, but I still might be able to handle the situation on my own. The first thing to do was to get down to Sarah and talk some sense into her. Then I had to arrange for a way to get us both out.

So . . . probably the best way to accomplish that was to go along with my own medical charade for a few more hours, to give me time to scout the scene and come up with a plan. A room would be a base to operate from.

Still, I was feeling plenty of trepidation as we ascended the marble steps to the second floor, which had a long, carpeted hallway with doors along each side. Then, when we started down the hall, I caught the sound of a baby crying.

"What's this floor for?" I remembered Alex Goddard had claimed it was to provide a postpartum bonding period, but I wanted to confirm that with my own eyes.

"This is the recovery ward and nursery. Here, let me show you." She paused and pushed open the door nearest us. I looked in to see a Mayan woman resting on a high hospital bed and wearing a white shift, with an ornate wicker cradle, wide and deep, next to her.

Marcelina smiled and said something to her that sounded like an apology for the intrusion. The room was lit only by candles, but I did make out how oddly the woman stared at me, as though she was seeing a spirit. Why was that? Because I was a *gringa* here in the middle of the forest? But it seemed something more.

"The birth of a child is a sacred thing for us." Marcelina was discreetly closing the door again. "When a woman carries a child she will take walks to the *milpas,* to the river, to the orchards, just so her little one can be in its world. Then, after her baby is born, our tradition holds that she should be alone with it for a week and a day. So their life's breath can become one."

I could sense her heart was deeply entwined with the people here at Baalum.

"Marcelina, how long have—?"

"Well, what do you think?" said a voice. I looked around to see Alex Goddard coming up the stairs behind us. And my anger welled up again. Everything about him was just too . . . manipulating.

He'd changed back to his black sweatshirt and jeans and was carrying a tray. The costume event was over. In an instant Marcelina slipped quietly around him and headed back down the stairs, almost like a rabbit startled by a fox. He smiled and moved past me.

"All those trappings just now, the fake green mask." I decided to challenge him head-on. Start *forcing* him to show his hand. "What's—?"

"Merely a little harmless theater." He looked back. "The forest Maya like to think they're being ministered to by a shaman." Then he indicated I should follow him. "By the way, in case you do get hungry, I brought you something you can have in your room if you like. Then you can make yourself at home and rest a bit."

Hold *on*. I was being given the illusion of freedom, but in reality I was nothing more than his prisoner.

"That room next to your office. With the steel door. What's in—?"

"That's the heart of Baalum." Pride in his voice. "The real reason I'm here."

"You mean drug research?"

He nodded. "Did you know the Central American rain forest easily contains a hundred thousand plant species? Over half of all pharmaceutical drugs are derived from plants, yet less than one percent of those here have been tested for pharmacological potential. Still, the old shamans and midwives all know of herbs they claim can cure everything from menstrual cramps to cancer." He smiled. "They also know which ones have powerful contraceptive properties, which is particularly helpful in my primary study, fertility and fetal viability. I take the specimens they bring and perform a rough screening in the lab to determine if they're actually pharmacologically active. If they do test positive, I then examine their effect on the blastocyst, the early form of embryonic cell formed just after fertilization, to see whether they affect cell division and viability and . . . the miscarriage rate here is very low, so some of these plants . . ." His voice trailed off as he pushed open the door of a suite at the end of the hall. It had a stone floor, a simple bed, and through the slatted windows the light of midday filtered through, along with the birdcalls of the rain forest. Any other time and place, I'd have felt like I was staying at a rustic nature retreat.

But this wasn't some other time and place. And what about Steve? Where *was* he? Maybe he was somewhere worse. Thinking about him, I was startled to hear myself say . . .

"Incidentally, I found out the man I've been trying to have a baby with didn't show up at his hotel in Belize last night. He was driving there from Guatemala City. I'm very worried. I keep hearing about how people get 'disappeared' in this country. He's—"

"Could his name be Steve Abrams?" Goddard turned back, still holding the tray.

It was a moment that stopped my heart. For a second I wasn't even able to speak.

"How . . . did you know?" I finally managed to say. "I never mentioned—"

"That's the name they gave me. I received a call this morning from Guatemala City. From Colonel Ramos's office, in fact. As you might suppose, he's well aware you're here, and he said you were seen dining night before last at a downtown restaurant with a man by that name. They think he's in the country because of you, and they're trying to locate him."

I felt the life go entirely out of me. My God, what was going on? Steve was now the subject of a manhunt in a police state. Did he even know?

"I told them you were here for purely medical reasons." He sighed with frustration. "And that they were being irrationally paranoid, but . . ."

"So they don't actually know where he is, right?" I was still trying to breathe.

"As of this morning. If they did, they wouldn't have called up here." He walked over and set the tray down on a rustic table next to the bed. "I wouldn't worry too much about it. He's committed no crime. They just want to make sure you realize your presence has not gone unnoticed."

Dear God. What had I dragged Steve into? If they found him, what would they do? I could only pray he was deft enough to elude them. If anybody could . . .

Then I looked at the tray. An empty syringe was there. Also, there was a large bowl containing some kind of soup. I was finally growing ravenous, but still . . .

"What's this for?" I indicated the syringe.

"I just need to take a little blood for some tests. Don't worry, it won't hurt a bit."

Hold on. How far do I have to play along to stay in his chess game?

Then I glanced down again at the tray. "And what's in that bowl?"

"Right now diet is crucial, so I've had Marcelina prepare you a healthy broth of soy extract and buckwheat and rain forest herbs that—"

"What kind of 'rain-forest herbs' exactly?" I was starving, but no way in hell—

"Medicinal ones. Part of your program of wholeness." He turned, with that faraway look of his, and opened the window slats. Beyond them I could see foliage, now alive with flocks of multicolored birds. The forest was in full cry. "You know, so many drugs are waiting to be discovered up here." He was gazing out. "Beyond this window is a giant pharmacy, but if it goes like the rest of the Peten, it'll soon be bulldozed to make way for more cattle ranches."

He came back and picked up the syringe. That was when I noticed it didn't seem to be entirely empty. It appeared to contain traces of a yellow substance, though maybe I was imagining. . . .

"Look, about the blood test. I don't think—"

"Consider it a free medical screening." He firmly gripped my arm as he plunged the needle into a vein. Seconds later he was capping off the syringe, red with my blood. "I'm running a batch of tests this afternoon, so one more sample won't make any difference."

While he swabbed my arm with alcohol, I looked down again at the bowl of broth he'd brought. Forget about it. I'd find something in the kitchen later.

"I want to go down and see Sarah." Get started immediately. Push and maybe I could catch him off guard. "I'm very worried about her."

"Of course." He nodded. "Whenever you wish."

"I was thinking, as soon as possible."

"Then I'll send Marcelina to take you, the minute she's finished downstairs. But I assumed you might want to at least unpack first."

With that he disappeared as quietly as he'd come.

I walked over and stared out at the birds flitting past the slatted window, feeling my hopes go up. The colors and the freedom. I wanted to be one of them, to take Sarah and just fly away. . . .

Then, feeling vaguely drowsy, I settled myself down on the edge of the bed. The next thing I knew, though, the chaotic music of the birds had begun to sound amplified, as though they were swirling down a long, echoing hallway. In spite of myself, I felt my consciousness begin to drift.

Shit, that needle he just slammed into my arm. It wasn't to take blood, you idiot. You suspected that, but he was too fast. Shit. Shit. Shit. Don't let him do it. *Stay awake.*

But now the tunnel was growing. I pulled myself up and staggered in slow motion to the door and tried it, but it seemed to be locked. I couldn't really tell, though, because the tunnel was swallowing me.

No! I banged my head against the door, hoping the pain would bring me back, but the room just swirled even more.

The tunnel. Now it was all around me, shadowy and dim. I thought I glimpsed Sarah at the end of it, wearing a white shift, beckoning me, but when I reached out for her, to take us away, all I could touch was empty mist.

Twenty-four

I'm on a bed, in a dreamscape room enveloped in pastel fog, watching a Melania butterfly the size of a man pump his massive orange and black wings above me. His voice is mellifluous, hypnotic, and I feel the soft wind of his wings against my face, cooling, scented, enveloping. It is the softness of eternal peace.

"Your body is a realm of fertility," he is saying, his tones echoing in the shadowy haze around me, sonorous and caring. "You are special." Then, iridescent blues and purples shimmering off his wings, his face evolves into the orange and black mask of a jaguar. "You are one of the special ones. Together we will create life."

Did he say "special"? Marcelina said I was . . . like Sarah . . .

Now his eyes are boring in and I'm thinking of the Chinese . . . Am I human, dreaming I'm a butterfly, or am I a butterfly dreaming I'm human?

As he moves over me, the rest of his butterfly form disappears and he's become a lithe jaguar whose lips are touching mine. The sheet over me melts into my skin as the soft spotted fur of his underbelly presses onto me. And his face has turned even more feline and sensuous, with dark eyes that look directly through me. I can feel his whiskers against me as he sniffs down my body, then explores my groin with his probing tongue.

Before I realize what's happening, his thighs press against mine and he knowingly insinuates himself into me. It all happens so naturally and effortlessly I scarcely . . . I see only an intense twitch of his animal ears, erect and directed toward me, as he enfolds me completely, his hot male breath urgent. As he grinds his thighs against mine, he emits growls, low in his throat, then nips lightly and lovingly at my cheek, his pale fangs benign and delicious.

I cling to him, bathed in sweat, falling into him, wanting him, but now . . .

He's changing. . . . My God. No! He's . . .

His face is becoming a jade mask with eyes that burn a fiery red, a spirit of evil. He's plunging something deep into me, metal, cold and cutting. Far inside, reaching, while my mind fights through the waves of pain that course down my lower body. I struggle back, but my arms just pass through empty air. *Stop.* The eyes, the hard metal . . . Time turns fluid, minutes are hours, lost, and I don't know . . .

Finally—it could be years later—he growls one last time and the room begins fading to darkness. Then a blessed numbness washes over me. He's gone. . . .

And I dream I am dead.

Sometime, probably hours later, I sensed my consciousness gradually returning. Around me the room was still dark and, remembering the "dream," I came fully awake with a start, my heart pounding. What had . . . *it* done to me? I was shivering, with a piercing, pointed ache in my groin. I needed air.

I rose up unsteadily and reached out, and realized I was in a hospital bed with metal bars along one side.

What! How did I come to be in this? Then I began remembering. I was at Baalum, in Alex Goddard's Niños del Mundo clinic. And I'd been trying to get Sarah and take her home.

Instead, I'd passed out and then . . . an attack, some unspeakably evil . . .

Get out of here. *Now.*

I settled my feet onto the floor with a surge of determination, and that was when I sensed I was in a different place from where I'd . . . Where—!

I gazed around in the dark, then reached out and felt something on a table beside the bed. It was a clay bowl full of wax. What . . . a candle. And next to it I touched a plain book of matches. My hand was trembling from the pain in my groin, but I managed to light the candle, a flickering glow.

My wristwatch was lying nearby on the table. Someone must have taken it off and placed it there. I picked it up and held it by the candle, and for a moment I was confused by the seconds ticking off. Then I realized the time was . . . How could that be! It read 4:57 A.M. Had I been out for hours?

I gasped, then raised the candle and gazed around. The walls were brown stone—or maybe they just looked like stone. Yes, now I recognized it. I was in the fiberglass-walled operating room I'd seen on Alex Goddard's closed-circuit monitor.

What was I doing in *here?*

My arm brushed against the table and I felt an odd sensation. Glancing down, I realized there was a Band-Aid on the inside of my left wrist. What was that about? Earlier he'd taken blood from my right arm, but then he'd just swabbed it off, so why this bandage? And what in hell was I doing in an operating room? I hadn't agreed to any procedures. Did he come back for a second—?

Or . . . *that* was what he'd done. He'd injected me with an IV drug. The bizarre vision I'd had was his cover for some perverse invasion of my body. My God, I'd been unconscious since yesterday afternoon. During all that time, what could he have done to me?

I was fist-clenching furious. Looking around the "operating room," I wanted to rip the place apart.

When I tried to stand, I realized my groin was tender and sore as hell, all across my panty-line, only somewhere deep, deep inside, in my reproductive . . . It was like after he'd given me those shots up at Quetzal Manor. I checked and saw no red needle-punctures this time, but the pain was much worse. That sick butterfly-jaguar dream was no dream. I'd been raped by . . . The *bastard*.

I pushed aside the pain, edged across to the door, and tested it. Unlocked. Good. Go find the SOB right now. Tear his head off.

I pulled back the door, took a deep breath, and checked out the hallway.

Whoa! How did *they* get here? In the dim light I made out two uniformed Army privates down at the end near the slatted windows, dozing in folding metal chairs, their AK-47's propped against the plaster wall.

Why were they here? Just a cool, breezy place to hang out? Or were they in place to guard me?

The breeze was causing the candle's flame to cast flickering shadows across the hall, so I quickly reclosed the door.

Now what? I was trembling as I returned the candle bowl to the table and sat down on the bed. Soldiers with guns were outside my room at five in the morning. In the farthest end of Guatemala. What was I going to do?

I gazed around at the "stone" walls and tried to think. My mind still felt clouded from whatever drug he'd given me, but it was beginning to . . .

Wait. I saw Alex Goddard come into this very room with embryos from the lab, which is connected by the steel door to his office. . . .

Where there was a *phone*.

Time to call the embassy, get some help to get the hell out of here.

I sat there thinking. All right. I'd need to wait an hour or so—now I'd get some low-level flunkie stuck with the grave-yard shift—but there was something I was damned well going to do immediately. With the lab right next door, I could try to find out why Goddard had just performed medical rape on me. There had to be some connection. According to him, the lab was for "plant research." But if that was all he was doing, why was the Army here? Right outside my door? I felt a pump of adrenaline that made me forget all about my pain. Before I got the hell out of Baalum, I was going to know what he was really up to here.

God, I feel miserable. I really hurt. All the more reason . . .

I took the candle, stood up, and moved to the opposite wall to begin looking for an opening in the fiberglass "stone." It appeared to have been made from impressions from the room atop the pyramid, rows and rows of those little cartoon-face glyphs, mixed in with bas-reliefs, but there had to be a door somewhere. I'd seen him walk right through it. As I ran my hand along the surface, I was struck by how their hardness felt like stone. But it couldn't be.

What was I looking for? There certainly were no door-knobs. I came across a hard crack, next to the bas-relief of a feather-festooned warrior, but as I slid my hand down, it ended and again there was more rough "stone." Solid.

Damn. I stood back and studied the wall with my candle. He'd come in from the left, which would be about . . .

I moved over and started again. This time my fingernail caught in a crevice that ran directly down to the floor. Then I discovered another, about two and a half feet farther along. It had to be the door.

I felt along the side, wondering how to open it, till I noticed that one of the little "stone" glyphs gave way when I pressed it. When I put my hand against it harder and rotated it, the panel clicked backward, then swung inward. Yes!

And there it was: the lab, CRT screens above the incubators, gas chromatograph in the corner. This, according to him, was where he tested the rain-forest plants the shamans and midwives brought in. But what about what he'd just done to me?

I was still worried about the Army guys outside, but I walked in, trying to be as quiet as I could. The first thing I did was head for the row of black boxes above the bench. Those, I assumed, were being used to maintain a micro-environment for incubating plant specimens. And sure enough, the dimly lit windows revealed rows and rows of petri dishes. They were clear, with circular indentations in the center. . . .

But wait a minute. Those weren't just any old lab dishes. And no plant extracts were in them either, just clear liquid. *That* was odd, very fishy.

I stood there puzzling, and then I remembered seeing pictures of lab dishes like these being used for artificially fertilized embryos. At the beginning, freshly extracted human ova are placed in an incubator for several hours, afloat in a medium that replicates the inside of a female Fallopian tube, to mature them in preparation for fertilization. Goddard had said something about tests on the blastocyst, the first cellular material created after fertilization. So was he using actual fetuses? My God. I felt like I was starting to know, or guess, a lot more than he wanted me to.

My thoughts were churning as I looked up and studied the video screens above the boxes. It took a moment, but then I figured out the petri dishes and their chemicals had been placed in the incubators between 4:00 P.M. and 7:30 P.M. Last evening. What—

I started counting. They were in racks, stacked, in sets of

four by four. Let's see. Five in this incubator, five in the next, five in the . . . There were over two hundred dishes in all!

Impossible. I looked down at them again, feeling a chill. Nothing seemed to be in them yet, at least as far as I could tell, but then human eggs are microscopic. So if ova *were* . . .

When he supposedly was doing that in vitro on the Mayan woman, was he actually extracting eggs?

Get serious. That was not where they came from.

By then I was well along the Kubler-Ross scale, past denial and closing in on anger, but still . . . so many! How could they all—

I turned and examined the row of plastic-covered jugs at the back of the lab, lined up, six in all. Now I *had* to know what was in them.

I was still shaky, but I steadied myself, walked over, pulled back the plastic, and touched one. It was deathly cold, sweating in the moist air. When I flipped open its Frisbee-sized top, I saw a faint wisp of vapor emerge into the twilight of the room . . .

Then it dawned on me. Of course. They were cryo-storage containers. He'd need them to preserve fertilized eggs, embryos.

I lifted off the inside cover and placed it carefully onto the bench, where it immediately turned white, steaming with mist. Then I noticed a tiny metal rod hooked over the side of the opening. When I pulled it up, it turned out to be attached to a porous metal cylinder containing rows of glass tubes.

What's . . .

Feeling like I was deep in a medical fourth dimension, I took out one of the freezing tubes. It was notched and marked with a code labeled along the side: "BL-11a," "BL-11b," "BL-11c," and so it went, all the way to "g." But nothing was there.

I began checking the other tubes. They all were empty too. So why was he freezing empty containers?

Go with the simple answer. He's getting them ready for new embryos.

I slid the rod back into the cryo-tank, then walked over and hoisted myself onto the lab bench next to the Dancing Shiva, creator and destroyer. And when I did, I again felt a stab of pain in my groin. The bastard. I was shaking, in the early stages of shock. More than anything, I just wanted to find him and kill him. . . .

I thought I heard a scraping noise somewhere outside, in the hall, and I froze. Was he about to come in and check on his "experiments"? Then I realized it was just the building, his house of horrors, creaking from the wind.

I took one final look at the incubators, and all the pain came back. The whole thing was too much for my body to take in. I sat there trying to muster my strength.

Don't stop now. Keep going.

I got back onto my feet. The phone. *Use the telephone.* Find Steve, alert the embassy, then get Sarah. Do it now, while you still can.

I was holding my breath as I walked over and pushed open the door to the office and looked in. It was empty and dark. Good. I headed straight for the black case of the Magellan World Phone.

When I picked up the handset and switched it on, the diodes went through their techno-dance of greens and yellows and then stabilized, giving me a dial tone. Thank you, merciful God.

I decided to start off by calling the hotel in Belize again, on the long shot that Steve had managed to get the hell out of Guatemala. Baby, please be there. My watch said the time was five-twenty in the morning, but he once told me they manned the desk around the clock. No problem getting through, though the connection had a lot of static. But then came the news I'd been dreading: no Steve Abrams.

"He still not come back, mon."

Where *was* he? I wanted to scream, but I was determined to keep a grip.

All right, try the Camino Real and hope you can get somebody awake who speaks English. Maybe he went back. Please, God.

I had the number memorized, so I plugged it in, and I recognized the voice of the guy who picked up, the owner's son, who was trying his best to learn English.

"Hi, this is Morgan James. Remember me? I'm just calling to see if there's a Steve Abrams staying there now?"

"Hey, *que pasa,* Señora James. Very early, yes? *Momento.*" There was a pause as he checked. Come on, Steve, *be* there. Please, please be somewhere.

Then the voice came back: "No, nobody by that name stays here."

"Okay . . . *gracias.*" Shit. It was like a pit had opened somewhere deep in my stomach.

I replaced the handset, feeling grateful that at least the phone still worked, my last link to sanity. My next call was going to be to the embassy, but I couldn't risk using up my opening shot with the graveyard shift. Maybe by 6 A.M. somebody with authority to do something would be there. Just a few more minutes.

Now what? I felt the aching soreness in my groin again, along with a wave of nausea. I had to do something, anything, just to keep going, to beat back an anxiety attack.

That was when I turned and stared at the computers, the little ducks drifting across the screens.

All right, you know what he's doing; now it's time to try and find out why. The real why. There must be records of what he's up to stored there. What else would he have them for?

"Clang, clang, clang." A noise erupted from somewhere outside the window. In spite of myself, I jumped.

Then I realized it was just the odd call of some forest bird. God, I wasn't cut out for this. Now my head was hurting, stabs of pain, but I rubbed at my temples and sat down at the first terminal.

I'm a Mac fan, hate Windows, so I had to start out by experimenting. In the movies people always know how to do this, but I had to go with trial and error, error compounding error.

After endless false starts that elicited utility screens I couldn't get rid of, I finally brought up an index of files, which included a long list of names.

    ALKALOIDS
    CARDIAC GLYCOSIDES
    PHENOLICS
    SAPONINS
    TERPENOIDS

Biology 103—which I hated—was coming back. Plant-extract categories. Looks like he actually *is* doing research on the flora here. But . . . still, what does he need my ova for?

I scrolled on. Scientific terms that meant nothing. Then, toward the end of the alphabetical list, I came to the word QUETZAL.

What was that? I clicked on it and—lo and behold—up came a short list of names. Six in all, organized by dates about a year apart, and each a woman.

My God. First I assumed they were patients from Quetzal Manor who'd come here for fertility treatment, though each was indicated "terminated" at the end, whatever that meant. But as I scanned down, I didn't want to see what I was seeing. The name next to the last was S. Crenshaw. She'd been "terminated" too.

The bottom was M. James. But I hadn't been "terminated." Not yet.

I slumped back in the chair, trying to breathe. How much more of this horror could I handle? Finally I leaned forward again and with a trembling hand clicked on S. Crenshaw.

A lot of data popped up, including three important dates. The first was exactly three weeks after the one in her passport, the Guatemalan entry visa. The second was ten months ago, the third eight months ago. After each was a number: 268, followed by 153, and finally 31.

The count of her extracted ova. Kill him. Just kill him.

A lot of medical terminology I couldn't interpret followed each number, but the note at the end required no degree.

"Blastocyst material from embryos after third extraction shows 84% decrease in cellular viability. No longer usable."

My God, had he made her permanently sterile?

While that obscenity was sinking in, I went back and clicked on my own name. The date was today, the number was 233. He'd just taken 233 of my ova. I stared at the screen and felt faint.

No medical analysis had yet been entered, but it didn't matter. I stared at the screen, feeling numb, for a full minute before clicking back to Sarah's page. Yes, I was right. The last date was just six weeks before she was found in a coma, down the river from here. . . .

No more mystery. He'd been using her eggs to create embryos, and they'd finally stopped working. Not "special" anymore. So her "program" had been "terminated." In the river.

My stomach was churning, bile in my throat, and I thought

I was going to throw up. I took a deep breath, slowly, and stopped myself. Before I got Sarah and we got the hell out of Baalum, I was going to smash everything in this lab.

It all had just come together. Those shots of "muscle relaxant" he gave me up at Quetzal Manor, they had to be a cocktail of his "proprietary" ovulation drugs. Then, with my ovaries ripening, he'd lured me here using Sarah. He knew I'd come after her. Next he'd "arranged" with Alan Dupre to fly me here. Finally, a sedative, and he'd harvested 233 of my ova, which he now had out there in those incubators. . . .

But what about proof? To show the world. Morning sounds were building up outside, so I was less worried whether the two soldiers in the hallway were still asleep or not. Truthfully, I was so wired I no longer cared. I clicked on a printer and began zipping off the files of each woman he'd violated, all six.

Disgust flowed through me like a torrent. Heart of Darkness. "The horror, the horror." Alex Goddard had used Sarah in the most unspeakable way possible, then tried to have her murdered. Probably he'd just turned her over to Colonel Ramos.

The same thing must have happened to those other women. All "disappeared" somewhere in Guatemala. But who would know?

One thing *I* knew. I was next. . . .

The printer was old and loud, but thankfully it was fast. Four minutes later I had what I'd need to nail the criminal. When I got out of here, somebody would *have* to believe me.

While I was stacking the printouts, I resolved to call the embassy right then, the hour be damned. I was sweating like a gazelle when the lion is closing in. Alex Goddard had just performed primal, surgical rape on me, and now the Army was right outside. I had to get the embassy.

And that was when I realized I didn't have the number. But it had to be in a phone book somewhere.

A quick look around the office didn't turn up one. I considered ringing the Camino Real again, to ask them to look up the number, but then I had an inspired thought. Steve had said Alan Dupre's number was easy to remember because it promoted his business. What was it? I couldn't remember.

Then it came back: 4-MAYAN, the six-digit number they used in Guatemala City. Call the sleazebag and ask him who can get me out of here. He's supposed to know everybody.

Dawn was bringing more and more forest-morning songs through the thin slats of the windows. I walked over and pushed them open, running my fingers out into the air. It felt cool, the touch of freedom, and I thought for a moment about bursting through to escape. Just get Sarah now.

Instead, I walked back to the phone, clenching my fists, and dialed Alan Dupre's number, praying and hoping it was where he lived. Steve had called him late in the evening, so it probably was. I'd thought I never wanted to speak to him again, but now . . . God, let him be there.

The phone, however, just rang and rang and rang.

Come *on*. Damn.

It rang and rang some more. Then finally—

"Who the fuck *is* this? We don't open till nine."

The first sound of his voice brought a wave of relief, but then his cocky attitude made me livid all over again.

"It's Morgan James, you shit. Why did you leave me stranded up here? You have no idea what—"

"Oh, you . . ." He paused for a cigarette cough. "You made me walk all the way downstairs just to bust my chops. What the—?"

"Talk to me, you prick." I still intended to strangle him. "I need your help. You owe me. You have no idea what—"

"Hey, lady, you didn't possibly believe taking off in that

fucking hurricane was my . . . Let's just say I was acting under duress. I all but didn't get back."

"Well, you can start making up for that right now by springing me the hell out of here." So, somebody *had* put him up to it, just like I'd thought all along. But who? "I want you to look up the number for the American embassy. And tell me the name of somebody there who—"

"Jesus, you truly don't get the picture, do you?" He paused for another early-morning reefer hack.

"I 'get' that you—"

"Missy, it was a high official at that very establishment 'suggested' I fly you up there. Why the *hell* else would I do it, for chrissake? You know I'm not a citizen of this fun house. Said party noted that if I didn't, he could make a few phone calls about my residency status, my pilot's license . . . Let's just say it was an offer I didn't see fit to take issue with."

"Oh, my God." I felt like a knife had just plunged into my back. "Was his name Barry Morton? Please tell me."

"Taking the Fifth on that one," he said, coughing again. "But you've got primal instincts."

I heard a noise outside and sank lower in the chair. What was I going to do now?

"Listen, do you have any idea where Steve is? They're looking—"

"No shit, Madame Sherlock. I had a long, deeply uninspiring interrogation by a couple of upscale assholes who showed up here in an Army Jeep. They wanted to know where the fuck he was, when I'd supped with him last. Let me inform you, love, you got my old heartstrings buddy in some decided doo-doo."

"I feel guilty enough about that as is, so stop." In spite of all Alex Goddard had done, I felt horrible about Steve, like a self-involved witch. "But do you know where he is now?"

"Haven't the foggiest fucking idea, never heard of the jerk. Shit, hang on." The line went silent, and I could feel my pulse pounding.

Outside the office door, I heard footsteps approaching down the hall. Please, God, please. But then they passed by, terminating where the two soldiers had been dozing. Next I heard the tones of a solid dressing-down in profane Spanish.

"Tú heres un pedaso de mierda!"

Then came a familiar voice from the receiver. I couldn't believe it.

"Morgy, *why* in hell did you let Alan take you up there by yourself?" His tone had a sadness, and a deserved pique, that cut me to the core.

I think I stopped breathing.

"Oh, baby, thank God you're . . ." I was expecting the door to burst open any moment. Men with AK-47's. "Do you know the Army's looking for—?"

"You're completely nuts. I got halfway to Belize and called the motel to see how you were doing, and they told me you'd taken off with this asshole. So I turned around and drove back here. It was after midnight and the Army thugs had just left. Morgy, I'm coming to get you. Soon as the gas stations open. I know a back road to Mexico. We've got to get out of this fucking country *immediately*."

"Don't try to drive up. It's too dangerous. Can you get Alan to fly you? Sarah's here and she's been turned into a space cadet. I don't know how I'm going to pry her away." I stopped to try to assemble my thoughts. "He's got soldiers watching me. I've got to smuggle her out somehow."

I couldn't bring myself to tell him what was really going on.

"Let me talk to Dupre a second. The fucker. I can't believe he did this to you. But maybe we can come up with something. Otherwise, I may just kill him with my bare hands."

I heard a cough, which told me Alan had been listening in on an extension. It teed me off, but then—he did have to be in on this. Shit. The idea of relying on Alan Dupre for *anything* . . .

"Well, do it fast. I broke into Alex Goddard's office to use this phone and . . . just hurry."

"You got it."

Now the sound of firm, officerlike boot steps stormed past the door, headed out this time, after which the two young soldiers began berating each other in high-pitched Spanish.

"Hace falta tener cojones!"

"Hijo de tú chingada madre!"

More and more light was creeping through the slatted windows. A glance at my watch showed the time to be six sharp, but the embassy was no longer an option.

"Listen," Steve said, coming back on, "there's some rain due for tonight, but he says he thinks we can try. He claims there's a clearing about a quarter of a mile down a gravel road that goes south. With the rain as cover, maybe we can put down just after dark. Think you can find a way to get Sarah and meet us?"

"I'm not even sure she can walk, at least not far, but we'll be there." I was flashing on her back in the square, proclaiming her happiness. Would I have to drag her out, carry her on my back? Well, I would. "There's some kind of 'ceremony' on for tomorrow morning. The Army's going to be here in double strength because of it, but maybe it'll make for some confusion that'll help. Still, she's—"

"Damn, this is going to be big-time dicey."

"Honey, let me tell you as much as I can about the layout of this place. Just in case."

Which I did. The main problem was, I didn't know exactly where Sarah was.

"Is there anybody there who could help you?" he asked when I'd finished.

"I'm not hopeful." I paused. "Listen, can you get your hands on a gun or guns?"

"What are you . . . Don't even *think* about it! That's the best way to *guarantee* we all get killed. I'm not taking on the Guatemalan Armed Forces. And you're not either. We've got to keep this very low-tech. The dark and the rain, that's what we use. They don't shoot back."

At that moment I wanted nothing more than to shoot Alex Goddard. I'd have done it if I'd had the chance. Happily. But I knew Steve was right.

"Okay, look, what time?"

"We'll try to set down about, say—"

There was a crackle as the yellow diodes on the phone erupted in a high-pitched whistle, cutting the connection.

No! My God, had somebody been listening in?

So when exactly was he coming? Around dark? That would probably be about eight o'clock. Or maybe nine . . .

I was closing the phone case when I heard a sound from outside, as though someone had passed the door, then come back to listen.

All right. Get going.

I gathered the printouts, then headed back through the laboratory, where I took a long, last look at the petri dishes being incubated. Should I just dump them now? But then he'd know for sure that I knew.

The time would come, and soon.

As I eased myself back into the fake-stone OR and closed the door, the dawn outside was steeped in forest sounds, clacks and whistles and chirps. That was good, because I needed some stray noise to mask what I was going to do next. Take control.

Twenty-five

I began by feeling along the fake-stone walls to find where the crevices were, the doors that enclosed the medical instruments. Somewhere, I was sure, there was a cabinet that held a complete set of surgical equipment.

When I found the first crevice, I gave the wall on either side a push and, sure enough, the panel was spring-loaded. Good. The side on the right of the crevice popped open to reveal the microscope Goddard had used. But nothing else was there.

I moved on down the wall testing for cabinets, trying to remember what Marcelina had done when Alex Goddard told her to prep the Mayan woman. One after another the panels snapped open till . . . yes, this was the one I wanted. Hallelujah.

The third drawer held the scalpels. I took out the largest I could find, heavy and steel, then wedged it into the metal sliding mechanism and snapped off the tip. Perfect.

I felt like I was holding the key to my escape as I carefully reclosed all the panels. Since there were no windows in the OR room, I slipped back through the lab—it had now become a haunted place of monstrous obscenity to me—and checked out the office.

It was still deserted, but now the hazy light of early day was mingling with the sounds of nature seeping through the slatted window. As I walked over to it, the cool, moist morning air once again felt like freedom. How long did I have before the clinic started stirring?

I'd originally planned to try to unscrew some of the slats, but that turned out to be unnecessary. The strips of wood were held in with crude, rusty clamps, and one by one I began prying them out with the blunted scalpel. I figured five slats should give me enough space to squeeze through, and I'd already removed three when I heard a frustrated voice in Spanish just down the hail. Uh-oh.

"Tengo que mear que mis dientes flotan!" It was followed by the sound of boots headed toward the office.

I ducked down behind a desk, holding my breath, but then the footsteps marched past, headed for the front door of the clinic. That was when I finally processed what he'd said: "I've got to piss so bad my teeth are floating."

So where was he headed?

Moments later I knew. I heard the noise of someone kicking their way through the underbrush till they were right next to the window, followed by the sound of a zipper.

My God, I thought, he's right here. Will he spot the missing slats?

I bit my lip as I listened to a member of the Guatemalan Armed Forces vigorously urinate upon the north wall of Alex Goddard's clinic. Well, I told myself, that's probably what they think of him. I'd like to do the same.

Then came a confirming re-zip, after which the sound of slashing boots faded back into the distance. If he'd noticed the window I'd just burgled, it hadn't alerted his curiosity. Moments later I heard his heavy footsteps returning up the hall.

Jesus, two minutes more and I'd have been out there.

I was trembling, but I managed to finish prying out the last two slats. I then pushed all five out onto the ground, hoping the clatter would be lost in forest music, and climbed through after them, trying to be as quiet as I could. I ended up going out headfirst and collapsing onto the ground in an unceremonious crumple. Thirty seconds later, though, the slats were wedged roughly back into place, and I'd discarded the broken scalpel in the jungle underbrush. Yes!

Now the cool air of freedom was all around me. My first small step.

How long before Alex Goddard discovers I'm missing? Will I have time to find Sarah, bring her to her senses, and hide her from him? A lot would depend on what kind of physical and mental shape she was in.

As I passed around the parking lot, gray clouds were thickening overhead, and I noticed that half a dozen new olive-green Jeeps were parked there. The Army was arriving in force, getting ready for God knows what. I took one look at them and felt my breath start coming in bursts. Steve, we're going to need our own kind of miracle. How are we going to get out of here?

I skirted the edges of the lot and reached the trail leading down into the village. And I was trying to quell my pulse. What was down there? With the dense rain forest arching over me, I felt as though I was entering a domain of Maya dreamtime where the past lived again, only with a sinister twist.

The air in the dark groves was thick with the buzzing of insects, harbingers of the coming rainstorm, but before long I caught a glimmer of daylight ahead. Soon I emerged into a wide arbor that, after another hundred feet, opened onto the central plaza and the pyramid. Now . . .

It was daylight, but it also was . . . The sight took my breath away. *What* was going on?

A milling horde of men was gathered in the square, and resinous torches were flaming on each of the pyramid's tiers of steps. A lot of drinking from clay jugs was getting under way, and the men were in the process of painting their faces, stripes of black and white, with dark circles around their eyes. Some also were applying rows of red-and-green-colored seeds to their cheeks with white glue. The bizarreness of the scene rippled through me like the shards of a dysfunctional dream. Jesus!

Alex Goddard had said the ceremony got "frenzied," and now I was beginning to realize. . . . What were they getting ready to do? Had I been wrong in thinking the classical Maya never got around to ripping out hearts? Did that explain the half-dozen young Army privates loitering there at the far side, rifles slung over their shoulders?

I melted back into the trees and studied the geometry of the plaza, reconsidering my situation. I needed to find some way to get around it and onto the cobblestone pathway at the far side, which led into the village. Finally I decided I could skirt the periphery if I was careful not to advertise my presence. Dawn had come and gone and the quick light of tropical day was arriving, but everybody appeared to be pre-occupied with their nightmarish preparations.

Thank God it worked. I weaved in and among the trees and in five minutes I'd reached the central pathway, now deserted. Still barely letting myself breathe, I turned back and gazed up at the pyramid. I had no idea what was next, but I decided it would be my signpost, to help me keep my bearings as I moved through the confusing, tree-shrouded huts of Baalum. Except for the men in the square, the village now seemed deserted, though a pack of brown dogs, curious and annoying, had spotted me and now circled around to sniff. *Don't* bark, damn it.

That was when I saw Marcelina, in her white shift, striding through the crowd of drinking men like an alpha lioness part-ing a posturing pride. My God. My heart stopped for a moment. Does Alex Goddard already know I've fled and has he sent her to lure me back?

No way. I clenched my fists and kicked at the surly, long-tailed mutts, still circling and nuzzling.

As she came closer, I saw she was smiling and carrying a brown wicker basket. What . . .

"I've brought you something," she announced as she walked up, her dark eyes oddly kind. "You must be starving by now."

"How did you know I was down here?" Looking at her earnest Mayan face, I suddenly wondered if she could have any *idea* what Alex Goddard had done to Sarah, and to me?

"You were gone from your room," she declared, settling the basket onto the walkway and beginning to open it. "Where else would you be?" When I looked, I saw it had a sealed container of yogurt, a banana, and two eggs, presumably hard-boiled—traditional "safe" food for *gringos* in Third World places. "I'd been planning to bring you down today," she went on. "They all want to meet you."

Was she coming to look after me? The more I examined her, the more I began to suspect something else was going on. Would she help me get Sarah out and away from Alex Goddard?

"I want to find Sarah," I said. Why not start out with the truth? "Does he . . . Dr. Goddard know I'm here?"

"He's not here now," she said, her eyes shifting down. "He left for Guatemala City early this morning. I think to meet with the Army. On business. . . ."

Yes. His big Humvee hadn't been in the clinic's parking lot when I went by. Why hadn't I noticed that? For the first time I felt the odds were tipping. Now was going to be the *perfect* time to get Sarah. Yes. Yes. Yes.

"If you want to see her, I can take you," Marcelina offered, replacing the lid on the basket.

Yes, perfect. I wanted to hug her.

"Then let's go right now" And while I was at it, I was determined to get through to this woman somehow, to enlist her help.

As we headed down the central walkway of the village, we passed the rows of compounds where I'd seen the women that first morning. None was in evidence now, and the gardens were empty, as though the entire settlement had been evacuated. It felt very strange.

And what about those bizarre proceedings now under way in the square? Was that going to interfere with getting Sarah out?

"Marcelina." I pointed back toward the milling plaza. "What's that all about? The drinking and the—?"

"It's begun," she answered, both simple and vague. "They're getting ready."

I didn't like the way she said it. Her tone seemed to imply I was involved somehow.

"Ready for—?"

"The ceremony. They like to drink a tree-bark liquor we call *balche*. It's very strong and rancid." She smiled and touched me. "Take my advice and avoid it."

"I plan to." Why did she think I'd even be offered it?

As we hurried along, two women abruptly appeared on a porch, bowed, and greeted us. Marcelina waved back, then went over and spoke earnestly with them for a moment. Finally she turned and motioned for me.

"They've invited you in."

Something about the easy way it all just "happened" felt as though they'd been expecting me. Had Marcelina's trip down to the village been part of a setup, wittingly or unwittingly?

"I told them we could only stay for a minute," she went on. I sensed she was reluctant, but felt we had no choice.

The last thing I wanted to do was *this*.

"Marcelina, can't you tell them we'll come back later?"

"It's . . . it's important." She was beckoning for me. "Please."

Well, I thought, this could give me the time I need, the personal moment, to get through to her. Even after I locate Sarah, spiriting her out isn't going to be simple. I've got to make Marcelina understand what's really going on, then get her to help us.

As we headed through the yard, the women smiled, then politely led us under the thatch overhang and into the hut. They both were short and Maya-sturdy, with white shifts and broad faces, and they exuded a confident intensity in their bearing, a powerful sense of self-knowledge. I tried a phrase in Spanish, but they just stared at me as though they'd never heard the language. Then I remembered my first attempt to ask about Sarah. The women hadn't understood me then either. Or had they?

The room they ushered us into had no windows, but there was cool, shadowy morning light filtering through the upright wooden slats of the walls, laying dim stripes across the earthen floor. A cooking fire smoldered in a central hearth, and from the smoke-blackened roof beams dangled dried gourds, bundles of tobacco, netted bags of onions and squash, and several leaf-wrapped blocks of salt. The room smelled of ancient smoke, sweet and pungent.

They immediately produced a calabash bowl with a gray liquid inside, pronouncing the word *"atole"* as they urged it on me, smiling expectantly.

"It's our special drink," Marcelina explained. She seemed to be wary, watching me closely as they handed it over. "It's how we welcome an honored guest."

I wasn't sure how politic I ought to be. Third World food . . .

"Marcelina," I said, taking the bowl and trying to smile. "I'm not really—"

"You must have a little," she whispered back. "It would be very rude. . . ."

Well, I thought, just a taste. I tried it and realized it was a dense gruel of cornmeal and honey-water, like a lukewarm gluey porridge, though with a bitter after-jolt. But I choked it down and tried to look pleased. Marcelina urged me to have more—I took another small sip—and then they produced corn dumplings wrapped in large leaves, together with a pile of fiery chiles and a bowl of squash, corn, and beans, all mixed together.

After one bite, though, Marcelina reached out and—her eyes downcast—whisked the bowls away, passing them back to the women. She said something to them, then turned to me.

"Eating too much would be as rude as not eating at all."

That was a cultural norm I didn't remember, and I suspected she'd just changed her mind about the wisdom of my eating local food.

I smiled at the women and used some of my so-so Spanish to offer them thanks.

"Muchas gracias." I nodded toward the bowls. *"Esta es muy delicioso."*

They beamed as though they understood me. Who could say? But they'd been intensely interested in watching me eat, even more than Marcelina.

Work on her. Now.

"Marcelina." I turned to her, only vaguely noticing she hadn't had a bite. "Do you understand why Dr. Goddard moved me down to the operating room yesterday? There in the clinic? What did he tell you?"

"He said it was for special tests." Her voice was gentle through the gloom. "You were very . . . sleepy. You must have been very, very tired. But he told me something in your blood work was unusual, so he had me bring you down for a pelvic exam. I gave you a sedative"—she was pointing at the Band-Aid still on my arm—"the way we always do. But then he said you were fine."

"Do you realize he did things to my body I didn't agree to?" I studied her trusting Mayan face and tried to get a sense of how much she knew about what was going on. That was when I first became sure of an increasing disquiet in her eyes, as she kept glancing away. Why was she so uncomfortable talking about Alex Goddard? "And I think he did some of those same things to Sarah."

"Dr. Goddard tried to help her in many ways when she was here before." Marcelina's tone had become odd and distant. "Now he wants to help you too."

Yes, there was definitely something uneasy in her eyes.

"Before he came here," she went on, trying to look at me, "Baalum was just a poor, simple village. Many children died of diseases. So I left and went to Guatemala City to study. To become a public-health nurse. Then after he came here, I moved back to help him with his clinic, the children."

She was trying to make a case for him, and I noticed she'd avoided the actual question.

"Now Baalum has become a special place," she said finally. "A place of miracles. And if a woman from outside comes, she can be part of that. When *Sara* was here before, I started teaching her to speak our language, and the others did too. She truly wanted to be part of his miracles. Sometimes we don't understand how they happen, but he has great medical powers."

One thing's for sure, I thought. He's got plenty of power over the *people* here, including you. The whole place has been brainwashed. I looked her over and realized she'd just gone on mental autopilot. She wants to be loyal to him, and she can't let herself believe there's something rotten in the "special" paradise of Baalum.

"Listen," I said, getting up, "I need to go see Sarah right now. Her father's been in the hospital, and he's not well. I spoke with him yesterday, and he's very worried about her. I know Dr. Goddard is treating her, but it's better if I just take her home immediately."

More and more I was beginning to suspect this detour for the two women had been a diversion, an attempt to stall. Marcelina had set it up. Maybe she wanted to tell me something, and she didn't have the nerve to do it point-blank.

"Families are very important," she said, sounding sincere. "We'll go now." She spoke to the women briefly, an animated benediction that seemed to leave her even more disturbed. As we headed out and on down the path, I again wondered what was really happening.

When we reached the end of the long "street," the arched arbors still above us, she stopped in front of an odd stone building unlike any of the others and pointed.

"This is where she likes to be," she said quietly. "Except for the pyramid, it's the most sacred place in Baalum."

The doorway was a stone arch about five feet high and pointed at the top like a tiny Gothic cathedral.

"What . . . *is* this?" I felt as though I was about to enter something from the Temple of Doom.

"It was once the royal bath," she explained. "In ancient times heated rocks were brought in, with spring water from a sacred cenote."

We walked through the portal and entered a room whose roof was a stone latticework that let the gray daylight just filter through. The space was vast, with carved and colored glyphs all around the walls, while the air was filled with clouds of incense from pots along the floor. It felt like a smoky pagan church.

At the far end was a large stone platform, and in the dappled, hazy light I could see it was embossed along its sides with carved and painted classical scenes and glyphs, glistening little red and green and blue pictures of faces and figures.

My eyes finally started adjusting to the shadows, and I realized the platform had been fitted with a covering across the top, a jaguar skin over bundled straw, and a tiny form was lying on it, wearing a white shift. . . .

Dear God.

"Morgy, I've been so hoping you'd come," Sarah said, rising up and holding out her hands. Then she slid her feet around onto the rough stone floor and managed to steady herself. Her shift was wrinkled now, but she still was wearing the brown slippers and the braided leather waist-cinch. She appeared sleepy, though her eyes were sparkling and she seemed to have more strength than she'd had when I first saw her out in the square. I looked at her and weighed the chances she could walk. Possibly. But I'd carry her if I had to.

"Sar, honey, we're going home now," I said, finally finding my voice.

She didn't respond at first, just turned to caress the decorated sides of the platform. "I've been wanting to show you this, Morgy. It tells my story." Her voice sounded as if it were coming from a long way off, as though through a dense haze.

"Please, we don't have time for stories." Was she hearing me at all? "Let's just—"

"See," she went on, ignoring me as she pointed down, "that's the Cosmic Monster, that one there with maize sprouting out of his forehead. And that man next to him with a flint knife is my father, letting blood from his penis. He's the king. And that one there is me, Lady Jaguar. He gave my name to this place." She paused to reverently touch the carved stone. "Look, I've just stuck a stingray spine through my tongue and put my blood in the copal censer there."

"Sar, please—"

"Here, see it?" She was pointing to a section at the very end. "That's the two-headed Vision Serpent up above me. He's the god Kukulkan . . . or something. I've made him come to me by giving him my blood. I'm—"

"Sar, what in heaven's name is going on with you?" I grabbed her and, in spite of myself, shook her. Jesus! The whole scene left me in shock. She was sinking back deeper into her fantasy world. Was she taking the drug again, I wondered, and fantasizing she was some dead Mayan princess? Please, God, no.

That was when I saw Marcelina walk over to a shelf along the wall and lift down another clay-pot incense burner, along with a small white brick. What—?

"Oh, yes!" Sarah exclaimed, moving quickly over to her. "Let's do it for Morgy."

Marcelina nodded warily and handed her the white brick, then turned to me. "She likes to do incense. It always calms her. This is copal, what the shamans use."

I watched while Sarah shakily began crumbling pieces of the sticky substance into the pot. My God, I thought, she's truly, truly lost it. Next she inserted dry tinder and began trying to knock sparks into it with a piece of hard black jade and a flint. But she was too weak, and finally Marcelina had to take the flint and do it for her. Then, as the gray smoke started billowing out, Marcelina began a long chant, shrill and strangely melodic. I felt a chill creep down my back. When she finished, she turned her dark eyes on me sadly, waiting.

"What were you saying?" I asked finally, sensing she wanted me to.

"I was singing from the Popol Vuh." Then she translated.

Holy earth, giver of life,
Help us in our struggle against
The God of the House of Darkness.

Wait a minute. What's she saying?

"Who's the God of the House of Darkness?" Could she be talking about Alex Goddard?

"I didn't want to do it," she blurted out, reaching out to me, her eyes even sadder. "But he said you're the new special one. We had to."

What the hell was she talking about? Had to what? Did it have something to do with my "visit" to the women in the hut?

"Please stay here with us," she pleaded as she took my hand. "Don't go."

Stay? Don't even *think* about it. I had Sarah halfway to freedom. While the Army was still getting its act together, we could lose ourselves someplace in the forest where nobody would find us, and when Steve got here tonight . . .

"Sar, come on, it's time." I pulled away from Marcelina and slipped my arm around her. "Nothing here is what you think it is."

"Are we leaving?" she asked, her eyes blank.

"Yes, honey, we're leaving. This very minute."

The dense forest was all about us, and I'd just carry her into it if I had to. In the coming storm, nobody was going to find . . .

That's when I noticed I was beginning to have gastric rumblings. Damn. Never, *ever* eat "native" food, no matter what the social pressure. That damned "visit" . . .

When I turned to ask Marcelina if she would help me get Sarah outside, I noticed she'd been joined by the two women, both still in their white shifts, who'd just fed me the sickly sweet *atole*. And more women were behind them, all staring at me, expectant, as though wondering what I would do.

Maybe it was my imagination, or the dizziness that was abruptly growing around me, but it also seemed they'd painted their faces with streaks of white, designs like the men in the square were putting on.

"She's going to be all right," Marcelina was saying. "But we have to get you back now. You'll need your strength."

I needed it then. My stomach had really begun to gyrate, and my vision had started growing colored. I noticed I was sweating, even though the day was cooling down. Actually, I felt as though I was about to pass out. *What* had those women fed me?

It was finally dawning on me that Marcelina's fearfulness back in the hut had nothing to do with betraying Alex Goddard. It was because she knew she was betraying *me*.

Well, damn her, I'm not going to let Alex Goddard win, no matter what.

"Marcelina, *please* help me. I've got to get Sarah out of here. Now. I don't know what poison drug he's giving her, but he's driving her insane."

"We'll take care of her," she said. But I could barely make out the words. They echoed, bouncing around in my head.

"I'm really getting dizzy." I glanced over again at the women standing by the door. "Please tell me what they—?"

"The elixir," she said. "For tomorrow at sunup. That's when you'll see his real power."

I'd begun experiencing white spots before my eyes—and for some reason I had a vision of the Army Jeeps parked up the hill. I didn't know how the two were connected, but in my jumbled thoughts they seemed to be.

Just get Sarah and get out into the air. Walk, don't think, and you can *do* it. . . .

I pulled her next to me and struggled toward the door, the women studying us, unmoving.

"Morgy, I've missed you so much," Sarah was saying, slipping her arms around my neck to help herself walk. "I'm . . . I'm ready to go home."

"I've missed you too." I think my heart was bursting as I urged her on through the stone portico. At last. Had something clicked that freed her from Alex Goddard? Maybe her mind was finally becoming her own.

When we got outside, the skies were growing ever more foreboding, storm clouds looming. Steve had been right about the coming rain, but now it seemed the perfect cover for us to just *get out*. I took a deep breath of the misty air and forced myself to start helping Sarah up the cobblestone path.

"Sar, you can walk, I know you can. Be strong. For both of us. I'm . . ."

I felt myself sinking slowly to the cold stones of the walkway, the hard abrasion against my knees, Sarah tumbling forward as I pulled her down on top of me, Marcelina's arms around me trying to hold me up. It was the last real sensation I would remember.

Twenty-six

Sarah was hovering around me, a sylphlike presence, as I watched myself drift up the steps of the pyramid there in the square, my senses waxing and waning like the waves on a distant ocean shore. There seemed to be rain, or fog, or smoke, but it had a luminous, purple cast one moment, a Day-Glo orange the next. In fact, all the colors were swirling and changing, shimmering from hue to hue. A pack of howler monkeys was cavorting up and down the steps on my left, like circus Harlequins in electric red-and-blue suits, doing pratfalls and huffing as they flew through the air and tumbled one over another.

Sarah was floating silently beside me, but where was Steve? Had he come? Were we escaping?

No. I sensed his face drifting across my sight like a cartoon cloud before dissolving into nothingness. He wasn't here. I was having the eeriest dream I'd ever had.

When I reached the stone-paved platform at the pinnacle, I felt Alex Goddard clasp my arm and turn me around to face the plaza below.

"They are waiting," he said, pointing toward the hazy square.

I looked down, and at first I couldn't see anything except rain and smoke, but then slowly a crowd materialized. The scattering of men I'd seen earlier had become an undulating sea of upturned faces painted with stripes and swirling circles of blue and white and red, a torch-lit garden of brilliant blossoms. They all were looking up at us, at Sarah and me.

Next he held out a mirror whose reflecting surface was a polished silver metal.

"Behold yourself, Morgan. As befits a royal one, a special one, your nose has been built up with clay and pierced with lustrous blue feathers and a giant topaz. Your front teeth have been filed to a point and inlaid with jewels, your royal skull has been shaped back and flattened."

I gazed into the mirror and gasped. I was monstrous, a Halloween harpie.

Then he moved over to a waist-high censer stationed there on the edge of the platform and began adding balls of sticky white copal resin, together with bark and grasses, which he ignited by the quick friction of a fire stick spun by a bow.

Finally he turned to me and held out his hands. "Now we will make a miracle, the miracle of Baalum."

Heavy smoke from the censer was pouring out into the rainy sky as we started a stiff pas de deux, the strains of a clay flute drifting around us. Was it the "ceremony"? Was I dreaming it?

As the incense billowed, our Maya dreamtime dance became ever more intense, and then a faint form began to writhe up out of the haze between us, an undulating serpent the deep color of jade. As Alex Goddard wrapped his arms around it, it began to form into two dark heads, then pirouette above us. Finally, as the two-headed specter opened its mouths and gazed down on the platform, Sarah stepped toward it and held out her arms.

"Sar, *no!*"

I screamed to her to get back, but as I did, the . . . thing reached down and swallowed her in flames. It was the Vision-Serpent come to receive her.

"Sarah . . ."

"Can you get up now?" said a voice, cutting through the haze that enveloped my consciousness. At first I thought it was more of the dream, but then someone was touching me and I opened my eyes to see Marcelina standing beside the bed I was in, dressed in white and holding a candle. For a moment I thought I was still atop the rainy pyramid, but then I felt the moistness of the sheets and realized the storm I'd been dreaming of was being blown in through the slats of the windows. I was shivering.

"Marcelina, where's Sarah?" The nightmare had seemed so real, and now I was hallucinating, having flashes of colors I didn't want to see. "I just had the most horrible dream. I was on the pyramid, and there was smoke and rain and some kind of ghastly—"

"It's the elixir. From the toad. It makes you dream dreams of the Old Ones." She took my hand. "She's resting now. He gave her something to calm her."

More drugs, I thought angrily.

Then I caught the "he." Alex Goddard must be back. Everything had gone wrong.

"I've got to get her and—"

"Not now," Marcelina went on, helping me up. "Come. I want to show you the true miracle of Baalum. Now is the time you should know."

The upstairs hallway was dimly illuminated by rows of lights along the floor as she led me forward. There also was total silence, except for the occasional whimper of a baby in one of the rooms. Where was she taking me?

When she stopped in front of the third door from the end of the hall, I tried to get my mental bearings. I was still hallucinating; in control of only half my mind, to the point where I wasn't sure I could find my hand in front of my face. But then she tapped on the door and when she heard a voice inside, something in the Kekchi dialect, she gently pushed it open.

When we moved inside, the room was dark and there was no sound, except a gasp from the bed when the woman realized I was a gringo. The dim slant of illumination from the doorway revealed a small night lamp just above the head of her bed, and Marcelina reached for it.

As the light came on, a pale glow filling the room, I noticed the woman was staring at me, her eyes wide and frightened.

"She's afraid you've come for her child," Marcelina whispered, pointing toward the bassinet. "She knows we have to give him back."

The woman was pure Maya, a powerful visage straight off that upright stele in the square. I walked over and took her hand, hoping to calm her fears. Then I lifted her hand to my cheek and realized my face was moist with tears. I held it there for a long moment, till the alarm in her eyes diminished.

Her newborn infant was sleeping quietly in a crib right next to her, on the opposite side from the table. When I looked closely at him, I finally understood everything.

I laid her hand back onto the bed and walked around. While the woman watched, I pulled away the stripped red and green coverlet and lifted out her groggy little boy, tender and vulnerable.

He made a baby's protest as I cradled him, then began sleepily probing my left breast, making me feel sad I had no milk.

"It's okay," I whispered, first to him and then to his mother. *"Esta bien."*

"Tz'ac Tzotz," the woman said, pointing at him. I could feel her deep, maternal love.

"His name?" I asked in English, before I thought.

When Marcelina translated, the woman smiled and nodded.

Then the blond-haired Tz'ac Tzotz started to sniffle, so I kissed him gently, turned, and took the woman's hand again. There was nothing else I could do.

Tz'ac Tzotz was Sarah incarnate. This was no hallucination. He had her special blue eyes and her steep cheeks, her high brow. I was holding her child.

"They are sent from Kukulkan," Marcelina was saying, "the white god of the plumed serpent. Then there's the ceremony on the pyramid and they go back."

The woman was staring at me, seemingly awestruck. Then she pointed at Tz'ac Tzotz and at me, saying something to Marcelina. Finally the woman bowed her head to me with great reverence.

"She says he looks so much like you," Marcelina explained. "You are surely the special one. The new bride."

I was still speechless, but then I noticed the baby had a little silver jaguar amulet tied around his wrist with a silken string, and on the back—as on Kevin's and Rachel's—were rows of lines and dots.

It finally dawned on me. They were *digits,* written in the archaic Maya script. What could they be, maybe his birthday? No, I realized, that was far too simplistic. This was the original bar code; it was his Baalum "serial number."

For a long moment it felt as if time had stopped. Sarah, and now me—we'd been lured here to provide the life force for Mayan surrogate mothers. This whole elaborate recreation wasn't about rain-forest drugs and research into fertility; it was just a cover to use the bodies of these intensely believing Native Americans. Alex Goddard had perpetrated the greatest systematic exploitation of another race since slavery. The difference was, he'd found a way to get them to give themselves willingly.

Baalum was definitely a place of miracles. There could scarcely be another isolated spot on earth where he could find this many sincere, trusting people with powerful beliefs he could prostitute. And all of it hidden deep in an ancient rain forest.

But I had to be sure. I turned around, leaving Marcelina to watch in confusion, and marched out into the hall and into the next room. The Maya mother there cried out in shock as I unceremoniously strode over to her crib and checked.

Her baby was the same. Sarah stamped all over him. My God.

When I went back, Marcelina was still trying to calm Tz'ac Tzotz's mother with her bedside manner.

As I stood looking at them, the extent of what was going on finally settled in. All those new babies at Quetzal Manor, even Kevin and Rachel—they all looked alike because they all were from the same woman. The one who was here before Sarah. And now *hers* were ready.

I was going to be next. The new "bride." Those fresh petri dishes down in the lab . . . My God, why didn't I destroy them when I had the chance?

So whose sperm would he use? Of course. It would be from the man Alan Dupre was going to deliver to him.

"Marcelina, don't you realize what's happening?" I wanted to pound some sense into her. They didn't *have* to let him do this to them.

"I know that with miracles must come sadness," she said, reaching to touch Tz'ac Tzotz's tiny brow. "We all understand that."

"It's not a miracle. It's science, don't you realize? *Ciencia.* He's *using* you."

"We know he does many things that are magic. He makes powerful medicines from the plants we bring him, and when women want to bear a child—"

"No, Marcelina." I felt my heart go out to her, and to all the others. "It's *black* magic. It's all a lie."

The first thing to do was go down to the laboratory and dump every last one of my petri dishes into the sink, ova and all. Destroy the nest, then call Steve and warn him. . . .

I glanced at my watch. NO! The time was 4:58 A.M. He was coming at nine o'clock last night. . . .

I was standing there in horror, unnatural colors flitting across my vision, when I heard . . .

"It's almost morning."

I jumped as Alex Goddard walked into the room, dressed in white, hair falling around his shoulders. He took Tz'ac Tzotz from his crib, checked the number on his amulet, and then absently put him back. Next he examined me, his eyes brimming with concern.

"How're you feeling?" He placed his hand on my brow. When I looked around for Marcelina, I realized she'd vanished.

"Where's Steve?" I felt the bottom dropping out of my world, my whole body trembling. "If you've harmed so much as a hair on his head, I'll—"

"He's here," he said quietly.

"I want to see him." Dear God, what had I done? I wanted to die.

"He's been given something to help him rest. Are you sure you want to disturb him?"

"I told you I want to see him." I could barely get out the words. *"Now."*

"If you insist. He's just downstairs."

We slowly walked down the marble steps, my mind flooding with more and more hallucinations. When we reached the first floor, he opened the door of a room adjacent to his office. I realized the window slats were open, sending a rush of moist air across my face. Then he motioned me forward and clicked on the bedside light.

Steve was there on the bed, comatose. I walked over and lifted his upper torso, then cradled his head in my arms. Baby, I love you. Please forgive me. Please.

His eyes were firmly shut and he didn't stir in the slightest. He was in a deathlike stupor, and there were large bruises on his face and a bandage across his nose. Then his bed shift fell open and I noticed another bandage on his groin.

"You've already done it!" I whirled back, ready to kill the bastard.

"As I said, he was injected with a mild sedative." He had walked over and started taking Steve's pulse. "Given the . . . condition he was in, I decided to go with the simplest procedure possible. After he was brought in, I made a small incision in the *vas deferens* and extracted a substantial quantity of motile sperm." He was turning down the lights. "Don't worry. I've performed the procedure before. The last was a Swedish tourist who was in a car accident up by Lake Atitlan and then lay in a coma in Guatemala City for weeks on end."

I listened to him, my mind racing. I'd thought Kevin and Rachel looked Nordic, big and blond. That Swede must have been their father.

"Those ova of mine you took, the way you stole Sarah's, and all the other women you've brought here—you don't use them for research."

"I have ample leftover embryonic material here for that." He started helping me onto the bed next to Steve. Now his face was undulating through my vision, as though I were seeing it in a wavy mirror. "Please understand, it's very expensive to run a laboratory up here. But the good I'm doing—"

"You're a criminal." I remembered the frightened eyes of the women upstairs and felt myself seething with anger.

"No! I am, in my special way, giving them back a small part of what they had taken away by people exactly like us. I'm providing them proof, living proof, their truths are still powerful."

He strolled over to the window and looked out. "The women come to me for my blessing whenever they hope to bear a child. They know that if they wish, I can cause their first child to be a descendant of their white deity Kukulkan. For them it is a sacred event."

"They *believe* that?" It was sickening. I felt a knot growing in my stomach, even as my hallucinations flashed ever bolder, bright rainbows that flitted about the room, then wound themselves around me.

"A great philosopher once said, 'All religions are true.' Who are we to judge?" He paused. "Let me try and explain something. Those patterns you see the women weaving on the fabrics down in Baalum, those patterns are actually just like the designs on that thousand-year-old pyramid. But though that pyramid had been buried and lost to them for so many years, they still made the designs all those years, because those symbols are a road map of their unseen world. Not the forest here where we are now, but their *real* world, where the gods dwell who rule the lightning bolts, the germination of corn." He was at the door, preparing to leave, but he paused. "They also understand the . . . special infants who come are miracles that must be returned. They receive but they also must give. Now they wish you to be part of that."

With that he closed the door with a swing of his long hair, a slam followed by a hard click.

Twenty-seven

As I watched him depart, hallucinations swirling through my brain like furious fireworks, I had a bizarre thought. In an ancient rain forest all things are still possible. The old fairy tales we grew up with mostly took place in a deep wood where evil could lurk unfettered. Today, though, the earth's forests no longer symbolize the unknowable dark within us. Nowadays, the ogres of our nightmares descend from outer space or even from our inner selves, places we can't physically know or subdue. Here, though, at this very moment, Steve and Sarah and I were marooned in a thousand-year-old forest where horror still lived.

I got off the bed and steadied myself, breathing deeply, forcing my brain to clear. Steve was wearing a shift, but his clothes were hanging from a hook on the door. For a long moment I just stared at the bruises on his face.

"God, baby, what did he do to you?"

No answer.

"Come on, love. *Please* wake up."

He didn't move, but his breathing was normal, not labored. I immediately decided I'd slap him around if I had to, anything to get him going and able to walk.

"Honey, wake *up*. Please." I pulled his feet out of the bed and slid them around and onto the linoleum floor. I didn't know what kind of sedative he'd been injected with, but if I had to shake him out of it, fine. This was no time for half measures. "Come *on.*"

I pulled him to his feet and dragged him across the floor to the slatted window at the rear of the room, where the predawn sounds of the forest beyond filled the air, mingled with the rain. What I needed was a gallon of black coffee, but the wet breeze would have to do.

It took ten minutes of working on him, with me barely able to hold a grasp on my own reality, but then his eyelids began to flutter. I kept talking to him, pleading and badgering, and when he finally started coming around, I began to walk him back and forth in front of the window.

Steve, I thought, I'm so sorry, so terribly sorry I dragged you into this.

"Can I please lie down?" His timorous voice startled me, but it gave me a burst of hope. Come *on.*

"Baby, just walk a little more. Try to get the blood flowing and flush the damned chemicals out of your brain."

"Morgy, are you okay?" His eyes had finally started to focus. And the first thing he asked about was me. I impulsively hugged him.

"I'm going to be." I pulled back and examined him. "You know where you are?"

He grinned with only half his face, and I could tell even that hurt. Then he stared around the room.

"Tell you one thing," he said, "this ain't Kansas anymore. Last thing I remember is, Alan and I were setting down. Then out of nowhere, your Colonel Ramos and about twenty kid soldiers with AK-47's were all over us." He groaned. "They took me and then he told Dupre to get back in the chopper and disappear. I think that son of a bitch tipped Ramos off we were coming. Then Ramos worked me over and gave me an injection. About five minutes later I passed out. It's the last thing I remember."

Ramos. Was he going to kill us both, now that Alex Goddard had gotten everything he wanted? I thought about it and decided this was not the moment to share that possibility with Steve. Instead, I turned him around and lifted up his head.

"Are you really awake?" I loved this poor, beat-up man. More than anything, I just wanted to hold him.

"I'm not . . . but I'd damned well better be." He tried, unsteadily, to straighten up. "Morgy, before he put me away, that Ramos bastard was talking about me, and you, in the past tense. Like we'd already been 'disappeared.' He didn't know I speak Spanish. What the hell's going on?"

I wasn't sure how to tell him. But I was getting that super energy God gives you when you realize life is no longer a game. We had to get focused.

"Baby, where's your passport?" I asked.

He looked around, then pointed to his battered camera bag in the corner.

"It's in there. Or was. Central America. Never leave home without it." He grimaced, then lightly pushed me away and stood by himself. "Jesus, do you know what they're doing? You were right all along. They're selling kids in the States. That Ramos prick is running the operation, not to mention Alex Goddard's slice of the action. And somebody at the American embassy here is handling all the paperwork, so they can grease everything through the INS. But I still don't understand how it is we're—"

"Honey, I know exactly what's happening." I'd long since figured out that Alex Goddard and Colonel Ramos were working hand in glove. But I still couldn't bring myself to tell him how he and I were going to be used. It was just too sick. "Listen, not long from now I think I'm supposed to be taken down there to the village for some kind of rite, as part of this whole disgusting operation, and then after that he's going to use . . . You don't want to hear. We've—"

"You know, Ramos and a bunch of G-2 thugs are here to take away a batch of little kids," he rambled on, not seeming to hear anything I was saying. He was off in his own world, trying to sort out things in his head. "But what I can't figure is, how can they just take children from here and nobody tries to stop them? Are these *indigena* so terrified—?"

"Listen, please." Now my hallucinations were returning in spite of all I could do, trails of light that glimmered off all the objects in the room, and I didn't know how much longer I'd be coherent. I'd have to talk fast. "We've got to get Sarah before daylight. She's down in the village. I tried to get her out of there yesterday, but—"

"Is she okay?" He stared at me and his eyes cleared for a moment. "I mean, is she able to—?"

"No, she's not okay. She's hallucinating worse than ever. I'm sure he's giving her more drugs. Really heavy stuff."

"So how—?"

"Hopefully, we're going right this minute. There's a river. But if that doesn't work out, there's something I can do to buy us a month's time. Alex Goddard's got a laboratory here, just down the hall, in back of his office. It's the evil center of this place. So if I can get in there and dump all his petri dishes, his in-vitro culture mediums . . . Baby, it's all so disgusting. But I'm going to take care of it."

I was starting to have real trouble just stringing words together into sentences. My hallucinations were still growing, the loud whispers of light, but I did manage to tell him how I thought we could get Sarah and elude the Army, if we did it before sunup, though my plan probably came out pretty jumbled. Yet I felt that if we did it together, we could take care of each other. . . .

Then, with my remaining strength, I launched into action.

"Let me check the hall. I just want to shut down his lab. Call it . . . call it insurance. Five minutes, and then we'll be out of here."

It also would be a kind of justice, to even the score for what he'd done to Sarah and to me.

I leaned Steve back against the wall, then walked slowly across the tile floor to the door and tested it. Surprise, surprise, it was locked. I again tried the knob, an old one, then again, but it wouldn't budge, just wiggled slightly. He'd locked us in.

Now what?

Then I remembered the time Steve and I were in an a similar situation. When we got locked in my room at the Oloffson in Port-au-Prince, he'd just taken his Swiss Army knife and unscrewed the knob, then clicked it open. He'd made it look like a piece of cake, but he had a way of doing that.

He was barely conscious, so this time I'd have to do it myself. I glanced around at his bag.

"Is your Swiss still in there?"

"I think . . ." His mind seemed to be wandering. Then he gave a weak thumbs-up.

I went over and zipped it open. Be there, I prayed. We really could use a break.

I rummaged through telephoto lenses and film canisters and underwear. Then I found it, zipped inside a water-repellent baggie and stuck in a side pouch.

I snapped it open and went to work, him watching me, his head nodding as he struggled to stay conscious.

The main difference between this time and Haiti was, here I didn't know what was on the other side and I was having hallucinations of multicolored snakes.

"You're doing great," he said finally, seeming to come a bit more alive.

And I was. Out with the screws, off with the knob, in with the small blade, and click. Maybe we just think men's mechanical skills are genetically hard-wired. Maybe it's all a secret plot to elicit awe.

I closed the knife and shoved it back into his bag, then turned to him.

"Honey, I'm just going to be a second. While I'm gone, practice walking."

"Be careful, please." He gave a cautionary wave. "They don't want us leaving here alive."

"Just get ready." I quietly pulled back the door and peered out into the dark hallway. It was empty, abandoned, no snakes, with only a light breeze flowing through.

When I stepped out, the fresh air hit my face and I had a moment of intensity that made me realize what I really wanted to do, first and foremost, was see Tz'ac Tzotz one last time. A last farewell to one of Sarah's children. Stupid, yes, a private folly of the heart, but I *had* to do it.

I was halfway down the hall, experiencing flashes of color before my eyes, when I heard a voice.

"They're all praying for you. It's almost time."

I turned back, startled, barely able to see. Finally I made out Marcelina, in her white shift. We were standing a few feet from the stairs, where I wanted to go, and I was tripping, my reality almost gone. I think she knew that, because she reached out to help me stand.

"Marcelina, where's Sarah?" I grasped her hand, which helped me to keep my balance. "Is she still down there in that . . . place?"

"She's been so looking forward to the ceremony. She wants them to bring her—"

"You don't know where she is?" I realized nothing was going to go the way I'd hoped it would.

"They all love her. They're taking good care of her."

"Well, I love her too. And I *have* to get her. Now." I was whispering to her, trying to save my strength. "Marcelina, promise me you'll stop all this. It's so horrible. So sad."

"It's our life," she whispered back, then turned her face away.

I didn't know what else to say, and I was terrified Alex Goddard might materialize, so without another word, I pulled away and started up the steps.

When I reached the top of the stairs, the hallway was lighted by the string of bulbs along the floor, and I made my way as fast as I could to my room at the end. I pulled my passport out of my bag, along with a charge card, slipped them both into my pants pocket, and headed back down the hall.

When I got to the door of the room where Tz'ac Tzotz and his mother were, I gave it a gentle push and peered in, but the glow from the lamp above the bed showed it and the crib were both empty. . . .

No! They must have already taken the children. Next they'd be coming for me. I realized I'd been a fool not to head straight for the lab. I should have just gone—

The room went completely dark, together with the hallway, a pitch-black that felt like a liquid washing over me. The main power, somewhere, had abruptly died, or been deliberately shut off.

Then I heard a thunder of footsteps pounding up the steps, hard boots on the marble.

I made a dash, hoping to slip past them in the dark hall.

I'd reached the top of the stairs when I felt a hand brush against my face, then a grip circle around my biceps. Somebody had been too quick.

I brought my elbow around hoping to catch him in the face, bring him down, but instead it slammed against something metal, which clattered onto the floor.

"Chingado!" came a muffled voice.

I drew back and swung, and this time my arm scraped hard against the flesh of a face and the bastard staggered backward, his grip loosening.

I twisted away and dropped to the floor to begin searching for what had fallen. Surely it was a pistol.

The marble was cold against my bare arms as I swept my hands across the floor. Then I ran my fingers down the edge of the stair.

And there it was, on the first step. My left hand closed around the cold barrel of an automatic. I shifted it to my right, grasping the plastic grip, not entirely sure what I should do with it. But at least I had a gun. I'd never actually held a real one before, but it was heavy and I assumed it was ready to fire.

I was halfway down the first set of stairs, on my way to the landing, when I felt an arm slip around my neck. I ducked and twisted away, stumbling down the last three or four steps, and landed on my feet, staggering back against the wall to regain my balance. All I knew was, the next steps loomed somewhere to my right. Just a few more feet . . .

But he was there again, moving between me and the final stairs. Get around him, I told myself, but at that moment he grabbed me at the waist.

Dancing in the dark, but the swirl had no music and no swing, just a quick, dizzying pirouette. I aimed the pistol as close as I could to his face and pulled the hard metal trigger.

"Mierda!"

Blinding light, a face lost in the burst of flame, stars filling my head. The fiery explosion tongued out past his ear like a brilliant sword of reds and yellows, sending a round off into space. The noise left a ringing in my ears and multicolored hues stuttering across my eyes.

It hit me who I'd just seen. It was Ramos. With a gun! Shit.

The flash of my pistol had given me the advantage for a second, since I knew it was coming, and with that edge I swung an elbow across his chin, then kneed him in the groin. It should have been enough to bring him down, but instead he merely sank to one knee and redoubled his grip.

Hey, I thought, maybe I know something he doesn't. How to take a fall. I'd seen enough movie stunts to know what you're supposed to do. It'd be risky, but I knew I wasn't going to win a wrestling match.

I opened up with the automatic, firing everywhere again and again and again, getting off five rounds in a crescendo of light and sound, like a huge firecracker in my hand, enough to illuminate the stairwell like a strobe and catch him off guard. In that fleeting moment I slipped a foot behind his ankle and shoved.

I think I yelled as I felt myself being pulled forward. Then I realized he was wearing a heavy bracelet that had tangled in my hair. I'd been planning to roll down the remaining stairs, protecting my head, and let him bounce, but the pull of his bracelet ruined it. I felt myself being swept into empty space, my gun flying away.

Then something glanced off my face, the wooden banister of the stair, which had mysteriously come up to meet me. I turned and felt his body beneath mine, arms flailing, a soft landing, till we rolled and I was beneath him again.

I struck out, a right fist, and he fell away, his bracelet disentangling as he tumbled farther down the stairs. Then I rose and tried to take a step, but it wasn't there. In the pitch dark the angle was wrong, off by just inches, and as I toppled forward into empty space I reached out, taking a handful of dark air.

Finally I felt something clenching my wrist, and the next

thing I knew I was being swung around. I twisted sideways one last time, but then my head hit the wall. The hard marble caught me just above the ear, and I saw the darkness of the space grow brilliantly light, then transmute to vibrant colors.

Or maybe the hall lights had come back on. I only know I felt a set of arms encircle me.

"Come," Alex Goddard was saying as he lifted me up. "They're ready."

Twenty-eight

When we reached the parking lot, several more Army thugs were waiting, grown-ups now, khaki shirts and dense mustaches, the regulation G-2 sunglasses even though it was still dark, with 9mm automatics in holsters at their belt. I took one look at them and I think I blacked out. Steve and I were about to "disappear," and possibly Sarah too. Probably in another hour or two. My tattered mind finally just slipped away.

Soon afterward, I sensed myself being transported in a large vehicle, and after that I was being carried, up, up, as though I were floating into the coming dawn. When I regained consciousness, I realized I was standing in a rainstorm near a small stone building. A dozen Army men were huddled inside, shielding their cigarettes from the blowing rain while they guarded a row of olive-green bassinets. Around me, censers were spewing copal smoke into the soggy air.

I became aware of the cooling sensation of the fresh rain across my face, and wondered if it might clear some of the toad venom (surely that was what it was) from my brain. Maybe it was working. Instead of seeing vivid colors everywhere, I was abruptly experiencing a hyperacute clarity of every sensation. The stones beneath my bare feet were becoming so articulated, I felt as though I could number every granule, every crystal, every atom. The paintings and carvings on the lintel above the door to the stone room—I recognized it as where I'd spent the first night—sparkled, leapt out at me.

"Stand there on the edge of the platform," Alex Goddard commanded, urging me forward. It was only then I realized we'd come up the back steps of the pyramid, where the G-2 men had parked their black Land Rovers, unnoticed and ready.

Looking down at the crowd of people gathered in the square, I realized they couldn't really see much of what was going on atop the pyramid. To them it was just a cloud of copal smoke and foggy rain. Although the sun was starting to brighten the east, the only real light still came from the torches stationed around the plaza.

Then like a ghost materializing out of the mist, Marcelina moved up the steep front steps, leading a line of Maya mothers from the clinic—I counted twelve—each carrying her newborn, the "special" baby she would give back to Kukulkan, perhaps the way Abraham of the Old Testament offered up his son Isaac in sacrifice to Jehovah. It was a sight I shall never forget, the sadness but also the unmistakable reverence in their eyes. I wanted to yell at them to run, to take Sarah's votive babies and disappear into the forest, but I didn't have the words.

Next the women arrayed themselves in a line across the front of the pyramid, facing not the crowd below, but toward Alex Goddard and me. Then, holding out a jade-handled obsidian knife, he walked down the line, allowing each woman to touch her forehead against its flint blade. I assumed each one believed it was the instrument that would take her child's life, ceremonially sending it back to the Maya Otherworld whence it came. Had he drugged them too, I fleetingly wondered, hypnotized them or given them some potion to prevent them from comprehending what was really going on?

I kept remembering . . . a hundred other insane episodes of immortal yearning leading to a mass "transport" to some other "plane." This, I thought, must be what it was like in the jungles of Jonestown that death-filled morning. And Alex Goddard was their "Jim Jones," the spiritual leader of the moral travesty he'd imposed upon the lost village of Baalum.

I was going to stop it, somehow. By God, I was. I stared at the women and felt so sad at the sight of the handwoven blankets they held their babies in, primary greens and reds and blues lovingly woven into shimmering patterns that mirrored the symbols across the sides of the stone room. Their faces, especially their eyes, were transcendent in a kind of chiaroscuro of darkest blacks and purest whites, as though all their humanity had been caught by their blankets and shawls, surely created for this ultimate moment. And the mother of Tz'ac Tzotz was there, carrying him, the baby I'd so wanted to hold one last time.

Next Alex Goddard emerged from the stone room bearing a basket filled with sheets of white bark-paper. He approached Tz'ac Tzotz's mother, then took a wide section of the paper and secured it around her face with a silk cord, covering her vision. Down the line, one after another, he carefully blindfolded the women, while they stood passively, some crying—from joy or sorrow, I could not tell. Finally, at the last, he also covered Marcelina's face.

So she's not supposed to know what's really happening. Nobody's supposed to know except him, and me. And, of course, Ramos and the G-2 secret police and whoever else is in on this crime. But, secretly, she does know. The God of the House of Darkness.

When he finished, he put down the basket, then turned to me. "Stand at the front edge of the platform and lift your hands in benediction. They all want to see you, the new bride."

I took a couple of steps, then looked back to see him adding more copal to the main censer, sending a fresh cloud of smoke billowing out into the rain. As the incense poured around us, the Army thugs who'd been loitering at the back of the stone room began coming forward, each carrying one of the bassinets. They set them down on the stones, ready to start taking the children. My outraged mind flashed on Ghirlandajo's "Massacre of the Innocents." Here, though, Sarah's children weren't being stabbed to death; they were being—kidnapped and stolen.

Revulsion pierced through me as though I'd been hit by a jagged shaft of lightning, but instead of being knocked down, I was energized. Or maybe the final effects of the toad venom were giving me a spurt of adrenaline. Letting his criminal charade continue one second longer became unbearable. What would happen to me, I didn't know, but I couldn't let it go on.

"No," I yelled, startling myself by the sound of my own voice. "In God's name, stop."

The rain was growing more intense, and I was soaked and bleary-eyed, but before I could think I found myself stalking over to Tz'ac Tzotz's mother, shouting at her. The next thing I knew I was ripping the paper from her frightened eyes. I hugged her as best I could, then yelled back at Marcelina.

"Tell them all to take off their blindfolds. This is obscene."

Then I went on autopilot, shutting out everything around me—the rain, the perilous sides of the pyramid, the pistol-carrying G-2 thugs, even Alex Goddard. The way I remember it now, it all took place in slow motion, like some underwater dream sequence, but surely it was just the opposite.

Anyway, I do know I snapped. I started shouting again, and with the G-2 hoods momentarily frozen, I started flinging the still-empty bassinets down the steep side of the pyramid, where they just bounced away into the rain. As I watched them disappearing, one after another, I felt marvelously emboldened. I would throw one and watch it go flying, and then I would throw another. Yes, damn it, yes!

I wanted to show anybody with two eyes that it was all a sham. Once they realized what was really happening, surely they would rise up and drive Alex Goddard from their home.

For a moment it seemed to be working. A stunned silence was slowly spreading over the square, while everybody around me was paralyzed, like waxworks. Maybe it's the same way you're temporarily caught off guard when a stranger on the street goes berserk.

By the time I'd flung away the last bassinet, the women had all removed their blindfolds and were staring at me, dumbfounded. Finally, Tz'ac Tzotz's mother whispered something to Marcelina, and she turned to me.

"She wants to know why you're angry. You're the bride. They only want to please you."

Angry? I was terrified, but also fighting mad.

"Marcelina, this is all a ghastly lie." I'd finished throwing and I was moving to the next stage. Get control. Could he risk killing me in front of all these people? "Tell them to take their babies and hide in the forest."

That was when I heard a cry that pierced through the rain and across the square beyond, and I turned back to see Alex Goddard shoving toward me. He's coming to murder me, since I've exposed him. But I wouldn't let it happen without a fight. I clenched my fists, waiting, feeling my adrenaline surge.

Instead, though, he just brushed past me, headed toward the edge of the platform. At first I didn't know why, but he was intent on something off in the mist, his open hands thrust up at the rainy skies.

That was when I heard the Guatemalan Army hoods yelling curses.

"Vete ala chingada!"

They also were staring off to the south, in the same direction.

Hadn't they noticed I'd just dismantled their sick pageant? I wanted a reaction that would drive home the truth to Marcelina, to the mothers, to everyone.

"Damn it, look at me," I yelled, first at him and then at the G-2 thugs. *"Mira!"* But their focus still was on something beyond the square.

Finally I turned, following their gaze, and for a second I too forgot all about everything else. An intense red glow was illuminating the morning sky from the direction of the clinic, a vibrant electric rose weaving its hues in the mist. Then I saw spewing spikes of flame, orange and yellow, dancing over the top of the clinic. There was a finality about it that momentarily took my breath away.

Then it hit me. Steve's in there. It was a horror that, in my initial shock, I couldn't actually process, the thought just hovering in the recesses of my brain defying me to accept it.

Then Alex Goddard turned back, shouting at the Army men in rapid Spanish—I recognized the word for fire—that galvanized them to action. They snapped out of their mental paralysis and headed down the pyramid, toward two Land Rovers parked at the back.

Next he turned around and fixed his gaze on me. At last he knew *I* knew he was capable of unspeakable evil, and I knew *he* knew I would do everything in my power to stop him.

"All my records." His voice sounded as though it was coming from another world, and it held a sadness that touched even me. "You have no idea what's been lost."

He was distraught, but also obsessed. With his wild mane of hair, he did, finally, look like Shiva the Destroyer. He stalked over and seized the obsidian knife, then turned toward me.

I looked for something to defend myself with. The bassinets, which I might have used as a shield, were gone. I only had my bare hands.

I had to get away from him, get down the pyramid and find Sarah and Steve. But as I started toward the front steps, the women were all clustered there, blocking my way.

Then, for no reason I could understand, the mother of Tz'ac Tzotz stepped out of the group and handed me her baby, saying something in Kekchi Maya and reaching to touch my cheek.

I was so startled I took the bundle that was Sarah's child. But then I thought, No! Alex Goddard will just kill him too.

"She said he must not harm you," Marcelina whispered, moving beside me. "You are the special one. She wants you to give her child back to Kukulkan."

She still believes, I realized. They all do.

Holding Tz'ac Tzotz, my eyes fixed on Alex Goddard, I'd entirely failed to notice a new presence on the pyramid, a ghostlike waif in a white shift who now stood silently in the doorway of the stone room. Sarah!

Marcelina had said she'd wanted to come for the ceremony. She was being helped to stand by the two Maya women who'd fed me the *atole*. Somehow, she'd gotten them to bring her.

"Morgy, are you there?" Sarah asked, gazing up at the rainy skies, the downpour soaking her blond hair, her eyes unblinking. At that moment, I felt we'd joined, become one person—me the dogged rational half who'd just gone over the line, her the spiritual part that needed to float, to fly free. "I wanted to be with—"

"Sar, get back," I yelled, and started to go to her, but there wasn't time. Now Alex Goddard was moving toward me holding the knife, as though tracking a prey, oblivious to Sarah, to everything. He'd concentrated all his hatred on me and me alone, and I hated him back as much. Death hovered between us, waiting to see whom to take.

But then the woman who had borne Tz'ac Tzotz said something in Kekchi Maya, pointing back at me and her child, and lunged at him. They collided together in the rain and next she slid down, first seizing his leg, then losing her grip and slipping onto the stones, her long black hair askew in the hovering smoke.

She's trying to save me, I realized. Why—?

Then I saw Sarah pull away from the women supporting her and slowly move across the platform.

"Morgy . . ."

She was walking in the direction of Alex Goddard, but then she stumbled over the fallen woman's leg and her hand went down as she sprawled across her. She must have touched something, because she recoiled backward, and only then did I notice the flare of a torch glinting off the obsidian knife now protruding from the woman's chest.

Sarah rose up, her eyes full of anger, and awkwardly flung her arms, searching. I could feel the passion that had been pent up all those months she lay in the coma, feeding her madness. She managed to catch hold of Alex Goddard's arm, and they began an awkward minuet, neither realizing how close they were to the stone platform's edge. I stood mesmerized a moment, then dashed toward them, but only in time to watch them vanish into the rain and haze. It was as though there had been some sleight of hand. One second they were there and the next they weren't. At first I thought my eyes were playing tricks on me, but then I realized it was real. They were gone.

"Sarah!"

I reached the side in time to see them land on the first

tier of stones below. She'd fallen near the edge, but she was solid and safe. Alex Goddard, however, hit with one foot on and one foot off, and the result was he slid away, then vanished into the dark rain.

It's her final act of self-destruction. She's joined me in my rage, but we've both been spared. *That's* the miracle of Baalum.

"Sar, *don't move.*" I finally found my voice. I was still holding Tz'ac Tzotz, who'd begun to shriek, his blue eyes flooded with fear.

Now several village men from the square were running, shouting, up the slippery steps. Their faces looked like they'd been painted at one time, but now the rain had washed most of it away.

While I yelled down to Sarah, again begging her not to move, Marcelina was asking them something, and their answers were tumbling out.

Finally I turned to look at her, the screaming Tz'ac Tzotz still in my arms.

"No one knows where he is," she was saying as she looked down over the side. "He's gone into the forest."

"Good." I pulled Tz'ac Tzotz to me and kissed him, trying to tell him to calm down. It wasn't working.

"Marcelina, here, please hold him. I've got to get down to Sarah."

She took him. Then I walked over to where his mother lay bleeding on the stones. The woman wasn't moving, the obsidian knife still protruding from her chest. She'd saved me, but now death had taken her. There was nothing anyone could do.

I was trembling, but I turned and began easing myself over the side of the stone platform and onto the first tier of the pyramid.

"Sar, don't move." I inched my way across to her. "Just

stay still." The rain was pouring again, but the electric bloom of sparks and flames from the direction of the clinic was unabated. It would be completely gutted. Was Steve awake enough to get out? He'd seemed alert when I left him.

"Morgy, is that you?" She was holding out her fingers. "I can't see you. Where are—?"

"I'm here, Sar. Right here." I reached down and took her hand, which was deathly cold. "Come on. Let me help you get up."

Carefully, leaning against the wet stones of the side of the pyramid, I gradually pulled her to her feet and away from the treacherous edge. Then it hit me what she'd said.

"Sar, what do you mean, you can't see me?"

"I'm okay. It's just . . ." She was gripping my hand now, and then she brushed against the stone side of the pyramid and put out her other hand to cling to it. "Morgy, I took it again. To go to their sacred place. But sometimes you can only see visions and then after a while everything goes blank."

That bastard. Alex Goddard had given her the drug again. Now she was lost in a world of colored lights, a place I'd just traveled through myself. She probably had no idea she'd just pushed him off the pyramid and into the dark.

"Your hand feels so soft," she was saying. "You're like warm honey."

"Sar, try to walk. We're going to turn a corner and then we'll be at the back of the pyramid. Next we'll come to some steps, and then we're going down."

As I inched our way along, scarcely able to keep our footing because of the rain, I wondered again about Steve. Please, God, let him be all right.

When we finally got to the steps, Marcelina was there, standing expectantly, holding Tz'ac Tzotz. He was still crying, intermittent sobs.

"He belongs to you now," she said, holding him out for me. "It's what she wished.

"What—?" I took him before I realized what I was doing.

As I cradled him, gazing down at his tender little face, I realized he truly was Sarah all over again. And I was so glad she couldn't see him. Never, I thought, she must never, ever know.

I finally forced myself to place him back into Marcelina's arms.

"You've got no idea how much I want him, but I can't. Let one of these women give him her milk, have a twin for her own child."

For that wrenching moment I'd held the very baby my heart longed for. But he was the last one on earth I could have. Just go, take Sarah and find Steve and go as far from Baalum as you can, before you lose your compass and do something terribly selfish.

"Marcelina," I said, reaching to hug her, "tell them these 'sacred' children are all from his *médico*. Look up 'in vitro' in your dictionary. That's all it is."

She hugged me back, though I wasn't sure whether she understood. Then I asked her to take Sarah's hand for a moment while I went back up the steps to the platform. I felt a primal anger as I took one last look at the women Alex Goddard had wronged, now clustered around the body of Tz'ac Tzotz's mother. Then I bade them a silent farewell, turned, and walked, holding my tears, back through the stone room.

The rear of the pyramid was deserted, the steps slippery and dangerous, but it was our way out. I began leading Sarah down, step by treacherous step. Everything had happened so fast I'd barely had time to think about Steve. Those flames, my God. It was finally sinking in, truly hitting me. Had he gotten out in time?

Then the slimy Rio Tigre, now swelling from the rain, came into view. I stared at it a second before I noticed the three young Army recruits leaning against the trunk of a giant Cebia tree next to the trail, their rifles covered in plastic against the rain. When they saw us, they stiffened, shifted their weapons, and glanced up at the top of the pyramid, as though seeking orders. Neither group had any idea why the other was there. Sarah and I were an unforeseen contingency they hadn't been briefed on.

What are they going to do? They have no idea what just happened.

"Morgy," Sarah said, gazing blankly at the sky, "the colors are so beautiful. Can we—?"

"Shhh, we'll talk in a minute."

I smiled and nodded and began walking past the young privates, holding my breath. Then a spectral form emerged out of the rain just behind them.

It took me a moment to recognize who it was. I was hoping it might be Steve, but instead it was a man dressed in white, now covered with mud, and holding a knife, not obsidian this time but long and steel. His eyes were glazed, and I wasn't sure if he even knew exactly where he was. Why had he come down to the river? Had he known I'd come here, too?

For a moment we just stood staring at each other, while the Army privates began edging up the hill, as though not wanting to witness what surely was coming next.

"Why don't you put an end to all the evil?" I yelled at him finally, trying to project through the rain. "Just stop it right now."

"Baalum was my life's work," he said. Then he looked down at the knife a moment, as though unsure what it was. Finally he turned and flung it in the direction of the river.

"It could have been beautiful," I said back. Thank God

the knife was gone. But what would he do next? "But now—"

"No," he said, staring directly at me, his eyes seeming to plead. "It is. It will be again. To make a place like Baalum is to coin the riches of God. I want you to stay. To be part of it. Together, we . . ." But whatever else he said was lost in the cloudburst that abruptly swept over the embankment. In an instant it was a torrent, the last outpouring of the storm, powerful and unrelenting. Nature had unleashed its worst, as though Kukulkan was rendering his final judgment.

"Morgy, I'm falling," Sarah screamed. The ground she and I had been standing on began turning to liquid, as though it were a custard melting in the tropical heat. As we began slipping down the embankment toward him, I gripped her arm with my left hand and reached up to seize a low-lying branch of the Cebia with my right.

Then, under the weight of the water, all the soil beneath us gave way, tons of wet riverbank that abruptly buckled outward.

Alex Goddard made no sound as the mass of earth lifted him backward toward the river. His sullied garb of white blended into the gray sludge of mud and rain, then faded to darkness as the embankment dissolved into the swirling Rio Tigre.

"Sar, hold on. Please hold on." I felt my grasp of the tree slipping, but now the mud slide had begun to stabilize.

I managed to cling to the limb for a few seconds more, the bark cutting into my fingers, and then my hold slipped away, sending us both spiraling downward, till we were temporarily snagged by the Cebia's newly exposed undergrowth. I still had her hand, though just barely, but the torrent of rain and mud was subsiding, and finally we collapsed together into the gnarled network of roots.

After a moment's rest, I managed to crawl out and pull her up.

"Come on, Sar. Try and walk."

Together we stumbled and slid down the last incline before the river's edge, then turned upstream along the bank. After about fifty yards, sure enough, the native *cayucos,* the hollowed-out mahogany canoes I'd told Steve about, were still there just as I'd seen them that first morning, bobbing and straining at their moorings. In the rain I couldn't tell how usable they were, but I figured going downriver was the only way we'd ever be able to get out. We'd have to flee the way Sarah had that first time.

For a moment I thought they all were empty—dear God, no—but then I realized there was a drenched figure in the last one in the row. When I recognized who it was, I think I completely lost it; all the horror of the last two days swallowed me up. I grabbed Sarah and hugged her for dear life, feeling the tears coursing down my cheeks. I literally couldn't help myself.

"They were tied up here just like you said." Steve wiped the rain from his eyes, then reached to take my hand. His bandaged nose was bleeding again, and he looked like he'd just been half killed. "I told those little Army *chicos* I was a big *amigo* of *el doctor* and they saluted and showed me where these were tied up."

"Thank God you're okay. What happened? Did—?"

"Ramos, the son of a bitch. He came in and . . . I guess it was time to finish me off. But I wasn't as drugged out as he thought." He was staring at Sarah, clearly relieved but asking no questions. "I brought along his nine-millimeter"—he indicated the silver automatic in his belt—"in case we run into problems."

I wanted to kiss him, but I was still too shaken up. Instead I focused on helping Sarah in without capsizing everything.

After I'd settled her, I pulled myself over the side and reached for a paddle.

"If we go with the current," I said, "we'll get to the Usumacinta. Hopefully the flooding will help push us downstream."

"Honestly, I didn't think the fire would get away from me like it did." He shoved off amidst the swirling debris. "Jesus. I heard them taking you away, and I assumed you didn't get to mess up his lab. So I figured there was only one way . . . I just threw around some ether and pitched a match. The place was empty, so . . ."

I looked around at the roiling waters, snakes and crocodiles lurking, and felt a lifetime of determination. Was Alex Goddard still alive? I no longer cared. . . .

Sunrise was breaking through the last of the rain, laying dancing shadows on the water as we rowed for midstream. Someday, I knew, what was real about Baalum and what I'd dreamed here might well merge together, the way they had for Sarah. But for now, true daylight never looked better.

Twenty-nine

We got picked up by a ragged crew of Mexican fishermen just before dark. Aside from being sunburned to medium rare, we were physically okay. The fresh air and sunshine did a lot to bring Sarah back, though she did have lapses of nonrationality, and once tried to dive over the side of their fishing cutter. They dropped us off at the tourist site of Yaxchitan, a Mayan ruin on the western bank of the mighty Usumacinta, where we joined an American day-tour on its way back to San Cristobal de las Casas. There we caught a prop flight to Cancun, and then American Airlines to New York. We had no luggage, but I flew us first-class, and I still have the MasterCard slip to prove it.

As things turned out, though, returning Sarah to normalcy—or me, for that matter—was another struggle entirely. For me, time, after that rainy morning in the Peten, became an essence that flowed around me as though I were aswim in the ether of interstellar space, pondering the conjunction of good and evil. I suffered flashbacks, late-night reveries of forests and children that must have been like those Sarah struggled to bury. For weeks after that, I had a lot of trouble remembering meetings, returning phone calls, giving David an honest day's editing.

For her own part, Sarah just seemed to drift at first, to the point I sometimes wondered if she realized she was back at Lou's loft. Then abruptly, one day she snapped into her old self and started sending for reregistration materials from Columbia. I really needed to talk with her about our mutual nightmare, but she seemed to have erased all memories of Baalum, except for occasional mumbles in Kekchi Maya. Perhaps that was best, I consoled myself. Maybe it was wise for us all just to let the ghosts of that faraway place lie sleeping.

As for Lou, I told him as little as I could about what happened to her there. He hadn't returned to work, had mainly stayed at his Soho place to be near her, as though he was fearful she might be snatched away from him once more. Frankly, I think all his enforced closeness was starting to grate on her nerves, though I dared not hint such a thing to him.

In the meantime, Steve returned to Belize to wrap up his photo essay, and David submitted a (very) rough cut of *Baby Love* to the selection committee at Sundance (our hoped-for distribution deal with Orion was, alas, in temporary turnaround pending yet another management shuffle). We did, however, squeeze an advance from Lifetime that lowered the heat with Nicky Russo.

Nevertheless, the story of how Alex Goddard touched all our lives still wasn't over. It was two months after we got back to the city that my dark dance with the man who thought he was Shiva, creator and destroyer, had its final pirouette, as though his ghost had returned from his rain-forest redoubt for one last sorcerer's turn.

Truthfully, it all transpired so fast I could scarcely take it in, but here's the rough outline of what happened. I was working late that Thursday evening in the editing room at Applecore, around seven o'clock. And I was feeling particularly out of sorts, including a headache and stomach pains from the leftover pizza I'd microwaved to keep me going. I was recutting some new real-life interviews I'd filmed to replace those of Carly and Paula. (Children of Light had gone defunct, by the way, the phone at Quetzal Manor disconnected, but I didn't need any more excitement in my life of the colonel Ramos variety. The replacement interviews weren't nearly as bubbly and full of exuberance, but they were actually much truer to the realities of adoption.)

Anyway, I listened to my stomach, and decided it was high time to toss in the towel. I got my things, locked up, and then I ran into David on the elevator, coming down from the floor above.

"How's it going?" he asked, ostentatiously checking his watch, an approving gleam in his eyes. I was glad he wanted to let me know he'd noticed I was logging long hours. Then he looked at me again. "Hey, you feeling okay?"

"I've been better," I said, thinking how nice it was that he cared. "Could be a couple of aspirin and a good night's sleep are called for."

"So now you're a doctor?" he said, following me into the lobby, "Providing self-diagnosis—?"

"David, give me a break. I just happen to feel a little off today, okay? It doesn't mean I'm at death's door."

"Yeah, well, the way you look you coulda fooled me." He headed down the street, toward the avenue. Then he called back over his shoulder. "I don't want to see you in tomorrow unless you look like you might live through the day. I pay for your health insurance. Use it, for God's sake."

After I found a cab, I began to think he might be right. This was no typical down day. So I decided I'd stop at the Duane Reade on my corner and talk to the pharmacist.

The second-shift man was on, a gray-haired portly old guy who knew more about drugs than most doctors. The tag on his jacket said "Bernd" and that's all anybody ever knew of his name. I sometimes called him "Dr. Bernd" by way of banter, but nothing I could do would ever make him smile.

The place was nearly empty and the pharmacy at the rear, with its spectral fluorescent lighting, looked like an out-take from a low-budget Wes Craven movie. Bernd, who was in back puttering, came out and looked me over.

I know it sounds naive, but I trusted him more than I trust half the young, overworked interns you get at an emergency room these days. I poured out my symptoms, including the story about how I'd been given fertility drugs and toad venom. Was it all coming back to haunt me, the dark hand of Alex Goddard?

He began by asking me some very perceptive questions, about things that had been puzzling me but I'd sort of managed to dismiss. Finally, he walked around the counter and lifted a small, shrink-wrapped box off a rack.

"Try this," he said, handing it over, "and then come back tomorrow. Maybe it's not such a big deal."

You're kidding, I thought, looking at the box.

I got home, collapsed onto the couch, and opened it. Believe it or not, I actually had to read the instructions. I did what they said, checked the time, and then decided to run a hot bath.

I filled the tub, dumped in some bubble-bath, put the cordless on the toilet seat, and splashed in. It felt so good I wanted to dissolve. Then I reached for the phone.

The clock above the sink read eight-thirty, and I figured, rightly, that Steve would be back at his hotel in Belize City. Sure enough I got him on the first try.

"Honey, you sitting down?" I said.

"I'm lying down. You wouldn't believe my day."

"You're not going to believe what I just heard from the pharmacist at the corner. Remember I told you I've been feeling strange, and some things were a little behind schedule? Well, guess what. We're about to find out something. We can't be together, but we can share it over a satellite."

"You mean . . ."

"I'm doing the test right now. You know, you take the stick out of the glass holder and if it's turned pink. . . ."

He was speechless for a long moment. Finally he just said, "Wow."

I checked the clock again, then reached for the test tube. This, I realized, is the most incredible moment in any woman's life. Is your world going to go on being the same, or is it never, ever going to be the same again?

When I pulled out the stick, it was a bright, beautiful pink.

"Steve. I love you. It's—"

"Max." He didn't realize it, but his voice had just gone up an octave.

"What?"

"That's my dad's middle name. I want to name him Max. It's an old family tradition."

"And what if it's a girl? Don't say Maxine or I'll divorce you before you even make an honest woman of me."

"Nope. If it's a girl, then you get to pick."

I couldn't believe I was finally having this conversation. It was something I'd dreamed of for years.

It then got too maudlin to repeat. He was coming home in eleven days, and we planned the celebration. Dinner at Le Cirque 2000 and then an evening at Cafe Carlyle. For a couple of would-be New York sophisticates, that was about as fancy-schmancy as this town gets.

I was crying tears of triumph by the time we hung up. By then it was late enough I figured Arlene would be home from her exercise class, so I decided to call her and break the happy news once more. Who I really wanted to call was Betsy, on the Coast, but I knew she'd still be driving home from her temp job. Arlene would have to do. Telling her would be the equivalent of sending an urgent E-mail to the entire office, but I wanted everybody to know. Two birds with one stone.

I looked down at my body, all the curves and soft skin, and tried to think about the miracle of a baby finally growing inside it, life recreating itself. God!

Arlene was going to break my mood, but for some reason I had to call her. If only to bring me back to reality.

I reached over and clicked open the cordless again. I was punching in her number when something made me pause. It was a nagging thought that I'd managed to repress for a while. Finally, though, it wouldn't stay down any more. There was something I had to check out.

I slowly put down the handset, climbed out of the tub, dried off, then plodded into the bedroom to dig out my private calendar, which had long since become a record of everything relevant to my and Steve's baby project.

It was buried at the bottom of the desk's second drawer, in amongst old bank statements. It was also, figuratively, covered by two months of dust, since that was how long it'd been since I'd bothered with it. I guess my attitude had been, what's the point?

I placed it on the desk, trying not to get it wet. Then I wrapped the towel more firmly around me, switched on the desk lamp, and sat down. I think I was also holding my breath.

I counted all the days twice, but there was no mistaking. The night Steve and I had spent so gloriously together in the Camino Real wasn't a fertile time. Not even close. I suppose that by then I'd become so despairing of ever getting pregnant, I hadn't even given it any thought. It was enough just to see him and hold him.

I just sat there for a long time staring at the white page, unable to move, random thoughts coming too fast to contain inside my tangled brain. Finally, though, I managed to get up and numbly put the calendar away. Order, I needed order. I then worked my way into the kitchen to fix myself something. I had a glass of water, then pulled down a bottle of Red Label and poured myself half a tumbler. Okay, somewhere down deep I knew it was the worst possible thing I could do, but I wasn't thinking, just going on autopilot and dismay.

I drank off a shot of the foul-tasting scotch, then realized how thoughtless that was and dumped the rest into the sink. Next, I moved into the living room and put on a raga, "Malkauns," concert volume, the one where the first note goes straight to your heart. Finally I collapsed onto the couch, the room now gloriously alive with all the spirituality and sensuality of the raga, notes piling on exquisite notes. For a while I just lay there numbly, enveloped in its lush eroticism. . . .

Eventually I started to think. Alex Goddard had planned to take from me, but had he also given? Had his "proprietary" ovulation drugs . . . causing all those hundreds of eggs to mature simultaneously . . . inadvertently let me get pregnant?

Then I had a dismaying counter-thought. Could he have done an in vitro while I was under sedation, when he harvested my ova? The ultimate link to Baalum. Was my baby Sarah's too? One of those last frozen embryos in his . . . ?

Then I leaned back and closed my eyes.

No, surely not. This baby was Steve's and mine. Ours. Had to be. His unintended, beautiful, ironic gift.

Surely . . .

Uh-uh. Go for a second take. Embrace life. Be Molly Bloom and shout it.

Yes!

Yes!

HORROR FROM PINNACLE . . .